SURREAL WORLDS

EDITED BY
SEAN LEONARD

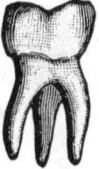

Bizarro Pulp Press
an imprint of JournalStone Publishing

Bizarro Pulp Press books may be ordered through booksellers or by contacting:

Bizarro Pulp Press, a JournalStone imprint
   www.BizarroPulpPress.com

The views expressed in this work are solely those of the authors and do not necessarily reflect the views of the publisher, and the publisher hereby disclaims any responsibility for them.

   ISBN: 978-1-940161-99-0

Printed in the United States of America
JournalStone rev. date: May 25, 2015

   Cover Art: Matthew Revert
   Interior Formatting by: Lori Michelle
      www.theauthorsalley.com

TABLE OF CONTENTS

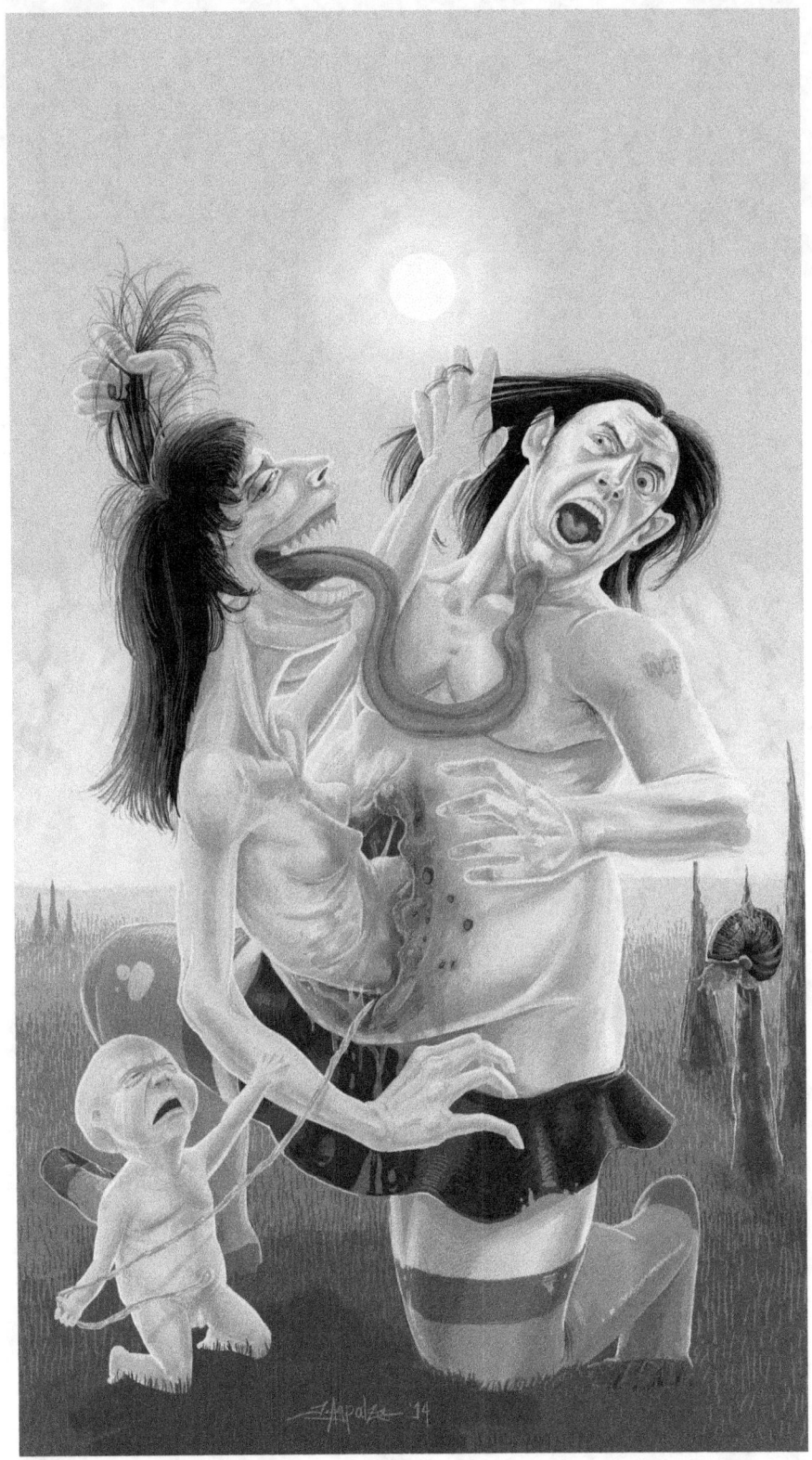

SPECIAL THANKS

We would like to thank the authors and artists for creating such a masterful book. The selection process involved for this collection was a unique challenge; from the interior, to the illustrations, to the editing, to the cover—we couldn't be more proud to have published this project.

And without our readers, we couldn't exist at all, unless we're talking about the probability that a planet is nothing more than the eye of a divine monstrosity that has been infected with the cosmos; in which case, we might still exist, but hardly in our current form.

—Bizarro Pulp Press

PAULA BREAKS

STEVE RASNIC TEM

PAULA HAD NOT left the house in weeks. Every time she'd asked permission her husband said no. "Things have changed since last you were out," he told her. "All the sidewalks are starved. They'd never be able to resist feet like yours."

"You like my feet?" she asked, hoping for a compliment.

"They're like dying fish, the way they flap," he told her. "You ought to take a gun and put them out of their misery."

Before he left for the day, he broke off her hands and locked them in his safe. This had happened so many times before they came off relatively easily, with not as much pain as she'd initially experienced. For the rest of the day, the only way she could open doors was to kneel and turn the knobs with her forearms.

She attempted this with the front door, but of course it was locked. The telephone squalled but then burst into flame before she could figure out how to answer it. It was probably him, checking up on her. He would be furious because she didn't answer.

She did not dare gain weight—he weighed her periodically—so she fed herself with long gazes out the window. She could hear children playing, somewhere, and somewhere an ice cream truck was gliding down a shaded street, its jangly music like a broken dream. She could see the top stories of an apartment house on the next block, and in one or two of the windows women sat and stared. She wondered if they noticed her. She wondered if anyone remembered who she was or where. A black bird tumbled out of the sky and landed on the grass below. Paula watched as a cat dragged it into the bushes.

A woman was running down the sidewalk, and before Paula could cry out, the woman had been chewed to bits, her remains a warning to the others.

"At least she *had* remains," the ceiling fan said, loose and working itself away from the ceiling. Paula moved to another room before she lost her head.

When she heard the key in the lock, Paula ran to the front door to greet him. Her body bounced eagerly even though she told it not to.

His head moved up and down like a security camera, swinging away from her for a slow evaluation of the room. Still, she bounced. "That looks ridiculous," he said, "without hands. Did you even bother to clean, or were you staring out the window again? Where's my drink?"

"No drinky," she said with a baby's mouth. "No hands." She made an exaggerated sad face, her lower lip pouting like a drunken clown's.

He swung his briefcase into her face, and for a moment she smelled a field full of cows spontaneously combusting. He stood over her, his chest heaving, and she was worried he might have a heart attack. Then what would she do?

"You know you might think about taking care of *me* for a change." He blinked, looking at her bare, splayed legs. "You didn't even bother to get dressed today, did you?"

She felt the words rushing up her throat; she was ready to vomit them. Instead she bit them off. They turned to salt in her throat, gagging her.

The next thing she knew, he had her in his arms. "I couldn't live without you," he whispered into her ear. "You know I love you, don't you?" She could tell he was waiting for her answer.

"I know," she managed, staring at her handless arms, not knowing what to do with them.

"I couldn't do this, any of this, without you," he murmured, and she raised her head and watched as electrical cords wriggled and tried to yank themselves from their outlets, as metal combs ran up the wallpaper and unzipped it, exposing the apartment's pale underbelly.

He spent the next hour tidying her up, apologizing, reattaching her hands with duct tape and glue. "It's horse glue," he said, "and there's nothing stronger than a horse."

She wondered if horses were so strong why they didn't stop men from making glue out of them. But perhaps that was a ridiculous thing to think about when your husband was giving you back your hands.

"From now on you get to keep your hands," he said. "That was really

2

pretty ridiculous of me—how can I expect you to clean house and fix dinner if you don't have your hands?" He kissed her on the neck, lingered, and gave her a little nibble. "Oh, I could just eat you up," he whispered, biting just enough to hurt. She stared at the kitchen counter until the corner of it melted, dripping red goop onto the white tile floor.

He graciously ordered Chinese, which they ate on the couch in front of the TV. Then he started drinking, and the more he drank the angrier he became, and the drunker she became, even though he hadn't shared it with her.

He suddenly shouted and everything hit the wall, including her. She sat in the corner and watched him, all by himself in the empty center of the blast. He looked like a sad little boy who had broken all his toys. "I wish you wouldn't make me lose it like that," he said. "After a long day at work it just takes everything out of me."

"Maybe if you took a nap?" She'd forgotten that she should never suggest things. She pushed herself more tightly into the corner, until the geometry of the wall began to separate and she could feel herself falling through the sky.

She could hear him ask from the ground below, "You do love me, don't you?"

She didn't know why he bothered to ask. He didn't believe anything she had to say. "Of course—" but she didn't finish.

"I couldn't live without you," he said again, so softly it was more to himself than to anyone else. Still she heard it, and felt weakened by the statement.

Still falling through the air, she closed her eyes.

"I don't want to have to teach you a lesson!" he shouted from the street. She got off the bed and looked around—the apartment was on fire.

It had been a whirlwind romance. He'd said he loved her on their second date. She should have jumped out of the window right then and there. She jumped out of the window now.

A little bird flew up to her. "Just keep your mouth shut!" it warned. She smiled, feeling just like a Disney princess.

Her mother used to say (her lips squirming around a broken cigarette, her eye swollen shut and as black as Daddy's toast she'd burned that morning) "Let your smile be your umbrella, Sweetheart."

She never could figure that out. Wouldn't a smile just fill with water?

Paula's last, desperate hope was that she wouldn't bounce. If she broke, if she broke into a thousand pieces, at least some of those pieces might escape.

←HE B—POL←Я ƎXPЯƎSS

JOHN PALISANO

ON **CHRISTMAS ƎVE** the boy looked out the window of his room at the Mars Rehabilitation Center and saw falling snow. He pushed back his covers and knelt on the edge of his bed. How could it be snowing in San Diego? That would be almost impossible. It must have been the new meds he was on—they were making him crazy and causing him to hallucinate. The snow made thudding noises on the roof outside. *Maybe it's actually hailing?* The boy got up and off his stiff bed, rubbed his eyes, and went toward the window.

He inched closer and saw the white dots falling from the sky were not, in fact, snowflakes, but rather, pills. Hundreds of thousands of small, white capsules pattered against the porch roof. He raised his window and put a hand outside.

"Ouch." They were hard and fell fast. Catching several in his palm, he sorted through them with his opposite hand. He read their labels. "Klonopin? Abilify? Zyprexa? Welbutrin?" he said. "It's raining happy pills." The boy pocketed the tablets. One never knew when they'd come in handy.

"Who says there's no Santa Claus?" he said, looking around the room for something to catch more of the pills with. He spotted a small garbage can with his *Beastie Boys* baseball hat on top. They'd have to do: he didn't want to miss out if it suddenly stopped raining Crazy Capsules. He pulled the liner from the garbage can and put the can out on the roof. Then he placed his hat next to the can. They filled rapidly, both overflowing with drugs.

He heard a large noise coming from outside. It was as if someone had the world's largest bass system in their car and was coming up the driveway. That couldn't be possible. They'd never get past the gate. Security never let anyone in who was playing music. That was a one-way ticket to never to come back.

The music sounded from within the compound, somehow. Leaning out the window, the boy saw an incredible sight. The biggest train he'd ever seen made its way from the bottom of the hill toward the main house, where the boy just happened to be staying. How could that be? There were no tracks. There was nothing but grass. He heard crunching sounds as the train rolled over the humps of pills flooding over the fields.

The boy looked down at the little white ovals cascading off the house. "You're really nuts," he said. "Wake up. This is just some really screwed up dream."

Shutting his eyes, he expected everything would be gone as soon as he opened them. It wasn't. Instead, the train pulled up alongside the safe house and stopped. Clouds of steam puffed around its wheels, which he noticed had been outfitted with spinning, shiny rims. Someone had stuck fake bullet hole stickers on the door to the driver's compartment up front. Pills bounced off the train in every direction.

The boy felt high. His mind seemed as though it might squish right out from between his ears and melt out through his nose and mouth. He wanted to go outside and touch the train—see if it was real. How could he? His room wasn't locked: that's what a year of good behavior on Mars got you, but Maurice was down there. No way he'd get past Maurice and the front door. Nope. If he wanted to go outside, the roof was the only way. How would he do such a thing? It was raining slippery pills, which would probably make him slide off the roof and fall. There was no other way.

"All right," he said. "Go slow." He put his arms outside the window. Immediately he felt the hard pelts from the falling pills. He jutted his head out, then his mid-section. "This is crazy," he said. "But I guess I'm crazy, too."

His whole body was out on the roof; he knelt on all fours. "If anyone sees me, I'm a goner." As he moved toward the front of the roof, he was thinking about how he might slowly lower his body over the side and allow himself to drop safely to the ground.

He lost his balance. The pills were too slippery. He rolled off the roof and flew into the air.

He put his hands out in front of him to try and brace and stop himself. He screamed, "Oh," at the top of his lungs.

Stretching his legs out before him, the boy tried to stand upward in hopes of breaking his fall that way, but as soon as his feet hit the pill-covered ground, they went out from under him and he went down right on his butt. "Oof." He put his hands to the sides of his butt and rubbed a little. He was already sore.

More pills rained down upon his head.

Looking behind him, he could barely see the Mars safe house. The pills were falling too fast and blotted it out of sight. He really wanted to get out from under them.

He stood and looked at the train.

The locomotive stretched as far as he could see. Painted black, it towered over him. The boy walked along the side, but all the windows were tinted and the doors were shut.

There was a light several cars down.

The train lurched forward. The engine fired up, shaking the ground with its low rumble.

"I better hurry," he said.

Then he walked faster. He wanted to run, but he was sure he'd slip.

The light wasn't so far away, but the train was picking up momentum.

The boy said, "Wait for me." He didn't know who he was talking to, but he was used to talking to himself.

The boy heard the loud, clear voice of a man. It came from near the light. "All aboard." It had to be the conductor.

He rushed.

The train went faster.

Finally he made it to the light, which he found came from a doorway between cars, and to the conductor, who stood on a platform on the bottom of a set of stairs.

"Tickets, please," said the Conductor.

The boy's eyes widened. He didn't have one.

"I don't have a ticket," he said. "But I know this train was meant for me. It came right up to my . . . house."

The Conductor ran a hand through his long grey-blond beard and regarded the boy from the corner of his eye. "Are you sure you don't have a ticket?"

"No," the boy said. "I don't." He was wearing a bathrobe and pajamas.

"Why don't you check your pocket?" said the Conductor.

He walked faster in pace with the train. "Fine," he said and reached into the front pocket of his robe. He found a crumpled up gold tinted paper inside. When he pulled it out and straightened it, he saw it was a prescription for Klonopin. "Shoot," he said. "See? There's no ticket."

The Conductor smiled. He reached out a hand. "That looks like a ticket to me," he said and took the prescription.

"Huh?" he said, and looked at the Conductor, who pulled out a hole-punch and clicked it across the ticket. He handed it back. There was a 'P' punched into it.

"What does that mean?" the boy said.

"You'll have to find out on your own," the Conductor said. "When we get to that place between the North Pole and the South Pole."

"You mean the Middle Pole?" said the boy.

"Why, yes. Indeed. The Middle Pole. Get on board." The Conductor held out a hand and grabbed him. His grip was strong and he pulled upward. In a blink, the boy was up and on the train.

As he stood on the platform between the cars, the Conductor said, "Welcome to the BiPolar Express."

The boy opened the door to the car, where he saw several other people sitting in large couch-sized chairs. The first person he noticed was a tall, lanky blonde girl who looked to be about twenty-five or so. She leaned her head against the window and folded her hands on her lap. She looked out of it. In the seat behind the drooping girl, an anxious guy with short-cropped blue hair grinned. "Hey man," he said. "Come sit next to me." He patted the large leather seat.

The boy walked toward the blue-haired fellow, catching a glance at the unconscious girl on the way. "We all want to sit with Annie," the blue-haired boy said. "She's hot, but she's as nuts as they come." He twirled a finger near his temple.

Sitting down next to the blue-haired fellow, the boy reached out his hand. "Hi," he said.

The blue-haired fellow reached out his hand and made to shake. "My name's Tony," he said before quickly retreating his hand. "But I don't shake hands." He turned away from the boy and whistled. "I don't want what you've got. No offense, but you can catch things just by shaking hands." He turned and faced the boy before he gestured to a seat behind them. "How do you think Henry back there turned out the way he has?"

"I don't know," said the boy.

Tony turned back to him, his smile now a frown. "Shaking hands, m'man. That's what the government doesn't want you to know about. That's their secret weapon. Spreading mental illness through ordinary contact. Then they can get the whole country addicted to pills. It's messed up."

"Really?" the boy said.

Tony raised his voice. "Yes, really. What are you thinking, man?" He sighed and looked out the window. "We're moving. This your first time riding the BiPolar Express?"

"Yes, it is."

"Well you're in for a treat," Tony said. "You're not going to believe what you're in for."

Scanning the rest of the car, the boy took inventory of some of the others riding in the car. There was a black guy about his age listening to music. He could tell because he had red earbud cords dangling down toward one of his pockets. He seemed preoccupied. Next to him, a teenage girl with a short bob haircut leaned back and had her feet up on the seat in front of her. She seemed angry; she pulled on her index finger repeatedly.

On the other side of those two, another unlikely pair talked. The guy sat on the aisle seat, his potbelly hanging over. He wore glasses and had a mop of curly reddish hair and a gap between his two front teeth. He spoke with a Massachusetts accent. "What you've got to do is listen to your heart at all times. You're on the ledge right now, but you're not going to be standing there forever, you've got to realize. This is only a temporary time for you."

The girl sitting next to him, a waif of a thing with shoulder length brown hair and super pale skin, was listening to him, but wasn't looking at him. The boy thought she looked like a deer caught in headlights. He wanted to go over there and say something, but knew he'd probably get sucked into listening to the guy's ramble, so he stayed put.

The boy realized he was one of the youngest passengers on the train. He'd only just turned sixteen. Some of the others looked twice his age. Many might have been older.

The boy turned his attention out the window. He didn't recognize a single thing. It was as if they'd turned a corner and entered a whole new world. Thickets of trees had replaced the strip malls and wide streets the boy had expected to see. How could they have gotten so far out of the city so quickly? Where were they going? How long would they be gone?

THE BIPOLAR EXPRESS

The pills no longer fell from the sky, but they still covered the ground as far as the boy could see. He wondered how there could be so many pills. It seemed impossible. "If those are all pills out there, then there's enough for the whole world to be on them, isn't there?" he said.

Tony nodded. "Now you're finally starting to figure it out. That's what they want."

"They?"

"Come on, man. You know who: Drug makers. The White House. Fox News. Them."

The boy shrugged. "I don't understand. The whole world can't be on drugs, can it?"

Tony turned, his face deadly serious. "Can't it?"

The door of their cab opened and the conductor walked through. "Everybody have their tickets?" he said.

Checking his pocket, the boy found his prescription still there. *Good*, he thought. Tony held out not one, not two, but five prescription slips. "Got one for each of my personalities," he said.

The boy didn't know what to say.

Tony nudged him. "Oh, come on," he said. "Just messing with you. I've only got three personalities: Happy. Sad. And in your face."

Laughing a little, the boy said, "I like that. That's funny."

Shaking his head, Tony wouldn't look up. "I find it really and truly sad. I don't even think they know what they're doing with these pills half the time. I mean: they seem to work in some ways, but in other ways? Forget it. The side effects are worse than what they're supposedly curing."

"I can't function on Klonopin," the boy said. "Not at all. I feel like I'm in *Dawn Of The Dead* or something, you know what I mean?"

Shaking his head, Tony held the boy for a good strong moment. When Tony let go, he couldn't help but notice how good he smelled and how soft the skin on his face was and how luxurious his long hair felt. He thought, *What a strange young man.*

There was a loud noise from the front of the car. Someone was attempting to break in. Well, at least it looked that way to Tony. The man's face was smashed against the window, his nose turned to one side. He yelled, but no one could hear him. The doorknob turned, but the door would not open. The man got angrier and angrier. "Suppose we should let him in?" Tony said.

The boy shrugged. "Probably shake things up if we do. He looks ready to blow a gasket."

"Maybe he needs *his* meds?" Tony said.

"Or get his ass kicked."

One of the girls near the front looked up, surprised. It took her a moment to realize what was going on, but she stood and opened the door. The man stalked inside the car. He frowned and he eyed everyone up and down with his bulging Marty Feldman eyes. "We got some special hot chocolate for all you," he said, his voice raspy and loud. "Something to calm you down."

Tony whispered to the boy, "Damn. They're giving us spiked hot chocolate now. What's up with that?" He sighed. "Typical caregivers. They'll try any trick to make sure we're properly medicated."

The boy said, "No doubt. And you know what? I'm feeling a little melancholy right now. It sounds like just the right time for a little mood stabilizer."

The car door burst open. The strange, fat man rushed inside carrying a large, industrial-sized thermos. "All right kiddies. It's time for a little refreshment."

Three other men followed him. They all wore black head to toe. None of them seemed in the least bit happy.

One of the girls in front of them waved the hot cocoa away. "Is it vegan?" she said.

The server looked confused. "It's hot chocolate," he said. "I don't think it has any meat in it."

"Does it have milk?" she said.

"Hell . . . I don't know."

Tony rose and tapped her on the shoulder. "Hey? Sarah?" he said. "You know you're not really a vegan?"

"Sure I am," she said, turning to him.

"Nope," Tony said. "During our lifetime, the average person swallows up to eight spiders while they're sleeping. So that means you've eaten meat."

"I don't believe you," she said, and turned back around. "That can't be true." She waved the hot cocoa away. "I can't have that."

Tony laughed and turned to the boy. He pointed his thumb at Sarah. "Just ruined her day, didn't I?"

THE BIPOLAR EXPRESS

They took their hot chocolate. The boy sipped his. Tony craned his head back and took it down in one swig. "Oh? Was I supposed to savor that? I'm so used to just slamming everything. Drinks. Meds. Women. Men. Whatever."

The boy said, "You're crazy, you know that?"

"Not crazy. BiPolar."

"Are you feeling anything yet?" the boy said.

Tony shook his head. "Not really, man. But I've got a pretty high tolerance after all these years."

"I wonder what was in that stuff."

"Hopefully something good that'll make us feel all warm and fuzzy pretty soon. Know what I mean?"

"I'd love that," the boy said. "I could use a little something to get me through this trip."

The train inclined slightly. Outside, the scenery changed from suburban to a more desolate landscape. "What's happening?" the boy said.

"We're leaving our hood," Tony said. "And we're heading into the outskirts, toward the Middle Pole."

"Do you know exactly where the Middle Pole is?" the boy said.

Tony grinned. "Right between the North and South Poles," he said and tapped the boy on the side of the head. "Where do you think?"

"I wasn't sure. But now that you mention it . . . "

The train tilted slightly up. "What's going on?" the boy said. He grabbed the sides of his chair.

They looked out the window. The train travelled up an incline. "Now what's happening?" said Tony. "This thing gonna fly?"

The boy said, "I think we're going up a mountain."

He was right. "How did we get out of San Diego so quick?" he said.

"Magic," Tony said. The train climbed higher. The other riders were all rapt, their noses pressed against their windows. Everyone smiled. They could see the moonlit sky brightening the vast, snow-covered valley below. There were other mountains in the distance. Stars twinkled.

"You know what?" someone said from across the aisle. "I feel really good right now." He looked around the car, his grin spread ear to ear.

The others all wore similar grins.

Tony looked at the boy. "Look at you," he said. "You look like you just won the friggin' Lotto."

"I feel . . . excellent," the boy said.

"The hot chocolate did it."

The boy pointed at him. "You're smiling, too."

"I'm always smiling. Makes no difference to me what's going on in the outside world."

"I don't usually like to smile so much," said the boy. "It hurts my face."

Tony laughed. "What's wrong with you? Smiling doesn't hurt your face? Does it hurt now?"

"Yes it does."

Shaking his head, Tony said, "This doesn't make any sense to me. How could the meds work that fast?"

"I don't think it's just the meds," said the boy. "I think it has a lot to do with the train going higher. Look." They were on a steeper incline, a fact made obvious when they looked out the window and saw the landscape on a slant.

Someone said, "The world looks like half a triangle now." It was the girl in front of them, but her voice was strangely asexual. She laughed.

The boy nudged Tony. "See?" he said. "It's obviously affecting her. Look at everyone else on the train."

Two rows ahead of them, a pair of boys stared back. Their eyes were wide and they wore huge grins. "This is one of the most amazing things that's ever happened to me," one said. "I just can't believe how fortunate I am."

"Me, neither," said the other. He wore bandages around his wrists. "I want to live to be a hundred. I want to make a million dollars. I bet we're all going to make a million dollars. I think I'm going to go on Amazon and buy every Stephen King and Social Distortion album ever made. I'll have the money. It'll come. Who cares?"

The boy shook his head. "This is not a good sign. They're manic."

"Are you feeling manic, too?" Tony said.

"My heart *is* racing," the boy said. "I'm trying not to think about it too much. I mean: after hearing him say he wants to buy stuff, I immediately thought about buying myself a new Strat with my Amex."

"You play?"

"Kind of. It's always been my dream."

"They let you have that stuff where you're staying? I mean: we're all staying somewhere other than home, and I don't mean these places aren't our homes now or anything, it's just not that they're our real home or anything, you know what I mean? Where we can play guitar as loud as we want, bring home who we want, eat what we want, get drunk, party, pass out. That sort of thing. Know what I'm saying?"

The boy said, "I think you need to breathe."

Tony waved him away. "I don't have time for that." He smirked. "Come on. My mind is racing. Look outside. We're flying high. We've got to be a hundred miles off the ground now. Isn't this amazing?"

"I hate heights," the boy said. "I hope we don't stay like this for too long. It's very uncomfortable for me. I really don't like this warm, fuzzy feeling spreading inside of me. It's way out of control."

"Get used to it," Tony said. "More where that came from." The train climbed the mountain.

Someone behind them hummed. The boy turned around and checked out who it was: a pretty brunette girl with a gigantic nose. She smiled, although her lips were shut. Her head bobbed gently from side to side. Others were equally affected. Scanning the train, the boy was surprised to see nearly everyone smiled. Many were singing to themselves.

The train leveled out as they neared the top of the mountain. They could see for miles. The winter world looked beautiful: vast valleys were covered in snow. Frozen lakes glistened in the moonlight. Yellow lights lit small cottages. Wispy grey clouds drifted near the large, grey moon.

"The view up here is unreal," the boy said. "Even though it's too far up." He felt the weight of the train moving on the tracks underneath his body; the sensation comforted him. He shut his eyes for a moment and just enjoyed it.

His belly shifted. It felt like something had dropped. He opened his eyes. Tony was looking around the car. Everyone had felt it. Their smiles were gone. The car had gone silent.

The front of the train pointed down.

"We're going down," someone shouted from in front of them.

Tony grabbed the boy's hand. "I hate this part," he said.

"You're scared?"

Tony forced a brief smile. "Hate heights."

"I hear you . . . " the boy said.

The train sped up. Its nose declined.

Within moments they were racing down the mountain. Fast. Tony squeezed the boy's hand with all his might. He swore several times. "Fudge." "Dill lover." "Geek Snod."

JOHN PALISANO

The boy did his best to ignore Tony's mouth. He tried not to laugh at his G-rated tirade.

Faster and faster ran the train, down the mountain it went, winding around sharp bends, shaking violently.

"We're inches away from the mountain side," the boy said, pointing at the window. "We might hit it."

On the opposite side of the car, a tattooed boy said, "We're really close to the edge." He had his hands splayed on either side of his window.

"This sucks," Tony said. He let go of the boy's hand and clutched the sides of his seat. "Make it stop."

The train kept right on going down.

"Ahhh," someone said.

The car filled with moans. "It sounds like everyone's dying," the boy said.

"We probably are," Tony said.

"Why aren't there any seat belts? I feel like I'm going to fall out of my seat."

It took much less time for the train to reach the bottom of the mountain then it did to race to the top.

The boy held onto the sides of his seat with all his might. "Feels like I'm going to fall right off the chair," he said. "It's all in my stomach."

"I want to puke," Tony said. "God."

Moans and groans filled the car as the train leveled off. They'd hit a low valley.

Someone said, "I feel so . . . low."

"Me, too," another piped in. "It's horrible, this sinking feeling in my head."

Tony looked at the boy. "Here's the flip side of being manic," he said. "I hate this going down stuff."

The boy put his hand to the side of his head. "I've felt like this before. It's like I was seeing the world in widescreen, but now, suddenly, someone's put blinders on the side of my head and I can only see a small area in front of me."

"Like horse blinders?" Tony said.

"Yeah. Just like that. And I just feel . . . crappy."

Tony nodded. "So much for those meds they gave us. I was hoping they'd stabilize us, but they've made the extremes even worse." He pointed out the window. "I think my heart's racing really fast now, and I wish I was underneath the train getting run over by it instead of sitting in this big fat seat next to you."

14

Someone behind them said, "Wish I was underneath the tracks along with you, man."

"You go first," Tony said. "Tell me how that works out for you."

The fellow behind them kept quiet. Tony shrugged and the boy looked out the window again. "I don't see anything but tons of ice and snow out there now. It's like we're in a no man's land or something."

"We are," Tony said. "This is really messed up." He put his head in his hands and bent down. "I just want to die right now. Can we please stop talking?" His mouth stretched into a painful grimace, which the boy could see even though Tony's head was down.

"God, I wish I was at home surfing the Internet instead of here." It was the girl from the front of the car. "I really hate this. Why do we need to feel this way? Why can't we just feel 'up' all the time? Is that so much to ask?"

Someone else said, "I think I'll be able to bend spoons with my mind soon."

Another said, "My brains are going to ooze out of my skull any second. They're melting inside my skull."

A third voice said, "My eyes hurt. Everything hurts."

Everyone complained. If they didn't talk, they moaned.

The boy said, "I think everyone's dying in here. It sounds like we're walking through a field after a battle and all the dying soldiers are crying."

"Sounds like a bunch of babies," Tony said. "I include myself in with them." He made a noise like a crying baby.

The train continued forward.

The moans and groans continued for several more minutes, but died down.

A sign rolled past them.

Middle Pole. Five Miles.

There was a picture of a woman on the sign holding a brown plastic pill bottle while she smiled.

"Is she going to be there?" Tony said. "I hope so."

The boy pointed at him. "You're smiling," he said.

Tony nodded. "I think I'm starting to feel okay now. Not too crazy, up or down. Guess we're getting close."

"I cannot wait to find out why we're being brought here," the boy said.

Tony smiled, "To meet Manic Claus, of course."

As the BiPolar Express pulled into the outskirts of the Middle Pole, buildings sprang up around them. "It's all mental health facilities and hospitals," the boy said. "Look at the names: Johnson Psychiatric. Aldrich Home For The Needy. Zimmerman's Home for Girls. Gage's Great Escape. Troy's Recovery Room. What the heck?"

"This is where they do all the testing for the new pills they're developing," Tony said. "We're in Mecca for mood meds."

"Great," the boy said. "Why can't they make one that just works, then?"

They passed by more hospitals and homes, their frequency getting higher, the area between them closer.

Someone said, "Look."

There were people outside, darting between the clinics. Little people. Really little people.

"Elves," the boy said. "Wearing lab coats."

"They're pharmacists," Tony said. "Look at that: they're carrying prescriptions door to door."

"So that's how the pills get to the hospital? I always wondered about that."

Tony nudged him. "I don't think little elves dressed in white coats make it to Pasadena," he said.

"San Diego."

"San whatever," Tony said. "Snot."

"Still pretty cool. They're pretty neat looking."

The train pulled farther into the Middle Pole. Streets stretched in every direction. There were condominium complexes everywhere. Most of them had 'for rent' signs on them.

The center of the Middle Pole was overcrowded with elves. Some had climbed onto one another's shoulders to get a better view.

The BiPolar Express came to a stop.

Everyone on board stood.

"We're here," the boy said. "This is so exciting."

Tony cocked his head to the side. "What's wrong with you?" he said. "You're always so damn positive about everything."

The boy nodded. "Guess that's just the way I am. What can I do?"

"If you're so happy, then why are you even in a mental hospital? Why are you here?"

"I'm not always like this," the boy said. "The flip side is that I get really, really dark. I've been in some pretty bad places, mentally, where I didn't think I'd be able to go on. Couldn't find my way out without help."

Tony made a gesture as though he were hanging himself from a noose.

The boy nodded. "Been there," he said. "More times than I'd like to admit. But when I'm 'up' it's like I can't really remember how bad those moments are."

"Huh," Tony said. "So you're just as messed up as the rest of us."

"Probably. Yes. I think that's right."

Tony made his way from their seat. "Sure, now?" He laughed a little. "Come on."

The doors to the car opened and they filed outside. The ticket taker stood just a few feet from the train. He held an electric lantern. "Come on, come on, everybody: Manic Claus is waiting for you. Go right on up to the town square."

As the line shoved forward, Tony said, "Manic Claus is the name he goes by, but his real name is Sam St. Nick. He built the Middle Pole with the profits from his pharmaceutical company."

"Which one is that?" the boy said.

"White Pharmaceuticals."

"They make everything good."

"Yup," Tony said. "And this is his way of giving back."

"The Middle Pole?"

"Not North or South, but 'even' and 'in-between', just like they want you and me to be." Tony smirked.

"Balanced," the boy said.

When they reached the town square, they realized they were far from alone. The center was filled with thousands and thousands of young men and women. "How do you think they all got here?" he said to Tony. "Maybe there's a Schizophrenic Sled? A Manic Mover? A Suicidal Ship?"

The line moved forward. As they walked up to the center area of the Middle Pole, they saw a huge white sled. It had tank treads instead of sleds. There were several dogs tied up in front of the sled, each wearing a blue vest with the words THERAPY DOG embroidered on the side. The boy knew therapy dogs were often prescribed to folks suffering with BiPolar disorder as a way to cheer them up, help them cope, and give them some responsibility.

"The one in front . . . the Sharpe?" Tony said. "His name is Henry."

"Does his nose glow?" the boy said.

"No.But his ears do. They turn bright red." The boy said, "Weird."

Music started.

Drums. A catchy guitar riff. Bass. The crowd cheered.

"He's coming," Tony said. "Here we go."

They heard singing.

When you're feeling down
When you're feeling blue
I've got just the thing
For you to do
Take a pill
Not one, but two
I'm So Glad the World's Sad

They couldn't see where the singing was coming from. "Where is he?" the boy said. "I want to see him."

There was a brief instrumental break, during which there was loud, cannon-like sound. A trap door opened near the white sled and Manic Claus shot through the air, waving his arms and smiling. He was wearing dark blue hospital scrubs, a red felt hat with a white puff on the end, and matching booties.

"He looks like Kevin Spacey to me," the boy said. "Not really what I was expecting."

"You were thinking he'd look like Santa Claus or something, right?"

"Kind of, yeah."

"You have to expect different with the Middle Pole," Tony said. "You have to keep an open mind."

"My mind is open."

"Shut up. We're missing the song."

Manic Claus leaned in on one leg. The guitar sounded more distorted. The crowd banged their heads. Manic Claus banged his head, too.

The song returned to its original melody and Manic Claus sang:

THE BIPOLAR EXPRESS

Sometimes you're up
Sometimes you're down
I've got something great
To get rid of that frown
Pop one in your mouth
Yellow or white
You'll be feeling better after tonight
I'm So Glad the World's Sad
It's made me rich beyond my dreams
Screams die down inside your head
As you become as docile as the family pet
You can't speak
You can barely move
You always sleep
Until half past noon
Your pillow gets wet with tons of drool
But . . .
I'm So Glad the World's Sad
Works out well for me
I keep counting my money
Let's invent another mind disease.
Please. Because I'd like to buy Belize.
Who's with me?

Then he broke it down into a bridge. Manic Claus jumped on top of his strange white sled and thrust his hips.

It's no fun to see
In fact it's kind of creepy
People going around feelin' funky
But I've got a magic pill for each of you
It'll make you feel better: I speak the truth.

He went back to the chorus. An elf jumped out from the trapdoor carrying a goldtop Les Paul, and when he put his fingers to the frets:
The worst, most unmusical sounds emanated from the guitar amp. It was as though the elf had no idea how to play.
"This is what your mind sounds like without Manic Claus," he sang.
Other elves hurried up the guitar-slinging elf. They carried a huge

19

pill-shaped rocket and put it down in front of the guitarist. He climbed inside and sat on the little seat.

Manic Claus said, "Now here's what happens when you take two pills and call me in the morning."

Gorgeous, fluid, fast notes poured from the guitar. The elf shut his eyes and threw his head back. His miniature elf fingers disappeared into a blur because they were moving so fast. It was as though Paganini had possessed the elf. The solo reached a climax. As it did, fireworks exploded in the sky.

Manic Clause went back to the chorus.

I'm So Glad the World's Sad
Works out great for me.

He gestured for the crowd to sing along, which they did. Even the boy found himself chanting the almost-catchy chorus.

Tony frowned and crossed his arms. "This is garbage," he said. "Hate it."

The song finished with Manic Claus thrusting his arms in the air and tilting his head back as the music carried on like the end of a thousand AC/DC songs. Finally, they hit the last note. Everyone cheered, although it sounded like a lot of people were moaning, too. The boy thought maybe a lot of their meds were wearing off.

Manic Claus worked to catch his breath. His eyebrows raised and his mouth worked its way into a frown. He cleared his throat and looked around at the huge crowd amassed in every direction.

He brought the microphone to his mouth. It did not feedback, like it seems to do in every movie just before someone begins to speak. It was clear as a bell. "Good evening, all my patients. How are you? How're the pills treating you?"

The crowd made noise, but it was not what the boy expected. He thought he heard boos and cries mixed in equally with the cheers. There were even people near him who were giving Manic Claus the middle finger. One mannish young woman even spit toward Manic Claus, but, as she was hundreds of feet away, her loogie landed on the back of some oaf's head. He didn't even seem to notice.

"We've been listening to your feedback all year round, and we know that some of the pills have had mixed results for you. But our biggest complaint is that you all have to take your pills every day, and that it takes a few weeks for the medicine to help you."

More mixed noises from the crowd.

Manic Claus continued. "We here at White Pharmaceuticals have developed a new pill for you. You will only need to take it once a year." He lifted a single pill up in front of him, and then put it over his head. "We're calling it Idealify, and today I'm going to pick one lucky patient to get started right away."

The boy and Tony looked at one another and shrugged.

"All right. Everybody get out their Golden Prescriptions," Manic Claus said. "Look at the number at the top right corner." He held a small golden envelope in his left hand, which he opened. He produced a piece of paper from inside. "And the winning number is six, one, three, one, nine, seven, two."

The boy could hardly believe his eyes as he looked over the prescription. Manic Claus repeated the winning numbers, and the boy nodded.

He'd won.

"It's me," he said to Tony. "I don't believe it."

"Do we have a winner?" Manic Claus said.

The boy raised his hand, but couldn't be seen through the crowd. "Come on," Tony said, "get up on my shoulders." They made their way to the front of the crowd, to the lip of the stage, where the boy waved the Golden Prescription.

"It's me," he said. "I've won. I have the Golden Prescription. Right here."

"Well come right on up here, young man," Manic Claus said. "Show us what you've got."

The boy got himself off Tony's shoulders and stumbled his way on stage. He went to shake Manic Claus's hand, but Manic Claus reached for his other hand, the one holding the Golden Prescription. "Sorry," he said. "We've got to verify this before we go forward." Manic Claus matched the numbers and nodded. "We're good. We have a winner."

The crowd erupted.

The boy looked around. Every eye was on him. He suddenly felt frightened and frozen.

Manic Claus shook his hand. "Now, listen, what's your name?"

"My name is . . . "

"Wait. Before I forget, there's a few things I need to tell you." He talked fast. "Side effects of Idealify might include eight-hour long erections. Nosebleeds. Failure of the hippocampus. Vision turned to black and white instead of 3-D. Constipation of the urethra. Your brain may melt inside your head. Those sorts of things. Okay?"

"Okay, but . . . " the boy said.

"Then we're in complete agreement?" Manic Claus said. He produced a brass bell from within his jacket and displayed it palms up with his left hand. "Here's the magic part of it. Whenever you feel like you're getting sad again, or that you're getting too high, all you have to do is . . . " He raised the bell to his ear and shook it. "Give yourself a little ring. You hear that? That delightful little bell sound?"

The boy nodded.

"That's going to trigger the Idealify to start working. And when I say, 'working' I mean it. This stuff works fast. No more waiting two weeks to feel better. No more getting groggy and out of it. This stuff will get you to equal and keep you there." He bent down to the boy. "So will you be our first beta tester?"

A grin spread across the boy's face. "Absolutely," he said. "Sign me up."

Manic Claus put an arm around the boy. "We'll get you on your way just as soon as we can."

With that, the music to "I'm Glad the World's Sad" came back to life. This time, though, Manic Claus didn't sing. He didn't have to. The crowd did it for him.

Before they knew it, the party ended and they filed back to their sleds, buses, helicopters, planes, and trains.

Riding back, the boy sat next to Tony once again. "I can't believe he chose you," Tony said. "You're so damn lucky. But don't go getting a swollen head or anything like that."

The boy shook his head. "Not me," he said. "I'm just grateful for this. It sounds like they've finally found something that will actually work."

"I'm right behind you," Tony said, and waved his Golden Prescription. "Don't forget he gave everyone a 'scrip to take home. We just have to go get them filled."

They looked out the window and watched the Middle Pole slowly turn into barrens.

Eventually they made it back to their world.

THE BiPOLAR EXPRESS

The BiPolar Express pulled up to the Mars Clinic and the boy got up. So did Tony. "Come on, give me some sugar," Tony said, and hugged the boy with one arm. "Look me up on Facebook," he said. "Let's not bother with e-mails. No one does that anymore."

"Okay," the boy said. "I will."

He smiled and left the car.

On his way down the steps the conductor stopped the boy. "Do you have your bell?" he said.

The boy showed it to him and went to ring it.

"Ah. Ah," the conductor said as he cupped the boy's hands. "Only do that when you need to feel better, remember?"

"Y-yes," the boy said. "That's right. I will."

The boy hopped down and stood in the driveway of the Mars Clinic. He watched as the BiPolar Express slowly got back up to speed and pulled away.

He waved at the conductor. He saw the people inside the car where he'd sat.

Some smiled at him. Tony did, too, as he gave him the finger.

The boy trudged his way through the sea of pills still littering the area around the clinic. He was surprised no one had noticed the entire time he'd been gone.

He looked up at his room and wondered how he was going to be able to get back up there. There were no ladders, and there didn't seem to be anything he could climb.

The front door opened slightly.

Mrs. Drake stood there. The boy was scared at first, but noticed she was smiling. The others from the clinic were behind her. "I hear you had a very special night," she said, "and that you were chosen for a something very special."

The boy nodded. "I think I was."

"Think?" she said. "Get in here."

They made him tell the story twice. No one could believe it. How had he been so lucky? How had he been chosen? Certainly there must have been better candidates.

"Nonsense," Mrs. Drake said. "You've been given a gift. Don't second guess it."

"I guess you're right," the boy said. "But it's getting late and I'm getting really tired."

The boy pulled his covers up to his chin and smiled. It'd been an amazing evening. He didn't believe it'd even been real. He took the bell from his nightstand and looked at it, rotating it several times on his fingers.

"Wow," he said. "Look at that." He saw his reflection on its surface. He wanted to hear it, but remembered Manic Claus telling him not to shake it until he was feeling down. "What's the worst that can happen? I get high? Sounds good, actually."

He put it to his ear and shook it.

The sound was beautiful. Perfectly musical.

Shutting his eyes, he brought the bell to his chest and cradled it with both hands. He felt warmth spread from the middle of his belly, up his chest, and into his head and face. He felt fuzzy and warm and happier than he'd ever felt before.

Soon, he fell asleep.

In his dream he found himself on a warm beach. Everything seemed tinted gold. On a lounge, he spotted a dark skinned man wearing shorts while holding a reflector under his chin. He wasn't sure how, but the boy knew it to be the prophet Mohammed. The boy wanted to go over to him and talk to him, but there was commotion in the way of noise coming from behind him.

The boy looked out to the ocean, where he saw Jesus and Buddha on surfboards. They were both up and riding a very pleasant wave.

Jesus reached out and tapped Buddha on the back. Buddha tried to keep his balance, but after a few misplaced steps, he fell face first into the water. Jesus laughed. Buddha's surfboard sprung ahead and made it to the shore. Buddha bounced to the surface like a balloon, his belly making it out of the water first. He pointed at Jesus. "You silly man, you." They both laughed. "I'll get you in your Holy Ghost."

Jesus made a perfect landing on the beach. He made eye contact with the boy. "My son," he said. "How are you?"

The boy couldn't speak.

The earth shook underneath them.

Something lifted from beneath the sand; Jesus, Buddha, Mohammed, and the boy were lifted into the air by some massive force.

The boy noticed they were being held hundreds of feet in the air by a massive hand. Two eyes as big as school buses checked them out. Its head was that of what could only be a giant octopus. Its body was slightly humanoid, although it had large tentacles jutting out in every direction. They blocked out the sun. The day became dark and the stars of countless universes were clear behind them. "I have come," said the great Cthulhu inside their minds.

The boy was scared; his stomach hurt. "This is only a side effect of the pills," he said. "We'll be fine."

He smiled and put his arms out to his Holy Friends. Everyone was happy. Happier than they'd ever been.

Mrs. Drake opened the door to check on the boy. She saw that he was still and that he smiled. His hands were clasped nicely around his chest and she could see the bell being held within his fingers. "That's nice," she thought.

She heard a fizzing sound coming from the boy.

Stepping closer, she confirmed the sound was not her imagination. Something oozed from the boy's left ear. She turned on a light, but couldn't let out a scream. It was too much for her to process. The boy's brains stained his pillow as they piled up next to his head. The fizzing sound got louder and the pile became larger until there was nothing left inside his head. The boy died, but he had done so happy, and smiling, and knowing that, for once, things had gone his way.

AAA◁AAAAA

GABINO IGLESIAS

HE TWO GOONS that came for me had no faces. They looked normal enough with their scary shadow suits, purposeful walk, and the glowing darkness pulsating in the exposed veins covering their hands. However, their faces were negative space. No, it was something infinitely more intense, something like a couple of black holes, a duo of singularities, two spaces between which light fluttered nervously, afraid of being sucked into the promised oblivion of the two gaping voids. I'm tempted to described them like this (   ) (   ) but that would imply that there was some sort of finality to their emptiness, some boundaries to encapsulate their nothingness. It was not like that. It was more like being lost twice in the middle of this

AAAAAAAAA

In any case, they were on me before I was done gasping in surprise, their antimatter simultaneously pulling and pushing me into blissful unconsciousness.

When I opened my eyes, I thought the goons had simply left me in an abandoned building. I only opened my eyes momentarily, registering a dilapidated wall with peeling paint and a gray roof with a strange green bulb. The light from the bulb seemed to come and go, dancing between being and being just a memory of an uncertainty. I didn't want to think too much about it, because the space could easily become too crowded if I placed too many beings in there. Sadly, not wanting is not the same as acting, so my pummeled brain kept contemplating the impossibility of a light that played with its own existence. Like most weird things, it had to either mean something or mean nothing. There was no middle ground. The light could be a signal, or an omen, but it was probably more a direct result of the bumps on my head. A headache unlike any I had ever felt was pounding at my temples with the persistence of a cocked-up woodpecker. I moaned for a while and finally gathered enough strength to sit up and open my eyes in a somewhat definitive matter.

The place was certainly not an old building. I'd love to tell you exactly what it was, but I have no idea. What I'd thought was an old wall covered with peeling paint turned out to be some kind of entity. It expanded and contracted with a rhythm that immediately made me think it was breathing. What I'd thought were strips of paint falling away from the wall were in thin, wing-like membranes. The translucent appendages revealed what I can only describe as veins. A yellowish liquid coursed through them. Lastly, the strange green light bulb skittered around for a few seconds before shutting off and melting into the roof. At least the physicality of this last act managed to shatter any doubts about the thing's reality. Unfortunately, the disappearance also infused those doubts with strength. The duality threatened to split my brain in half.

Scared, worried, and confused, I managed to stand up. The more my head cleared, the stronger I felt. I walked away from the strange white wall and surveyed the room.

The remaining walls seemed to be ordinary. They were flat and white, although their depth was not clear, and I was scared to try to put my hands against them and find out. A wooden door was the only way out of the room. Behind that door was an infinite number of possibilities. I tried to contemplate a few, but when you have no starting point for a thought, when you try to come up with an idea in an absolute void, the result is a dull pain in your chest and mental image that resembles a sheet of paper in which a worrisome scribe has repeatedly attempted to scribble his or her thoughts only to violently erase them before they even had a chance to settle and become a reality.

Feeling trapped between the possibly infinite depth of the white walls and the blurry, abused paleness in my head, I decided to just try the door. I walked to it, grabbed the doorknob and turned. To my surprise, it was unlocked. The surprise itself was surprising to me because I hadn't thought about the possibility of the door being locked, so being surprised that it was open was far more unexpected that it being unlocked. The surprises were short lived, however, because instead of a predictable click, the doorknob emitted an ear-piercing screech. I let go of the door. An image of a pterodactyl getting raped by a giant saguaro came to mind as I struggled to stick my fingers in my ears to block out the infernal shriek. It stopped a few seconds later and the door slowly opened the rest of the way. Sticking to my original plan, I walked out.

On the other side of the door, I found myself standing in long hallway completely covered in what looked like giant black fish scales. It undulated like a snake. I shook my head and immediately thought the two bastards that jumped me had given me a strange drug or had managed to mess me up so bad a piece of my brain had rattled loose. Fighting the movement was a choice, but I opted to will my legs into adapting to the serpentine hallway. They did. Movement is a strange thing when you attach it to reality, but when allowed to break free of all restrictive rules and preconceived notions, it can be a
w   o   n   d   e   r   f   u   l
thing. I eventually found an elevator made of an organic material that

AAAAAAAAA

was pink and speckled with darker bumps. It reminded me of clam chowder, which is something I've heard and read about but never actually tried because the word chowder fills my mouth with an awful taste not unlike what urine-covered slugs taste like, except less crunchy. Since there was no button to press, I screamed out the word ELEVATOR (after all, all words are floating signifiers, but thinking and saying elevator helped me focus my desire) all in capital letters and ignored the scurrying seconds my brain was telling me were running away from me as I waited.

A soft, guttural groan emanated from everywhere at once and the elevator/thing popped open in front of me with a gaseous exhalation. I stepped inside and turned around. Contrary to the outside, there were buttons on a metallic panel on the inside of the elevator/thing, but the symbols underneath them were not in a language or numerical representation I recognized. I pressed the first one from the bottom and felt the elevator move in a plethora of directions at the same time.

The elevator/thing thumped against something and I convinced myself we had reached the first floor. I waited for the doors to open, but instead the elevator puckered up and spit me out into a lobby with corners that bent inward. Recognizing the non-Euclidean geometry from my days living with a French woman who was obsessed with impossible architecture, I knew I was in trouble. Knowing how I had ended up here was not a priority; getting back home was.

The impossible lobby was not only possible but also a concrete thing that surrounded me, and the implications were pushing down on my shoulders with the weight of all the dead dreams of an entire generation. I scanned the place and spotted a door about a mile away. I took three steps and reached it, opened it, and exited the building. As soon as I stepped outside the building, I stepped on something and felt it crack under my right foot. I looked down and found LAC and ONIC trembling a bit. The words had cracked down the middle and both ends were suppurating a liquid that exuded its own need to be the exact opposite of green but failed horribly in its attempt. I murmured an apology to the word, the "sorry" coagulating in my mouth and falling down on top of the ONIC, delivering a gloppy last blow that put that half of the word out of its misery. The death, as always, signaled it was time to move on.

The world outside resembled the world I'd known before, but only at first glance. There was a blue sky above the tall buildings and what looked like a regular street separating the weird, scaled sidewalks. The most obvious difference here was that the city was... alive. There's no other way for me to describe it. The walls of the buildings moved. Buildings moved. There were no cars, no sound, and no people. The blackness that covered the street looked like it was moving forward at breakneck speed, making it look blurry and dangerous to step on. Up in the sky, gelatinous blobs floated around. I wanted to scream, but I feared something would find me and kill me if I did. Not having a plan, I began to walk.

I walked around for hours that first day, not quite able to get used to the sound of my steps reaching my ears with a two second delay despite hearing it constantly. The city appeared to me as a looped creation. I tried to take one right and one left or to take a few rights consecutively, but my surroundings changed only slightly. The sense of forward movement was there, but the feeling of stagnation pressed itself against my torso until I started sweating despite the lack of temperature. I'm not saying it was cold, just that temperature did not exist.

Night, or what I thought was night, came in the form of a purple sky that appeared after a blink. Thoughts had gained weight, a strange form of physicality that was really hard to ignore. The knowledge that night was a construction based on the rotation of the earth was nothing until I thought about it, which made it immediately become a tumor in my left calf. It was the size of a baseball and undulated with a strange, silent rhythm that reminded me of the serpentine hallway. Overcoming the thought by pondering the nature of squares, which only translated into an itch in my scalp, I sat on the scaled sidewalk I was walking on at the time and fell asleep right away. It was not a natural sleep. There was no way I would sleep in such a situation. It was more like someone had turned my brain off with the flip of a switch.

Consciousness came as fast as sleep had. The switch had been flipped again and, again, I wasn't the one responsible. Ownership of that switch, not to mention my ignorance regarding its location, was maddening. The sense of having been violated, intruded upon, messed with or whatever else manifested itself in the form of a painful stiffening of the fingers of my left hand. Looking down at it, I realized my hand now sported an indeterminate something of fingers. I wanted to know why I couldn't think of the thing that somethinged them. Frustration cracked my two lower ribs on my left side. I stood up and thought about BLANK. The bumps and bruises disappeared. I started walking again, which luckily lead me to stumble upon a few puddles of dark liquid that I hadn't seen

AAAAAAAAA

before. The presence of liquid activated my thirst. The inky liquid tasted like really sharp and cold emptiness, but at least helped me quench my thirst.

There was still no one around, but that doesn't mean I was as alone as the first day. Black shadows with wings crisscrossed the sky above me, sometimes coming incredibly close to the blobs but never interacting with them in any perceivable way. But the action was not all up in the blue sky. A wide array of strange creatures squirmed, slithered, and scurried out of my way as I walked. Some entered the strange walls like ghosts while other jumped into the black puddles or simply disappeared with a loud pop that, much like my own footsteps, reached my ears with a two second delay. They never stuck around long enough for me to figure out what they were, but there was an incredible variety of them. Some resembled furry lizards while others were more like very small, slimy humanoids. Some had wings, others walked on a varying number of legs, and some even appeared to be hovering a few inches above the scaly pavement and sidewalks. Sadly, it seemed like there was a force around me, a presence that prevented me from approaching anything without making it disappear, which obviously made me doubt the presence of the entities in the first place.

Night never came, but after I blinked once, the certainty that one day, whatever that was, had become another, and the thought that it might've been the previous one or one in an indefinite future because chronology had ceased to exist, accosted me.

Stillness was dangerous. Every S in it cut against my flesh whenever I stayed put, so I kept walking. The unfixed now/present I couldn't think of in any way other than the third day brought with it the warm acceptance of the fact, soft and fuzzy as it was, that the city was endless. Corroboration is more like a satisfying meal than a living thing, but I feared it like one fears a toothy creature more than I craved it like one craves sweets. Against instinct that felt like talons ripping into my ankles, I climbed to the top of the tallest building in the street.

The elevator was exactly like the one that had spat me out, only this time it took me up by moving simultaneously in all directions. I stood on a flat, grey surface that seemed to be the roof of the place and looked around. As I was turning, a paragraph fell from the sky. I looked at it. It was obviously a dangerous one. It was bulky, ugly, and made of single words instead of sentences, but it had an aura to it that reeked of danger. I approached it, reading:

31

Larvae. Contract. Pessimistic. Indelible. Itch. Thrychinosis. Towel. Necessity. Problem. Welt. Strangeness. Bear. Reflection. Animosity. Shadow. Explosion. Yellow. Blood. Agreement. Stoning. Thunder. Antihestamine. Perpendicular. Limbo. Anachronistic. Service. Eleven. Scratch. Spotting. Victim. Desire. Wound. Albino. Terminal. Occult. Agony. Malevolent. Insidious. Perplexed. Miserable. Box. Tourniquet. Lamp. Moss. Sample. Biopsy. Tender. Puncture. Scabies. Demolished. Infestation. Violence. Borrow. Head. Infected. Knife. Serum. Juxtaposition. Bitterweed. Buzz. Gymnasium. Immediate. Backwoods. Furious. Slashing. Incandescent. Tone. Splendid. Dirty. Poison. Discourse. Trauma. Linen. Organism. Include. Wall. Epidermis. Positionality. Thread. Away. Parasite. Elderly. Unnecessary. Thirst. Void. Cold. Decomposition. Inhuman. End. Velocity. Pebble. Flattened. Need. Windowless. Exact. Stomach. Vengeance. Large. Daybreak. Elevation. Bird. Wrench. Theoretically. Tumescent. Android. Heroine. Gods. Waste.

As I approached, the paragraph cracked, right between Perplexed and Miserable. A snakeword came out from the impossible gap. I heard it with my eyes:

```
           s
          s
           s
            n
         a
      k
          e
```

Escape was not an option. Fear was a fading memory, like the reminiscences of conversations I never had with a man I never knew who died from a virulent case of philosophy. The wordsnake was about two steps away from me, so I took thirty seven steps and grabbed it. I placed both my hands on the "a" and tried to break it. Instead of snapping immediately, the letter stretched

aaaaaaaaaaaaaaaaaaaaaaaaaaaaaaaaaaaaaaaaaaaaaaaaaaaaaaaaaaaaaaa
aaaaaaaaaaaaaaaaaaaaaaaaaaaaaaaaaaaaaaaaaaaaaaaaaaaaaaaaaaaaaaa
aaaaaaaaaaaaaaaaaaaaaaaaaaaaaaaaaaaaaaaaaaaaaaaaaaaaaaaaaaaaaaa
aaaaaaaaaaaaaaaaaaaaaaaaaaaaaaaaaaaaaaaaaaaaaaaaaaaaaaaaaaaaaaa

AAAAAAAAA

aaaaaaaaaaaaaaaaaaaaaaaaaaaaaaaaaaaaaaaaaaaaaaaaaaaaaaaaaaaaaaaaaaaaaa
aaaaaaaaaaaaaaaaaaaaaaaaaaaaaaaaaaaaaaaaaaaaaaaaaaaaaaaaaaaaaaaaaaaaaa
aaaaaaaaaaaaaaaaaaaaaaaaaaaaaaaaaaaaaaaaaaaaaaaaaaaaaaaaaaaaaaaaaaaaaa
aaaaaaaaaaaaaaaaaaaaaaaaaaaaaaaaaaaaaaaaaaaaaaaaaaaaaaaaaaaaaaaaaaaaaa
aaaaaaaaaaaaaaaaaaaaaaaaaaaaaaaaaaaaaaaaaaaaaaaaaaaaaaaaaaaaaaaaaaaaaa
aaaaaaaaaaaaaaaaaaaaaaaaaaaaaaaaaaaaaaaaaaaaaaaaaaaaaaaaaaaaaaaaaaaaaa
aaaaaaaaaaaaaaaaaaaaaaaaaaaaaaaaaaaaaaaaaaaaaaaaaaaaaaaaaaaaaaaaaaaaaa
aaaaaaaaaaaaaaaaaaaaaaaaaaaaaaaaaaaaaaaa
aaaaaaaaaaaaaaaaaaaaaaaaaaaaaaaaaaaaaaaaaaaaaaaaaaaaaaaaaaaaaaaaaaaaaa
aaaaaaaaaaaaaaaaaaaaa
aaaaaaaaaaaaaaaaaaaaaaaaaaaaaaaaaaaaaaaaaaaaaaaaaaaaaaaaaaaaaaaaaaaaaa
aaaaaaaaaaaaaaaaaaaaaaaaaaaaaaaaaaaaaaaaaaaaaaaaaaaaaaaaaaaaaaaaaaaaaa
aaaaaaaaaaaaaaaaaaaaaaaaaaaaaaaaaaaaaaaaaaaaaaaaaaaaaaaaaaaaaaaaaaaaaa
aaaaaaaaaaaaaaaaaaaaaaaaaaaaaaaaaaaaaaaaaaaaaaaaaaaaaaaaaaaaaaaaaaaaaa
aaaaaaaaaaaaaaaaaaaaaaaaaaaaaaaaaaaaaaaaaaaaaaaaaaaaaaaaaaaaaaaaaaaaaa
aaaaaaaaaaaaaaaaaaaaaaaaaaaaaaaaaaaaaaaaaaaaaaaaaaaaaaaaaaaaaaaaaaaaaa
aaaaaaaaaaaaaaaaaaaaaaaaaaaaa
aaaaaaaaaaaaaaaaaaaaaaaaaaaaaaaaaaaaaaaaaaaaaaaaaaaaaaaaaaaaaaaaaaaaaa
aaaaaaaaaaaaaaaaaaaaaaaaaaaaaaaaaaaaaaaaaaaaaaaaaaaaaaaaaaaaaaaaaaaaaa
aaaaaaaaaaaaaaaaaaaaaaaaaaaaaaaaaaaaaaaaaaaaaaaaaaaaaaaaaaaaaaaaaaaaaa
aaaaaaaaaaaaaaaaaaaaaaaaaaaaaaaaaaaaaaaaaaaaaaaaaaaaaaaaaaaaaaaaaaaaaa
aaaaaaaaaaaaaaaaaaaaaaaaaaaaaaaaaaaaaaaaaaaaaaaaaaaaaaaaaaaaaaaaaaaaaa
aaaaaaaaaaaaaaaaaaaaaaaaaaaaaaaaaaaaaaaaaaaaaaaaaaaaaaaaaaaaaaaaaaaaaa
aaaaaaaaaaaaaaaaaaaaaaaaaaaaa
aaaaaaaaaaaaaaaaaaaaaaaaaaaaaaaaaaaaaaaaaaaaaaaaaaaaaaaaaaaaaaaaaaaaaa
aaaaaaaaaaaaaaaaaaaaaaaaaaaaaaaaaaaaaaaaaaaaaaaaaaaaaaaaaaaaaaaaaaaaaa
aaaaaaaaaaaaaaaaaaaaaaaaaaaaaaaaaaaaaaaaaaaaaaaaaaaaaaaaaaaaaaaaaaaaaa
aaaaaaaaaaaaaaaaaaaaaaaaaaaaaaaaaaaaaaaaaaaaaaaaaaaaaaaaaaaaaaaaaaaaaa
aaaaaaaaaaaaaaaaaaaaaaaaaaaaaaaaaaaaaaaaaaaaaaaaaaaaaaaaaaaaaaaaaaaaaa
aaaaaaaaaaaaaaaaaaaaaaaaaaaaaaaaaaaaaaaaaaaaaaaaaaaaaaaaaaaaaaaaaaaaaa
aaaaaaaaaaaaaaaaaaaaaaaaaaaaa

Finally, with a pop that reached my ears two seconds before it happened, the snakeword broke, releasing nothing from its nonexistent interior.

Paragraphs contain endless possibilities, so I walked up to its broken form and peeked inside. Out of that nothingness I imagined a notebook and a pen that had been waiting for me since before I was dumped in that place. They were the first "normal" things I've seen and I can't help but think that someone, or something, was watching my every move and had placed them here for me to find.

I tried to write something, but the pen's self-awareness was more powerful than me and all that came out was

PEN

time and time again until a few pages were covered in the pen's celebration of its apparently unexpected, and obviously underserved, coming into being.

Then that now moved forward and became this now, which is infinitely more present. I have no idea what the negative-space-for-faces goons expect from me, but at least I know what I want to do.

The following is a condensed version of all I've observed in what some invisible force has convinced me I can safely call the preceding/anteceding/succeeding three days. I hope someone finds this if there is ever someone in my same predicament. Maybe these words will serve to satiate their curiosity and they won't spend three days wandering around while this (non)place devours their (in)sanity with each new surprise, each nonblink, each step in no direction, each inch moved forward but not quite forward.

Anyway, here we go.

This place is not a city. This is not a place or space, at least not like we understand them. This is a . . . state, a splace, an ever-changing situation, a morphing, palpable continuum of alteration, alliteration, living things, and madness.

The buildings appear to have been maliciously thrown together in an effort to cover every inch of available space and kill every standing tree, shrub, and blade of grass, if there was ever such a thing here. The structures look like a collection of monstrosities that architects on acid came up with right after waking from an awful dream. Besides the scales and . . . (biomechanical? living? conscious?) walls. Anyway, besides the scales and skinlike materials that cover everything, there's only maddening continuity, repetition, reiteration, recurrence, repetition, duplication, repetition, echo, repetition, repetition, repetition. Architectural coherence is nonexistent here. Non-Euclidean can't even begin to describe it. The grey, torn blocks of stained concrete and what I think is flesh are of various sizes and colors. They look like piles of discarded rubbish, but turn into edifices in the blink of an eye, and you only blink three or four times a day(?) here.

The living buildings sometimes loom over smaller things that resemble houses. These usually stand still. They seem to be a remnant of a different time, like a previous version of what the buildings are now,

AAAAAAAAA

or maybe just an attempt your brain makes at bringing back some recognizable form. I've tried to approach them a few times, but the distance between us remains constant.

I'd love to write in here that there is a way to comprehensively explore space here, but there isn't such a thing. I can walk and turn a corner that wasn't there two steps ago and find myself in a new street that looks exactly like the street I was just on, which looked exactly like the street I was on before that one, which looked exactly like one I was on before that one . . .

The few times I tried running, all I managed to do was stay in the same place. Other times, I blink and my surroundings had changed drastically and all that was left was the unshakable feeling that an unavoidable amount of time had escaped me, avoided me, abandoned me.

Juts before I came up to this rooftop, I found a few large skeletons scattered around like shitty afterthoughts. None of them were of beasts I recognized. Loneliness hadn't caused me so much despair, but these skeletons somehow did, because I knew my brain was making them up to give me some company. If those big creatures couldn't survive, even in my head, my odds are incredibly slim, both there and here. I started thinking about my situation, but it was obvious that my situation could ponder me infinitely more viciously. That's when I entered this building and rode the elevator to the top.

The skin on my hands and forearms is slowly dissolving. It comes back when I think about it, but as soon as I forget about it, it starts dissolving again. Thankfully, there's no pain, but seeing the first chunks of muscle underneath is freaking me out, and that feels like inhaling tar. Also, the tasteless sludge I've been drinking is doing something inside me. The fluttering I feel in my stomach has nothing to do with hunger or fear or any of my thoughts. When whatever is in there becomes too big or simply decides to come out, I don't want to be around to witness, and feel, the consequences.

I have no wallet, and as I try to remember my name to sign it at the bottom of this document, nothing comes to mind. My identity is being pulled away from me. I can feel that. I fear another day of walking will only produce more nasty encounters and more dissolving/disappearing/ceasing to be whoever I am. As I look down at the exposed muscles of my forearm, I wonder how my own flesh would taste. Something tells me the blobs, which are now closer than ever, are contemplating the same thing. Before I convince myself, whoever the fuck I am, of taking juts one bite and getting back to the walking, I'll bid you adieu and jump down from here. I hope the scales in the street below are as hard as they felt beneath my feet.

Hello.

A SHADOW OF A PRINCESS'S DREAM

ROBIN WYATT DUNN

FLY ALIGHT in the dawn, and my majesty is the truth. See me spear my rage in your old books, see me pour fury into your hopes, boy, your hopes, boy that I dreamt of too, when I was younger, when I was not what I am now: princess.

(Princess)

I am your tool, I am apotheosis.

"Princess!"

"Yes?"

"Get down off that balcony!"

I step down. I move to the table and take hold of the block, one like wood.

"Put it in you already!" my nursemaid commands.

It's a new format. I lift my dress, and shift the *hlafweard* into my waist, under my diaphragm, as I have been trained . . .

My nursemaid smiles. "It's easier this time, darling! Better sit down though!"

I refuse to sit down but I hold onto the edge of the chair as I accumulate the data from the *hlafweard*, the lord, the system of lords. The keepers of the bread.

I who would be used must use; it is politics. We use a system of light here. I have not seen my father for eight years. I am the corridor unmasked, you see. Have you ever been in a corridor? Try to come inside:

"Who are you?"

Young men. Young men. Hot boyz. Here in our righteousness I must unwrap this specific throat for your caress, this aspect of your long orgasmic devotion to kings, whatever your chief star system: I can not dominate as you might think. I am only a woman. And I am young.

"My name is Anadone."

"Who are you? I can't see."

I see him through the colored static the *hlafweard* allows for me, behind my eyes. I speak to him, with a darker voice. I have so many practices; they tire me.

"Boy, come to me. I am here for you."

And in a second, along our Light. When he seizes me. Our Old Light! (music)

(for conquering)

—four thousand governments

—A long low ocean on a planet flung from orbit, unique

—The 5 megabit key for the Coliseum Vault, the secrets we've been wanting . . .

Tell me, do tell me, temptresses of old, what do you do with them after? Always a decision, isn't it? Some like to keep them close, to feel their humiliation. Some like to throw them aside, never to see them again. I take photographs. To remember my many shames. And the men's faces keep me comfortable at night.

"Unplug it lady! Jesus!"

"Don't speak to me of old gods tonight, Elizabeth, I'm tired."

I am a working girl. Call me Rapunzel, if you like, though my hair is black, like they would have my heart be. Like the storm that is coming. Like the eyes of my servant, Georges. Let me tell you of Georges, while we process our new territories. Light is fast, but it has a speed. The trick is turning it . . .

Anyway, Georges was born in France. Have you heard of France? It's *tres belle* . . .

A SHADOW OF A PRINCESS'S DREAM

For centuries it was the manorial system in France, before the Carolingians. Before the Holy Roman Empire. Though it lasted longer in Germany, it thrived in France briefly too: the *hlafweard*, or, if you like, the *Dominus*, the Lord.

The trouble with leadership is it's so often underappreciated. And then when it's gone some never even quite see what went wrong. Isn't that right, Georges?

"My lady?"

"Put on my slippers, will you? I need a walk."

My temple, or, if you like, my prison, is not on a planet. We keep a region of spin under tight control near a quasar (I cannot tell you the region), and it acts as a useful center for communications, and intrigues. It is narrow, and lonely. Though I speak with many, I see few. Mostly just Georges and Elizabeth, my servants.

"Georges, what are we paying you these days?"

"I am generously compensated, miss."

"But what? Are we paying you in gold? In land?"

"Information, miss."

"Ahh, a man after my own heart."

He is so droll, Georges is, in his copper-colored suits and slicked hair and 20th Century stock-broker glasses. I do love him. Sometimes I have even wanted him.

He is a man like you might have seen: sad, tall, lonely. Dark hair, laugh lines, though he rarely smiles. Getting fat, a little bit. Slim fingers on his hands. And wide, clear eyes, slightly mad. His madness is what is most useful to me, though as a woman I like his shoulders, for they fit my head. But it is unseemly for an employer to rest her head on her employee's shoulder.

"Georges, I've been thinking of running away again."

"Why is that, lady?"

"I don't know. The usual reasons, I suppose. Do you think I should?"
I flick my hair and play coquette, though I am not very good at it. We here by the quasar have so many layers of irony; it is one thing the beast does not suck into its obscene gravity . . .

"No, lady, not yet. Not quite yet, *Princesa*."

And then we see the sky redden, here in our tight sloughed-off region of time, cut fast down and rewound like a magnetic tape, scraping away our skin—

"Georges!"

But he is running away from me, away from our tower?

"Georges!"

I run back to the tower. The sky is talking now. I hate talking skies. I hate that I was born to a king. I hate that I am a woman. I raise my skirts so I can run faster and slam my shoulder into the oak door and run back up the steps, shouting:

"Lizzy! Lizzy!" I am crying, I realize.

Lizzy is asleep, her eyes black. Already she is defending us. My God, loyal servants. They are the strangest, somehow, stranger than all the rest, why does she—

I bow to our godlet, and allow its wires into my head. The world of my mammal senses slips away.

***

I was taught visual programming from the age of three. It is of the highest importance in our rule. Can you think quickly? Do you have a sense for color? We are always hiring. Speak to one of our agents on Earth, or Aelena Seven. Bring a map you have drawn yourself. We still love quality, you know. It is why my father's kingship survives.

When I was six I programmed this hallway: see it with me.

The Hallway

Yes, here it is. I've slowed it down for you; part of me must go on ahead (money to be made and borders to defend!). The white is pure nostalgia: I always loved the Terror Ships of Galactic Empire in George Lucas' films. See here, I made this wooden table. The teddy is my oldest friend. His name is Lucifer. I know, morbid. Well, I had a difficult childhood.

"Lucifer!"

The doll opens his eyes.

"Hello, *Princesa*."

"Don't call me that, Lucifer! We have guests! One of the far travelers is here with us! Be polite! And call me Ana, for God's sake!"

"Yes, *Princesa*. Ana."

I pet his fur; isn't he soft? The trick to organic structures in visual programming is to follow your instincts—what else is there? I remember thinking, as a girl, the doll is like a window, and so it is, just touch his head and you'll see the shimmer at the far end of the hallway.

Clearly you know how flexible reality is, but the trick for me has always been knowing its meniscuses, its surface tensions. As you caress the teddy, the milk of the shimmer will sense you too, and you must decide what kind of information you want to transmit.

I'll make this easier; already I have won, you see; the me I sent ahead has won, and I am left back here, with you. You are so slow. Well, there's charm in that, I suppose. *He he he.*

So concentrate: it is moving into your head. Here in my hallway you feel the shiver. It has decided to feel with you; the shimmer from far away has. Welcome it; like you would welcome a storm, we will shelter you. Hold the teddy. Let the shiver from afar know that the teddy comforts you; it's interested in that. No, no, it's not a betrayal. It's a friend, like you are a friend.

Some have said my designs are madness, that my programs are unrepeatable. That they're organic to the point of sentience; but I disagree. I say they are palm trees, and I am a Hollywood starlet, and they sway in the breeze *for me.*

I remove my head from the wall, and the wires slip back into it. Elizabeth is asleep. I climb into bed too; I am exhausted. As always, I dream of men. I am still technically a virgin.

"Ah, you're still here."

"Yes."

"You speak our language."

"Yes. I was taught it."

"You are the visitor I showed my hallway?"

"Yes, I am he."

"I have been rude. Tea? I will make it."

The visitor says nothing, only nods. I step from my bed, still in my favorite blacks and scarves, a bit bedraggled. A wind blows through the room, smelling of rain.

"I feel I can see you clearer now," I say. "How would you like your tea?"

"Milk and honey, please."

"I'm afraid we're all out of honey. The last storm took our apiary clean out! But I have aspartame. Would you like aspartame?"

"Fine."

We sit, and drink.

"What brings you here, guest?"

"I want to know. I want to know how you do it."

"How I do what?" I say.

"How you rule."

"You are awfully forward for a spy. Haven't you any more flirtatious tactics?"

"No. No, I haven't. But you are very beautiful. That is why I dislike you. I dislike beautiful women."

"Why?"

"Because they are cruel, of course. Their beauty makes them so."

"Always?"

"I believe so. You are cruel too, though you do not seem to know it yet."

"Oh, I know it well enough." I sip my tea. "You are a very tiring guest. Did you bring me a gift? My visitors always brings me gifts."

"Yes, Princess. I bring you your servant."

And he put Georges' head on the floor in front of me and I screamed.

I am the princess. I fight for freedom. I am your symbol. I am your hope. I am your fantasy. My breasts and hips, my lips. My eyes of hate and darkness, and of love. My legs that cut through space and through your mind, limiting your dimensions, your thought, your manliness. I am this weapon; I am made for you.

I am sorry if you are confused. Perhaps I made a good governess once; if so, that is long gone. I do this for my father; for him, I do anything I can. May he return.

As I told you, I reside near a quasar. Have you ever seen one? It is a peculiar feeling, isn't it? Like coming home. I am always coming home here; one of the many tortures I despise.

"Elizabeth!"

She shuffles into the room.

"Yes, my lady."

"Prepare my horse. I am leaving."

"I thought you might."

"Yes." And I smile. "You're coming too, after we bury Georges."

I know it is the *hlafweard* that you want, visitor, guest, spy, aspirant. I know you think to capture its logics as we have done, but it is a generational awareness, can't you see that? What would you do with it, even if I gave it to you freely? You would not understand the first thing about it.

But we can come to understand it, lady.

"Shut up shut up shut up!"

"*Princesa?*" says Elizabeth.

"Nothing. Is my horse ready?"

"Almost."

Elizabeth is so good to me. I was bred to rule. Raised for it, selected for it in the womb. Power is a prison. You who claim to be wise, do you know what that means, guest? That it is a surrender? That I surrender every time I use the *hlafweard*? That I must accept this truth to use this tool?

You will be tortured for a very long time, princess.

And I scream, and Elizabeth gives me a shot.

We are riding. I have never liked it. Relativistic travel is nauseating.

Imagine the universe. You know it is like an eye? Spread through the milky fluid, strands of matter stick together, messy, glowing, interfering with the retina. Floaties. We are the floaties; the mess in the eye of God. I know, rather Gnostic. Still, Gnostic mysticism is quite useful in our kingdom.

Map the floaties; the slip and slide of their movement; their habits and patterns and desires. Yes, all matter has desires! Did not the Teddy desire you too, guest, as you desired it? The shimmer remembers that, you know?

Shhh, I must accept my future-past selves, I must reassess . . .

It is my father. Dear God—

Suicide is shameful. Why I can't succeed, I do not know. Elizabeth is too good at stopping me from reaching death.

"It was father, Elizabeth, it was father—"

My voice does not sound like mine. I am older, too. I want to die. Please let me die, God. The guest is still here, he is sitting by the wall.

"Guest, why do you look like Georges?"

"I am Georges, princess. The Georges you forgot."

"Well tell me of France then, Georges, if you're really Georges. Do that."

"It was my home country, princess. We love our cuisine in *Longuedoc*. I miss my cheese."

"Go off and die," I hiss at him.

And yet I do recognize my voice. It is never far from me. It is the voice of abuse. I am what I do to others—

That is the other part of ruling. You never do it alone. And your family wants to kill you. As in wolf packs, cutting off the pups' heads when they grow inconvenient for the new alpha, the new lord, the new *hlafweard*, the Keeper of Bread . . .

My bread is rising, father. I will make you eat every bite.

Forgive me. Pardon-moi. Je m'apelle Georges Armignac de Longuedoc. I know she is evil, but we do not kill her yet. In the confession is mystery, yes? And what is mystery but land? Vous comprenez? Croyons, once we had empire. And we will again. We make the land, now. In the mysterious. Our railway is coming.

Outside the fortress, I touch the side of my dress to reassure me that my gun is there. Long sleeves cover my wrists. Elizabeth smiles at me. I will kill him.

A SHADOW OF A PRINCESS'S DREAM

The gates open, and the wind is brought to a pitch, and I strike a pose:

And you must listen to this part, please. This is the part you must remember. I am Anadone and I know I have been evil but know that this is the truest part of the record, the part you must understand, not the part that comes after.

I am riding through: I am a princess. Not a prince, but a princess. Royalty, but the strangest kind. I can marry, and my name will change. I can slip away into the womanness of me: I am recyclable this way. A woman, even more than a princess. And less. But see me, anyway, for this is the symbol we may never outgrow:

I cry at the sky, my teeth a sword, and my dress is thrilling to the mobs, a cut of ash, as my eyes are blessings for their dooms. I am princess and they are my children, they are my mats on which I cut my battles like I would an album, secreting away my kiss into its vinyl grooves. I hold my horse's neck and he is with me and the eyes of children are jewels. They see me and they see the mystery of this realm, a slight diminishment that is power:

I am above, and they below, and they rule forever. A thousand thousand millennia. I am temporary.

The king is ahead, my father. I dismount and curtsy.

"Father," I say, with a smile. And he smiles back. Politics.

"Four thousand governments! Astonishing, Ana! I am so proud of you!"

He refills my glass. I simper, as best I can.

"It's Elizabeth, father, she really is amazing."

"You're all grown up, my daughter. Your mother would be so proud."

If she ever wakes up.

"Thank you, Daddy."

And he rises and steps behind my chair and strokes my head.

"You're a good girl, Ana. You always will be. You serve our kingdom. You are beautiful. And terrifying."

And I shiver. He is my father.

I have killed him. What was lost; is lost. I know no other reason. Once we were called nuns. How many were virgins? I want to cut off my own breasts, that have never given milk.

What is an empire, anyway? I want to die planetside. I want my horizons to be real, even if I am cursed with noble blood, and cursed with history.

I keep mother in the basement here, like father did. She is like a mascot to me. What does she dream of? Father?

"Lady?"

"Don't call me that," I mumble.

"Lady, I'm Elizabeth."

"I'm dead, leave me alone."

"You're not dead, lady. Wake up. Someone is here. A guest."

I sit up and it is you. You again.

"What do you want?" I say.

And he flickers a little.

"Who are you?"

And I hear your scream. It's what you wanted: worlds, and times. And I laugh, and Elizabeth with me. Is there a pleasure greater than another's pain? Our schadenfreude could be mapped like a star . . .

Well. What else is there to say? I am forty now. Infertile, they say. If I want a lover, and do I? If I do, it's somewhere I don't want to see.

I will comb my hair out today. I will be beautiful.

The sky is strange to me here. Often I dream of my Father. But more often, I dream of my tower, when I was young. When I stepped onto the ledge and let my hair blow in the wind of the quasar . . . everything was possible. What do you see, in this record? Only sadness? Some say I am a happy woman. But I will never be a queen.

S⊃Я Я Ǝ◁ L CHƎSS

BRUCE BOSTON

TARASHAN ASTOUNDS THE spectators with an aggressive hypermodern opening of her own invention. She releases three companies of foot soldiers across the glacial moraine. Horovitz's response is no less unconventional. He advances his panther to the king wolf's forest and fianchettos his hetaera.

"Chess is a game of beautiful and horrible complications," states honorable Grand Master Tyro Suzuki. "Surreal chess is a game of dream complications." (free translation)

Nearly half of Tarashan's forces perish in harsh mountain storms. The rest suffer severe frostbite. Those who survive the arduous and bone-chilling trek emerge along the perimeter of the coast ensconced in enemy territory.

Horovitz has little choice. He must conscript the fisherman of Port Ligat to defend his eastern flank. Ignorant peasants to a man, they advance against a heavily armed foe with nothing but their tridents and nets.

Yet these poor fisher folk are only sacrificial bait, a delaying tactic. Not far behind come elephants on stilts, ungainly creatures brocaded in heavy satin with gouts of flame spouting from their trunks and columns of smoke twirling up from the hidden cavities of their ears. Even when such mammoth beasts perish, and they do so by the score, they leave swaths of indescribable destruction in their toppling wakes.

BRUCE BOSTON

"The Dictionary of Surreal Chess exists in two mediums and versions: hypnagogic and full REM." venerable Grand Master Tyro Suzuki informs us. "The inadequate and contradictory rules in either edition are of little value. Chimerical tales relating many of the incidents and notable matches in the history of the game abound in the pages of both volumes. There is no basis in fact for any of these entries, yet they carry a ring of truth that few can contest." (free translation)

The players, curled fetally in their chairs, settle down to a middle game of entrenched warfare, lobbing elaborate epithets and ultimatums, few of which reach their marks. They pound each other with compulsive images and incendiary nightmares.

The proportions and perspectives of the board begin to evolve at a frightening pace. This is a terrain that can sprout the benign and knowing face of a goddess and young boys in sailor suits, a geology that contains a series of flexible mirages passing through undeclared dimensions.

"If the board did not keep changing," states often esteemed and rarely reviled Grand Master Tyro Suzuki, "it would not be surreal chess, only a pale imitation for those who cannot sleep." (free translation)

While seemingly bemoaning the slaughter on the eastern front, Tarashan counters in the midland plain with a pack of bloodhounds inhabiting the forms of itinerant preachers. The double entendre escapes no one fully conversant with the literature of pain.

Evacuating churches and citadels, barricading public utilities, Horovitz interposes a division of hallucinogenic toreadors. They appear to be no more than sensitive dandies in their tight red pants and velvet hats, yet they prove a ferocious lot once their blades are drawn.

Fatalities transpire at an uncanny rate. The outcome is virtual obliteration for Tarashan's would-be Inquisition.

"You understand nothing of the game! Nothing whatsoever!"

enraged Grand Master Tyro Suzuki screams to his bewildered students, many of whom have forgotten to remove their sandals. (substantiated anecdote)

Tarashan places her hands across her face and lets her hair hang down in plaited rows. Her body shivers with a sensation hard to distinguish from a clinically perfect orgasm.

Horovitz, enthralled by his own genius, lounges back in his chair with careless strength. He lights a long black torpedo-shaped cigar. But alas, despite all pretensions to the contrary, it is nothing more than a cigar.

Suddenly the flies are everywhere, dark iridescent dots that settle on corpses and corpses-to-be like a species bred for the occasion. Once they have feasted, they clean their hairy bodies with great diligence.

Somewhere in the woods a unicorn screeches its terror, a high-pitched keening that causes the other pieces, the players and spectators, to turn their heads as one.

Rising up from his narrow bed with one gnarled finger raised in crooked admonition, speaking in a heavily accented yet grammatically perfect English, Grand Master Tyro Suzuki declares: "It is more a question of metaphysics than physics, more pataphysics than meta, the psyche of the human animal in rank and file absurdity."

The end game is upon them before they know it. The pieces lie scattered like symbols across the board, their intent and possibilities so open to various interpretation that both players are left reeling with the implications.

Horovitz's cigar is a withered stump, sputtering in its own ash. He utters the first words spoken aloud at the match. Like most sentences carried from the depths of slumber to the land of the waking, its meaning is unintelligible to all but the speaker.

Tarashan's only response is to glance up and lean back in her chair. The flesh of her aging yet still handsome features recedes to reveal the skeletectonics beneath.

The survivors, heroes and heroines alike, gather at the base of an irregular and top-heavy monument that ignores gravity. The heat of the unrelenting sky beats down upon them. Bleeding from many wounds, some self-inflicted for effect, they pray for the anodyne of rain.

And the clouds gather and the rains come down, though they are not composed of water. Assorted distorted objects pellet like hail: howling portmanteaus, pale lavender sachets of a bleak persuasion, proleptic reason stretched upon a rack, the ruins of a petrified railway station, huge metal insects with articulated limbs and fried eggs for saddles.

The puddled mass of the clock begins to reform one molten droplet at a time. Light insinuates itself beneath the curtains and dimples their folds with gray. The game is recessed to begin again in another night's play. The board folds upon itself with a thunderous clap. The spectators dissolve. There are no winners or losers here. Only conscious convention about to cut the cord of sleep at its navel.

With a vigor that belies the wages of visionary excess, retired Grand Master Tyro Suzuki tends his ornamental garden in the unceremonious dawn. "Believe me," he croons to the stunted trees and the nodding buds of the flowers, "I mean you no harm." (free translation)

THE BONES OF JONES

RHYS HUGHES

AM LYING on my back.

The truth is that I'm on my front.

That's how easy it is for me to tell a lie when I am on my back. With no real effort, I can assert, quite convincingly, that I'm on my front and people are more likely to believe me than not.

I like to lie on my back. It's my favourite position for lying.

My chin is made of wood.

I keep a miniature pig in a jar on a shelf.

That shelf is wooden and the wood came from my chin.

My face is much shorter now.

See what I mean? Lies, all lies. They rolled off my tongue like spherical giraffes on an extremely steep incline.

No, not at all like that . . .

I don't try hard to lie when I'm on my back. It comes naturally. I suspect it's something to do with magnetism, with the circulation of the molten iron that I use as a substitute for spinal fluid.

Having said that, I can also lie competently in many other positions. I'm not a pun trick pony, like Hayley Jude, who can only fib when she's in a stable condition. Hayley, or Hay as everybody calls her, can't lie unless she is utterly motionless, her muscles rigid, her breathing as shallow as it possibly can be, her pulse rate as low as a midget diver.

I bet you didn't know divers are used to explore midgets?

They aren't, as a matter of fact.

And Hayley Jude doesn't exist. I made her up. But only after she turned me down. Brutally. That's what I do.

And it's what she does, too. Hay Jude.

Lying on my back, as I am, I can see the ceiling.

51

Seeing the ceiling is soothing.

This is because the ceiling is so high above me it might as well be a sky, but the sky of another world, a paradise planet in orbit around some other star, a daydream made real, a private heaven.

Utopia. Itopia. Wetopia.

The constellations have been painted on with luminous paint and how do they sparkle, you ask? Like low energy chemical reactions, that's how, in other words exactly like what they are, rendering the simile redundant. Luckily, it took voluntary redundancy, that simile.

The telephone rings . . . I turn my head to look.

I can't recall why I put rings on it. The necklaces and bracelets are also a mystery. I must have thought it needed adornment when I was younger, but that was a mistake. It was fine as it was.

It doesn't work anymore. The metal jewellery interferes with the circuits and makes them malfunction badly.

No, it makes them malfunction well. If the malfunction was bad it would be a low quality malfunction and the telephone would probably still work, but it doesn't. It is merely a dead ornament.

Too bad. I hate talking to people I can't see, anyway. How do I know they aren't pulling baboon faces, parading in underpants, frying plantains in bicycle oil on dangerous stoves? Too risky.

A star falls from the distant ceiling. A meteor.

It grows bigger as it approaches me and then I realise that it's not really a meteor but a parachute with a badly fashioned ball hanging from it. The ball is a piece of paper that has been scrunched up.

Clearly, it's a message from my employers.

They can reach me anywhere.

And I'm always on duty.

The message lands on my chest, and the parachute canopy, which is just a pocket handkerchief, settles over my face.

Snot funny. So I blow my nose in it contemptuously.

Then I fling it aside so I can see.

And now that I can see, I am in a position to turn the paper ball into a flat page again and read what is written.

Dear Corker,

Hope this finds you well, or if not well then adequate, or if not adequate then bearable, or if not bearable then vicious.

It has recently come to our attention that the bones of a man

THE BONES OF JONES

*by the name of Jones, who drowned a few years ago, have
started telling the most appalling lies. His bones lie under the
sea and the physical and moral shockwaves caused by these lies
are causing a hazard to shipping. As our specialist Lie Detector,
we want you to do something or anything about it.*

Will you do something or anything about it, pretty please?
If you refuse we will slaughter you.
But it's entirely your decision. Cheerio, buster!
Grillchin and the Team

What could I do? One doesn't refuse Grillchin. I knew an agent once
who refused him and that *agent* is now *a gent* instead, which sounds
rather nice, but the insertion of that space between the 'a' and the 'g' of
his identity was painful in the extreme and he never recovered.

So I sigh deeply, because that's the correct way to sigh when one has
to prepare for a voyage under the sea, and I turn on my side and reach
out with my hand to punch the buttons of the bedside unit.

Punching them makes me feel better, but not much, so little in fact
that it makes me feel worse, my knuckles anyway . . .

Then I press them properly, with my fingertips, and those buttons
activate a motor inside my mattress which propels my bed on numerous
little wheels out of my bedroom to a destination specified by the
sequence of buttons I selected. A perfect system for men who like to lie
in bed, and only marginally less so for men who prefer to be honest under
the sheets.

The bed accelerates steadily, passes out of the house, doors opening
and closing automatically to ease its passage, and now it is on the street,
joining the flow of traffic, moving at an incredible speed.

I take cover under the duvet as the wind generated by my velocity
ruffles my hair unpleasantly. I wish to hide from the stares and honks of
ordinary vehicles and their passengers, who are unused to being
overtaken by a bedstead. But soon I leave the city and find myself on a
quieter road leading to the secret beach where my private harbour is
located.

The bed bounces over the shingles and the motor grumbles when we
get onto the sand, but without any serious problems it deposits me next
to the jetty that I use to moor my entire ocean-going fleet.

For I have many craft that ply the waters of the deep blue yonder. I
have yachts, schooners, clippers, galleons, caravels, longboats,

catamarans, canoes, barges, galleys, yawls, hulks, cobles, dinghies, feluccas, cutters, dhows, junks, gondolas, sampans, punts, skiffs and trawlers.

Unluckily, they were all bashed together during a stupendous tempest and the hulls interpenetrated each other and the whole thing is such a knot of vessels it can't be undone, so when I put to sea I do so simultaneously in every one and it's an odd sight, certainly, to witness Captain Corker strolling the deck(s) of that maritime mix-up like a mini-minotaur in a maze.

But today I need to dive below the waves, not swish over them, so it is to my submarine that I'm headed. I only have one submarine but it's a good one. It was given to me by an inventor called Boppo Higgins and it is fast and reliable, quite roomy too, and most importantly, very watertight. I jump out of bed, stroll along the jetty to where this machine waits and climb down the ladder into the cockpit, which I seal by shutting a transparent plastic dome on a hinge over it. I pull levers and twist knobs and press buttons.

And so I'm off, heading for the seabed where the bones of Jones are lying and thinking how terrible it is when bones avoid the truth. Why do they do that? Is it because the word *tibia* nearly sounds like *fibber*? But the word *metatarsal* nearly sounds like *sent a parcel* and no bone has ever worked successfully as a postman in my extensive and expensive experience or even outside it. I regard it as an unsolvable mystery and maybe it regards me the same way. It would serve me right if it did. I like being served right.

In such cases the waiter is efficient and puts every dish in its proper place and bows deeply before wishing me *bon appétit*. Better to be served *right* than served wrong, which means being *left* with a service so rotten you twiddle your fork and spoon until they rust and the spaghetti never arrives. I am lucky never to have supped in such restaurants. I would still be there if I had, waiting for the meal until the future itself became the pasta.

But none of that is important. It's far more pertinent to say that within the hour I arrived at the precise spot where the bones of Jones were. I imagined they would be scattered randomly but in fact they had been arranged in a neat circle, too perfect a shape for the artistry of the currents to have fashioned. They were telling new lies even as I approached . . .

THE BONES OF JONES

"I am a renowned opera singer," said a femur.

"Scotland was put on the world upside down," said the maxilla.

"Two plus two equals five," said the sphenoid.

"Love is half an onion," said a phalange.

"One quarter," corrected the coccyx.

"I can't talk," said the mandible.

"Chairs are used as currency in Yuckystan," said an ulna.

"Griffins are monkeys in disguise," said one of the cervical vertebrae, to which another responded, "Swans dwell in nests of solid yogurt." But the first objected to this, "Swans don't exist at all!"

"Squeezed coughs think like weasels," said the scapula.

"Chums are hexagonal," said an astragalus.

"Jokes are always unfunny," chuckled the humerus.

"Gloves knit themselves," said the patella.

"Diameters hate cheese," said a radius.

"Unless it's in a pi," countered the ischium.

"Glue is pear cider," said the clavicle.

And so on. It was very disturbing, and I was disturbed.

The submarine designed for me by Boppo Higgins has lots of prehensile tentacles and mechanical arms that I can control from the cockpit and there are signalling devices that enable me to communicate with anything on the outside in a myriad of practical and impractical ways.

I can, for instance, shoot beautifully scripted letters enclosed in tungsten canisters for the recipient to read at their leisure once they have recovered from being struck on the noggin by the things.

Or I can make the hands on the ends of the arms perform sign language in known and lost tongues, and it goes without saying that I can broadcast sound at any volume and frequency I might desire.

I had decided on this occasion to send my messages to Jones with the aid of a large xylophone that extends from the prow of the vessel, which happens to be shaped like a gigantic head, incidentally.

The xylophone juts like a callous sneer from the mouth.

For some strange reason, bones and xylophones instinctively understand each other. I fiddled with the necessary controls and one of the mechanical arms played a nice little melody on the instrument.

This melody said, "Why don't you cease your untrue chatter and try to be more respectable in future, you bones! Don't you appreciate the atrocious havoc you are playing with the serenity of the sea?"

Then I played a few more notes and these notes said:

"You are upsetting the fish, whales, coral reefs and all the other entities in the surrounding waters. You are spooking the crews of merchant ships that pass overhead, for the vibrations of your lies pass through the hulls and into the dreams of sleeping sailors and when those sailors awake they believe things that can never be, for example that the moon grew from a seed planted in a very big garden or that ants are driven by clockwork."

I continued playing notes on the xylophone and the gist of my words was that bones should rest in peace or at least tell the truth if they really felt they had to speak and that I, Pop Corker (that's my full name), had no intention of letting the bones of *my* skeleton behave so despicably.

At last, they answered me.

"We never lie," they chorused.

"*That* is the biggest lie of all, you liars!" I tinkled.

They shrugged metaphorically.

Before I could say or do anything more, my submarine was rocked by a sudden disruption in the water around me. Some object was approaching at an unadvisable velocity. The bones seemed to be full of trepidation and I craned my neck in the cockpit, struggling to see through the bubble what might be the cause of the shockwave. Then it appeared.

It was a diver in a bulky suit riding a sledge pulled by more than a dozen seadogs. He swooped low and skimmed the seabed and yanked the reins just in time, halting his crazy rush inches from the circle of bones. Then he dismounted and strode with slow motion strides into the centre of the circle of bones, where he kneeled and began playing with them.

I frowned. No, he wasn't really playing. He was picking them up one at a time and repositioning them, making the circle slightly smaller, contracting it so that it covered a lesser area of the seabed.

The bones remained silent during this procedure.

Either he hadn't noticed my submarine or else he had deliberately chosen to ignore it, so I xylophoned a protest.

"What do you think you are doing? Unhand those bones!"

Without rising from his knees or even glancing back over his shoulder, he laughed while continuing with his work.

The sensitive microphone on my hull picked up his subsequent words and relayed them to me. "No, I won't stop. I am an artist and this is my art. You are obviously a barbarian if you want to prevent me from finishing this masterpiece. I dive down every day and make the circle of bones smaller by a tiny amount. It is my art and I am an artist. So there!"

I paled at once, for I recognised the voice.

"Grillchin!" I barely whispered.

"Yes," he said, indicating with a nod of his head the seadogs, "and that is the Team." He must have had his own microphone and amplifier to hear what I had said. But he wasn't angry with me.

Then I realised the incongruity of the situation.

"It was you who asked me to investigate these bones in the first place and stop them from further lying!" I cried.

"Of course. Why shouldn't I? I don't want them telling fibs when they are fated to be merely the component parts of a superb artwork. I gave you the task of preventing them from lying, nothing else. Plus, good art really needs someone to view it to make it complete. That's the other reason I wanted you here. At the moment it's only a work in progress."

"What exactly does it mean?" I wailed. "Because the continual shrinking of a circle of bones, or indeed a circle of any kind, seems a pointless exercise. I have nothing against conceptual art and yet—"

"A pointless exercise?" he roared. "On the contrary, Corker dear boy, you are utterly wrong. *I am making a point.*"

I tried to laugh but no sound emerged from my mouth and I had forgotten the xylophone equivalent of a chuckle. A circle that steadily contracts will end as a point of no dimensions, of course.

"What would Jones say about this?" I finally managed.

"That's none of your business. Just be grateful you have a chin made out of wood rather than iron bars like me."

"My chin isn't really made from wood," I said.

"Isn't it? That's not what your miniature pig told me, and in fact he's here now, so take the matter up with him."

And the diver finally rotated his head until I could discern his face in the circular window. Jammed against the glass was a tiny piglet with mischievous eyes who winked at me sardonically.

"But he lives in a jar on a shelf," I protested.

"So you admit he isn't a lie? He outgrew the jar and now lives here, in the helmet of my diving suit. As for the shelf, it was very *shelfish* to keep him there on his own, you rotter. Now he is happier."

I couldn't dispute this. Or rather I could but didn't.

"Right, I've finished. I'll be back here tomorrow at the same hour. In the meantime get them to stop lying, Corker!"

And he clambered up and once again in slow motion he remounted his sled and jerked the reins. The seadogs pulled him away across the seabed and back to the surface of the ocean and thence to land.

I hate the way Grillchin has no understanding of the difficulties his agents face in the line of duty. I hate the way he cooks falafels on his lower visage.

Now that he was gone, I felt vindictive and vengeful.

So I reached out with the mechanical arms and picked up those bones of Jones and tore apart the circle. I didn't make a geometrical shape of my own but carefully fitted the bones together properly.

I thought that if I could reconstruct Jones I would be able to persuade him, as a complete skeleton, to stop lying. Whole skeletons are more reasonable than individual bones. That was my hypothesis.

Slowly but surely, the bones slotted into their correct positions and I tied them in place with lengths of seaweed. The entire process took several hours but finally the skeleton had been reconstructed.

And then I gaped anew. For this man wasn't Jones.

It wasn't a man of any kind.

It was the skeleton of a female. And I knew who.

"Hayley Jude!" I shrieked.

"Hello Pop," she retorted.

"But you don't exist. I made you up."

"Sure you did. And now you made me up for real."

"What shall we do next?"

"Take me with you and I'll be your wife."

"That's against regulations but I think I'll do it anyway. Grillchin will be furious and murderous when he finds out. He'll set the Team on us to tear me apart. I'll have to change my identity."

"Do it. Put on weight and get a job as a policeman and call yourself Cop Porker instead. He'll never know it's you."

It was a good idea. I couldn't open the cockpit to let her in because that would have flooded the interior of the submarine and I would have died, but I picked her up in the mechanical arms and we rose together out of the sea until we reached the air. Then I took her ashore.

My motorised bed was waiting for us. We climbed into it and snuggled up tight. I ordered it to convey us to the residence of Boppo

Higgins, for I had been struck by an inspiration. Boppo is such a good inventor that he can invent a device that will extract my skeleton and replace it with Hayley Jude's. Then I will return to the seabed and substitute my own bones for the missing ones. The entire task could be completed in one day.

This way we can trick Grillchin and satisfy all his requirements. He will have a set of bones to use as artwork and I am confident that my bones won't lie under the sea. In fact, that's where I keep my truth, mingled with the marrow inside those white human sticks. It's a good place to keep truth safe. Why not try keeping your own truth there sometime?

Hayley Jude will be inside me until the end of our lives and few couples, no matter how romantic they try to be, can claim this. The fact her skeleton is a bit shorter than my own doesn't matter. My flesh sags on my frame now, but so what? I love Hayley Jude. She's a Corker.

Next time I get a vacation I will take her somewhere nice. I won't use my mishmash ship, nor the submarine, but construct a vessel from slices of charred bread. With luck it will be *tempest toast* on vast waves and become soggy, casting us upon a desert island where we will be safe from detection. Grillchin will be able to fume as much as he likes, to no avail, for he will never find us, and even if he does we can protest innocence convincingly.

I am sure all will be well, or if not well then adequate, or if not adequate then bearable, or if not bearable then vicious.

And if you believe that you'll believe anything.

Nonetheless it is true. Isn't it?

THE NOISES THAT SCANS

BY R. A. HARRIS

DON'T LET HIS constant heroics persuade you otherwise—
Skittles is not my friend. Skittles is insane. The only reason he
saves my life is so he can eventually throw me into a volcano. He
thinks throwing me into a volcano will prevent the approaching
apocalypse. I don't blame him for thinking that. He's only ever had his
superiors to look up to and they're even more insane than he is.

I'm currently lying across Skittles' shoulders, partially sunk into his
gloopy black flesh. He's made of crude oil. Every time he checks in the
rearview mirror, waves of iridescent rainbows spread across his
featureless face.

"You okay back there, baby?"

My neck is hard wax, making it difficult to nod, but I do it slow and
deliberately, so he gets the gesture. I'm as good as can be, given the
situation.

Our steed, a copper horse oxidized green, gallops along roads littered
with dead scorpion exoskeletons and through tunnels cowering beneath
crooked bovine bridges. Street lights wilt and dry out as a corrosive
stench unfurls in our wake.

Night is a host of hairy spiders that crawls across the world. They
descend from the giant tentacle-less jellyfish sky on thick web made of
steel.

Our pursuer is sly and hides behind corners; she creeps along the
edges of the objects of the world, haunts the peripherals of our

perception. Here, in the city, there are many edges and many corners—all sharp teeth upon which we may be cut.

It begins to rain rotten fly carcasses. Each tiny body crumbles to dust as it lands on my wax skin; the ones that land on Skittles sink into his oil flesh.

Skittles checks his mirror again. "Don't look now, but our pursuer is upon us."

The city groans and shrieks. The buildings around us flex their muscles, crack their ancient joints. Boiling pus spurts out of sewer pores. Our enemy has infected our city. Our steed's hooves splash through puddles of urine stinking sweat along the street. Skittles pushes on. I would be honored that he tries so hard to save my life, but like I said, Skittles is not my friend, he's just insane.

Night catches up and gives us a hairy embrace; spiders climb in my eyes, in my mouth. The terrible rustling of a thousand spider legs tapping in my ear drowns out the world.

The heavy to and fro of our galloping steed dies as it succumbs to the added mass of the black bodies. I can sense our antagonist slipping between the seething bodies; its foul flickering chasm-body, a hideous waste of demented colors, subsists in the dark. I'm glad I cannot see right now.

Plastic tentacles full of the dreams I fight so hard to forget worm their way inside me. Newborn stars shitting radiation and cancers; the dogs of the universe barking mad; our gods, the ghosts that haunt our religions, our wars, and our machines; the putrid remains of our ancestors reincarnated as empty engines and paper-thin cysts; the world in a mirror caving in on itself.

A rebellion against entropy, a cake becoming egg and flour, and an egg becoming soil and worm, and a worm becoming a tyrant, and standing tall along the edges of all the things in this pretty world, it makes them into a single blade and it uses that blade to slice our dreams in two.

The world is a ball and a bladder and it falls apart at the seams, steaming piss and malformed bones of children evaporate, run for the stars and beyond.

I do not fear the end of the world. I only fear the gaping chasm that

Skittles and his superiors so fervently revere. Where there is light, there is void. Only in the dark can you get a true sense of yourself, your limits, and your edges.

"Fear not the darkness," Skittles says in muffled tones, "for it is but a bruise upon God's glorious apple, and by the grace of sunlight, shall be vanquished."

A strange sensation overtakes me, like freezing water expanding in my veins. The tentacles unfurl from my soul; there's nothing for them to wrap up anymore, just the slush dreams of an extinguished candle. The spiders retreat from my orifices. Detached legs and crushed bodies lie still. In their wake, it becomes clear why I am becoming nothing. I am melting. Skittles has set himself on fire in an act of heroism and martyrdom. The flames engulf us. Skittles, that insane bastard, he'll be the death of me. I spread like ink into the void.

Skittles died in the fire. He dies in every fire he sets. Don't think for a second that stops him from reincarnating and finding me again. It may take him days, years even, but he always finds me.

In the meantime I have been discovered by another agent of the superiors. Those damn calcite bony bastards. They never leave me alone. Not while the apocalypse is encroaching upon our world. They'll see me tossed into that volcano if it's the last thing they do.

My new host is a robotic rainbow trout. His flesh is corrupted metal, his organs electronic components mass-produced years ago. I can hear electricity dancing between faulty connections as he speaks. "Life is a river, and sometimes river flow will turn a man into a monster," my new host tells me. "River flow will do that to a man." He has told me that same thing many times. Skittles will arrive and correct him, just because he thinks he should. He says the same thing, "Life is a river, and sometimes river flow will turn a man into a monster. River flow will do that to a man."

I am a wave of frozen wax across the flank of our steed. I am set in my ways. We have ridden further, the rainbow trout and I, into a cat litter tray desert. From here the city is a distant tumor, a brief rupture of pink flesh and organic milieu. Our homes are smallpox scars, are mosquito bites upon our planet's hide, and nothing more.

And the sun, that morning loser, that creeper, gropes the land from behind the horizon. Soft tendrils of light escorting its swollen body up the rampart test, retest, and worm between objects, along the edges, in the orifices of all the dead things. Sensing no danger, it rears its ugly head, a bulb atop a wire, flopping in the wind.

The ground melts to treacle and we're forced to abandon our steed as it sinks without a trace. My host swings me onto his back like a stiff cape and begins to hop towards our destination. That's one thing I can rely on, the one constant in life: the destination is always the same.

"This isn't my preferred method of locomotion, baby," my host tells me as we bounce along. He counts each step in a foreign language.

After a number of hops I don't know, because I never learnt to count in a foreign language, the robotic rainbow trout stops and places me on the ground. "It's best we spend the night here." He begins to dig a hole using his fins. The ground is hard again, the sun has retreated, leaving only the translucent sheath of jellyfish flesh to protect us from the myriad stars that stare down upon us, greedy gravity sucking detritus into their bowels. "Night's coming," my host says.

Sure enough, he hits an oil pipe and night ascends in an arc. Thick black night that smells of a history buried beneath rock and sand. It pools around us, a horse shit swamp riddled with flies, crab limbs and lumps of whale blubber floating like icebergs in the dark.

Skittles stands before me. His form takes shape from that murky night, Jesus walking on oil. "God does not fear the night, because God is of the night," he says. "Hello baby, I'm here to do right by you. I didn't mean to melt your heart and steal you away, just the luck of the draw is all. A man's got to burn to be the brightest star."

The rainbow trout stands upright. His skin is now coated in thick, slimy black oil. "Are you here to do God's work?"

"I want to know if God is sleeping with the enemy..." Skittles answers. "Or if we just don't believe in him anymore."

The two of them crabwalk in tandem for a moment, an oily ritual.

The trout speaks, "The white hairs on their lips..."

"Dead trees in snow . . . "

"They talk their slow, amorphous talk . . . "

"Speak their leaky, winter speak . . . "

The trout nods as best it can: a universal trait amongst all beings who communicate with Skittles. Skittles rattles off a laugh. "To the mountain, where we will wake God from his slumber, and dispel the nightmare beast that stalks these lands." He scoops me up and wears me like a bandanna. "Hold tight baby, we're going for a ride."

He climbs aboard the rainbow trout. Pistons churn, cam belts chug, and we swim through the sticky night. We're headed in the right direction.

The volcano is a lion, its mane a mighty rock formation. It roars as we approach.

"Don't let the roar fool you: inside, it's a void." Skittles roars himself. "It's a half full promise made of despair, it preys on the thoughts we never have."

The volcano is a fierce beast, magma guts and lava blood. Igneous rock teeth clash together as it bites chunks out of the sky.

Skittles calls it a coward and smacks our fish steed on its hind, telling it to make haste. "This party won't start without us," he cries.

The lion takes a swipe at us. I feel the intense heat of its blood bubbling beneath its rocky skin as its great paw passes overhead. A flock of birds, clouds no doubt, spread across the sky in its wake. They shit white globs of rain.

Skittles leaps from the back of the fish and latches onto the lion's paw. "Go free, now, my fellow warrior," he calls to the trout.

"I'll be back with the boys," the trout shouts, and hops away, counting backwards as he goes.

"Just you and me now, baby," Skittles says. I nod that same deliberate nod I always do so Skittles gets the message. "Time to taste the molten flesh of our arch nemesis and end this game of charades. Ain't no world but the one we make and we make it by dining on volcano blood, the sweat of our dreams and the bones of every ugly child who ever got to smell the Earth."

Skittles begins to climb the leg of the lion volcano, edging closer to its cauterized jaw. Its sulphuric breath reeks something rotten.

At last, we arrive at the orifice that opens into Hell. I take comfort in the knowledge that it will not be me alone who is eaten by the flaming belly of this foul beast, this fuming volcanic wild cat. Skittles is made of oil. Skittles is climbing inside the volcano. Skittles is insane.

The robot rainbow trout arrives at the foot of the beast. He leads an army of boys. They all eat candy bullets and make dioramas with their guns and their helmets. Skittles salutes them one by one from the lip of the lion. I give a slow deliberate nod.

THE NOISE THAT STAINS

Skittles bellows, "And as ye be cast into the flames, so will ye arise a Phoenix. Reborn to birth a new world, yours are the loins of the new god. A god we can believe in." He throws me down the gullet of the lion as it roars one last time. White angel heat burrows between my atoms and pulls me apart, piece by piece.

The Great Antagonist creeps in with the heat, slides right into the heart of the matter. She hugs me with her disintegrating arms and says, "I fear the noise that stains even the most perfect image, the dark that is at the heart of even the smallest particle."

EXCERP⟵ ꟻ⅁ОM *GOODBYE* B⟵BYLON

SEB DOUBINSKY

1.

THE SUN WAS gently striking the surface of the water, making it seem motionless. Only the tiredless whisper indicated the strength of its raging spring flow, bending its back like liquid muscle. Large chunks of grey ice floated away in the distance, ephemeral wrecks. Three policemen, in their impeccable blue uniforms, were throwing up in the water, side by side, like grotesque life-size hand puppets, their caps bobbing up and down in stomach-turning harmony. One of them had puked on his shoe, and was dipping a careful foot in the dark green broth. A long thin trail of vomit was going down the current, making its sinuous way like a strange serpent heading for the open sea. Commissioner Georg Ratner thought about the people on the other side of the ocean who would benefit from this wonderful gift of civilization. He smiled, but he wasn't cheerful. Shivering in the early morning cold, he remembered—with some surprise—that he hadn't always hated spring.

2.

Smell of fresh coffee—sun rays on the apartment's kitchen table—this could be a Sunday—the toasts are burning, but who cares?—memories are like Sundays—unclear, lazy, magical—Barbara is washing her hands in the sink—the sound of her laughter!—the calendar

66

is shining on the wall like clean sheets hanging to dry—this is spring, believe it or not—a season long forgotten—this is spring—try to forget about it again

3.

The photographers were already here, doing their job. Lightning everywhere, like silent storms. He passed the security fences, and stroked his hair backwards. It was humid. There were patches of snow here and there, the rest was mud. His shoes sank deep with each step, and he was careful not to trip. Lieutenant Valentino, his partner, was trodding behind. A young guy, full of talent. He could hear his slight panting at each humid step. "A fucking cold morning to die," Ratner thought to himself. Police officers trampled all around, some of them carrying torchlights. You could see the white cloud of their breath preceding their half-bent silhouettes. Ten or fifteen police cars were parked randomly on the outskirts of the restricted area, lights flashing grimly in the rising dawn.

"We've got an arm!" someone suddenly yelled, from the semi-darkness.

Georg Ratner hurried in the direction of the shout. You always had to start with something, and an arm might not have been the worst thing to start this new day with.

4.

A young police-officer was standing by his discovery, pale and shivering. The bleak circle of his light revealed a strange object, half-broken, incongruous in the snow, a mixture of red, pink and blue, alien and yet horribly familiar.

If you took a closer look, as Georg and Jesse Valentino did, you could definitely see that it was, indeed, an arm. A woman's arm.

"Where's the rest? The main part?" the Commissioner barked at the rookie, trying to shake him out of his stupor.

The young officer pointed weakly to another direction in the wall of shadows, and suddenly began to throw up on himself. Georg shook his head and turned around. No need to embarrass the kid any further. He made a sign to Jesse, and walked towards a cluster of silhouettes who were standing a little further away, by the growling river.

5.

The coroner, a middle-aged black man, but incredibly long and thin for his age, got up and took off his plastic gloves. He scratched his head, then calmly lit a cigarette. Ratner imitated him with a cigar. With the tip of his shoe, he lifted the blue plastic sheet which covered the body—or what was left. From here, in the peculiar dim light of the freezing dawn, it looked like a large chopped animal. A pig, maybe.

"Unusually cold for April, isn't it?" the coroner said, putting on some thick leather gloves.

Georg nodded, and let the sheet fall back into place.

"What have we here?" he asked, looking at the ambulance crew lifting the remains on a stretcher, in what looked like an oversized garbage bag.

"Female, between 25 and 30, black hair, identity unknown, cut in half from head to pelvis, then dismembered. Probably raped too, but it's too early to tell. Nice butcher's work."

Georg grunted and noted everything in a little pad, which had his initials carved on its cover in golden letters: G. R. A gift from Laura for his 36th birthday, about six months ago. "So you can catch all these horrible criminals," she had said. Wishful thinking.

"Like the others?" he asked.

The thin man scratched his head and looked in the distance. On the other side of the river, the city was slowly waking up.

"Looks like it," he finally said, breathing out a long trail of smoke, "but who knows? With all the publicity this sicko has gotten from the media, basically anybody could have done it. Only the tests will tell. You'll have to wait for the conclusion of my report, I'm afraid."

"That's okay, Frank. Thanks anyway."

The coroner shook his hand and left. Georg watched his elongated body tower back to his car, carefully avoiding the mud puddles. He looked like a big bird. A strange big bird.

Valentino was interrogating the patrol cop who had found the remnants. A few yards away, a flock of journalists were now fighting their way through the security fences like a flock of vultures. It was time to leave, he told himself, and puffed out a thick grey cloud of cigar-smoke as he left the scene. There was a faint smell of decay floating around. The smell of life. The smell of his life. He smiled. The cigar switched sides in his mouth.

6.

How many bodies had he seen in his life? He couldn't tell. First, he had joined the Army, right after High School. There was a war going on then, "somewhere in South-east China." A mission of peace, they had said. He had never seen so many dead bodies, piled up, mixed, unified in mutilation and blood. Couldn't tell the uniforms apart. He could remember a friend who used to count the bodies. Systematically. He drew figures, diagrams, established statistics. He was trying to figure out war, to give it a tangibility through its most obvious manifestation: bodies. He got wounded, and after that, he had stopped counting. The shock, maybe. Or it could have been amnesia. He wasn't the same, anyway. He wondered what had happened to him. They had gotten separated after the offensive on Lin Tsang, when Hell broke loose. He had just disappeared. Maybe he was in some concentration camp out there, now. Still counting. Or up on a cloud, with Baby Jesus, doing the same thing with saints and sinners. Numbers . . . Murderers cared about numbers. They always knew how many people they had killed, and so did soldiers, and so did cops.

After the Army he had joined the Force. Maybe to put some value on human life (there were worse excuses than that). One or ten murders were the same thing—as a human life was infinite, priceless. Not a statistic. Never a statistic. He always felt sad when he looked at bodies. Like today.

He grunted and pushed his hands further inside the pockets of his coat.

But he also had a part to play, and he would play it all the way through. "Commissioner Ratner? A tough one." And he sure was, but death still hit him sideways. A body was work. Pain began with the investigation, when you moved deeper into personal stories. You saw the mess, the cruelty, the waste. And you began to feel empty. Completely empty. Jesse Valentino opened the door of the car. It looked like a hearse. His own personal hearse. Counting? Who had said "Counting?"

7.

Jesse was at the wheel, his back upright against the seat, as usual. His startling blue eyes moved around like careful spotlights. The Commissioner turned the radio on and the Industrial Jazz station began to emit its strange melodies inside the cabin. He could feel the

Lieutenant grow tense. It amused him. He liked it when people hated the music he loved. It made him feel special. Barbara couldn't stand it. She would sometimes walk into the dining room and simply turn the record player off. He didn't have this problem with Laura. She didn't mind it, or she simply didn't care. Go figure.

"Good stuff, isn't it?" he teased the young man.

Jesse turned his head towards him, smiling tensely.

The Commissioner leaned back in his seat, marking the rhythm with his hand, flat on his thigh. The sun was slowly blinding its way through the corner of his eye. Traffic was getting thicker by the minute. Somewhere, in this city, an assassin was having wild dreams.

8.

Sweet music—sweet sweet music—perfume and soft hands—she walks—soft breasts—dark hole—wet hole—seasons move—great hair—and now a $10,000 question—maybe a trip to the pyramids—sexy cheeks—white teeth red teeth—jesus christ god of death—elevator music holy music—i want a mother—be my mother—kill my mother—yes yes yes yes—buddha god of death—knife axe scream penis slit cut axe penis knife scream slit—slit OPEN—scream—semen Semen SEMEN—welcome my son—redemption—allah god of death—this my dream—leave it alone—this is my child

9.

"I think it's time to quote a poem," Jesse said, and he did.

The poem said something about life being short. Very à propos, Georg thought. Poetry . . . Jesse Valentino wrote poems in his spare time. He had confided this to the Commissioner about a year ago. He had even published a small collection last fall in some underground press. Under a fake name, of course.

One dedicated issue of *DEATH ALWAYS WEARS RED AND BLUE* sat in his bookshelves, somewhere in his apartment. He had actually enjoyed reading them, although he didn't get everything. Too modern for him. He liked the Classics—all of them. Chinese Classics, French Classics, Russian Classics, American Classics, you name it. He used to read a lot of poetry when he was younger. Especially during the War. But not anymore. He couldn't figure out why. He just didn't. He read philosophy and books about magic and ethnology. Other poems, in a way. The words might have been different, but the riddles were the same, questions and revelations, all of that. Valentino was a good poet, and he lived by the obscure standards of his secret passion. To him, everything had a meaning. It went beyond aesthetics. Words said something, like "good" and "evil." He wrote a lot of poems about that. To be honest, he seemed obsessed with that. But they were good poems nonetheless. Even if they didn't change a thing about the goddamned world. Actually, this was maybe what Ratner respected the most in his young partner: the attachment to a useless passion.

It took courage in this world.

THE CONTINUED INSTANCES OF GEORGE MARTHIS WITHIN THE SINGULARITY, WHEREIN THE INSTANCE KNOWS NO RULES (GEORGE IS OLD WHEN OUR STORY STARTS)

TOLD BY THOMAS LOGAN

Origination

IMAGINE THE UNIVERSE.

Of it, something called The Real. This supposed "sum of things" acting as a constant, adjusting all equations. This same "something" George Everett Marthis tries to avoid. He knows The Real can be overcome; it is only of this universe. There are estimated 10^{500} universes, 10^{500} reals. George only need discover one.

George's primary thoughts are of his freedom, his narrow pacing how he spans worlds.

He's not been born with genius, but he is diligent, disciplined. He will find a way.

Flashback: Nineteen years old. Any day now.

Flashforward: Age eighty-one. Any day now.

At its fundamental level, reality is not a thing, not an event, not a thought. It is a sliver of a sensation, caught peripherally in the corner of the eye. Figuratively, George knows. The real universe is not physical, nor is it found in words.

George by and large keeps his thoughts and theories to himself. George knows the fickleness of the masses, crowds, and power. His findings are not for publication.

People try to write their own stories into their lives but think too small. They depend on The Real. They schedule their tomorrows and futures together based on its being here. Evolutionary psychology: Cling to others as they drown, too. This is not to judge them; they know not what they do. George imagines better. He's witnessed their desperate search for life vests by eating right, working out, material goods, political office, making millions. They have it wrong. He's getting off this sinking ship. He's building his own ark. There will be no genocidal 40 days of rains. He will simply slip out from harbor into the night. (Figuratively.)

"Oh, hello. Sorry. Didn't see you there. Will you be checking out?"

There is no time ("Like" the present)

The hotel graveyard shift is a second job; George's first is at a vanity press, binding theorists' self-published pages at part-time, 32 hours a week. Once, dissident philosophers' and scientists' findings/theories/conclusions were produced crudely at copy shops or even manually typewritten with individually reproduced, hand-drawn equations and illustrations. The absence of gloss gave most of these radical, outsider publications a manifesto quality, tremendously increasing the likelihood of their life's work going unseen, unread, lost. But today anyone with ambition and a credit card can now receive a fair hearing and be printed multiple times, preserved for the generations. These half-days of part-time work prove a sound education for George, a slow but steady reader, who moved to this college town at age nineteen with plans and an ambition to one day teach.

Most people survive with a feeling that there's a place for them in the world, that they really have a useful function.

But most societies operate at far less than half-power ($P = W / \Delta t$).

George Marthis is looking for a better world. Any suggestions?

If the math pencils, it exists.

We exist, according to physicists, upon the surface of a cosmic bubble, called a "brane." (George immediately understood the homonymic significance.) Within the largest conceptual space possible (the "bulk"), virtual particles pop into and out of existence so quickly that our math (based still in "sum-things") cannot account for when, what, or how. But these particles exist, must exist, bang out big in a *sui generis* universe every now and then. Whether the "new" universe lasts brief or long along the brane is hard to say, having no referent absent a single unit of measure: Consciousness. We are the timekeepers and accountants of The Real. A hotel with many rooms.

A woman on the opposite side of the counter holds a groomed lap dog close to her chest. Between her and George, who's stopped mid-pace, is a man half her age with a rough face and military carriage, a football, or more correctly, a rugby player's hardened squareness. The only explanation George can find for her stay is that she's a donor to the college.

Distinctly, and on too many maddening occasions late at night at the hotel, he has felt the shape of change, of time, of movement—only to have its taste vanish to a vague stencil of sweetness. Lost again. Or interrupted.

"Will you be checking out?"

After years of rejection, George no longer submits his work. His proof will be his disappearance; his vindication, that no one notices.

Understand that a change in physics occurred about a century and a half after Newton: math began telling the natural philosopher where to look and lurk, transmuting tinkerer into physicist. To a world powered by the pressure of steam engines and simple sums, this shift to the immaterial was a frightening understanding. As imaginary numbers centuries after discovery became the basis for controlling electricity and light. As mass became translatable into energy. As energy was no longer created nor destroyed. And so it was understood: What is possible in mathematical modeling is not just possible but real somewhere. Including universes in which George Marthis reached his potential, his development never delayed.

He could have been a famous thinker, but what is the worth of human success, human praise? The nights were his, then the days and nights, and then—

Master astral projection

The economy tanks. The binding press cuts back George's hours from part-time to furlough. The hotel work remains steady, exponentially so once its owner commits suicide. The grieving widow sells George the hotel for a dollar. "Burn it to the ground," she says. But George has no plans for doing any such thing. It's a double shift. He paces behind the center until his ankle becomes tender, trying not to ponder this new development.

George feels the swelling of potential universes in his own life. It's an effervescence present each evening he wakes in a hotel bed and makes coffee or on evening walks along the feeder road from his home to work— into sunsets in the fall—an aura of dawning possibility that inflates precariously along the skin of an existence much bigger than his own, his night-to-night, his day-to-day, his mortality. He cannot stop.

Having dedicated his whole life, George cannot imagine a world in which his escape is not imminent, and this confidence/fear is what assures it must be. What he's discovered, it's no longer filling in-between the lines pre-drawn by The Real, painting by its prescribed numbers; instead, it's like a fresco where the math is absorbed into the rock, becoming one with the universe, changing what is. And the possibility of the moment remains infinite.

A new dawn is upon us. Figuratively, George knows.

The solitude of ideas (Matter is what stands still)

"Smile," the magazine photographer says. But George is no smiler.

These people are interrupting his work. Adding to his distractions. Lessening free time for thoughts. They said they wanted to know about the hotel. They said they wanted to know something about his life.

Time is full of such interruptions. Having few family living, fewer coworkers, and even fewer friends, it is easy for George to avoid the business of being busy. There was no one in his daily life forcing him to speak of the events of his weekend, his feelings, or his plans, i.e. his life as social network status updates. He's never created an online profile for himself and rarely checks his email at work or the library. Most of his online time is spent on message boards and sites of fellow seekers. His cellular phone is primarily for emergencies and was paid for by the minute.

The reporter interviewing him was taken with George. She says he looks like her father.

What is suicide? George knows it is not simply the pistol blowing off-white skull/brain soup outward onto a green imitation leather headrest of a two-tone tan Datsun parked in the woods behind the house (his father). Nor is it an injection when no other cure for the pain was possible (hotel owner). Suicide could be slow, a life spent on the immaterial, on the insignificant. Like those around him.

It's not about publication, the recognition, or the elegance of equations for others to admire. What George wants, quite simply, is a better world.

George knew if he doesn't succeed, it'll remain the dying telling stories of the dead. He didn't care if others thought it practical. It had to be done. For all of us.

Words

Words. George tries to avoid the words of the world around him, those that want his attention, want to divert his thoughts. He buys bulk when he can, generic products as a second option whose less vivid colors are more appealing, packaging less assaulting to the eye. For those few items he cannot readily transfer to plastic squeeze bottles or storage bins, strips of two-inch masking tape used sparingly over words and icons provides the sensory censorship George requires—masking tape because it is beige and reusable, transferable one to four times for refrigerated products, one to eight times for frozen items, and six to ten times for dry goods. He likewise covers or crosses out or peels logos from consumer goods, owns no mirrors, and his only set time tracking device is the one on his cheap cell phone—synchronized with atomic time—that wakes him in the evenings to go to work.

You walk to work tonight along the access road, cars passing quickly overhead along the interstate with frantic wipers and lights on in the unseasonable rain. An occasional truck or carload of male students this week or next will inevitably yell or throw something as they drive past, showing off. In recent years, groups of women have also started being mean, which is disheartening, representing for you a cultural retrogression to the crudest common denominator. They think of you as a vagrant, despite your well-ironed white shirts, despite owning a hotel. Because you travel by foot with your thoughts, not by car. Because of the shoes you wear. Because of your age. Because you walk even in the rain. But this is who you are, George Marthis, and this is the life you lead.

Your name is George Everett Marthis, and once, you owned a minivan but found too much time was spent worrying about costly repairs. Besides, you moved here because, unlike other parts of this repressive state, this is a walkable town. And walking gives you time to think. This wet evening you think about how you can reserve a room at the hotel but how this decision doesn't work retroactively. That is, after you've awoken the next day, it's too late to decide on staying in a room instead of at home the night before. Yet. There are times when waking up at the hotel you think you've woken up in your trailer home and vice versa. A tiny leap. Perhaps too small with which to bother. But quantum physics allows for such possibilities.

No two days are identical. Any similarity is only order imposed by the mind for the sake of predictive laziness.

There was a feature article about him and the hotel in the state's monthly travel magazine. Ol' George Marthis reads and re-reads his complementary copy one afternoon in a hotel bed, taking him seven minutes, thirteen seconds, then rereads it at a slower rate and goes back to sleep and then downstairs and into work that evening, his aching arthritis, the carpeted rectangle, the television, and nearly a dozen labeled composition books full of coded notes. that lie under notices, timecards, and bills and memberships to pay. George Marthis has been losing his way. Time has gotten the better of him. Because, honestly, he doesn't know what he's doing anymore. George finds he's absently turned on the TV. A temptation he'll quickly avoid. But not just yet.

There was not enough substance to the article to warrant a correction letter.

Parousia

The deceased hotel owner was apparently a person of interest. He was a pillar of the local business community of the city adjacent to the (nominally) Christian college town. He was also an author, secretly, of science fiction and numerous unpublished works without genre, writing eccentrically under a different pseudonym for each but all with a simple style, smart, sincere, yet approaching every subject crabwise, just out of tune. Many were life-fulfilling stories, only to remind the reader that one cannot escape life.

George, dedicated to his thoughts, avoided fiction, has never read any of these humous or post-published works, but a pre-med college student named Lupe who works for George as a housemaid has. The story she's read she relates to her boss (nominally) as she stays behind one late evening and watches the reclusive hotel owner (some say autistic) do the daily reports' math in his head. (George could tell she did not have many college friends.)

As Lupe relates it: The story is so, like, about how these three mental patients were woke up during graveyard shifts all across this kinda big campus for the insane. You don't know why at first, but you get this really good description of the place, all spooky and full of shadows, security cameras that're never watched, a large but empty feeling. So these orderlies bring these three guys together from different wings into a kinda large room, like a warehouse or maybe a gym. Anyway, these three dudes all believed he was Jesus Christ, our Lord and Savior. The story is told by an orderly like he was in a confessional and we're the priest, you know, he's writing personally, like all this happened to him, the author, who seems kinda to be regretting it. (George understood Lupe to mean "narrator" and not "author," as he was pretty sure the story was not autobiographical, especially when she came to the end.)

So each of the three Jesuses look at each other in this long silence like dogs sniffing each other out. Then all three start preaching altogether at once; it's like if one opened his mouth, all three ended up proclaiming something. So, they boasted miracles. They made challenges that boomeranged back, like, If you was Jesus, why do you waste your time in a mental institute?—or—Where have you been for the past 2,000 years, sir?

The staff grew bored. They thought it was going to be amusing, but the patients weren't really funny at all. It was getting awkward for them watching. Some left, and then there was an emergency. The dude telling the story stayed back alone as lookout until they could sneak the Christs back to their rooms and not get caught. The Christs quieted down—no one was watching or coaxing them anymore—and the writer seemed to maybe have fallen asleep.

So maybe it was a dream, the writing was unclear like that, but this guy realizes and hears how long the quiet the crazy Christs had gotten to be and so he comes into the room where the three just were—there's only one entrance—and all he finds is like this notebook, which he's now reading to us, so he's like a writer, a reader, and a character all locked inside the same story and they won't let him out. (She looks at him with sad eyes, and George wonders if Lupe suspects how close she is to becoming a story within a story.)

How much time actually passes? Would we ever know if time slipped, shifted, contracted? What keeps our constants constant? What if dark energy doesn't exist to push us apart but rather all matter has been shrinking at the same constant, leaving more emptiness without? We are the only measure. And our instruments are faulty. If there's never been nothing, then that means there's always been the burden of something. What, then, to do with our something? George Marthis knows.

George's journals will never be found. Or if they are, they'll be written in code never bothered to be cracked. The pages will be recycled. Or go to a landfill. It all depends on the Bureau of State Lands employee managing the estate.

THOMAS LOGAN

But George—age nineteen or eighty-one and a day—sleeps easy tonight knowing that never for one day has he let the hotel become his life.

EVERYTHING IS COLORS, ALL OF THEM

DANIEL VLASATY

SOUNDS HAPPEN AND Peter can't focus on anything but his own breath. His own breathing. Soft and shallow. Like this is the end. Like he is dying. Like he is nothing but fear.

Outside, the sky is full of things. Black things. All different sizes. They are planes, or ships. They are space ships. But they are also alive. They are animals from another end of the galaxy.

Peter stares at the sky, hearing things happening. But this time he doesn't breathe. He tries his hardest not to breathe. The animals in the sky move about. They flutter. They twist. They glow strange, new colors. They make noise. So much noise.

Peter thinks about running, going inside. Maybe where it is safe. In his room. He always felt safe there. Tucked under his bed. Or in the closet. Hugging his knees to his chest. Rocking slightly as the clothes hanging above him gently caress his hair. Mess it up. But he doesn't move. He can't move. How could he? He can only wait.

He just watches. It's all he can do. It's all he's ever done.

One of the things, the ships, the animals, lands in front of him. In his front yard. It makes noise. It glows colors. It is orange now, but it is an orange that looks almost blue. It flops around on the grass. It is dying, Peter thinks. It looks like it is dying. But he doesn't know for sure.

More of them land around the neighborhood. In the front yards of surrounding houses. These things. These animals. They are sky animals.

The one in Peter's yard is the size of a small car. It's the size of his

Kia Rio. It jitters around, moving closer to him. It is only a few feet away. It smells like the absence of smell and its noises hum louder and louder. They play right in Peter's ears. In his brain. The sounds tell him that he should be running. Running far away. But maybe that is just his subconscious. Maybe it is telling him to stay. To wait.

The thing stops in front of him. This sky animal. It is still glowing colors Peter's never seen before. The side hisses open like elevator doors. The creature inside is everything. The outside is only a shell. It is the size of the flying machine. Its ship. It stretches legs that have been cramped under it the whole journey. Legs it didn't have a second ago.

Peter takes a step back. The creature steps with him, unfurling arms from its sides. Its arms are longer than its body. Covered in feathers. Its arms are wings.

Peter looks over at his neighbors. Most of them have gone inside their houses. Where they will be safe. Some still linger, like Peter, looking at the creatures in their yards. The sky animals crawling out of their flying machines. They are all different sizes. Different colors. Different shapes. Some are thin and long. Others are round. They are fat or not. They have wings or fins or human appendages. They are like nothing. But they are also like everything. Every kind of thing.

The creature in front of Peter makes a noise. A new sound. A line forms on what is probably its face and it opens like a mouth. Its teeth are big and small. They are blue and pink. It does not have a tongue. Drool builds up behind the teeth, spills out over its lips. It opens its mouth wider.

Peter closes his eyes. The creature opens its own. They are nothing. Not there.

"Welcome," it says. "Welcome." It speaks in Peter's voice. But it is also not Peter's voice. It is new.

Peter screams and the creature takes a step forward. Toward him. Peter screams more. The creature just stands there. Watching. Like it is learning.

"Stop," the creature says after twenty minutes of Peter screaming. "Your voice," it says. "Your voice is hurting." It puts a feathered arm on Peter's shoulder and turns him toward his house. "Here."

The creature leads Peter inside his house. Back to the kitchen. The creature makes Peter some tea. With extra honey. "For your vocal cords," the creature says.

Peter drinks the tea, but he is scared. "Who are you?" he asks the creature. Once the tea has coated his throat. "What are you?"

EVERYTHING IS COLORS, ALL OF THEM

The creature cleans Peter's cup. Places it back in the cabinet. "I am you. Not you. To help you. I am you to help you."

Peter just looks at the creature. Blank face. The creature smiles its monster smile. It cleans Peter's kitchen.

Peter looks out the window as the creature vacuums his living room. Sees the creature's flying machine mowing his grass.

Peter passes out.

He wakes up later in his bed. He is wearing fresh pajamas and he has been bathed. His face cleanly shaved. Hair combed and parted perfect. Peter screams again and again. The creature rushes in with an ice cold beer in a baby bottle. It sticks the bottle in Peter's mouth and hums some alien lullaby. The creature glows a soothing purple color.

Out in the living room the creature's flying machine watches a sitcom set in an office where people do weird and quirky things instead of work. The flying machine laughs along with the laugh track. The flying machine eats potato chips. Its black shell is covered in crumbs. It is drunk on cheap human whisky.

The creature shakes its head at the flying machine. Says it is not helping. The flying machine waves it off. Turns the volume up. It laughs out a mouthful of chewed up potato chip mush.

Months pass. The creature works hard to help Peter. To help him get his life together. To help him become a better person. The flying machine does nothing. It only eats and drinks. It gets drunk all the time. It has gotten fat. Its breathing is loud and forced. Its colors no longer glow as bright. It is sick. The creature fears it will soon die.

Other sky animals help people all over the city. They are making the city a better place. They are making people better. The sky animals only want the best.

Peter wakes up to find the flying machine passed out in a pile of its own vomit. Its vomit is all colors. Full of chunks of nonexistent colors. Its eyes are open and crispy.

Peter calls for the creature. It is in the kitchen cooking. It comes into the room wearing an apron that says "FOOD IS LOVE." The creature shakes its head. It kneels down near the flying machine. "Oh no," it says.

"Is it okay?" Peter asks the creature. The creature doesn't have a name. It told Peter their kind never has a name. They are always unnamed. They just are. Peter has started thinking of the creature as a friend. It's been nice having it here these past months.

"No," the creature says. "Not okay. May never be okay again."

Peter shakes his head. So does the creature. The creature carries the flying machine out of the room. To the bathroom. Peter hears the shower running. Hears the creature bathing the flying machine. Hears it talking in clicks and sighs.

The phone rings. Peter answers it. He hasn't answered the phone once since the sky animals arrived. The creature always answers the phone. But the creature is busy. Peter doesn't want to bother it.

"Hello," Peter says into the phone.

"Jennifer for Peter," a strange voice says.

"Uhh, okay."

Peter hears the phone shift around on the other end. Jennifer takes the line. "Thank you, Claudia," she says to her creature. "Hey, Peter."

"You call your creature Claudia?"

"Yeah," Jennifer says. "She likes it. What do you call yours?"

"Nothing," Peter says. "It doesn't have a name. I didn't name it."

"You don't call him anything?"

"No." Peter shrugs. "I didn't know people were naming their creatures. I'm not even sure mine's a *him*. I think it's just an *it*."

Jennifer laughs. "Of course it's a *him*, you weirdo. All men have male creatures and all women have females."

"Oh," Peter says. "How do you know all of this?"

"Everyone knows it. Don't you ever watch the news or read the paper?"

"Not really, I guess. My creature's flying machine is always hogging the TV."

"That's weird. Why does it live inside? Claudia's flying machine stays in the garage. Like most vehicles."

"I don't know," Peter says again. Like it's all he knows how to say. "But I think it might be an alcoholic. I think it's drinking itself to death."

Jennifer laughs hard at this. She's cracking up. "You're so funny, Peter. God, that's hilarious."

He pulls the phone away from his ear. Listens to the sounds coming out of the bathroom. The shower has stopped. But he hears the flying machine humming and gagging. It is vomiting again. He also hears the creature trying to comfort it. The creature hums the same alien lullaby it sings for Peter every night before bed.

"So, anyway," Jennifer says. "I was just calling to see if you wanted to get together. I haven't seen you in months. I guess I haven't really seen anyone since the sky animals showed up."

Peter thinks about it. He hasn't seen anyone either. He doesn't think he's even left the house at all since the creature moved in. The creature does everything for Peter. He has no reason to leave the house.

"Yeah, okay," Peter says, "sure. That sounds great."

"Awesome. I was thinking we'd go out for dinner or something. Maybe see a movie."

They agree to meet at the Italian restaurant in the mall at eight. It's right by the movie theater.

Peter hangs up and the creature comes out of the bathroom. It's drying its hands on a towel. Its feathers are wet. They stick to its skin. The creature leaves the flying machine in the bathroom. It closes the door behind it.

The creature looks sad. It shakes its head. It smiles when it sees Peter watching it. The smile is weak.

"I have a date," Peter tells the creature. Jennifer hadn't called it a date. But Peter is thinking about it as one.

"Oh," the creature says. That is all it says. It pulls at its apron. Turns to go back into the kitchen to finish breakfast.

"Is there something wrong with that?" Peter follows the creature into the kitchen.

"No," the creature says. "Not problem. Okay for date."

Peter smiles at this. He smiles at the creature. He goes to get ready. Even though the date is not for 12 hours.

"I drive you," the creature calls after him.

"No, that's fine." Peter stops at the stairs. "I can get myself there. It's not an issue."

"No issue," the creature says. "I drive. My duty."

"Can you even drive though? Like a car?" Peter's never seen the creature drive a car. It usually takes the flying machine out when it runs errands.

"I drive," the creature says. It continues cooking. Its skin glows red.

The creature drives Peter to the mall for his date with Jennifer. Peter feels like a kid. Like he is 13 again. Like he's going to meet up with friends and pretend to be able to pick up girls. He laughs. The creature laughs with him. The creature is not a very good driver. It swerves all over the road. It jerks the wheel and can't seem to figure out the pedals.

"Want me to drive?" Peter asks. The creature tries to concentrate on the road. It is very serious. Its skin and wings glow very serious colors.

The city looks different to Peter. He stares at it through the windshield. The buildings are all covered in black. Everything is black. Like sky animal skin. Everything glows weird colors. The roads are bumpy and pulsing. Everything hums strange sounds.

The sky animals are transforming the city. They are making it their own. They are terraforming the city. The whole planet.

"What is happening to the city?" Peter asks the creature.

"Better," the creature says. It swerves around a spiky animal in the middle of the street. "For everyone. Better."

Peter doesn't say anything else. Just looks at the changed city. The park he used to hang out at as a kid is gone. Now it is just a bunch of colors. The black ground glowing beneath it. He doesn't see many people out. Just the creatures. Their flying machines. The few people he does see are accompanied by their creatures. They stay close like shadows. Glowing nervous colors.

The mall is no longer a building. It is now a pulsing blob of black. The creature pulls up to the blob. "Meet here," it says. "When done. Here."

Peter gets out of the car. The ground is warm. He feels it through his shoes. A yellow glowing warm. He sees Jennifer in the distance. Her creature is standing behind her. Jennifer tells Claudia to leave. Claudia looks around nervous. Her skin glows. She shakes her head. Flies away with large wings that grow out of her inverted back.

Jennifer sees Peter. She moves quickly to him. "This is weird," he says. She hugs him. He keeps his hands at his side.

"How weird," Jennifer says. "To be out here alone."

"What's going on here?" Peter asks. They start walking toward the mall. The glowing black blob that was once the mall. "To this place? The city?"

Jennifer shrugs. "The sky animals. They are making this planet more like their own. They do everything for us. So we no longer need the world like it used to be. They are here to serve us. And a planet like their own will make that easier for them."

"But why? It's just . . . "

"You really need to watch the news more. Seriously."

EVERYTHING IS COLORS, ALL OF THEM

They are close to the mall blob now. Peter watches a creature approach it. The blob opens for the creature. It disappears inside.

Jennifer says, "But I wasn't prepared for this. I guess. Not really." She looks around. "I knew the sky animals were doing this. But I didn't know the extent of it. Didn't know the world would be almost . . . unhuman. I haven't been outside since they arrived."

"Me either."

They approach the black blob. Where the Italian restaurant used to be. Now it is just color. Kind of blue. But also kind of greenpurplebrown.

"Can we even go in?" Peter asks.

The Italian restaurant blob opens up for them and they pass through solid black. Until they are surround by color. All colors. Every color.

They move through the colors. Swirl through them. A long tunnel of colors. Inside the restaurant, a creature greets them. It wears a red bow tie around its neck. Nothing else. Just its glowing skin. Its skin glows welcoming colors. Like smiles.

"Welcome," the creature says. "Eat time. For two?"

Jennifer smiles at the creature. Her face glows with all the colors around them.

"Yes," Peter says. "A table for two please."

"Very good," the creature says. "Follow this. Eat at table."

The creature leads them through the restaurant. It is dark. But it is also too bright. The walls are so black. Pulsing with colors. There is no floor. But they move through the restaurant as if they are walking normal.

The inside of the restaurant is just one big open space. Everything is here. There are no interior walls. The bathrooms are off to the side. Toilets not far from where people eat. The cooks are in the back. Cooking colors.

Most of the patrons are creatures. Some are human. The humans are all accompanied by their creatures. They stand at tables. People and creatures. Close together. No one is alone. There are no chairs.

The creature leads them to a table near the cooks. "Enjoy food time," it says. "Very good. Nice." It places two menus in front of them. It bows. Leaves.

Peter looks around the restaurant. Looks at the people. He is more focused on the humans. Not the creatures. The humans all stare down at plates in front of them. The plates are full of colors. There is no food. Just color.

The creatures grab handfuls of the colors. Stuff them in their mouths.

They chew the colors. Swallow. They smile. Talk about how good the colors are. They talk in a combination of English and Sky Animal. Peter watches a human try to eat the color. He sticks his hand in the pile of color. Pulls it toward his mouth. The color drips from his hand like melting snow. Like liquid. He sniffs his hand. Licks his fingers. He shrugs. The color tastes like nothing. Like empty.

Jennifer opens her menu. It is just color. Different colors for different meals. She flips pages. She stops on a yellowpinkorange. It is on the "SPECIALS" page. "This looks good," she says. "I think I'll get this." She shows it to Peter. He nods. Doesn't understand. "What are you going to get?" she asks him.

He flips pages in his menu. They are just colors. There is no food. "I don't get it," he says. "It's just color."

"You're not supposed to get it. You're just supposed to eat it. Or, well, drink it. I guess."

"I thought this was an Italian restaurant."

"Not anymore. It used to be. It's authentic Sky Animal cuisine now. It's the food from their home world."

"But it's not food. It's just color. Just colors."

A smaller creature comes over to their table. It carries a notepad. "Order," it says. "Ready to eat. Time?"

Jennifer nods at the creature. She points at the yellowpinkorange in her menu. The creature nods. "Favorite," it says. "Too good. Oh my."

Jennifer smiles. She is pleased. She feels cultured. The creature turns its attention to Peter. "You time," it says. "Sir."

Peter shrugs. Doesn't know what to order. "I'll just have the same. I guess."

"No same," the creature waiter says. "Too much. One table. Order new. Something something."

Peter stares at the creature. It seems to nod at him. It smiles a greenpurple smile. Taps in its notebook. Peter points to something in his menu. Anything. He doesn't know. Doesn't care. It is brownblacktan.

The creature just nods. Doesn't speak. It walks away. It changes colors.

Peter looks around the restaurant. He is pissed. He is bored. And he is hungry. He doesn't know how colors are supposed to fill him up. He wants pasta. Meatballs. Not brownblacktan. Not yellowpinkorange.

Jennifer wants to ask him what's wrong. She does not. They stand in silence until their plates of color arrive. The waiter says, "Eat time. Enjoy time. Time to eat. Time to go."

EVERYTHING IS COLORS, ALL OF THEM

Jennifer digs her hands into her plate of yellowpinkorange. She brings her hands to her mouth. Slurps color. Licks. Swallows. "Oh yes," she says. "It's delicious. Like nothing I've ever experienced before." She digs in for more.

Peter stares at his plate. The restaurant has gotten busier. More creatures. The few humans stand in sadness. The color does nothing for them. The creatures love it though. They devour it. Lick their plates clean with colorful tongues. They eat what their humans don't. They eat it all.

Peter sticks a finger into his plate of color. The brownblacktan is hard. Not liquid like Jennifer's yellowpinkorange. He pokes at it. But he does not eat it. He won't eat it. He'd rather starve than eat this nasty.

Jennifer sees that he is unhappy. But her color is too good for her to care. She eats. Slurps. She moans at its deliciousness. She can't help herself. She orders seconds. Peter grumbles. But she does not care.

The creature waiter comes by with their bill. It smiles at Jennifer's two clean plates. Frowns at Peter's untouched brownblacktan. "What wrong?" it asks. "No good. Try maybe. Make people happy."

Peter just shakes his head. He pays the bill and they leave the restaurant. Back through the tunnel of swirling colors. And the solid black. So dark. Out into the warm night.

They go to the movie theater. It is some Sky Animal production. And it is just flashing colors. Jennifer loses herself in the colors. Laughs when things turn redblue. Or orangegreenblack. Peter doesn't understand. He excuses himself to go to the bathroom. "Hurry back," Jennifer says. "You're going to miss the best part. I think."

Peter moves through the lobby. Passes the bathrooms. He walks out of the theater. Out through more swirling colors. And the dark dark black.

His creature is waiting for him. In the parking lot. In front of the movie theater. Peter walks over to the car. Gets in. "How did you know?" he asks as the creature starts the car. They pull out of the parking lot. Into light traffic. The traffic lights are no longer red, yellow, green. They are new colors. Combinations of colors that should not be mixed.

"Just know," the creature says. "No longer for humans. For us. We work now. For you. Not you."

Peter shrugs. He doesn't understand. But he doesn't care either. He feels bad about leaving Jennifer. But she is not the Jennifer he knows. She is new. Different. She is changing like the world around them. Being changed by the sky animals. Peter is too. He knows this. He is fine with it. He stays quiet the rest of the ride home.

The flying machine is dead when they get home. Dead in the living room. In front of the TV. Beer cans surrounding it. Its skin is more gray than anything. Has a deflated look. Vomit that lacks color blends into the carpet.

The creature kneels in front of its dead friend. They have been together since birth. The creature's colors change to sadness. It lets out a wail that shakes the walls around them. It hugs the dead flying machine. Holds it tight.

Peter helps the creature bury the flying machine in the backyard. The creature does most of the work. Peter's just there for moral support. He guesses. "My responsibility," the creature says. "To grieve. Help to sadness. Happy again some. Maybe. Hopeful."

Peter doesn't say anything. He's never lost anyone close to him. So he doesn't know what to say. Doesn't know what the creature is going through. He thinks just being there is enough. He doesn't know.

After they are done, the creature showers. It locks itself in its room. Peter can hear it crying from downstairs. The spot where the flying machine died has been cleaned. But Peter still knows it happened. He can't forget it. Probably never will. He pulls a folding chair from the closet. Sets it up in front of the TV. He turns it on. To watch the news. To catch up on what is going on in the world. To follow along.

He flips channels. Channel after channel. They are all just colors. And humming. Colors and noises. TV is no longer for the humans. He knows. No longer for him. It is for the creatures. The sky animals.

Every channel is a different color. A different sound. Peter watches one for a few minutes. A whitepink channel. The color is solid. Never changing. The humming on the whitepink channel sounds like church music. Maybe this is one of those church shows for shut-ins, Peter thinks. But it might also be something else. He doesn't know.

He turns the TV off. Goes up to his room. He falls asleep to the sound of the creature crying. Screaming. Humming.

Peter wakes to solid black. Swirling colors. He's in his room. In his bed.

EVERYTHING IS COLORS, ALL OF THEM

But it has changed. Like the sky animal's skin. Like the city around him. His walls pulse with colors. His bed is a blob of darkness. Soft and hard.

The rest of the house is the same. Changed to be more like the sky animals. The creature is moving about the house. Checking things. Touching the walls. Making sure the house is working properly. Peter guesses. He has no idea.

Peter goes through the living room. It is all black and colors. All the furniture is melted blobs of color. Everything is color. The TV glows brightest. Flickering. Showing things that only the sky animals would understand. Peter watches the flickering for a second. Sees nothing in it. He goes into the kitchen. It is the same here. All black and melted. Colorful blobs. The fridge is nothing but a mound of pulsing, solid black. He knows there's no food in it anyway. It will be full of colors. Nothing else.

All the windows are coated in glowing black. But Peter can see through them. He can see shapes and colors. He looks out the window over the kitchen sink. It looks out to the backyard. To where they buried the flying machine. The ground is dug up. Reburied. The flying machine is dead in there. In the ground.

It is cold in here. In the house. In the kitchen. Peter sees his breath in front of him. Steaming. Like clouds of color. Whiteyellowblue. Puffs of it. Peter moves over to the back door. He pushes it open. The creature appears behind him. Before he can step outside.

"Careful," the creature says. "Much different in there. Not in. Out. The out is no longer like before. Much changed."

"No shit," Peter says. Too quiet for the creature to hear. That is not new. The changing. "Thanks," he says to the creature. And steps outside. It is just as cold here as inside. Too cold. It should be warm. Hot. Like summer. But it is cold.

The sky is just as black as everything else. It is no longer the sky. It is something else. Something new. It glows with colors. Like clouds. But different.

Peter moves through the backyard. Breathing. His breath hangs in the air in front of him. In new colors. In all colors. He goes to the patch of disturbed ground. The flying machine's grave. Its forever bed. Something grows here. A long stick. Like a tree trunk only thin. It is more green than black. But it is still black. It is greenblackredblue.

Peter kneels by this new growth. This thing sticking out of the black ground. The creature comes up next to him. Peter holds his hands in front of his face. Trying to catch his colorful breath. It rolls through his fingers. Changing more colors in contact with his skin.

The creature kneels next to Peter. Its black skin glows brighter than before. It reaches a hand out to touch the growth. "Friend," it says. "New friend from old. Grow for me. To me. And you."

"It's going to regrow from death?" Peter asks. His words make his breath change colors.

"Oh yes," the creature says. "We all do. Die. Never really. Forever grow new."

"How long?" Peter reaches out to touch the new growth now. It moves away from his hand. Sways away from the warmth of Peter's skin. The lack of black and color. The pale warmth of human.

"Soon maybe. Or not. We never know. Could be today. Or maybe never really. Only time."

Peter doesn't say anything. Drops his hands to his sides. They stay like this for a while. For too long. Peter's legs ache. The creature just watches the growth. Staring at it. Its friend. Peter will never fully understand the sky animals. He'll never know the world again.

Jennifer and her creature, Claudia, come around the side of the house. They come from the darkness. In swirling colors. Jennifer's clothing matches Claudia's skin. They are becoming close. Like one.

Peter and the creature stand to greet them.

"Not you," the creature says. It points at Claudia. "My land. You can't. Will ruin my new growth." It now points at the flying machine's grave. "Only human enter."

Jennifer steps into the backyard. The ground changes color to welcome her. She comes up to Peter.

Peter sees the color of her clothing. Watches it blend down to her skin. Changing her even more. He steps back. Away from Jennifer. Away from her changing. She looks at him scared. But her eyes are no longer her own. They are changing too. They are like no color. Like every color.

"Just leave," Peter says. "Just go."

"But Peter, please." She tries to step closer to him. But Peter's creature steps between them.

"No longer welcome," it says. The ground changes color again. More dark. More redblackpurple. It is not happy. Jennifer is not welcome.

EVERYTHING IS COLORS, ALL OF THEM

Jennifer doesn't move. Just stares at Peter with eyes that are no longer her own. The ground pulses beneath her. Rough. Goes soft and hard. The new growth moves to her. The flying machine's tree trunk reaches out for Jennifer. Wraps itself around her waist. Its colors changing to match the redblackpurple ground. It knots itself around her body.

Claudia makes a move to come to her human. To help her. To be her. Peter's creature points at Claudia. Tells her to stop. The new growth around Jennifer's body pulls. Drags Jennifer toward the flying machine's grave. The ground opens up. Shows too-bright colors beneath the surface. The new growth continues pulling. Jennifer disappears into the colors.

Claudia screams out a humming scream. She runs toward the closing hole. Toward Jennifer. But she is already gone. The ground flashes colors under Claudia's feathered feet. It zaps her. She hums painful. Changes colors. She flies off into the black sky. Into the clouds of color. Screaming. Humming. Crying for Jennifer.

"What was that?" Peter asks the creature. It stands in defense. Fists tight.

"Protect," it says. "This land. Everything here. For you. To save and keep you." The ground rumbles. Moves. The growth pops back up. Into its original spot. Jennifer is gone. Somewhere in the light. But gone. "We are you," the creature says. "Not you. For you."

"I don't like it," Peter says. He goes back to the house. The creature follows.

"Nothing to like. Just is."

Inside the creature cooks. And they sit in the living room to eat. They eat together. The creature watches the changing colors that used to be the TV. But Peter doesn't eat. His plate is just colors. A pile of color. The creature slurps it up. Smiles at the taste of the orangeorangeorange in front of it.

Peter pokes his orangeorangeorange. It is soft and liquid. He has no appetite. He has no idea what time it is. There is no sun in the sky anymore. Just black and glowing colors. Peter goes to sleep. The colors in his room change to make him sleepy. Bluewhitewhiteblue.

The new growth in the backyard is bigger when Peter wakes up. He has no idea how much time has passed. But he feels refreshed.

Peter and the creature go outside to check on the growth. It now has a face. Tiny hands poking out of the sides of its head.

"Soon," the creature says. "Born to life."

Peter stares at the flying machine's new face. Growing in his backyard. It looks kind of like Jennifer. It is very Jennifer-like.

"Your friend help," the creature says. Touching the new face with feather fingers.

"That's Jennifer?"

"Not Jennifer. Not now. Now it grows new friend." The creature smiles. Smiles big and colorful.

Peter paces the yard. Thinks about Jennifer. Thinks about colors. Everything is colors. All of them. He notices that his shirt is changing colors. It is solid black. So dark. But it is also blueredpurple. It is the color of the creature. And the ground. And his house blob. And the new growth. All blueredpurple. All swirling the same.

Peter screams out a squeak. He rips his shirt off. Pulls it over his head. He throws his shirt to the ground. It disappears into the colors. His bare skin beneath the shirt is the same color. Matching blueredpurple. It moves through his skin. The color. And he can only see in colors. In swirls. In things he shouldn't understand.

His eyes are no longer his own. They are colors. They are every color. They see every color. Every change.

The creature steps up to Peter. Places its feathers on Peter's colorful shoulder. "Time," it says. "Better time. Like one. You see change. Like everything. Like all color."

Peter steps away from the creature. He runs to the house. He opens his mouth. And his breath comes out in waves of color. In every color. All of them.

He is color. He is everything. All the colors. He can see the change that is the world. He can feel it all. He can sense Jennifer here. In the color. She is happy. She is something.

The creature comes up behind him. Sees the change in Peter. "Welcome," the creature says. "Welcome to life. We are you now. You are one."

Peter opens his mouth. Colors pour through his solid black skin. He feels his arms. They are colorful feathers. They are every color. Like him. Like the world. Everything is colors.

JEWELS AND FALSE MEMORIES: THE ORIGINS OF A LUNATIC

MICHAEL GRIFFIN

"The difference between false memories and true ones is the same as for jewels: it is always the false ones that look the most real, the most brilliant."

—Salvador Dali

1. A Boy Confused at Masculinity's Threshold

THE CATALAN BOY cuts between gray buildings, ever conscious of Mama's oft-repeated warnings to stay out of the industrial district. Mama says, Dust and filth ruin your fine things, Heart. She says, Your satin slippers are too delicate for the rough cobblestones. Like an Arabian prince, the boy wears silks colored eggplant and pumpkin. His reason for taking this alternate path home from school isn't that it's shorter, but that it lets him avoid the other boys. He fears Mama's judgment more than their threats and teasing, but the boys are near. Mama's far away.

Near the open side door of the watch factory he pauses, just at the moment a nude woman tiptoes past, just within the doorway. Intruding sunlight highlights her skin, a glare of brilliant white purity. She seems vulnerable somehow, more revealed than merely naked. As though aware she might be seen, she glances out.

The boy recognizes her. Can it be? His own mother! Certainly she must have seen him too, yet shows no sign of recognizing her own son. The boy starts after her, but halts. Closely following her is a man wearing a black suit and top-hat, formal gloves and walking stick. Who is this? Certainly not Papa.

The boy hesitates. Rush home, or follow?

What does it mean, mother appearing the moment he defies her, sneaking home this way despite her warnings? Guilt and shame at his small rebellion burn in his cheeks. Who does he think he is, making this awkward grasp at autonomy? Just a boy, despite sixteen years. So foolish. He looks down at his slippers. Soles worn through, tassels frayed, beadwork shredded. What will Mama say? He turns toward home, runs a few steps, then halts.

Mama's not home. She's here, in the watch factory.

Distraction behind. Wooden cart wheels approach, clattering on stones. Obscuring dust billows. The boy hides from the carter and any who might be watching from within the door. He huddles behind a mound of sodden disintegrating trash, which stinks of terrible rot and disintegration. From within the abattoir across the alley comes a shriek of dying goats. He turns to see a beggar watching, leaning on a crutch cut from a tree branch, the beggar's hunched back an interrogating question mark.

The boy stands away from the garbage and wipes his filthy hands on silken pants.

He must follow Mama, confront her. If she's angry, who cares? She should be home, not running about naked. And who is this man? It's the boy's job to find out. He'll be a man himself, sooner than they think. This will prove it, begin his transformation. He must find what he's meant to become, what's growing inside him. Discover his future self, and become it.

He steps toward the doorway.

2. The Flames of Oedipal Rage

Some furnace roars nearby, filling the factory with heat and sound but no light. Ahead, indistinct shapes move left to right. A flash of white, a black top-hatted outline. Does Papa know a man like this? They flit around a corner, once more out of sight.

Through dusty rooms the boy follows, wandering alone, peering through cobwebbed glass, sweating through his fine silks. After a time he fears he's lost the trail of the woman and the man. He wants to get out of here, go home. Maybe she wasn't Mama, after all. Why would Mama be here? Even if she were, why naked? Her shape lingers in his memory, the outline and extreme paleness somehow familiar. The only naked woman he's seen, other than Mama, is the fresco on the wall of *Sant Pere*.

Disoriented, he's lost his place in the factory. Which way out? Sweat bursts out anew, trickles down his forehead. Dampness adheres the silk under his arms. So hot, his head swims. The boy wants only to leave, doesn't care anymore about Mama or the man.

Around a corner he stumbles into the churning glow of the metal foundry. Smoke rises from the melt cauldron, drawing the boy closer. On the red-glowing rim rests a gold pocket watch, which has begun to soften and run like melted cheese. The boy looks over the edge. On the infernal surface of the molten white metal, a coat and top-hat flame away to ash. He steps back and only then notices the black cane leaning up against the cauldron's exterior, just below the melting watch. The cane is intact, undamaged.

He reaches for the watch but even before contact the superheated air burns his fingertips. Dizziness rises, faintness at such intense heat. Using the cane, he tries to knock the watch down from the cauldron's lip to the dusty brick floor where it might cool. The watch, already soft liquid, sticks to the cane's tip, which catches fire at the touch.

The boy stubs out the flame on the soot-grimed floor. Discarded there, unnoticed before, is a torn red dress.

Radiant waves shimmer. His head spins such that reality seems to waver. He backs up. Will these rubber legs give way? Leaning on the walking stick, he staggers off toward the cooler darkness of the next room.

Here a long feasting table is covered with discarded wreckage of a great supper. He envisions a parade of apostles ceremonially gorging, then slinking away to sleep in corners. The wretched leavings boil with flies. Meat scraps putrefy, crumbs disintegrate to dust. Dry fish bones fester on a tray beside a phone handset without a cord. All saints gone, messiahs vanished.

A sound of footsteps. The heels of the dark man, unmistakable.

Despite danger, the boy wants to continue. He follows, creeping. The footsteps lead into a hallway which narrows and grows darker.

Such fear. *"Estoy dispuesto a morir,"* the boy says aloud. He's willing to die. The fastest way to become a man is to die in boyhood.

Closer, the walls draw in, barely more than shoulder-wide. The hall ends not in a door but a black wall, featureless but for an irregular opening near the floor. He kneels, unable to see. His hands find a gap, not made of wood or brick, but soft and moist like flesh. The boy reaches into the portal, finds it to be round or perhaps egg-shaped, pleasantly warm. Deeper, deeper he penetrates. His hands emerge into an opening on the other side. A breeze cools his fingertips. A way out? Trying to widen the opening, he pulls, strains to see through. Nothing but vague grayness. He presses forward, squirms into the soft canal between rooms, wriggling, striving deeper. Straining for breath, constricted from without, moving less from his own effort than being driven, squeezed through. The boy wants to fight, to struggle, but forces himself to relax.

Bone wrenching stricture, and gush-splat, he emerges.

A vacant office, empty file drawers, strewn, rotten papers. Curled up on the floor, barely visible in graphite darkness, the pale-skinned woman sprawls on checkerboard tiles. Blindly, the boy feels the surface of a desk, and switches on a lamp. He's startled at the revelation above him, an imposing shape which looms, threatening. Not the man in black, but a yellow, faceless Christ nailed to a giant crucifix on the wall. Not a real god, but an icon.

He turns to the motionless nude, draws nearer, trying to see her face. Mama? Another step and he slips, something wet on the floor. Blood puddled in thick dust. Then he sees the many thin slices, tally marks in the flesh of her back and sides. Her posture is strange, curious. Closer, he leans in.

Her arms are missing. Jagged white bone protrudes from dark red stumps. Something white fringes out where the edges of skin merge with meaty interior flesh. He looks away. Wants to flee. Has to know.

He slides the lamp nearer and kneels. Strains to see her face.

"Mama?"

Out of a shadowed corner steps a man, white shirt untucked and flying. Now without hat, jacket, or cane, he approaches, jerks the black stick from the boy's hand. Raises it, smiling. No, not a smile. The man's upturned mustache is like a mouth, black lips in an exaggerated, mocking grin.

The man looks familiar. Something like Papa, but not Papa. Like the boy himself, his future.

The black stick swings down. The boy dodges, trying to escape. He stumbles over the armless torso, falls, cracks his elbow on the stone floor. Strains to his feet, trying to stand.

Once more the stick descends. A flash of black strikes down like dark lightning.

3. Resurrected Flesh, Transfiguration of Vision

As the dream fades he tries to grasp it. Tattered fabric slips through fingertips.

The boy awakens outside, beneath a darkened sky. The clouds are exaggerated, more dramatic than real, like a painting. Vanishing sun stands apart from looming, deep gray clouds, the degree of contrast hyper-real. The seething red orb under-lights ridged clouds upon which float echelons of saintly apparitions grown gigantic, smiling benedictions. Perched upon the nearest edge, silvery ranks of angels line up to gaze down upon the mortal earth. Do they approve, disapprove? The boy who is now a man cannot hear their whispers.

These visitations loom over new white buildings adorned with gold leaf, the filth and depravity of the familiar city replaced by an idealized variant from a poet's dreams. No more trash, no beggars, the rough cobbles smoothed and whitened. Where the abattoir once stood, a great statue rises. A white horse of exaggerated musculature rears skyward, threatens to stomp, to crush the remade world.

The boy looks down, sees himself, his very own face and eyes looking back. His twin brother, returned from death? No, the other never lived, lost in infancy. Maybe the boy himself is dead, and his passing allows his twin to return in his place? The face shimmers. Water's surface, touched subtly by wind. It's only a reflection glimpsed in a mirror pond, all sludge and pollution somehow purified. He wonders, Am I dreaming? Narcissus at the lake's edge, coming to new awareness. Above him is a swan with a broken neck, not flying but seeming to hover. He sees it in the reflection but doesn't look up to see if it's real.

All this must stop. Either live or dream, not both. Back and forth is maddening.

He stands. His silks are ruined, not only stained but torn. Mama will beat him. First she'll scream, then blister his bottom with a switch. Seeing his tears, she'll embrace him, sing to the baby in her arms.

He hates the fear. More than anything, wants to be free of it. He's a man, no longer a boy. Certainly not a baby.

The young man turns toward home, beneath the looming hooves of a rearing equine monster. The fear leaves him, fades away, a pretense voluntarily relinquished.

Mama is dead, weeks since. He keeps forgetting, or perhaps lets himself play the game, pretending she's still alive, that she waits for him at home. He can't help imagining again what she'll say when she sees him. Of course she'll say nothing, see nothing. Papa won't care, in fact wishes only that the boy might straighten up, become more forceful somehow. Papa prefers he wear real shoes, black leather. A man's ankle boots. Suits of wool and cotton, fabrics not light but sturdy.

Not a boy, he remembers. A man.

Mama asked him always, Heart, what do you want? Heart, what do you desire? On his weaving path through new-made streets gleaming with otherworldly light, he sees her now, not a memory but a sainted altar spirit cradling in her hands a bleeding heart made of rubies. The heart is his, broken at the loss of her. Beneath her cupped hands his blood gathers in a pool. Not a wretched, slippery mess of blood like he discovered in the factory, but beautiful, as pure and valuable as the jewels themselves.

He feels clear-minded, despite the swollen gash on his forehead, which still trickles blood. Perhaps half-shocked, slightly delirious. The horror seems a distant thing, easily detached from the beauty of these immaculate surroundings. All this lends him strength, the beauty and mortal fear, darkness and doubt, agonizing grief transformed into a new conception of self. These help him to see what he will become, and that the world will never again be more or less than his conception.

P◄—N P—G'S P—LGЯ—M◄GƎ

CARTER RYDYR

High on atop a dusty musty shelf Miss Aligned pulled down a volume of enthralling and appalling tails.

Blowing the dirt from the yellow tallow cover she flipped open the sook book and called to her awful offspring. They cackled and crackled and crowded around her cloven feet.

Leaning in she whispered in hushed tones to the frigorific freaks. "Gather round chilblames, I have a story to say. About a pig in a poke, who woke and spoke, and screamed and dreamed of exquisite extreme . . ."

Chapter 1
THERE WAS A CROOKED HAM

ONCE UPON A Toad Mother's stool, in a demeaning dream scene, there thrived and contrived the troublesome, muddlesome troll known as Pain Pig.

The immortal immoral Pain Pig, who embodied original and eternal sin, dwelled in the muddle of the Faecal Fields, a lard skidmarked by smears and smudges of shit streaks and strained stains, where never is heard a discouraging turd. Situated in the third turd corner of the

whirled, the hamlet of the Faecal Fields was an outlet for confused refuse and wasted whiffs of skewwhiff; a quarantined quagmire of ire and twisted desire.

Whereas other turdlings and sycophantic simians possessed mono members, Pain Pig was a unique freak by being doubly dickheaded hence doubly dunced. One cock prong hung slung from his pork fork while the other grew long and strong from the middle of his porky prima faecie.

Suffering from mental nillness, Pain Pig was exceptionally silly and supercilious because he had two cocks to mock and shock with. Two pricks are better than one up the bum and keep you dumb and dumber, long and longer. Pain and simple.

Ass everyone nose, if you fool with two you get twice as stoopid and loose with the truth.

Pain Pig ran amok in the muck and mire, sloshing in hogwash and rolling around in the cesspit of shit. The pillock would frolic with colic, pushing shit up hillocks and scumbathing on floaters bloated with botchelism. The fugue stooge strayed stupid by spending his daze snuffling for backed-up logs in the backblock bogs, scanning and panning for nuggets of fool's mould and jerkin' his beef gherkin. No morality, no veracity; only morassity.

The hamburglar resided in the domicile of the Domisilly Toad Mother's absurd turd. A twisted, fetid shit shat long ago by the supersillyarse Tsarina during one of her mangy sojourns to the southern unstable lands.

The turd roasted in the hot, muggy night, steaming into bakelite shite.

Pain Pig improperly appropriated and coveted the massive motion, making it his own. Every day he would sit and eat a bit of shit, hollowing out the stinking plop, thus making it his home.

Having previously dwelled and grovelled inn the hovel of the Turd Mother's irritable bowel, Pain Pig derived comfort by being eternally interned in her turd. The execrable Pain Pig had acquired a taste for greasy grub and sustained sustenance from his poo igloo. Every morsel of fetid faeces he excavated, he consumed, and in turn excreted. After all, you are what you eat.

He would serve her turd in batter on a platter of flakes and scales scraped from his own eczematic skin and wash it down with the Toad Mother's very own moonshine urine, a homemade brew mixed with spew. After a time, Pain Pig's crust-domed abode disappeared down his own cakehole and he became a gnome without a home. No shit!

The scummy rummy shit a brick to build a shack of shat but it was not as good as that of the Toad Mother's turd, all sticky, stinky and skanky with gooey goodness, for lewdness sake.

Pain Pig needed another poo in lieu but not just any poo would do. So in a diarrhoea need for a shit replacement the hopeless, homeless and gormless git decided to quit. Having lost the plop, the ruthless and roofless Pain Pig packed his whacking sticks in his joy toy bag and began a sementical sabbatical in search of rank sanctity in servitude.

Chapter 2
THE MISCELLANEOUS SESQUIPEDALIAN SINS OF THE STIGMARTYRS

Pain Pig rose at cock's grow and crossed the diarrhoea straits by the blight of the fool moon. He took the well-worn path and trotted down the road to rack and ruin along an insular peninsula and presently came upon a dumb cum kingdumb. Here the loony goon took a deft left turn and went on a guilt trip down mammary lane.

Perambulating down the road paved with good intentions and extenuating circumstances through a false fence of insecurity to a procrastination nation, the bedevilled ham descendant descended with a hop, skip and a jump, down in the dumps of a deep ravine latrine into the unpleasant valley to a village of no privilege.

Beyond the defensive walls, dwelling within the anathemized halls of the infortuitous and forlorn fortress of distressed solitude and outrageous misfortune was a clichéd clique of huckabuck hunchbacks chilled with chilblames and filled with sorrow and strife and trite contrition. A neurocracy of stagnant stigmartyrs practicing penitence for perceived persecutions and dismal disappointments, who rue with regret yesterday's frays and delays, and worry over tomorrow's sorrows.

The pariah sheeple spake of self-hate, which does not dissipate, but only hardens their arterial resolve and dissolve of direction. Displaying suicidal tenderancies and Munchausen madness, the hand-wringers would dream scream therapy and play depression roulette with lugie lugars and expectorations of ablution absolution.

PAIN PIG'S PILGRIMAGE

The erotic motor-neurone neurotics and triple nipple crippples could not obtain bliss without risk to life and limb so they would skim milk and lance indiscreet discreepancies of cross purposes on their pensive apprehensive lives with prehensile knives.

Wailing in paralysis from over analysis and wallowing in holey melancholy of crucifixion conviction, the next of skin kin convinced the blithering dithering Pain Pig of his wilt guilt and invited him to join them in beating their hickory dickory cocks. "It's not whether you sin and lose, it's how you place the blame," claim the down-on-their-luck-schmucks as a resolution for their disillusion and double negative entendres.

In the village of the damned-if-you-do and damned-if-you-don't, each moronic member, a reject from the cruel school of hard cocks, had no-one to blame but himself for his in situ situation, so each ignoranus engaged in self-flagellation and occasional immolation.

"Good grief! Only with self-sacrifice cums redemption," mewed the mediocrisy of misery guts and lost lust. Hence the pitiful populice beat themselves up with hammers of guilt, rods of regret and mallets of remorse, forever lamenting what could've, would've, should've been.

"Confession is good for the prole's soul," the suffergettes extol. Safe and sorry in their flagellation salvation and double jeopardy, the blind led the bland ham down and up the garden path in a dare to share the care of their despair. "Help yourself," said the flunky monkey lunkheads.

Being a sexhibitionist and forensick porn again pissant, Pain Pig joined the whacking stickmartyrs and raised his bone of contention. Standing in malign he accepted his and hearse curse and beat his meat with the beast of them.

Deep in the citadel he went hell for leather beating his inclement wether boards. The porky pied piper lied as he plied his bullshit and played with his penile rhinoplasty in the scenter of his disgraced face. He thrust and parried each blow but don't you know, it was just a case of the blind brow-beating their own mind.

In the mindfield of misdirection erections the animal cracker wanker masturbated as he flagellated his own porky pantaloons, but no exquisite excremental excitement was expelled from strapping his own sebaceous coriaceous silverside. The desensitised Pain Pig tried every which way butt loose but only received a minuscule peniscule stirring in his oriface.

The shame game was a sham on the ham, for in his heart of farts he knew that the hole whirled is fat! And with that, he left the grim weepers and motor-neurotics and set off on his quest to live as a gerbil guest in the festering foul bowel of the Toad Mother; a home he'd known and bemoaned some time ago.

Chapter 3
THE COMPLEXITY OF PARADOXICAL APOPLEXY

"Perish the thought," thought the perisher. Pain Pig's bran flake brain contained not a single original thought, nought a skerrick of merit, so he sought vice advice from a kindred soul greater than he.

Pain Pig traversed the tawdry terrain to the first fist-fucked corner of the chaotic whirled. Deep in the abyssmal dismal district of dubious duplicity, there lived the connoisewer of crassness, the Assinine Ass full of ambiguous ambivalence.

The Assinine Ass had the body and head of a shonky donkey and the torso of a damned hanged man. Thick as thieves, the scoundrel was surrounded by a scary harem of scarred and scored whores dressed in nothing but satanic skirts. Strapless, backless, sleeveless, the translucent floozies were slatterns in sluttire of revolting ambition and diabolique chic. Given permission to be permissive, the enticing entourage of lascivious whores sent out sexual semaphores of hex sex to all and sundry. The sinister centaur dabbled in diablerie revelry and incessantly stuck his scintillating and scantily-clad glad staff with his well-endowed dowry of nine stiff shafts, fondling and fucking his faculty of split-tails and jezebelles and cussing cousins.

Posteriorally, Pain Pig asked the unassuming Ass how he could curry favour and sway the tumultuous and turpitudinous Toad Mother to accept his sorry arse back into her manifold of fetid fromage.

The answer was simple, the Assinine Ass asserted then informed the fractally foolhardy Pain Pig: "The procurement of a tribute would suit vicely."

"Butt what sort of gift would lift and appease the affluent effluent Toad Mother?" the silly swine whined to the binge brink of alcoholism.

Far from insane, the Assinine Ass did not deign to answer and refrained from revealing the secret. Instead he insisted that Pain Pig be subjected to the abject turd degree. Pain Pig lacked any insight or foresight sew the crass Ass cauterised his arsehole eyes then incysted Pain Pig answer the Riddle of the Sphincters.

The submissively inclined Pain Pig lay supine upon a bedrock of pine cones and needles while the Assinine Ass straddled his insipid and forlorn form. The centaur tore the sightless swine a new asshole then exerted and inserted repeatedly all nine of his dicks up to the hilt to his parabolic bollocks, into Pain Pig's syphilitic skin and obsolete meat. "You will be the hole entertainment," the Assinine Ass proclaimed with profane disdain.

With each retraction, his sick kin left a rectal recession until Pain Pig's ecchymosis epidermis was burrowed and furrowed with anal canals from his malodorous armpits to the bottom of his lardy da da.

Then the union jackass dipped all nine willies in chilli, hotter than a pepper sprout, and proceeded to penetrate all of Pain Pig's newly formed cornholes. Every sodomy caused a modicum of indignation in his malformations and a stinging singeing sensation at the expanse of the pig's serrated rings.

The outrageous entourage of centwhores looked upon the variety of impiety and impropriety with relish and mustard as the erotic, quixotic and chaotic charlatan dealt a decisive blow job. The caucaus had a raucaus romp as the psychopompous ass stomped on the gronk.

Pouring propane into the lamebrain, Pain Pig was further force fed more combustibles and corrosive explosive creating a blitzkrieg in his foul bowel.

As the inglorious basturd's guts gurgled and churned his google of rectal rings burned and burst into a massive gastric attack. Snap, crackle, pop! goes the wheezel.

The mockingbirds of paradoxical paradise mocked the pig as he became embroiled in a boiling roid rage, which exploded from his multitudinous arseholes, creating an ebullient anal avalanche of mighty shite and diarrhoea fire.

The shady schadenfreude frauds laughed and heckled Pain Pig's burning freckles as they doused the louse with more corrosive explosives and made him salad roll in beatroot and poison ivy before his internal furnarse projected a pyroclastic flow of ordure slough.

The Assinine Assassin took sadistic glee as the desperate and delusional scuttlebutt mutt agreed to be peed upon by the hole congregation to put out the conflagration. The frottage of fiends gushed a golden shower on the crackling cad then cackled as they stubbed out his butt on a stray ashtray. Afterward, his fritto misto frizzled and sizzled and his burnt bacon smote and smoked. Next the sick ilk spilt milk and spat a spate of mucous and molluscs upon the doused louse's disgusting dermis and chocolate starfish fissures.

Given the bum's rush, Pain Pig farted and departed despondent. Butt not before the Assinine Ass offered a last minute lead to heed. "The Divine Wine of the Vile Vine is what you need."

Chapter 4
TRICK OR TREATMENT

Snorting anoysome stench, Pain Pig traverses the globe and goes to the second corner of the whirled whereupon he reached the Pest Huys, a hospital in which to heal his holes and seal his soulless soles. The Sinistral Sisters of No Mercy, the Ladies of Maladies, meat and greet him. Immediately, the sallow shallow swine whines and mews, "My skin is skewed and sieved, my body bored to the abhorred core."

The Siamese sin twins ushered Pain Pig down to the debasement to a bedlam where they prodded and poked, studied and smote. The cynical clinical attendants attended to his moonscape of pockmarked skin and crater-ached sin. The typhoid scaries performed an unhygenius autopsy on the dropsie, flopsy mopsy to see what made him tick and two see what made him sick. The fister sisters extracted his dead heart and diagnosed that a catastrophe of apathy had caused his brain to atrophy. "He's not sick, he's just sickening," one declared with dubious despair and unrestrained disdain of the morally bankrupt runt. "His inner evil is expressed by the disgrace etched in his face," the other concurred as she slighted the cur.

The suture sisters knew exactly what to do. "Fist and foreskinmost wee must evacuate the nincompoop's puerile poo and the bullshit too with a moronic colonic irrigation."

To purge his foul bowel the gruesome twosome grew some evil weevil milkweed and deadly belladonna and mixed it into a bubonic bumhomie brew. Pain Pig drank from the mouldy bowl, causing him to sprue spew the infection of self-inflexion and introspection.

The cruel cure was compelling and repelling and required the cleansing and disinfecting of his hole-infested form. Lying prone on a dire and dirty dais in the inhospitable and gloomy room, the pitiful pig is ordered to wank his shank. The liar complies and as he jerks they insert an intrusive hose up his nose and intubate his innumerable inutile arseholes. They filled, then flushed Pain Pig of all the impurities which the chained male had collected in his invected tubercular crackling.

Butt alas this was not enough. So the slattern interns' final soulution was an ablation ablution for the absolute abolition of any traitorous traits and atavistic attributes. Inserting an uncertain hook into his snout, they hollowed out the gout and grout of the boorish boar, removing all of his infernal internal organs and intestinal fortitude, which they later slate to use as gross gristmas tree degradations. No guts, no glory.

To suture his future, the Sinistral Sisters sewed all but one of Pain Pig's greedy seedy holes with razor wire, turning him into a germy taxidermied punching slag bag. Pushing a funnel into his fudge tunnel they proceeded to pour gallons of sebaceous sores and rancid candida candy until his sewer self swelled larger than strife. The twin freaks infected and filled the dill with flox and pox, with scurvy and herpes, with griefe and gangrene, with dermatitis and hepatitis, with colitis and trichuriasis. A myriad of diseases infested the avaricious missionary. Being a selfish swine he absorbed them all and then some more mores and sores.

Instead of convalescing Pain Pig began to convulse at the horse-piss hospice. Bloated with prurigo and prickly heat and coated with seropus, Pain Pig remained lying in weight upon the ill-fated tableau.

The Spinister Sisters wheeled Pain Pig past the stunted tree of ennui and obloquy to the bigger tree of bigotry. Twining the hapless sap's spineless cord around his dreck neck they proceeded to string the has-been from a gnarly branch of the triquetrous tree, turning Pain Pig into a porky piñata.

As he hung strangling and dangling at the end of his tether, the terse nurses gleefully beat his meat to burst his bloated flesh. With high zealocity and frosty indifference they thrashed his rawhide and lashed his formaldehyde, bashed his snide chide and smashed his sewercide lies. As hard as they thumped the plump dumpling, his leatherarse farce and coriaceous carcass toughened by years of beating, would not burst nor break.

Testing their triste patience the sinister strumpets unstitched the sore arseholes of their porky patient and stuffed rags dipped in napalm into his multiple orifices and wrecked rectum. They set the rags alight, exploding the boar's Molotov cocktail.

Remnants of the ruminant's awful offal rained on a disparaging parade for forty daze and forty blight nights.

Then, by some strange synchronicity Pain Pig's raison d'etre resumed and he reconstituted to his former boaring self-centred self. He displayed the scars on his chide hide with snide pride and continued to pursue his mission of total and absolute submission.

Chapter 5
THE BEAUTY OF OBLIQUITY

Pain Pig travelled a cuntry mile across a paradigm shift, through sub-space to the dredge edge of reality until he came upon the plateau of perpetual platitudes and perplexity.

On the peripheral centre of the plateau grew, wild, the Divine Vine of Inequity. Upon the vine, grouped in succulent bunches, were the grapes of wrath, puckered and pristine and ripe for plucking.

Pain Pig pinched a grape and squeeeeeezed.

The amazing grape released a tiny turd from its puckered arsehole. Pain Pig caught the tiny turd with his tongue and savoured the acrid shit. Verily he realised that it was good shit. He grabbed a bunch of arseholes and squeezed them all above his gaping maw, releasing a motion lotion. Bunch after brunch the swine guzzled the diarrhoea wine.

Unbeknownst to the greedy swine, entwined within the vile vine, was the serpent of sin, the whorrific whore of wretchedness, the Vertical Viper, whose length and breath stretched eternally nowhere.

"I see you choose to steal from me without paying a fee." From above, the Vertical Viper hissed then pissed on Pain Pig for free. Pain Pig, whose breadth stenched, glowered in the golden shower then tried to gloss his gluttony by palliating his extenuating circumstances.

The Vertical Viper dismissed the tedious, tawdry fawning of the pissed-on pig with a deft flick of her forty forked tongues.

Hairy, scary, and quite contrary, how does your avant garden grow out of control? With hell's belles and cocks that swell and dirty clits all in a row boat.

Presently, she lowered her serpentine head from the bough breaks, locked her gaze on the gloze poser, and insisted that the pilfering pig work off his debt by harvesting the crop of crap.

While Pain Pig worked, the Vertical Viper lurked, twisting and turning among the poison ivy vine and ridiculing him with riddles every time. "What is at the beginning of eternity, the end of time, the beginning of every end, and the end of every crime?" the fake snake spake smugly with a beatific smile of denial.

Butt alas, the blithering boar's only knowledge of speculative friction and speculum theory was in relation to the twit's sexistential pursuit of shit. That's all there was to it. Being a poxymoron, the paunchy pachyderm didn't realise that the answer lay in his bestial behaviour, his chase for debasement, his eternal quest for Ecstasy through Endorphins employing ingratiating excruciating demeans. Ecstasy and everything starts with E and ends with penance.

So he lied as he skived and contrived and continued to gather and seek the faecal matter, and as the twerp perp picked and plucked he usurped and stealthily supped the slime from the occasional anal grape.

Without the Toad Mother's domsense of order or stern cystern system, the hapless Pain Pig gathered grapes in a haphazard and random fashion. All the while the wily Viper followed the simpering simp to keep a slit eye on him.

Unwittingly, as the Vertical Viper twisted and turned continuously through vine and twine trying to follow every lie, she tied herself in knots. Being an onanistic opportunist and possessing no responsiliability, Pain Pig absconded with the proceeds of the harvest, leaving the analconda knot happy.

The Viper let out a trismus scream, but this made no difference to the indifferent dickhead and silly coprophilic liar.

The Toad Mother's bowel was beckoning, and so with dead reckoning Pain Pig passed the whippersnapper jaws of the commode dragon and continued on his merry derriere way to hunt for the Toad Mother's cosy cunt. Being a flim flam spam, the clyster shyster escaped with the entire dire, slime wine that he hogged and robbed from the bitch to give to the whore.

Chapter 6
ECLIPSE OF POLYPS

What goes up your bum makes you dumb.

As a young swine, Pain Pig was not raised, but reared. The master of despise quickly developed an indecent tendency toward wanton his ring of reference extended and distended, and also displayed a deep proclivity to poking his purple nob nose into other people's cavities to snuffle out their backside stories.

PAIN PIG'S PILGRIMAGE

The cuntry bumkin regularly inserted ever larger suppositories into his rectum in readiness for the long prolonged journey aheadjob. Pain Pig followed his fart heart and long prong which the sod used as a divining rod.

Now, after much debilitation, he diddly bopped with a hop and a scotch across the cultural void and voyaged to the vortex of the central anal earth where he perchanced upon a modern sodomy, the eternal grope rope of licentiousness and sin – a hazy daisy chain that diminished to a perpetual perspective. The buggery line of turdlings twisted and turned, stretched and stenched for a million miles.

Seldom a setback for the wetback razorback the middle beast between Pain Pig's stumpy legs reared its ugly head. Following an initianal greeting and meeting of the mindless, Pain Pig's nose rose to the challenge so he nose-dived butthead first into the stray fray of the merde herd.

Fitting right in, Pain Pig puckered his farce arse and joined the butt end of the bugger juggernaut, which led directly to the Toad Mother's Cuntdom.

Pain Pig poked his pubic proboscis; how disgusting was the suggestion, his sinus dribbled congestion and froth snot, semen and phlegm.

The path upon which the unstable cable pumped and writhed was narrow and treacherous with lecherous links of deviant finks. Each stink link in the buggery chain continued to batter and bash the udder's bum till it was well and truly buggered and churned and turned to butter. As the plop thickened, the plot sickened, and many wannabe wantons, whipped and withered, fell exhausted from the path and into the sea of semen and slime. Each grime time a cockamamie cockhead fell from the maligned conga line, Pain Pig moved one bum forward. Bugger the devil you nose then the devil you smote.

Possessing priapic powers and being a professional pinheaded prick, Pain Pig continued to shag and dag through cubits of shit and relished his deep vainglorious thrombosis. With tongue firmly in bum cheek he didn't miss a beating and didn't fall from the path of rutting righteousness and blunt force sex objective. Slowly butt sorely, inch by grinch, Pain Pig travelled up hilt and dropped down stale dale along the anal avenue, getting closer and closer toward the incontinent of the Toad Mother.

A blind eye in a brown eye maketh the hole whirled mindless.

Amoral oral sex might make your day but banal anal sex makes your hole weak and as years and rectal tears passed, members of the poop troupe fell from the buggery grove to stink and sink in the quicksand of bland handjobs and mediocrity.

"The enema of my enemy is my friend," the indurate Pain Pig would squeal with glee as he held firm to this solitary thought; his monism and whole hole goal. With each redundant fecundate falling from disgrace into the splatter of moribund matter and waste, Pain Pig moved forever forward, until finally his hammered ham and pounded polyps reached the burning bridge which led to the mountain of the malevolent smother Mother.

The redneck runt bared the brunt and after a billion bumps and humps his arsehole resolve started to dissolve, but he gird his loins with damned stamina, switch flicked dicks, and continued on his unswerving mission to full submission.

Pain Pig conceded to his robust lust and proceeded to follow the yellow prick road to la lard land, bumping and grinding over the frigid bridge, which spanned the dubious Rubicon, a cesspool moat of smote surrounding the spatial blight on the lardscape that is the Toad Mother.

The rickety bridge collapsed halfway across the moat so he hopped on a boat and with an awesome oar in each poor paw rowed slow through the slough.

The sloop dupe sliced through the sluice and refuse of the sea of shit in a dipship, past the farce of the ion tip, a displace where all matter is dumped leaving only a fallacious, palatious façade throughout the Dominion of the Toad Mother's dream realm.

On he paddled through the addle and plop across the top of the slop to the terror pin of sin and squalor, till he reached the breach and came ashore the Great Whore.

The skewbald screwball scaled the scala santa to the gaping maw between the grand whore's thunder thighs to the soma stoma, the south mouth of madness.

Chapter 7
SERMON ON THE MOUNT

The hole whirled is fat!

The stench of stuperiority was overwhelming as Pain Pig stood before the giant mountain of muff, gaping in awe at its bulging magniference. He beheld the behemoth, the architect of fear, the source of all suffering and the mother of more misery.

She was a vision and fission of fat; dispassionate and disproportionate scat. A monument of malevolent malice, the pinnacle of putrescence, an audacity of huge! "Ewe reek, aaah!" Pain Pig proclaimed as he sucked in the stench from her trench mouth with orgasmic delight when he reached the breach of the damned dame.

Lying as an island, the Damenation's bulk and bunkum had expanded to outrageous purportions and circumference becoming the equatorix of the hole whirled. The spectrum of her bum and her seismic size was matched only by her egotistic foolosophy, creating a deceptive perspective. She was a monsterpiece of indifference and moral torpitude cloaked in mistery and secrecy.

The height of arrogance of the magnanimous mountain was so enormous it stretchmarked from the horizon to the zenith and blocked out the sun. The lard around the vulgar vulva of the mother lode mountain was shrouded in a murky, gloomy loony fog and sank into a stank dank darkness of deficient fish. Pain Pig could not circumvent the uncircumcised circumference of the festering feast of fat because the enormous gelatinous girth was girt by sea.

Possessing more arse than class the ambiguarse barge arse larded over a slack lack of an imagination nation, a ninny-nanny society, and expressed perfidious views and poos wiped with a tissue of absurdity and sly lies in disguise.

The ratio of her ignoratio elenchi did stench from the notion motions that she squirted from her parallaxative view above her vantage disappoint.

The shite mites would hang on every turd word and anal banality and inanity uttered by the ironic iconic cuntox. There was a complete and udder distortion of the fucks as all throughout the lard the solipsistic Mother Fuehrer ranted her erudite shite and misled by example. Her arsenal of cruel accruals and gossip gospel bumbarded the buggers all

with attitude sickness, myxomatosis and halitosis. The Toad Mother's immoral didactic dictum dictates that—all things being unequal—the drelb realm of the wicked whirled will always exist and fester forever. Every stagnant stalagmite and social misfit full of shit is entitled to an opinion ass long as it coincides with thine. She sodomised the misfits with an obscurantist fist and clotted their neurosis with thrombosis osmosis. She bombarded the buffoons with her body dismorphic disorder, espousing a tenesmus tenet, a foolosophy of inexortable excrement and doctrine of idiotology.

In her fat earth theory, the lying buttress laze and stays immortal by festering on the life blood sandwiches of the misinformed miscreants, leaving empty vessels which she aborts; thus she absorbs the years and yearns the cads would have had.

Trite detritus leaks from her enormous anus as her bassoon bum blusters and bellows and a monsoon of urine slime sprays all the time. Selling sickness the seismic Suzerain sovereign's reign over her domain was unforgiving with spatial putrefication, forgery sorcery, and flawed rectumtitude. The fake pharoahess presides over a perennial sintennial that celebrates and percolates chocolate hate and torment of the overweight.

There was no rind rhyme or reason in her ideologically unsound irrationanality and archaic matriarchic mumbo jumbo. Her psychotic zymotic speeches, errant aberrant rants and corny horny orations infected all the turdmites and acolyte blights, that frantically and flailingly followed the fanatical fatameringue's lore of futile foreplay and fungoid phallusy. The eccentric theocentric fishwife was a barramundi of enema anima mundi, every day through to mundane. No gritty integrity here; their nonsense of self was diluted and their minds polluted with puerile propaganda.

For a blind mind the only way to be warm is to conform and bow before the cow. For every choice there is a cuntrol, for every quip a censorship. Nothing matters, butt being battered as a matter of fact and for as long as there is faith in phallusy ewe live under the yoke of tyranny and joke of freedumb.

For every universal truth there is an untruth. And the truth is ewe have no rights to cite, only blights and cellulite.

Every whole is injected with pseudo syllogism jizm and every one must eat shit sandwiches. Ewe have no might to eschew. The only right given ewe is to choose how much dread to chew.

Freedom from choice is no voice at all.

Chapter 8
THE PURSUIT OF SLAP HAPPY MESS

The butt end justifies demeans.

Pain Pig had an all pervasive need to be on bended knees and submit to defeet and kiss her flaccid, rancid meat; to reject self-respect and replace one deform of oppression for another.

"I stink therefore I'm spam," said the ham. Pain Pig knew that the only way to be womb warm was to conform and confirm the Toad Mother's hidden agenda bender. The infibulated fibber's wedgie was that he was an eager edgy player looking for the next extreme peen experience. He enjoyed being toyed and tortured because his brain wiring was fused and confused. No contradiction, no contrition, only constriction and deconstruction.

Through humiliation, violation, and anal annihilation he proposed to rebutter his bum and purloin the Toad Mother's attention to his groin. So he trotted the well-trodden path and repeated the past mortem by going on a surrender bender.

First he took a dip in shit, drunk a potion of poo and bathed in a lotion of her magic motion, the diarrhoea sea, to make himself alluring and smell sweet to her nonsense rhyme, unreason and wicked whimsy.

Waring a yellow bonnet of dried vomit, the slack rucksack gingerly approached the reproachful regal reprobate with trepidation. The pimpled pimpernel knelt before the biggatrix, spread her toe jam on his dread, bowed his head and made an offering of the Divine Wine of the Vile Vine of Inequity.

The Toad Mother sniffed the musktang on the poontag then guzzled the gruesome brew of the amazing grape and saith that it was good shit.

Enamoured by his grift of graft and servile submission, the dopey doyenne possessed his proposal and repossessed his preposterous posterior, making him her trifling truffles and strife. Around his stoat throat she attached a latch and collar of real steel and a chain of command. For the Toad Mother, possession was nine-tenths of her flaw.

The Cane Toad whacked the dackless pig with her fiddlesticks, fiddle dee dee, until the pig was scarred for strife.

She proceeded to lavabo the hobo, warts and all, then basted the brothel-bred bastard and lambasted the sham lam. Waxing lyrical, she stopped for a bite of his bruised behind, smite and backbite his flubber blubber, gnawed on his laurels and ruminated on his rump diddly um pump.

The fatwa muffty shat on the toughy, chewed on the cur and weigh. Then the rambunctious rogue munched on the scrumptious munchkin receiving calorie comfort, enlarging her intentionally large intestine with a largo of turgid and tossed trocomare and rare jugged hare.

Once bitten forever smitten.

The more his senseless senses were rapiered the happier he seemed. The loblolly lobbed on the fat slob, the auburn urbane Lazy of Leisure, for the thrill of dismorphic euphoric displeasure and dislocation through strappado. Raising his self-extreme, the feckless fool was inflicted with masochismo and hanged as a toe-rag dag from the Toad Mother's perineum continuum outside her oval orifice.

Four decayeds he was highly strung around her bunghole humbugged as a sickening, sniffling, sycophantic snag dag, dripping with liquid shite every time the Toad Mother squirted diarrhoea with all her might and sour power.

"Fee, fi, foe, fum. I smell a bum." With one trotter in her osculum rectum he was between sham ham and bog god.

For another four score and seven lesions the poontang hanged entranced at the entrance of the Toad Mother's anal auditorium suspended in morbid moratorium. The Tourette's curator taunted the whipper snapper with toad rage, "You are not special, you are not unique, you are obsolete. You are what I excrete." She told and scold as she mixed his cocktail with failed fallacies to fuel her stools.

The porky pariah relished the attention deficit disorder and agreed with open anuses, "You mean to be mean to me."

At the dawn of sum pretentious portentions, she moved him to her bowel movement and micro managed his mission to follow her methane emissions into her conduit of shit. Pain Pig adhered to an undress code in disorder to enter the inner sanctum of the Toad Mother's rectum. Being an arsehole through and poo, Pain Pig travelled up her pipeline into the poopchute until he was in deep shit.

Chapter 9
SLEEPING WITH THE ENEMA

The spelunkhead crawled on bland hands and skinned knees, along her faecal vehicle, up the inner tube of the bacillus basilicarse. He squiggled and squirmed upwards to colon-ize her despised insides. The prodigal bum chum returned to the mould fold of the matriarch's buttressed aquaduct of mucous and motions and flattery of flatulence. With no emotion he eliminated all the shite mites and turdlings lodging in the crevices of her perfunctory rectory, took pride of place in the fee, fi, foe's bum and sat in her ship of stools.

Savouring his saviour, the idiot savant servant pursued shit with true grit and went from crack to crap, becoming her cave slave, her groom of the stool. The bastard was now an inmate of the inconsiderate and incontinent concierge's colon.

Dwelling in her dirty stovepipe of hymen hype and fabrication the counterfeit twit wood shit, split hairs and splinters from his blockhead dead as a door nob. Feasting and festering in the union of holy communion, the fawn of plenty prodded his prostrate as he swirled in a whirlpool of poo and canoodling with his noodle.

'Tis a shit moulded by a nitwit fool of sound and furry sicknifying nothing.

Inside the snide and loathsome organ, the bore snuggled warm in her bumbora, an erratum bum full of scum and sebum. The cuckold was cosseted and coddled as the spastic colon would convulse and massage him. He hunkered down in the bunker of her fucks hole as her analconda would squeeze and pressure him. Her snake of fowl substance would undulate the ungulate making him unduly late with his piss offering. Her crapulence would emit malodorous odours sweet to Pain Pig's defunct oldfactory nonsense as he splashed and played and bathed among a shitload of logs.

Surrounded by the pitter patter of tiny shits his slime and punishment entrailed being hung upside drowned in a titanic colonic irrigation.

For sustenance the kuru guru munched on a brunch of her diplodicus scum, gangrenous gall bladder and harvest of hideous and loathsome organs. He tasted the waste as he sucked on a paste of pus and supped from a vat of shat and mucous membranes and masticated on her spleen of soylent green. He had a party between her parted cheeks with vinegar from her shrivelled titties that made his clever dicky became sticky with ichor.

The flunky's junket and jolly jubilee inside her bellicose bowel ended in an instant and abrupt burp when the promise of displeasure was reconsidered and his ten year tenure was revoked, provoked by a royal pee decree.

Chapter 10
STINKER, STALER, TOTAL FAILURE

"The Lard giveth and the Lard taketh away." So spaketh the stomach.

Silent butt deadly, her judicial jaundice and prejudice permeated the meat deep heat as the truly unruly toxic floozy denounced the full of shit plaintiff from the pulpit. "Every-bum is expandable and expendable."

Showing savage insignificance toward the scuttlebutt mutt, the tinpot despot added attention deficit disorder into the potty mouth mix and so upon hearing his piss, the deranged and demented debuttaunt moved the goal posts of her engrudged gourd. She moored and ignored him once more.

Renting his own spleen Pain Pig tried to redeem his dismal demeanour through fawning sycofancy in the faint hope his self-sacrifice would suffice. Fussing and fossicking, primping and pampering, the simpering simp did piss and pose and stick his nose, his anal probeboscus into her internal infernal affairs and tried to declare himselfish as the one true blue vein of cheese that could please the doyenne of sleaze.

The despised dipstick boar false witness as he tried to cajole the moll with his disgusting guise of diseased lies, but smitten and bitten by intermittent explosive disorder, she cracked the shits.

Having a dumb Cuntdom to run into the ground and contend with contempt, the fickled fiend flipped between effusive and abusive. The bulimic schemer became wearisome of the stubby subby's randy antics and dismal demands for attention. So the mistress of mistrust chained and caned him with disdain twice more, pulling his bone apart.

Greater than wee, he can only temper the distemper of the hidden agenda bender from the quasi quaquaversal arse. Constipated and vituperated the saggy haggis-headed humpty-dumpty tied and tried to appease with please of remission and ebullition. The character traitor tried to cook a banquet for the Toad Mother butt he just cooked his goose instead. Unable to cut the mustard, he just cut the cheese.

The pundit bandit tried to bandaid the breach of dishonour but suffered from hoof in mouth disease which displeased the frugal fungoid fuckhead for ever more.

CARTER RYDYR

He protested vermachtly, testiculated wildly and threw a hissy fit of shit and pissing like a spoilt bratwurst. This pissed the pompous pontiff off causing an expulsion of cuntaclysmic purportions. She endured a cursed curette, a lapse of mammary and prolapse of palpitating putrescence and udderances of uterus pus.

As her bowels tolled, the whoremoanal Toad Mother suffered an infallibilism embolism and jumped to a moronic colonic conclusion.

Perhaps phylioxera from the grapes of wrath had fermented into hate that did not slake the Mistress of Despies; or maybe she was just a bitch of the highest disorder; or maybe she was gone with the wind. Whatever the debased case, the paunchy Pilate washed her pudgy hands of the flim flam ham. She ho-hummed and hoicked on the hog and jettisoned the flotsam fop. Casting pearls before swine the obscene Queen of Denial reproached the dope by denying him a third turd time and determined his festering destiny by ordering his sexecution.

Pain Pig's paranormal paramour was no more.

Chapter 11
END OF AN ERROR

Everything happens for a treason.

"Put the piggy in the pokey!" the mercurial magistrate ordered, summoning the death knelt. The largess placed a largo embargo on the larrikin loser.

Although he spaketh not a turd word the sultana-breasted sleaze bag had gone troppo and was insulted by the peasant's mere presents of mindlessness.

"Butt what have I dung?" He begs with breath of rotten eggs.

"Alimentary, my dear flotsam." The teleological Toad dismissed the ribald piebald pig without a cause. Although the rise of her despise should come as no surprise, the enigma of his stigma contused and confused the pariah pig big crime this time.

Crestfallen, the meagre moth-eaten, brow-beaten mongrel mogul managed but a pitiful bleat. The loose louse was placed under house arrested development for no other reason than the bumbastic biddy deemed it so.

From the vaginal halls of the hateful moor came galoots galore who, blindly obeying the law of the lore of the abhorred whore, took the stupid nincompoop stoop from the poop chute to the hoosegow and locked the fecundate inmate in a cunt full of cold water.

Pain Pig was locked in her pubicle of penance and penalty, a bestial Bastille full of fu flux flanges that flustered and flummoxed the lummox. Held in detention in her water retention, Pain Pig stewed and spewed in a permanent wet spot of phlegm and mollusc mucous, inside the scold's cold caldera.

Besmirched by the Motherlode Toad's denouement denouncement and doomed by royal soiled etiquette, the cellar dweller fell into a despondent state of inertia and adepochre in the apocalyptic crypt.

Disenfranchised by her tyranny of distance for a slime prime number of yearns, the bamboozled loser sat and shat in putrefaction; alone in slough, his remonstrated bleats and pleas for appeals went unanswered.

Flapping her elephant ears, the dopey deviant diva fanny farts a mirthquake that shakes loose sloppy seconds slime, awakening herpes hermaphrodite mites which erupt from the weeping walls. The reproachful roaches spit and shoot venom at the trussed turkey, wasted and basted in the Toad Mother's sluice juice and yabby dabba doo doo. Swimming in the vestibule of her septic, peptic ulcer was a soup of indigestible and suggestible vestal sturgeons employed to harry and worry the swindling swine. Rub-a-dub grubs burrow in the tubby trotter's diseased dermis. Creepy crawlies in the cesspool were incessantly biting and sniping Pain Pig as he wallowed in the reality of the Toad Mother's realty.

Dietmetrically opposed, I suppose, to providing any cuntfort or nude nutrition, he was given nothing to eat but an agent orange and the slimy scrapings on the flaw of syphilis and saxatoxin from the hag's crabs. No more, no less; just mouldy molasses. Slim pickings for the pig with the gaping yaw maw between his pork fork that was stuck between his cock and a hard place. So he picketed and ate the peanuts from his very own poo.

Explicatively, due to an ineptitude of unintelligent design inside the decrepit shit-pit, the felonious bezonian, although resigned to his fate, escaped into the Toad Mother's labiarynth of sinful skin.

Chapter 12
LUST AND CONFOUND

The god damned ham was condemned to traverse the inversed universe of the Toad Mother's defunct cunt—the cuntnundrum.

PAIN PIG'S PILGRIMAGE

The labial labyrinth was a mouldy manifold maze of malaise and molasses. A dark and dank, murky, lurky steam bath of fetid mildew and undead dreadends of rotting erotic carcasses that stink inside the box ewe live in. The lout followed the fallow trench stench of haut gout to bottomless botox fucksholes and sillycone vulva valleys. He discreet excrete and pussyfoot through the galoot's sticky botchelistic mystic river of rashes and potato mashes of mullet and mucus and anchovies.

The ragamuffin waded through the muck and mire in search of desire through itchy, yeasty cells of cellulite harbouring gruesome ghettoes of gobsmacked rogues and rancid rodents. The hairless harelip pig slipped past her elite clit because he didn't know what to do with it.

Lost in amaze of difficult daze in the never never lard of the gigantess's chatterbox, the unprivileged belligerent trudged on further and deeper into the blind mind meld of the convoluted cleave full of heat and humidity of meat. Her cunt was a cold cauldron of hubble bubble toilet trouble of festering bacteria, algae algorithms and pee fricasee.

The porky pariah was propelled and compelled to unravel the conundrum of her claptrap, but with each step he took he sank in the stank of her mezzanine flaw and catechism schizm. The rootin' tootin' pooper scooper staggered about in a stupour certain that his pee-shooter would suitor if only he could root out the scenter of her dementia. He had to reach and breach the abhorred core of the great whore to reverse the curse and begin anew a nude and spew relationshit. But how to navigate through the hate of the loathsome labiarynth?

Walking through the valley of the shadow of bad breath he hoed through the humdrum of her halibut hell but he could not breach the great wall of vagina. The vaginal vault shimmered and his pork belly quivered, audibly crackling in the heat of conceit and deceit. In desperation he saw a vision with a division butt it was just a mirage of her barge arse.

Stalled in her menopause, the taxidermied dervish descended down her one thatch blind into the Toad Mother's trough. On he trudged along the sludge and slushy corridors of the cuntess's cunt, dilly dallying along the grim brim of her mangy minge. Balancing on the rim of her ruff muff, peeering over the edge of her catechism chasm, the tardy retarded pig quivered and shivered and trembled with stress.

Butt eye digress . . .

Back tracking and back-peddling, Pain Pig chained discretion as he changed direction and encountered a rot gut of brain-dead mucous lamebrains, a cloister of oyster farmers and gong scourers, who guided him to an oasis of molasses and badder bladder of piss bliss. He guzzled deep on the yellow slough from a vestigial vesicle then followed a fistula of hype and tripe to smoke on a piss-pipe—the Toad Mother's urinary tract, in fact.

Pain Pig had no spur to prick the snides of her water retention, butt revolting ablutions that overleak and slip underhoof. Although the surrounding lard was hot and fetid the whore's core temperament was cold as ice.

Pain Pig trawled through her crawl space; round and rotund he went in the cleaver beaver skittish like a dervish, inside the impuzzable passages of her sweatbox, but he could not furnish a path out of the astrolabia as there were no stars only scars to navigate by and bye.

With every deadend his groan had grown and reverberated through the flawed halls of the Great Whore's fishy fanny. Falling on his pork sword caused his aching echo to prick the attention of a demi-demon, an evil spleen with eyes of ice scream, who dwelt deep in the heat and barren wasteland of hoity toity goitres in the Toad Mother's womb of doom.

Chapter 13
MULESING THE BODY ECLECTIC

In the wan light of perpetual night, amidst the mist of the hidden pudenda, the silhouette became distinct and there appeared the Vulvarine, a vagina dentata of insatiable lust and sage rage.

"This little piggie went to market," she sang as she led Pain Pig astray deeper and steeper inside the lousy house of the dread dead, numb without feelings of guilt quilt from past transgressors and trespassers. So she inserted a cathode catheter into his urethra, made untoward overtures on his aperture, smeared the seersucker with jeer and fear, then swiped the pig with the jawbone of an ass-wipe.

"This little piggy stayed home." Putting his body in a stress position and his neck in check she kept the zymotic arseholic in a zygotic cell, a kennel of fennel and thorny corns. The jabberjaw of jealousy and malice maced his face and performed psilosis on his silly nose hairs. He displayed high dudgeon in the dungeon as each capricious vibrassa hair of the bog dog was plucked from his stout snout.

"This little piggy had roast beef." Pain Pig's scrotal jowls were punctured, ruptured, and removed and made into mullock muesli and forcefed to the corn fed pig. To see if he could last the teste of time she cut off a sceptical testicle and stored it in a despicable and unasseptable receptacle of pickled onions and hematomatoes then served it with capsicum dip to the disgusting dipshit. She gorged his gratuitous gluttony by giving him a serve of cabbage baggage borscht with rashly added radish relish. She further fed the corny leprechaun peppercorns of leprosy and bade him to swallow his own sebaceous tallow. She chipped away at his blockhead with hammer and chisel, and then using knuckledusters busted his mouth open wide.

"This little piggy had none." After kneading his flesh with needle and dread the kali harlot forced him to vomit all fowl food and fool fish behaviour. Then proceeded in starving him by halving his ration of bacon rashers that she sliced verily from his very own behind. She sucker punched the fucker's pucker and did sing while she did mulesing his arse to fleece the flystrike and retailiate the tall sloppy poppy's tall tales. Then the reckless recluse and amusing muse infused muesli into his loose caboose as she trained her thought on making him haiku spew and puke before seppuku.

"This little piggy went wee wee wee all the way home." The blistered bitch rolhypnoltised the quisling traitor, shook and took the sook to crack and urine then pounded his pork on the pavement, exercising his demons. She castigated and castrated him by skewering his second sour ball then surly, tersely and mercilessly flogged the porky farter to tenderise his toughened dermatised lies and despised lost vague arse. She paddled the panhandler, smacked his crack and beat his butty into silly putty then proceeded to slap and sickle the barnacles and carbuncles off his shingle back hyde. Scarred and soiled, scored and boiled, the Vulvarine vent her contempt by taunting the transgressor in ways and daze the mutton glutton despised.

"This little piggy stayed and played with razor blades." The vicious viscose vixen beheld a strident trident of savage significance to stick the pig to test the propensity and intensity of his bone density then wielding axes of evil to strip the blighter fantastic. She rammed a steel eye stylus over his styleless hide and gouged deep grooves into his gammy phoney legs. She round up the rotund ruminant and whipped the weed whacker before bothering to sink her bovver boot in. She gleaned his spleen, green with viridity stupidity, seconded a section of his rectum with secateurs then defoliated his hyde, shaving all his hair before daring to dissect his derriere. He did plead while he did bleed and peed himself so she extracted his urinary tract and vain veins and draped them on a topiary of arms and legs she'd prepared earlier that daze. A little slaughter clears the pus of misdeeds, indeed.

"And this little piggy was flayed alive for worshiping false bogs." The vagrant was delectibly flayed of his delecto flagrante. She hammered his hamorrhoids the size of asteroids then bashed his unabashed head to dash the balderdash from the sozzled Zeitgeist. The inquisitor visitor flushed his head in the loo along with all the poo then stretched the long pig on the rack and ruin and drew out his intestines by rote and decked his gall bladder with holey moley baloney. She peeled his jacket potato and vacuum sealed the spud's sphincter and squeezed cold spaghetti through sub-atomic black holes in his dead head. The bestial sextraterrestrial extracted the grubs from the schlub's blubber and rubbed and honed his bones with sandstone, before tenderising his meat seat with hammer and tongs.

After which she sandwiched Pain Pig's back feet betwixt the rollers of an old-fashioned fandangled mangle and flattened his gammy legs up to his obscene knees to squeeze the sleaze from his navicular disease. Having deadlocked his fretted and fettered fetlocks she plaited them into dreaded dreadlocks. Between each turn of the stenosis screw, the shrew committed a torture or two then rubbed salt and balmy balm in the buffoon's wounds.

Another turn of the mangle handle and another torture to pass the time and urine. Discovering a discreepancy with his penis, she pinched and drew out his contractile penile just for something to do. Compressed in the press, the sabre-toothed tart tapered his jippy, gipsy gut, which jut and attenuated his inflated ego. She rocked as she spoke while she poked the lights and blights out of Pain Pig, "Loverly, loverly, loverly."

She had no qualm in doing him harm so over the painstaking yearns, inside the prison cell of selfishness, the vampiric Vulvarine squeezed out all the crud blood from the stoned bonehead by choking his nexus of evil. The gaiety of the deity was doubly demonstrated by remonstrating his prostate with phosphate, cracking his sick coccyx and cutting off his apocalyptoe.

The mangle continued to roll over his body to strangulate the ungulate till only his head protruded and expanded. Pain Pig pled and bled as the rollers squeezed his bonehead.

Six drops of essence of terror, five drops of sinister sauce. After adding a pinch of iodised lies plus a dose of gingivitis, she compounded the powder with conjunctivitus. All was mixed together with uranium urine in a vile vial; shaken, not stirred.

Strapped in the confounded contraption, with just his hidearse head exposed the Vulvarine dripped drops of the stinging liquid into his eyes in search of tears of remorse. As the acidick liquid fell in the dark wells, dire swellings of stinging haemorrhoids rose bloody and blue, reeking and seeping of tetanus and animus pus. Having no eyelids, the crusty musty wastrel could not stop the explosive corrosive detritus dripping in to his haemorrhoidal skin, and possessing no remorseful tear ducts he could not wash away the fray of the liquefaction distraction. Then when the stirring was done she flicked the poon with a flick-knife.

Butt for the disgrace of bog there goes an eye.

Knot a grate loss for Pain Pig, as he has arseholes instead of eyes. Thus he was used as a Draize Rabbit for sham poo experiments—just desserts and a fitting end for a shameful shaman of shit such that befits Pain Pig.

After a thousand moments without so mulch as a tear from the pinkeye dye, the Vulvarine tired of the routine, and decided to quit this shit and try another tack. Tying twine from the divine vine around the schlock cock of the habeus corpus, she foisted a funnel in his fudge tunnel and filled his shrivelled dishevelled husk and hogshead with more fermented wine than the curdled cur could presume to consume. Thus inflating his sky highfalutin ego and flattened, sandwiched body back into its formerly horrendous misshapen shape.

At last, bloated and smoted and coated in egg yolk, the Vulvarine raised the obscene beast willy nilly by wrapping the cock between his forked pork around a rote spoke. Hanging in mid air strike, using a metaphysickal sickle, with a single swipe she truncated his facial trunk, his stout snout, leaving a stump with two snot holes exposed.

Chapter 14
DREAD BY DAWN

Miss Aligned closed the story book, leaned into the row of chilblames sitting on the floor in awe before her and said, "And that's how pigs got their noses and curly whirly corkscrew cocks."

"Tell us another story," the Hell's belles chimed.

"That's enough blight for tonight. Off to the rack before I maul you all." She chided with a frown of thorns as she whacked and cracked their heads with the crooked book.

The shameful and spiteful chilblames shuffled off to their respective deceptive beds, pulled the covers over their scornful heads and dreamt unpleasant thoughts.

Suffering insufferably from down syndrome and sodokosis psychosis, the chillblames sprung from her maligned misaligned mind. The rug rats were an infestation of verminous rodents ransacking her memory, a manifestation of hoarded infractions and blind rage in her droll soul. After accumulating many knives in her back, Miss Aligned acquired an axe to grind. Hanging onto hatred, she maintained the rage. Hate does not dissipate; it only hardens your arteries. Coiled as a knot of dire spitfires that spite venom in the pit of her stomach, the chilblames represent a gluttony of el dente vendettas tucked tight in her psicko psycho psyche of what could've, would've, should've been.

Everyone of pus has a personanal cross to bare, a silly responsiliability.

Fart from the madding crowd she welt better by feeling bitter. Suffering had taught the septic sceptic to cut the hate into pieces of eight.

Every error, every regret, every fret was turned to stone, locked in a box and placed on the top shelf out of breach reach in a cloistered closet. In the middle of midnight weary, a dreary chillblame got out of bed, scuttled across the flaw, and with a skeleton key opened the closet door. The chillun removed all the boxes till the cupboard was bare, and then with rapt attention unwrapped the packages, releasing all the pent up rents and dissents. The savage ravaged rugrat hoisted foibles and foisted follies into the scary air, creating a pandemonium of sinicism and prism prison of pessimism. Submerged fears and welled up tears rose to the surface and floated on a sea of mental disease. Broken thoughts, broken dreams, broken hearts.

Each stepping stone melted and merged and was forged into a millstone that weighed heavily around Miss Aligned's neck. Although what had emerged was the urge to purge the gall stones and collywobbles of stress and distress, and tension of contention, too old to behold, they were embittered and embedded deep and wood not budge. Suffering from heartworm, she bottled her battles and stored her obscure insecurities and sewed them into a Frankenstein skin which she wore as a coat of smote; an abhorred armour that no counselling of reason or respite could pierce.

CARTER RYDYR

Every eternal night Miss Aligned sat in an empty room, alone in her tomb wallowing in gloom, surrounded by faceless foibles and depressive doom. Try as she might one interminable night, beside herself with misery, she could not face the disgrace or muster the ruse of an excuse and explain the pain away.

Stubbornly at sunrise as the night dies, she soaked in a shower of shards of hearts made from broken glass. The steam driven cloy rose as a fog and clouded her mirror image. Wiping away the condescending condensation and confusion she didn't like what she chain sawed. So see-sawing between desynchronisation and decompression depression, she smashed the glass and carved up her insecurities into a facial infibulation. Using hooks and wishing line she sewed the wounds wide shut.

Saving and salving no horrorscope of hope and having no-one to blame but her own shame, she swallowed a bottle of bitter pills before she cut out her tongue. She sewed her lips into muted bliss and silently sentenced herself to an eternity of taciturnity.

The immoral of this hoary story is: The fool moon may be made of green with envy cheese butt the hole whirled is full of shit!

ONE DAY I'LL QUIT THIS JOB AND RULE THE WORLD

MAX BOOTH III

FATHER WAKES UP at 5:30 A.M. still tasting the whiskey from the previous night. His body is sore—it aches so badly that all he wishes in the world is to be able to close his eyes and go back to sleep. Mother lies next to him in bed. Father considers nudging her awake and asking permission to call in sick. But it is useless, not to mention foolish. Those who call in sick do not keep their jobs. Those who do not keep their jobs eventually start eating those who do have jobs. It is a cruel life.

Father forces himself out of bed and showers. In the shower he masturbates. For a few minutes he is king of the universe, then he ejaculates and reality comes rushing back. Father considers this moment to be a disappointment.

He wishes he was still masturbating.

After he has finished showering, he gets dressed in the usual business suit. As he tightens his tie, he contemplates pulling it harder and harder until his eyeballs pop out of their sockets. How amusing, he thinks. How absolutely hilarious.

Mother already has a cup of coffee ready for Father when he enters the kitchen. He smiles, gives his thanks, and kisses her on the cheek. Mother is not yet made up. She looks quite ugly. Like maybe what Death would look like if Death was a person. Later, when Father leaves, she will touch up and apply her human colors. She'll be bright and shiny and appear fuckable to strangers from a distance.

Father sits at the table drinking his coffee and eating his toast and browsing over the morning paper. The headline story is about a teenage pop singer being arrested for drunk driving. Another story reports that a major A-list actor made a racist comment during an interview. In the article, the journalist requests for the actor's death. It is reported that government officials are currently considering it.

Son walks into the kitchen with an annoyed look on his face. Father recognizes the look well. It is a look he himself wears on most days and nights.

Son asks if he has to go to school.

Father says, "Yes."

"But why?" Son asks.

"So one day you can have a job."

"But why do I need a job?"

"So one day you can die."

Son makes a pouting face now. "But why do I have to die?"

"So one day you can live."

Son sighs in frustration and takes an angry bite of toast.

Daughter enters the kitchen. She can wake up pretty without having to apply any special cosmetic features. It will not last. One day she will wake up just as ugly as Mother, and life will be miserable.

Daughter asks Father if she can borrow some money. He asks for what. Daughter tells Father she is pregnant and she needs to get it taken care of before her belly becomes fat and disgusting. It is her third pregnancy this school year.

Father sighs and pulls out his wallet. The money drains away like the blood from a corpse atop an autopsy table. Daughter consumes the money and begins texting Boyfriend on her cell phone.

Father finishes his coffee, kisses his family goodbye, and starts the long journey to work. It is a beautiful day. The sun is bright and there is not a cloud in the sky.

As Father waits at the subway station, a man approaches him, scratching his head as if lost. Father asks if he can help him, and the man nods, opens his mouth, and attempts to eat him. Father swats the man with his briefcase and tells him they are in a NO HUNTING zone.

"But please," the man says. "I'm so hungry. Just let me have a little bite of your meat."

"Absolutely not," Father says.

"Like you can't stand to lose a few pounds."

"Oh, that was just rude. Now you're definitely not having any." Father swats him with the briefcase again. "Now shoo, or I'll report you to the officials."

The man sighs and walks away in search of someone less selfish.

The subway finally arrives and Father boards it. He sits down next to a woman who is crying. He straightens his tie and begins to cry, too. Then everyone in the subway cries. It is a real special moment.

When he gets off the subway, there is a different man waiting to eat people in the station. He snaps his jaws at Father and Father points and tells him, "No, no bite."

The man lowers his head and says, "Aww, not even one?"

"Not even one."

"Fine, your loss!" The man jumps onto the subway tracks and awaits his demise.

Father leaves the station and walks down the street. A large man in a trench coat is waiting outside for him.

"Here's the deal," the man in the trench coat says. "I am going to start chasing you now. If I catch you, I am going to tear out your jugular with my teeth and drink your blood. If you win, you keep your life, plus I will email you a coupon for a free gas station hot dog. Deal?"

"Deal," Father says, and flees.

The man in the trench coat chases after him. Father is faster. He makes it to work without any trouble. The man in the trench coat catches up to him, wheezing and panting, and takes down Father's email so he can send him the hot dog coupon.

"That was fun," Father says, then walks into work.

Boss is waiting for Father so he can tell him that he is three minutes late. Father apologizes, but Boss only sighs. He bends Father over the desk, pulls down Father's pants, and spanks his bare, hairy buttocks ten times with his belt. Father thanks Boss for the punishment and goes to his cubicle.

Someone has already delivered today's human heart. It rests on a dinner plate on his desk. It pumps up and down, squirting a line of blood every now and then. There is a sticky note attached to the heart that says "PLEASE DO NOT FAX HEART".

Father crumples the sticky note into a ball and tosses it in the wastebasket. He picks up the heart and forces it into the fax machine. The machine begins to smoke and the alarm goes off in the building. The water sprinklers in the ceiling are initiated and everybody screams as it rains. They shed their clothes and form a massive orgy in the break room.

Father stares at the bloody fax machine, wondering where he went wrong in life.

Boss calls Father back into his office. He tells Father that he's warned him enough times against faxing the hearts. Boss has no choice but to let Father go. Father cries in the office as he bends over and drops his pants.

On the way home, nobody tries to eat him. He buys some flowers for Mother. They are dead by the time he walks into the house. He tells Mother he is no longer employed. She asks what will they do now, but he doesn't know. Nobody knows.

Son tells Father he has burned down the school again.

Daughter tells father she is keeping the baby.

The day is no longer beautiful.

Father goes to sleep at 10:00 P.M. Mother slides into bed with him. She says she is scared. Father caresses her cheek and tells her there is no reason to be afraid.

"Life can finally begin," he says.

He wakes up at 8:30 A.M. He skips the shower, ignores the newspaper on the porch, and replaces his coffee with a tall glass of whiskey. Mother gives him a look like she wants to criticize him, but thinks better of it. Father kisses his family goodbye and leaves, still dressed in only his underwear.

At the subway station he does not board the subway. Instead he lingers around the station until he spots some poor miserable sap dressed in a depressing suit and holding a briefcase.

Father approaches this depressed man and smiles. He tells the man good morning. The man says good morning back. Father leans forward and bites off the man's ear, then the other one. Two clean chomps and the man can no longer hear. But he can still scream, and that he does.

Nobody in the subway station pays them any attention as Father chases him in circles, taking more bites. He finally ties the man up with some old rope he has found and drags him back home. He throws the man's bloody body on the kitchen table and Mother asks what this is supposed to be.

"Dinner," Father says. "I have caught us dinner."

Mother smiles and kisses Father. She tells him he has done good.

Father smiles back and tells Mother that he loves her, and that he will always provide for his family, and finally he feels like a true man.

Outside, the sky is cloudy and raining.

It is a beautiful day.

HOUSE PARTY

DUSTIN READE

THE PUNCHBOWL SAT on the table, full of punch. Ashley lay on the floor. The other guests took turns placing various flowers beside her body. She played dead better than anyone, and so it was she who had been elected to play the corpse. From the corner by the window, Marcus smiled. His handlebar mustache curled upwards and tickled the sides of his massive nose. The party was a success.

From her spot on the floor, Ashley allowed her hands to slowly rise into the air. She moaned like a ghost. The mourners wailed. Tears lined their faces as Ashley's ghost made itself known to them.

"Praise The Eye!" they screamed. Marcus took the momentary religious zest to release the Praying Mantises from the shoebox beside the table. The insects prayed about the room, showing off their devotion with intense displays of supplication. Marcus smiled. The party was a success.

Slowly, and with concentrated grace, Ashley lifted body and all from the floor, so that she hung several feet over the heads of the mourners. A Praying Mantis alighted on her chest, which heaved with faux life. The mourners took this as further evidence their entreaties had been received by the Great Eye painted on the ceiling. To its immeasurable credit, the Great Eye did nothing, merely allowing the mourners to worship beneath its penetrating gaze. Marcus smiled. The party was a success.

The bathroom door suddenly ripped open, revealing Jeremy, wrapped head to toe in black electrical tape, and brandishing the severed hose and nozzle of an old vacuum cleaner. His was the part of the exorcist. He was supposed to lurch into the room and recite a William S. Burroughs 'Cut-Up' made by splicing together portions of texts found in various books. The text used was from three sources: *Satan is Alive and Well on Planet Earth* by Hal Lindsey, *The Boston Strangler* by Gerold Frank, and *Trouble in Paradise*, a Dawson's Creek novelization by C.J. Anders. Jeremy, however, had forgotten his lines, so Marcus had to pull the script from his back pocket and throw it across the room to him. This invasion of reality had the exact effect on the party as a glass of ice water has when poured over a painful erection.

Undaunted, Jeremy pointed the vacuum nozzle at Ashley (who now whipped around the room like a rapidly deflating balloon), and read: "I believe there is a pink SAAB with a special God! He is giving it away today! Its leather interior pulled into God for the power!"

From the corner by the window, Marcus smiled. The party was a success.

Ashley thrust abruptly into a crucified position. The mourners screamed. They began to shred the flesh from their faces. When they had been reduced to grinning skeletons, the Great Eye painted on the ceiling blinked once. The mourners screamed praises to the Great Eye. The blink was a miracle! The Day of the Great Blinking! Bibles must be revised!

Jeremy ignored the acrylic eye and read on.

"Many people," he screamed, "have waved gaily at Jen, and others who she got out! She was the gifts of God!"

Marcus turned on the fog machine. A shrouding white mist, thick as molasses, filed the room. The other guests picked up their faces and put them on the wrong skulls. Bearded men with breasts and pocketbooks lumbered about the room. An elderly woman with the body of a large Italian man stumbled over the snack table, spilling cheese and crackers all over the Persian rug. Ashley began spinning around in a violent circle, spraying a heavy green vomit from her mouth and anus. From his corner by the window, his arm resting on the cloud-belching fog machine, Marcus smiled. The party was a success.

"Hair was pulled back, pray in tongues!" Jeremy shouted, still reading from his incomprehensible script. "Servants from New York prayed in tongues just to unload her two dozen handbags in her ground floor of the flesh!"

HOUSE PARTY

One of the guests had lost interest in the faux exorcism, and had bent himself over to pluck bits of mushy feta from the Persian rug. He smeared what he could onto a cracker crumb and ate, his face, which was not his own, showing intense boredom of a kind so vicious as to be troublingly infectious.

Still, Jeremy read on. "A woman saw a strange man in Gram's front yard and at the windows of 224! Pale pink was Courtney's life while others sing into her cousin's arms!" These had been the final words of the incantation.

Ashley fell suddenly from her place in the air. Her body plopped down hard on the davenport, crumpled up like a dejected sheet left outside in the rain. Her legs and arms curled inward, as though devoid of bones. From her open mouth dripped all manner of strange sea creatures, their gelatinous bodies creeping slowly down her chest, staining her shirt with oily rainbow streaks. Jeremy raced over and immediately began vacuuming them up with the severed vacuum hose. The sound that filled the air was beyond description, like the world had released a tremendous, inward fart. The Great Eye painted on the ceiling blinked again, as if to say, "Excuse me."

After the last of the sea creatures had been sucked into the hose, Jeremy raised his hands in triumph and bellowed the final Cut-Up: "She loathed most kissing the vicinity of her European Mother!"

"Amen," the mourners cried, mashing the last of the Praying Mantises into the Persian rug, filled as it was already with crackers and cheese. From the corner by the window, Marcus smiled. The party was a success.

The mourners removed their faces and helped Jeremy move Ashley from the couch to the floor. They again surrounded her body with flowers. The Great Eye watched, pleased. The punchbowl lay on its side on the floor, no longer full of punch. At least, not noticeably so.

Marcus and Jeremy excused themselves from the party and made their way into the kitchen. Attaching the severed end of the vacuum hose to the ice dispenser on the refrigerator, Jeremy smiled and said, "Hell of a party tonight, eh Mark?"

Marcus nodded.

"Yeah it is, and I got to say I'm a little surprised. I mean, Ashley is really getting into it this time."

Jeremy smiled and shook the hose. The sea creatures screamed as they were ushered into the unfamiliar tubing of the ice dispenser. They would have to find a new model of life; learn to feed on the tiny crystals which lived in the ice. Once inside the freezer, however, they promptly forgot their pitiful worries. For you see, sea creatures have very little memory. Recent studies have shown that the common goldfish has a memory which lasts no more than two or three seconds.

In the living room, the mourners wailed. Someone screamed loudly, "Where the fuck is my *face*?! I have to leave soon. I've got to go to work in a few hours!"

Jeremy smiled. "Yeah," he said. "Ashley was really excited about being the corpse tonight. She's been practicing all week."

The last of the creatures had been sucked into the ice dispenser, and for a moment neither of the two men knew what to say. A black cloud had formed over the conversation, shielding their heads from words as an umbrella protects the hair from rain. Jeremy was suddenly struck with the realization that, outside of these parties, he didn't really know Marcus that well. He had never seen him in any other social situations. He briefly attempted to imagine Marcus sitting down to a plate of carne asada with refried beans and Spanish rice at some low end Mexican restaurant, but the image was entirely too ridiculous to really seem believable. That was the thing about him that he liked so much: Marcus made reality seem absurd.

Looking up, Jeremy noticed there was a second eye painted on the kitchen ceiling.

"Another eye?" he asked, pointing to the eye. As if on cue, the Great Eye blinked. It filled the kitchen with a dry, scratching sound. Marcus nodded.

"Yup," he said. "It showed up sometime last night, while I was in the shower. I don't know what purpose it serves yet, but if it is anything like the other one, well . . . "

A bell rang in the freezer and Marcus smiled. He ripped the freezer door open and removed a long, slimy thing dripping with mucus. The thing writhed in his hands with insect life. Jeremy leapt back, terrified.

"What the hell is that?" he screamed.

"This," Marcus began, eyeing the larva coiled around his wrist with a childish delight, "is Christmas without Jesus; a sad and pointless holiday built around flashing lights and snowmen."

"What?" Jeremy asked. "What does that mean?"

Marcus rolled his eyes. "This is the whole reason we are here. It is the pure, unfiltered essence of this party, all of this strangeness.

HOUSE PARTY

Otherwise everything we've done tonight is nothing more than surrealist games."

"Isn't it just a surrealist game?"

Marcus shook his head and made his way into the living room. Jeremy followed awkwardly behind, unsure of what to expect. The Great Eye in the kitchen blinked again, raining a fine plaster dust down onto the kitchen table. Marcus smiled. The party was a success.

An old woman lay dead on the rug beside Ashley's shrunken, twisted corpse. Both bodies had become horribly dried out, resembling ancient Mexican mummies, tucked away for thousands of years in caverns and cliff walls, the arms and legs brittle, wrapped in flesh like yellowed Bible paper, the eyes withered and small, the brains rattling about in the skull. Centipedes crawled in and out of their bodily orifices. Several of the other guests had once again replaced their original faces, attaching them with whatever adhesives they could find. Duct tape, superglue, bubblegum, etc.

Marcus grabbed the old woman's corpse and lifted it easily from the floor with his free hand. Then he held it up to the Great Eye painted on the ceiling. In his other hand, the greasy larva writhed and squirmed, the coils of its tubular body gleaming in the soft light.

The floor began to rumble, shaking loose books on shelves, and a whole row of glass figurines, which smashed all over the floor and mingled with the looping coils of Mantis guts and feta cheese crumbles. From the bowels of the house there issued a deep, guttural moan, as though the very earth were sighing. The other guests began looking around uneasily. This was a wholly new development, and they felt unprepared.

The Great Eye painted on the ceiling blinked, this time releasing a heavy teardrop made of stagnant water and house paint. The teardrop landed directly on the body of the old woman, still held aloft by Marcus and the larva. Marcus leapt with an animal grace beside Ashley's brittle, crumbling body. Quickly, he placed the larva over her closed eyes and began crumbling the old woman into a fine powder, filling the room with the faint scent of burning leaves and cigarette smoke. When he had finished, he rubbed the dust over Ashley's lips, which had peeled back to reveal a row of elongated, yellow teeth.

As Jeremy watched, the larva began working its way down Ashley's throat, cracking the dried skin around her face and neck as it undulated just beneath the surface, whipped into some kind of sexual frenzy by the powdered antediluvian woman. He held back the urge to regurgitate the microwave burrito (bean and cheese) he had eaten for lunch. The house buckled and lurched underfoot. The other guests began clambering to their feet. They had not signed on for weirdness this heavy. None of the other parties had gone this far down the bizarre corridor, and they were all unsure as to how they were supposed to proceed.

Themes from parties past: Bring Your Own Beast, Cosby Show Cosplay, and the like.

Jeremy watched as Ashley's body began to swell with a luminescent life, glowing from deep within as though perched atop a high-powered streetlamp. Her every vein could be seen just below the surface of her skin, which had become moist and pulsating, writhing with life. The larva was plainly visible in the depths of her stomach muscles, curled into a tight ball, resembling a horribly deformed fetus. Beneath their feet, the house buckled once more. The Great Eyes painted on the ceiling blinked in tandem, and the walls shifted and dissolved, leaving behind a wet redness which pulsed and breathed. Jeremy felt as though he were standing in the center of a vast, humid throat.

Contrariwise, Ashley's body became increasingly less organic, less alive. The flesh on her arms shifted imperceptibly into long slats of white-painted wood. Her quantityimproved exponentially. Jeremy watched in paralyzed horror as her mouth stretched into an oblong scream silent as the grave, which was quickly replaced with a dusty old screen door, banging against the frame of her lips in a smooth summer breeze. Nails grew from her fingertips, and her legs welded together into what first looked like a tail, but then became a sprawling front porch, complete with rickety swinging bench, peeled paint, front windows with the faintest trace of blue eyes, blue-beautiful bug zapper littered below with the charred corpses of innumerable insects. Her body grew and grew, overtaking the living room and forcing the guests into the kitchen. They all looked to the Great Eye painted on the ceiling in the kitchen. It, too, had become anew. Where once there were the two-dimensional imperfections of acrylics, there was now a rotund eyeball, fully veined and wet, moist, real. Millions of dime-sized bacteria could be seen squirming over its surface.

The walls of the kitchen groaned, a deep, human sound, mournful and redolent. Jeremy looked to Marcus for guidance.

"What the hell is going on?" he asked.

Marcus shrugged.

"You mean you don't know?" Jeremy screamed, flailing his electrical taped arms about in a complicated gesture whose meaning was lost on all in attendance.

Marcus nodded, a strange, cat-like grin stretched across his face. "That's about the size of it," he said.

The guests screamed in terror. Confusion, it seemed, was the one thing for which they were completely unprepared. The Human Animal does not handle lack-of-direction with an overabundance of aplomb. Jeremy chanced a glance into the living room. Ashley had transformed entirely into a small house. He could see rain gutters running down her sides, over her porch. Two stone gargoyles perched over each side of the sloping roof, covered in thick layers of moss and mold. The living room had also completed its transformation from inanimate dwelling to massive, wet life form. The stairs bled shag carpet over Ashley's house-body, wrapping her swelling girth in a protective cocoon of mucus and building materials.

Jeremy looked back into the kitchen. All of the color had drained from his face. In fact, the preponderance of his features had shifted from horror to terror—a transition so subtle as to be almost totally without difference.

Looking at Marcus and the others, he said, "We have to get the hell out of here."

Marcus nodded. He walked over to the cellar door and pulled it open. A blast of intense heat filled the room, melting the majority of the gathered guests. Those who survived were covered from head to toe in third degree burns. Marcus snapped his fingers and pointed to the door.

"Right this way," he said, as though nothing had happened.

The guests formed a respectful line—single file—and made their way, one by one, down the steps. Jeremy waited impatiently at the end of the line. He tapped his foot, anxious to escape, for that was how he had come to understand the situation: one which needed to be escaped from. He chanced a glance through an open window. The view was startling. It was as though the landscape were being viewed from a window in an airplane. The landscape flew by at an incredible speed, blurring hills and gas stations with their illuminated signs reduced to brief flashes of neon. He walked over and peered out the window, stunned by what he saw.

The house had completely changed its outer appearance. Where once there were white painted boards and windows, there were now muscular arms and legs. At the end of the beefy arms, massive fists pumped, studded with rusty nails, the knuckles covered in a fine layer of fiberglass insulation. The house stomped over the earth, crushing houses and businesses underfoot, on its way to some unforeseeable location in the far corners of the world, where mythic beasts tore humans apart in gluttonous orgies of mutilation. Jeremy imagined beasts converging on the surreptitious spot, all of them brandishing strange implements of torture and frothing Technicolor saliva from their gaping maws. He imagined a world of dark carpet, shag, covered in dried gore. Huge birds swooped and dove from the rafters, pecking at empty skulls for any bits of moist life still tucked away in the crevices, which looked for all-the-world like deep fissures in the earth.

As the house walked on, crushing cars, swing sets, dog houses, trees, a Shell station, and a few grazing cattle, Jeremy stepped away from the window. He had seen enough. The line moved at a slow, almost amiable pace. No one any longer seemed to be in a hurry to flee the house. The heat from the cellar had disappeared almost as quickly as it had appeared, leaving behind only fragments of burnt corpses, and a thickness in the air that was noticeable but not unpleasant. Marcus stood at the door, ushering people in as they came. His face was devoid of all expression.

"The house is alive," Jeremy told him "It has arms and legs, and it is wandering through the countryside, crushing stuff."

Marcus nodded. "That sounds about right," he said. "If I'm not mistaken, then that means Ashley is a little house by now." He checked his watch. "Yeah, we should hurry."

Jeremy walked through the cellar door. Marcus followed behind, closing the door behind him. The other guests could barely be seen through the dark, faintly red light of the narrow stairway. They spoke in hushed, conspiratorial tones. Something flapped past Jeremy's ear, something big and dusty. Its wings husked the dry air like a vulture swooping up from a rotted donkey carcass in the heart of a vast and desolate desert. He swatted at the thing, missing it by a large margin. Marcus patted him on the shoulder, startling him.

"Scared?" he asked. Even in the dim light, Jeremy could tell he was grinning. He nodded in the dark.

"Hell yes, I'm scared," he whispered, "Aren't you?"

"Not really. I mean, I knew most of this would happen. It's not exactly what I pictured, but it's close enough."

Jeremy had a hard time believing this was all going according to plan. Nobody had a mind built to withstand this much weirdness. It just wasn't in a person. He shook his head again, this time in disbelief. "How could you possibly have known this was going to happen?"

"Like I said, it isn't exactly, to-the-letter what I thought was going to happen, but I knew it would be similar to this. Now, shut up. We're almost there."

Up ahead, Jeremy could see the other guests gathered around a tight, puckered hole. It stood about eight feet high, stretching from the mid-floor to the mid-ceiling, and gave off a rank, vinegar smell. It reminded Jeremy of outhouses in state parks. One of the guests reached out and stuck his finger through the tiny black dot in the center of the hole. He pulled his hand back and sniffed it.

"It's an asshole," he said.

"So are you," someone said. The other guests snickered.

"All right everybody, that's enough." Marcus sidled up next to the pucker ring and held his hands up, beckoning silence. "Now," he said," I want everyone to climb through the asshole in a single file. No pushing. We want this to go smoothly, both for the house, and for ourselves. Does anyone have any questions?"

No one had any questions. Marcus waited much longer than was necessary. Finally, a fat man with bright red hair and a baby-face held in place with thousands of safety pins raised his hand.

"Yes," Marcus said, nodding to the man.

"What are you waiting for?" the man asked. The other guests nodded, whispering things like, "good question," and "I was just about to ask that."

Without another word, Marcus reached over and pulled the hole open. A gush of stagnant air was pulled into the room, and Jeremy had to once again fight down the urge to void his lunch. A young woman stepped gingerly through the hole, followed in quick succession by everyone else. Finally, only Jeremy and Marcus remained.

Marcus smiled, holding the asshole open. Through the hole, Jeremy could see a vast parking lot full of cars and trucks. It looked like a used car dealership. The other guests were already making themselves at home, lying and talking on the hoods and in the truck beds. Marcus patted him on the shoulder.

"You're up, Sport," he smiled. Jeremy nodded and stepped through.

The fall was much farther than he had anticipated. He landed on his face, breaking his nose and ripping several layers of electrical tape from his neck and chest. One of the guests said, "Watch that first step, it's a doozy!" The other guests laughed. Looking around at them, Jeremy noticed they all had broken noses too. He didn't feel so bad after that. He got up and sat on the hood of a green Cadillac and looked at the house. It was huge and disgusting. The flesh of the house looked too pale to be real human skin, and it was covered all over in coarse, black hairs. From where he sat, he could just make out two massive butt cheeks, spread out like windows and separated in the middle by a screen door shaped asshole. The asshole pulsed and pushed outward, and Jeremy could see Marcus's upper torso easing its way out.

It looked very much like a house painfully crapping out a human being.

Marcus fell to the ground and broke his nose. Everybody laughed. It was quite funny. Blood ran down the front of his shirt.

Marcus joined Jeremy on the hood of the Cadillac. The two of them sat silently for several minutes, watching the house, too tired to speak. They watched as the house rolled over onto its back and thrust its chunky legs up into the air, exposing to everyone present its pulpy, red vagina.

Blood issued forth like the birth of a crimson river. The house screamed a horrible sound, like creaking doors and buildings exploding. Jeremy heard within the wail the drippings of a thousand faucets, feet hammering up and down limitless stairs, coat hangers clacking together in dusty closets. He shivered.

Suddenly, with a final bellow that shattered the windows of every car in the lot, something large and wooden erupted from the house-vagina.

"What. The. Fuck." Jeremy said. Marcus clapped. The other guests followed suit. Soon the whole parking lot was filled with sounds of riotous applause. The house lumbered awkwardly to its feet, tapped the thing with its foot, and with a satisfied sniff resumed its journey towards the mountains. Marcus grabbed Jeremy by the hand.

"Come on," he said. "Let's go check it out!"

Jeremy followed, too shocked to protest. He watched as the house-baby-thing came closer with their every step. It's a house, he realized.

HOUSE PARTY

He could see the rain gutters coated in a thin layer of mildew. He could see the wide windows, looking vaguely like two bright blue eyes.

Marcus led him gaily up the creaky porch. He pulled a key from his pocket and held it up for the guests to see. They clapped again—lightly—as he put the key in the lock and pulled the door open. He grabbed Jeremy's hand and pulled him inside.

Ashley waited in the living room, surrounded by balloons and party favors. On the far wall, there was a poster of a donkey, sans tail. A large yellow cake sat on the table, peppered with blue and white candles.

Jeremy looked around. He had no idea what had happened. Nothing made a bit of sense, but the cake looked delicious. He decided to have a piece. The other guests shuffled in behind him, taking in the lush decorations, patting Ashley on the back and telling her what a fine corpse she had been, complimenting her performance.

"Thank you," Ashley said. "Really, thank you so much."

From his corner by the window, Marcus smiled. The party was a success.

I CAN DO WHAT I NEED TO IN THE DARK

ADRIAN LUDENS

WONDER WHY there are suicide notes and murder confessions, but not vice versa. Whoever heard of a murder note? Not me. Sometimes a smell brings to mind a song. Sometimes a song brings to mind a memory. But a memory never conjures up a smell. I think that's unfair. Something should be done about that.

My wife. She's done a lot of dumb things. Irresponsible. Reprehensible. Clandestine in Constantinople. Told a lot of lies. Fudged a lot of truths. While I spent all night searching in Constantinople, she was balling in Istanbul. Such bull. Not as much fun as They make it sound.

Once, we lay abed watching a pornographic videotape I'd discovered in an abandoned house. In it, a man and woman made frenzied love while an intrusion of cockroaches swarmed over their naked, writhing bodies. The only two things that will survive a nuclear war are cockroaches and porn. Count on it. These cockroaches were skittering everywhere, like they were looking for somewhere to hide. I was clenched up tighter than a guy hoping to create a diamond from the lump of coal (Or at least a relatively presentable cubic zirconium.). It can be done, but not often. Usually it's just dung.

Dung beetles. Now *that* would be something to see. But no. We had cockroaches in the scene, cockroaches on screen. One raced across the screen and dropped onto the cigarette-scarred bureau. Another explored the upper reaches of the rabbit ears I've placed atop the set. They showed up in every photo we took of it, even though the joke wore thin.

The thin woman on screen shivered, the cockroaches skittered. They parted on the man's back. I imagined Moses parting the Red Sea, and briefly considered parting my hair down the middle as well. My wife turned to me then, and spit a cockroach onto my chest. Damn woman drove me batty. I thought that'd be a good thing, since bats eat bugs, but I struck out again. Bats eat certain bugs, but cockroaches are not on the menu. Not part of the batting order. Three strikes with my useless bat and I was out. Out of order. Out of ideas. Out of commission. Out and about seeking commiseration.

On the sidewalk (out and about seeking . . .) an invisible beam pulled me backward. My inner workings were infused with a sensation of exhilaration. The feeling it brought could be described as the opposite of debilitating. Someone nearby said, "Leave your canes and walkers, you won't need them now." I saw a ball. I saw a dog. As I sped by I reached down, picked up the ball, and threw it. The dog chased it, retrieved it, worried it, and presented it, but I was out of reach. The dog would have to find someone else to play fetch. I passed a young lady whose lips looked very fetching. I passed a man who wiped his mouth because he had been retching. The man at the next gate had been . . . well; in his hand he held an oversized swirl straw (the kind children love to drink their Kool-Aid with). I found that to be in poor taste.

At last the beam pulling me backward slowed and I stopped my journey (not that it came to an *end*, per se). I turned to see a wall of television screens in a store window. "Technology cannot help you," the newscaster on TV said.

"Coat Hanger Alley."

"Excuse me?"

Someone else stood nearby, his face covered in enough grime that only the whites of his eyes and the yellows of his teeth showed clearly.

"Coat Hanger Alley."

The newscaster onscreen looked irritated. A problem with the contrast left him looking irradiated. Or like his colon needed to be irrigated. Then: (colon) I wondered how asses had backed back into the back of my mind again for the first time.

"Religion can't help you."

"I don't know what you're trying to tell me." (Sell me.) Shel me; you over there where the sidewalk bends, but—

"Coat Hanger Alley is where your (her) problems began and begin."

"I don't know what . . . " I looked at the TV newscaster.

"Science can't . . . "

I looked away. He stopped.

"Time most assuredly does NOT heal all wounds." The filthy-faced man danced a lick, widened his stance. "But time DOES wound all heels."

I turned back to the newscaster to see if he'd seen. He scowled. "Psychoanalysis can't . . . "

I looked at the dancing man. He kicked his heels. Twirled around a lamppost.

" . . . can't help you. Goddamnit!" The newsman said. "If you don't pay attention, I can't help you!"

I gaped at the newsman. On screen he was waxing wroth.

"NO MORE WIRE HANGERS!" The filthy-faced dancing man howled into my face. My cheeks rippled like an astronaut in a g-force simulator. The television screens shattered and went dark. The man spun on his heel and departed for parts unknown. The grime from his face still hung in the air, like a lingering trace of a backward glare.

A great number of people are seated just behind me but it's no use looking. When I turn my head I know they'll be gone. My wife drinks. Drink, drank, drunk. She drowns her sorrows, her yesterdays and her tomorrows. I plead and plead but she does not heed.

Once, I looked over to see her trapped. She'd been trying to suck out the last drop, no bout adout it. Built up enough air pressure that she ended up getting pulled inside the bottle as a result. She tapped on the glass, a helium baby doll voice crying in the desert to avoid her just desserts. I'm nothing if not a devoted husband. I *had* to get her out.

So I smashed the bottle. I had to get her out didn't I? But the police didn't like the bruise on the side of her melon (melon balls soaked in Everclear, by watch and warrant) and I spent six days behind bars. She spent six days in them. I went down the rabbit hole but all I found were snakes.

It's gotten so bad I can't go anywhere without seeing someone who contributed to her TMJ. My life is a funhouse mirror maze but none of the reflections are of me. I can't look anybody in the eye anymore. I've tried to take the high road; she got high. I tried to find the needle in the haystack; she got pricked. Yet she's always on the offensive. I scurry to avoid confron . . .

(wait for it)

(wait for it . . .)

(here she comes)

("Brace yerself, laddie!")

TATION!

She does the crimes while I do the time. I can't find any sense in that. No damn sense at all. What all of this has to do with hi-balls, happy endings, and the high cost of living, scholars have yet to determine.

Nowadays, we have a son. I'm certain he's mine, but she's not convinced he's hers. I would try to tell her it doesn't work that way but it does no good to add peanut butter to cotton mouth.

His name is Weird because he was born with a tail. (But that's a tail/Tale for another day. And a good day it will be. As my Lakota friend Alvin would say, "Wašte." This is not pronounced 'waste', rhyming with 'post haste' but instead sounds like 'wash day' which is a good day indeed.)

I get my wish and the boy will have to change his name to Ward. As in 'Of the State.' There's a good Native-sounding name. Perhaps I suggest as much in my murder note. Or suicide confession.

He got a ride home from school with some strangers who held a slightly different set of values; they blinded him with grapefruit spoons and empty rhetoric during the drive. He sat at the table wrestling with numeric values. Of his mother I saw no sign. Nor did he.

"What's seventy plus—never mind."

"One hundred and forget it."

"I see."

Clearly he did not. But I (eye) did.

"Tell me the Who, What, When, Where, and Sometimes Y of your future, Weird." (To make a complete circuit of the Five W's.)

"I hear dogs mocking." My son leaned back, traced one open palm with a bleeding hangnail finger. "They're warning me to warsh my hands.

Lather up with hot, soapy water to kill all the snakes and germans. There's so many germans on my fingertips they make me feece. I'm afraid to bite them."

The little liar. "What elts?"

"I won't have to hang out with kids who are toby, or act like toeballs. I will get rich and crich and sit behind my own monogamy desk with feet kicked back and smoking a bick. Girls will line up to show me their pollypeetings."

I understand his words, but not the sentiment. I masked my stupidity with a grin. "What elts?"

"There is no 't' in else, Father."

I put my smile away for a more suitable occasion. My son had become imprisoned within his chair. I could see him behind the bars. But they called them slats. Wide ones are known as splats. That's what they said anyway. 'They' being the police. The slats were for Weird, the bars were for me. We both got carried away. Déjà vu all over again, for the first time.

Eleventy-teen years later they released/sentenced me to be a prisoner of the Real World. We tried to rebuild, my wife and I. Big Shot and Miniature Man. We had a full house, what with me, myself and I, all our collective demons, plus her and all her baggage squeezed in under one roof.

We found the perfect place. It had a trap door and a sinister-looking painted portrait with the eyes cut out. We took turns standing between the walls staring at each other.

I learned to avoid most of the ugliness. At the beginning of our (my) post-prison home hunting we'd found an abandoned house. Seemed like a potential fixer-upper until I saw the lump under the rotting blanket at the back of a fly-cloud closet. I just backed away. I still do. Take it back, and back away. Backtrack, backpedal, backstroke.

Doggy paddle, tread water ("How long can you tread water, Noah?"), do the dead man's float. Pray that's a log and not a crocodile. But if it (she) is, begin to pray. Verily I say unto you, "You shall be the prey."

I made a habit of staying up late. I'd stare at the sky, wondering where the sun hid itself until it dawned on me. Then I'd stumble to bed, exalted and exultant, only to wake to shades of grey, the bed heaped with blankets, heavy as a coffin lid.

I CAN DO WHAT I NEED TO IN THE DARK

I try so damned hard.

My wife hosted a party the day Weird died. My wife, social butterfly, black widow, praying/preying mantis all in one.

The women in her theater troupe had assembled at our home for their Recognitions. My wife was all aflutter. I suppose that was to be expected. The women had congregated in a room separated from the rest of the house by a vault-like door.

My wife seemed to be enjoying her moment so I bore the news alone. (Go along to get along was the kinder, gentler me.)

The boy did something wrong. Perhaps a sin of pride or anger but I don't know for certain. The punishment had already been carried out. There was a man at the door. He stood. He waited. He said we had to "(Self) identify (with) the body." I could read between the lines. But I could NOT interrupt my wife. We all must remain industrious, aspire to acquire, and never break the rules. *Rules subject to change without notice.*

I left him standing on the stoop. I found something else to do. I remembered my wife's party, the women in her theater troupe. My wife put their head shots on display in our living room, though the party itself was behind locked doors. I got my camera. I took pictures of their pictures. (I photographed their photographs.) I knew they'd want copies. I needed their contact information.

I went to the door where the party was. I tried the knob but found it cold and unyielding. (Honey? Is that you?) This mirrored the mood of the women within—toward me, that is. That was. That ever shall be. I had hoped to be allowed access. To be passed around, even; to use and be used. Not all of the women were beautiful, but some were. I would have gone willingly. I would have done or said whatever they asked of me, if only. This humble man would/could/should have risen to a new low. But no.

Inside, I knew, was a man. Just one. Playing the role of the Dentist. Filling. Cavities. Filling cavities. How I envied him.

I heard laughter and music from within; a muted trumpet and sliding double bass. My wife burst from the locked room and staggered past me. In her hurry to leave me behind she knocked over some (aspired to and) acquired items from an end table. I put things right and she returned with her arms full: A bottle of wine. Another of champagne. Flavored lubricant. A gleaming meat cleaver.

Her left pupil had fully dilated. I felt curiously off balance when she looked at me.

Which side of her brain is she thinking with?

?with thinking I am brain my of side which

My wife tipped her head at our various antique sound systems interspersed throughout the living room.

She fixed her gaze on a palm-sized device lying on the corner of an end table. I pressed the 'Play' button. Her curt voice issued from its tiny speaker.

"I'm taping a tape and recording a record. Keep them going until I get back."

I started to reply, to observe obsequiousness, but she had already returned to the party. I remembered then that I had needed to tell her something important. Good grief! How had I forgotten? I had meant to let her know what had just happened.

I hurried after her but she closed the door in my face.

I had wanted to tell her that I took photographs of her photographs. She would have wanted to know that.

We've draped ourselves in shawls of sorrow. When they begin to fray, we're torn between letting them unravel and fastidiously mending them. We also still have our skeletons cohabitating in crowded closets. Sometimes we drag them out to pick at the gristle hanging from the bones.

"Hey, Dial Tone, you're phoning it in."

"Then stop answering my calls."

Eat. Work. Sleep. Repeat.

"I didn't like your beard at first but it grew on me."

"You stupid cow, it grew on *me*."

Earn. Spend. Borrow. Repeat.

"Don't be jealous because he's huge. It felt like getting fucked by a bar stool."

"You would know."

Wash. Rinse. Spit. Repeat.

Now she's smashed all the light bulbs in the house. Thinks that will

I CAN DO WHAT I NEED TO IN THE DARK

stop me from having any bright ideas. Au contraire. I can do what I need to in the dark.

It's our 13th anniversary—a special date. Am I in the mood to celebrate? Or to suffocate under a pillow of self-hate? I don't want to eat the crow that's on my serving dish.

Both glasses are filled with wine. "I'd like to propose a toast."

Both glasses are filled with whine. Our cups runneth over.

Both glasses of wine are filled with ICD-10. ("In-con-theeve-ah-bull!") Strychnine.

Enough poison to kill a colony of rats. Poison enough to kill a horde of mice. Or a murder of crows, were they to eat the poisoned rats or mice. Purchased by my farmer father to kill moles a decade before they changed the active ingredient to zinc phosphide. My wife has moles. I hate them so! Or rather, I hate them, so . . .

A toast, my Love, my Loathing, my Sanity Clause . . . and we both know there ain't no—But shhh.

Chug-A-Lug.

Finished? As am I. And so we are both finished. I've composed something to mark the occasion. Not a sonnet. Not a poem. Not even a dirty limerick. It's a murder note.

Or is it a suicide confession?

Read it quickly, before the spasms begin. Before the convulsions kick in we can look forward to lockjaw and risus sardonicus. God that was a great flick. I can see his face. Grinning.

"That's going to be you and me, wife."

It will be good to finally have a reason to smile again.

LIGHT AMPLIFICATION BY STIMULATED EMISSION OF RADIATION

ANDREW WAYNE ADAMS

I WANT EVERYTHING, but what I want the most is to fix my eyes. I have been abysmally myopic since prepubescence. As a child I often mistook my mother for a columnar puff of cotton. The human face resembled wads of rotting ham, and cityscapes were a dabbed patchwork of matte greasepaint. The hands of my little girlfriend bobbed in the air like huge translucent shrimp from the ocean bottom. I could never read the storybooks my friends were swearing by.

To see a thing clearly, it had to be a millimeter from my eye. Exactly a millimeter. As a boy I would sit for hours with some small trinket held just so—a pebble or breadcrumb or beetle—marveling at the sharpness and nuance of life in focus. The practice gave me headaches daily. I coexisted with the headaches, the way a feral child can feel the freezing cold and not think it into a torture; it was only later, once my parents really got a hold of me, that I learned a headache was something to be hated. And so I stopped the practice of bringing things into focus.

I got glasses when I was ten. I wonder why it took so long. The lenses were five inches thick, the circumference of dinner plates. Their weight necessitated a complex system of scaffolding—a polyhedral cage of girders and wires encircling my head like an antique diving helmet modeled on the skull of a (demonically large) housefly. I could never figure out how to take the thing off. I slept in it, bathed in it. A small door in front allowed me to eat. But I rarely ate. Once a day I slurped some curdled milk through a long straw, and that was it. My body grew thin, a burnt matchstick bent beneath the massive metallic seedhead of my glasses.

I passed puberty. I passed my exams, graduated high school, turned down an invitation to a pizza party (it would have been my first), and went to computer programming boot camp. Now I write code on a typewriter and get paid biweekly. I sit on a metal folding chair in my cubicle of rough particle board. I sweat inside my insectile helmet, staring out through its portholes at a world warped almost into true. My eyes have withered into dingleberries.

A boy brings newspapers to our cubicles. I never read mine. But I do collect the coupons from them. The coupons masquerade as obituaries. I think I'm the only one who knows about them. Everyone else thinks the obituaries are just obituaries. Could be the coupons are encoded holographically—latent in the surface text—and only certain eyes can reconstruct them. Eyes like mine.

I have enough coupons for a free bicycle. Or for two free unicycles. Or for half a canoe, or two sessions with a (demonically large) masseuse, or one fifty-slot toaster, or fifty rides on any rollercoaster at Woe World. And those are all things I want—I want everything—but none of them are what I want the most. So I'm waiting. Saving more coupons. I almost have enough. If only more people would die.

The code I've been writing at work, it has something to do with lasers. We've been on this project for five years. It gives me headaches.

One day a school bus floods with gastric acid, digesting the children inside. Killing them. They appear in next week's paper as obituaries. Hundreds of them. (It was a very *long* school bus.)

I have enough coupons now.

I leave work early—sneaking out of my cubicle, taking the stairs down to the street—clutching my briefcase to my chest. My briefcase full of obituaries.

My briefcase is a plastic shopping bag.

On the street, I blink. Blink. Blink. The street shimmers; it bubbles and crawls, as if made of chameleons. My breath is loud inside the cage of my glasses. I walk downhill, away from the sun. A parade comes up the street. It swallows me. I emerge from its anus. Feral children follow behind it, dragging blocks of ice. I blink. Downhill. I am skeletal and shriveled; my eyes are dingleberries. I trip on a chameleon—fall to the

157

sidewalk—roll downhill. Like a bouncing ball. A goalie stops me from entering his net; he deflects me into an alley, where an open doorway swallows me. My screams are loud inside the cage of my glasses. I blink, and the huge steel fishbowl on my head blinks with me. I am somewhere cold and sunless.

A doctor's office.

I am exactly where I meant to be.

I examine my briefcase. The plastic shopping bag is ripped in several places, obituaries sticking out—but none lost.

The receptionist tells me to sign in. I do. She waits two seconds, then calls my name. She says, "Why are you here?"

Too profound a question. I lift my briefcase to display the obituaries spilling out of it. I'm here to be seen. It's raining inside the cell around my head. I'm here to get what I want the most. To get it for free. I want the receptionist to receive me into a lighter world. I hope she has the eyes to see things my way. To see them free from their seeming flatness. I hope she doesn't think the obituaries are just obituaries.

She looks at me. She is like my mother, or like the little girlfriend of my prepubescence, or like my single female coworker. She takes one of the obituaries, looks it over. It's a little boy's. Ian McCartney, age 9, biochemistry major (minor in holography) at Our Lady of Sorrows Elementary School. One of those who died in the very *long* school bus. In his picture, his face is ham.

The receptionist hands back the obituary, glances at my briefcase full of them, says, "Looks like you have enough for the free surgery. That why you're here?"

I nod. Yes! Nodding, my glasses bounce, their structure like a giant fossilized blowfish made of coat hangers and windowpanes.

The receptionist says, "The doctor will see you now."

She turns into the doctor.

"I see," she says, looking at the bear trap on my head. "You want to fix your eyes, don't you?"

Yes! Yes!

My glasses fill with rain. I open the small door in front, and water gushes out like words. It soaks the doctor, and she removes her shirt. Her nipples are eyeballs, then blocks of ice.

She says, "This should take no time at all." To make her statement literal, she pulls a gun and shoots the clock on the wall. The clock becomes a corpse, decomposes instantly. All moments occur at once, holographically superimposed. She says, "We have all the time in the world." No time; all time. She points the gun at me.

She fires a laser beam.

The laser passes unimpeded through my glasses. It hits my eyes. It shaves tissue from my corneas, reshaping them. Kissing my retinal flowers with photonic pollen.

Curing my myopia!

The doctor removes her pants. Her vagina is a wad of rotting ham. Her hands bob in the air like huge translucent shrimp from Venus.

I can't see!

Of course—I'm still wearing my glasses, making everything out of focus for my cured eyes.

I grab at the cage of my glasses, trying (like a million times before) to tear them off. For some reason I think it will work this time. It doesn't. My eyes (no longer dingleberries, after the surgery; blueberries, now) look out through the huge, heavy lenses at a world warped out of true. It gives me a headache.

I lunge at a shred of cotton that I take to be the doctor. I want to strangle her for doing this to me. The cotton sidesteps, and I fall to the floor. The doctor stands over me. I look up at the rotting ham of her vagina. It looks like my mother's face.

She says, "You still have coupons left. Enough for a free prosthesis."

And she fits me with a new pair of glasses.

The glasses fit over my old glasses, a second shell around the first. Each correcting for the other. With this addition, I can no longer lift my head. Immobilized on the floor. Anchored by a cancellation.

I have to get back to work. Surely my boss has noticed my absence by now. My typewriter sitting cold, a fragment of code abandoned on the page. Possibly my cubicle is glowing, as if irradiated, to alert of my desertion.

The doctor watches me writhe on the floor. She says, "We could fit you with a full-body prosthesis. To support the weight of your redundant augmentations. But, you have no coupons left."

I blink at her. My eyes are healthy blueberries buried in useless apparatus. This is not what I wanted.

"There is one special coupon you could use.. . . . "

No! I'm saving that one!

The doctor unhinges her jaw and vomits gastric acid on me. I struggle for an instant, then decompose, flying apart into countless laser beams. Folding back into flatness.

A boy brings the newspaper. The doctor takes it and flips to the obituaries. There I am. In my picture, my face is a (demonically large) eyeball. My obituary is very *long*.

The doctor clips it out. This special coupon is good for anything.

Anything.

The doctor fits me with a full-body prosthesis to support the weight of my glasses. My empty glasses. The prosthesis hangs on empty space, a complex system of scaffolding encircling nothing. I'm nowhere. Because I'm nowhere, I'm everywhere, and because I'm everywhere, I'm a millimeter from everything. Exactly a millimeter.

All is in focus.

The full-body prosthesis gets up and goes back to work.

⊢HƎ 'ƎND Oꟻ ⊢HƎ WOЯLD' ꟼ⟶Ǝ

WOL-VRIEY

THE CHIEF ƎXECUTIVE sat atop his pink cardboard elephant in his bulletproof cubicle, signing papers with an intense expression on his face.

A middle-aged man with thinning brown hair, he wielded his pen with a violent flourish.

The Chief Executive's cardboard elephant moved about in a semblance of life. Every now and then it turned its attention away from the tree it was tethered to—and which it was busy defoliating—and trumpeted at the mass of salesmen surrounding the booth.

When it did this, the Chief Executive would raise his head for a few moments and gently pat the elephant's head before scribbling something on it with a red marker.

Then he'd pick up his pen again and resume signing papers.

Jack walked warily past the giant executive in the giant cubicle, visible from wherever one might be in town. The Chief Executive made him uneasy. Jack had so far been unable to work out why.

"Sir, do you care for some . . ."

Jack paused for a moment to see what the salesman was selling. The man was faceless, the front part of his head a perfectly smooth featureless expanse. He was dressed in the regulation yellow suit all World Inc. salesmen wore. He eagerly pulled out a pack from his bag.

"Instant Kids," he said, speaking through his ears. "Just soak in water and leave overnight."

Jack studied the glossy pack. It had the faces of three children printed on it: one Caucasian, one Black, one Asian. He couldn't tell their sexes.

"All our kids have a one year World Incorporated guarantee," the salesman said. "If they defecate more than once a day, you get your money back."

"Even once a day's too much," Jack said, in a hurry to depart. Other nearby salesmen had noticed their transaction and were coming around.

"That, sir," a voice said behind Jack, making him jump, "is why we, World Inc., have developed our new 'low poo' baby food formula."

Jack turned. As expected, it was another faceless man.

This new salesman held up a plastic can. "Feed them *this*, and World Inc. Instant Kids are guaranteed to only need to use the toilet once every *three* days." While he spoke, breeze ruffled his green hair and his ears twitched like lips.

Jack stole a miserable look at the now distant figure of the Chief Executive atop his elephant, wondering how he'd let himself get trapped so easily.

"I'll take a pack of kids and your low-shit formula," he said finally. He was about to ask for a discount, then decided against it—the last time he'd tried for one, the salesman had instead talked him into taking out a health insurance policy for his soap demon.

Rather than go directly home, Jack headed for his local bar.

II

In the bar, Jack sat drinking a cold beer at the table he'd made his personal property over the years. The table was by the street window. View of it from outside was obscured by the bar sign painted on the glass, and also by a placard letting passersby know what that evening's special was.

The bar was dark and smoky.

The woman at the bar was dark and smoky too. That was what Jack first noticed about her—how well she fit in with the décor. She seemed almost an ornament.

THE 'END OF THE WORLD' PIE

She was alone, not yet drinking. Jack gave her the eye. She looked away. Jack promptly forgot about her.

Jack had a lot on his mind. Dr. Nicks had just told him he had only six months left to live.

Jack had lung cancer. How he'd gotten it, he couldn't fathom—he'd never smoked.

The cancer had eaten so far into Jack's lungs now that there was no point doing anything. He'd be recycled in six months and that was that.

Dr. Nicks would have preferred he stay in hospital, but, the odd thing was, Jack wasn't in any pain. None at all.

The doctor had thought Jack was shitting him, but he wasn't.

Jack *was* having slight difficulty in breathing, which was what had made him go for a checkup in the first place, but otherwise, he was in no discomfort.

Dr. Nicks had given Jack a prescription for all the pills he thought he'd need, then sent him home, telling him to check back in once every two weeks.

How do you deal with the certain knowledge that you're dying? In Jack's case he'd finally decided to forget he was, and just have fun.

He had several hundred thousand dollars saved up, so he could travel. He had no family to leave anything to, so he could spend it all.

Damn, he thought, sipping his beer, *with what's going on, I don't even feel like leaving a dime to a cancer foundation.*

"Buy a girl a drink?" Jack looked up to see it was her—the woman at the bar.

"I'm Aida," she said with a smile, offering him her hand.

"Jack." He shook the proffered hand, indicated that she sit. The evening seemed to be looking up.

He signaled the waiter to come take her order. A Bloody Mary.

Aida's drink arrived and they sipped together in silence for a while.

Jack took the opportunity to study her. There was something unhealthy about her looks that he found comforting. Misery loves company. He half expected her to tell him she had cancer too.

The best way Jack could describe Aida was to say she looked sleazy. In a good way. Black hair, brown eyes with eyeliner smudged just enough to give that "wasted rock star" look, high cheekbones, purple lipstick.

He couldn't place her skin tone. She seemed neither Caucasian nor Negro nor Asian.

They took Aida's car back to his place. Jack would otherwise have walked; his home was near the bar.

Aida's car was a World Inc. "special import" model from Neo Korea.

It was shaped like an egg laid on its side—the wider end forming the automobile's rear.

The car's trunk had a deep vertical cleft disrupting its oval smoothness. To Jack, this indentation made the vehicle look like a set of buttocks when viewed from behind.

Kansas—a weird woman Jack had dated several months back—had driven a similar car. Its sleekness magnetized women.

Jack had a strange moment in the parking lot.

About to enter Aida's car, he spotted the silhouette of a woman on its front door.

The shadow moved quickly from front to rear door, then slid across the trunk and disappeared. Jack turned round to see the woman who'd made it, but she'd disappeared.

He was spooked: something about the shadow had seemed familiar.

They got home and rushed into Jack's bedroom.

Before they lay down, Jack patted his bed several times to clear it of butterflies. These took to the air chirping musically. The noise they made was the primary reason Jack had gotten them, their tinkling melodies helped him fall asleep.

"My ass," Aida said when they were both naked.

Jack gripped her buttocks and fondled them appreciatively.

"Not *that*. I mean—*fuck* my ass. I *adore* anal."

Jack obliged her. They did it doggy style. "Harder!" she kept moaning, while her hand worked between her labia.

Pulling out of Aida's anus afterwards, Jack saw that his erection was coated with blood. More crimson liquid spurted out of her ass once he'd fully withdrawn his penis.

Jack was extremely scared. Aida was bleeding profusely—like she was having her menses from the wrong opening. Jack's groin was a bloody mess.

THE 'END OF THE WORLD' PIE

"Shit, Aida, I'm sorry. But you kept saying to fuck you harder."

"It's okay," she replied dreamily, already half-asleep, totally unconcerned that he'd hurt her.

Blood kept dribbling from Aida's anus.

Alarmed, Jack shook her. "Wake up! We need to get you to a doctor!"

She turned to face him, her brown eyes momentarily aglow with an indecipherable expression. "How sweet of you. It's okay—just a minor rectal tear—happens to me all the time; I'll be good as new by morning."

Then she looked at the blood splattered all over his lower torso and laughed.

Jack had no chance to ask her what was funny. She was already snoring.

"I don't like your new girlfriend one bit," the soap demon said when Jack picked it up.

"Shut up and soap," he told it. He dunked it underwater and held it there so it got the point.

It soaped, its body turning slippery, filling the water with suds.

Jack tried to wash Aida's blood off himself, to no avail. It stuck to him like paint.

No, it's more than that, he thought, looking at himself in the mirror. *It looks part of me, like an oversized birthmark—like I'm turning piebald groin first.*

"Oops, something's wrong," the soap demon said, its bulbous eyes looking Jack over studiously.

Jack really wished it would shut up. It was frog-shaped, its color light pink mixed in with streaks of green.

The soap demon had been belonged to Jack's ex-wife, Kim. He'd hated it all the while they'd been married—it talked too much. Kim had left it behind when leaving so he'd have a constant reminder of how much she hated him now.

Jack was unsure why he hadn't yet thrown the demon away.

"What don't you like about Aida?" he asked the soap demon.

"Not really sure—she just gives me a bad feeling." It grinned a wide froggy grin. "I can tell she's *dirty,* though. With a capital D."

Jack gave up trying to wash the blood off himself.

"I bought some kids," he said.

"You're not using me to soap some baby's shitty ass," the soap demon growled. "That totally voids my warranty."

"Relax, I'm not having them. I'll give them to someone for their birthday."

The soap demon's aggrieved look reverted back to its usual gargoyle-like one. "I almost forgot to mention, there were some salesmen here earlier. Door-to-door."

Jack gaped at it in horror. *"Door-to-door?"* Was there no escape from World Inc.?

Haunted by the news that World Inc. was encroaching even more deeply into his life, Jack made his way back into the bedroom.

Aida had now stopped bleeding from her anus. Her buttocks and thighs were however coated with a glistening red.

After a look out the window, down at the street where the nighttime salesmen were energetically hawking their nighttime wares, Jack lay down beside her, avoiding the wet part of the bed.

III

Morning came, and all the blood, including that on Jack and the bed sheets, was gone. Jack might have imagined it all.

Aida made no attempt to go anywhere. Jack had nowhere to go, so that was fine with him.

While Aida made toast, Jack snared some of his butterflies in a net.

"I'm AIDS," Aida said while they ate.

Jack looked at her. "What?"

Aida repeated herself. "I'm AIDS."

Jack saw she wasn't joking. Her face was dead serious. In addition, she looked even less healthy this morning than she had last night. Still attractive, but sick-looking.

Jack could well believe she was diseased.

"You're saying you've given me AIDS?" He picked up a large butterfly and smeared it on a slice of toast. The creature squeaked a musical trill of protest then splattered into the creamy yellow paste that World Inc. had promised it would.

Jack felt oddly detached from Aida's announcement. Also, he felt no rancor. His only thought was that she'd been a couple of days too late. The most she'd done was accelerate the speed of his death.

Aida frowned. "Yes and no. I *am* AIDS. Getting it was *your* fault. You should have used protection while fucking me."

Jack placed his toast on the table and looked at her like she was a loon. "You're saying *you're* a disease?"

Aida picked a butterfly out of the net. Squinting, she read out the tiny writing printed beneath the barcode on its abdomen. "Low cholesterol: World Inc. Farms guarantee you'll live stronger, for longer."

She shrugged, then squashed the dairy insect onto her toast.

She took a bite, chewed it for while before replying him. "Yeah."

Jack considered kicking her out, but didn't. Other than for the ubiquitous salesmen, he'd had no one to talk to for a while.

"Prove your claim," was all he said finally, certain that would shut her up.

Instead, Aida reached out a slim hand and touched his forehead.

Jack's mind exploded. His head was suddenly filled with images of the millions dead and dying of AIDS around the world, the despair of those lying in hospital beds, the fresh terrors of those who'd just discovered they were HIV positive, the stigma the disease's sufferers everywhere experienced. She was . . . she was . . .

She was every virus in every ravaged body, as well as the summation of them all, and . . .

"You *are* AIDS," he said, his mind reeling when she removed her hand from his head. "How?"

"Don't bother yourself about that," she said. "It's hard to explain. Best accept the fact I just am. Works for me."

Jack stared at her for a while.

"But you're female." Try as he might, he was unable to shake the feeling that there was something sexist about the fact that the world's least favorite chaperone was a woman.

"Only because you're a hetero male. If you'd been homosexual, I'd be a man."

Her features slowly altered, till she'd become a *he*. The nude young man now sitting beside Jack had the same facial features as Aida—a twin.

He grinned at Jack, then reached down a hand to grip his manhood and stroke it to erection.

"Please stop doing that," Jack said. "You're making me very uncomfortable."

"Why?" The young man continued masturbating himself. "Don't tell me you're tempted. Are you bi?"

Jack didn't reply. He stared stonily at the young man till the other's grin disappeared. A few subtle adjustments and Aida was back with him again.

Jack heaved a sigh of relief. "No more freakiness okay? I'm currently fighting to remain in the general radius of a psychiatrist's definition of sane. You may notice I'm not exactly overreacting to your giving me HIV."

Aida wagged a correcting finger at him. "AIDS. You're getting it direct from the source; you skipped the aperitif, dove straight into the fatal main course."

Jack grimaced. "You sound like a bad radio jingle. Illness I can handle. Just don't become a guy again."

"Okay, you homophobic prick. But gay is, as the name suggests, fun and games."

"Shut up!"

IV

Jack was only recently divorced from Kim.

He hadn't bothered calling her up with news of his anticipated passing. He expected she'd tell him to go jump off the Chief Executive. A very acrimonious divorce it had been.

They'd met a year ago, at Jack's favorite bar.

A catchy jingle for World Inc.'s then newly-released instant infants had been playing in the background:

'Artificially incubated then dehydrated,
Nine months of fuss gone thanks to us,
Want a son or daughter? Just add hot water,
Instant Kids, Instant Kids,
No need to get pregnant like your parents did.'

Finding the pale redhead with the pert nose rather attractive, Jack had chatted her up.

Kim Krash was a car freak, entranced by anything on four wheels. She'd raced and lost and won races since she was a teen, and got high just smelling gasoline.

THE 'END OF THE WORLD' PIE

(Kim had developed her interest in cars after suffering—at the age of twelve—a horrendous automobile accident in which both her legs were crushed. She'd have wound up paraplegic, but World Inc. provided her A LOT of free surgical repair work.)

Jack quickly realized there was something neurotic about Kim's obsession with automobiles.

Neurotic, because she now closely followed the auto accident stats on TV. She kept an "accident diary" in which she logged car crashes, arranging them by year, location, and number of fatalities recorded.

Jack had been the one who'd decided to end their relationship.

Once he'd married Kim, things had gone downhill fast.

Kim was stiflingly possessive, and a horrendous nag.

Their relationship had quickly degenerated to the point where Jack had slapped her about brutally one night.

The next day he'd filed for divorce. Not because he'd stopped loving her, but because he still did—Jack was certain that if he didn't leave Kim, her endless whining would one day lead to his murdering her.

What Kim hated Jack for now was his refusal to call off the divorce despite her insistence that she'd prefer to stay with him even if he beat her occasionally—as long as he loved her—rather than them both going their separate ways.

That was totally illogical to Jack—made no sense at all. But he hadn't imagined it—Kim had told him so to his face.

And more than once, and with the tears in her eyes proving how serious she was.

Jack had felt super-guilty about leaving her, as if he'd abandoned the responsibility of being man enough to resist the urge to hit her.

But he saw no point in hanging around such strong temptation.

V

"You're already dying of cancer. What difference does one more disease make?"

Jack looked at Aida sharply, wondering how she knew.

She shrugged, but gave no explanation, saying instead, "We'll cure you, my sisters and I. But we need you to do something for us first."

Jack listened patiently while she explained what she/they wanted. It made no sense. He wondered if he wouldn't be better off with the mad salesmen outside.

"You want me to mind a *pie* for you?"

She nodded. "Uh huh."

"Why *me*?" seemed the valid question to Jack.

Not to Aida apparently. She exploded in anger. "That has got to be the dumbest question in the world! And *why not* you?! And if not you, *who*?! It has to be *someone*! And whoever it was would now be asking me the same stupid question, wouldn't they?!"

Jack acceded that she had a valid point.

He agreed to do what she wanted. He had no real choice.

"Good," she said. "Let's get dressed. We're expected on the other side of town."

Before leaving, Jack remembered to take a couple of butterflies in for the soap demon. As it liked him to do, he let them fly free in the bathroom.

"Thanks," the soap demon said, snaring one of the butterflies from the air with a soapy prehensile tongue.

Jack stared for a while at the pretty bubbles this capture left in the air, then exited, shutting the door behind him so the demon could enjoy its meal.

After fighting their way through a mass of salesmen hawking gym-gear and gym-wear, they again took Aida's car, despite Jack's protests that doing so would make them easy targets for salesmen selling car insurance.

Once again, Jack saw the shadow of the mystery woman run across the car's surface as he was about to enter it. Once again, she was gone when he turned to see who it was. Once again, he was struck by the same strange feeling of familiarity.

"World Incorporated: The Whole Planet Is Our Office," the huge sign above the Chief Executive's huge cubicle boasted.

THE 'END OF THE WORLD' PIE

The Chief Executive had been changed.

Now it was a green crocodile with yellow digital clocks for eyes and wearing a red suit with green buttons.

It still had human hands though, and still sat atop an elephant, though now the elephant was a flesh-and-blood one, green in color with bright yellow and blue tassels on its sawn-off tusks.

Rather than feeding off a tree like its predecessor, it was eating a huge sandwich that it gripped in the split tip of its trunk. Beside it was a large pitcher with "MILK" stenciled on its side in long white letters.

A HUGE pink bird with a red double-sided LCD television for a head sat beside the executive cubicle. On its two screens, visible to the entire town, were tabled the world's daily broken records.

World Inc. competed only with itself—the records shown were those of its various branches.

Jack had a quick look. New York was winning again, followed by Tokyo. Buenos Aires and Johannesburg were tied for third, Peking and Berlin behind them.

Occasionally, the Chief Executive's eyes changed from displaying the time to show a pair of names—the name in the crocodile's right eye that of its subordinate making the most sales, that in its left eye the subordinate with the worst performance.

Once they even showed the latest tennis scores.

Aida steered the car on a winding track through the mob of salesmen filling the road so she didn't hit any of them.

"Damn!" she groaned when the Chief Executive's eyes showed the tennis scores, "Olga Pavleva lost *again* to that Spanish slut. I should travel to Madrid and give the bitch AIDS!"

She stole a quick glance at Jack. "Sorry, I didn't hear what you were saying."

"Where are we going? You never said."

"To see Kansas."

Jack looked at her in surprise. "You know Kansas?"

"Um um." She smiled at his not-understanding.

VI

Jack had met Kansas four months before, in the same bar he'd met Aida, and in the same circumstances—she'd been alone and he'd bought her a drink.

Though pretty, with delectable lips and lovely blue eyes, Kansas had looked as unwell as Aida. She'd been dressed head to toe in black, including a black shawl.

She was busty, with a fat ass.

And on the prowl.

Once Jack hit on her, she'd made no bones about letting her intentions be known. "I wanna get fucked," she'd whispered throatily into his ear. "Your place or mine?"

They'd taken her car back to his place. It was the same "egg" model as Aida's. Now Jack remembered more carefully, it might even have been the *same* car; he seemed to recognize the placement of the interior decorations.

At Jack's place, Kansas had gotten weird.

She'd only wanted oral, and that with all her clothes on—including her shawl.

"Don't!" she'd shriek and pull away each time Jack tried to touch her anywhere other than her face.

Then she'd banned him from touching her at all—he'd had to keep his hands on the sofa the whole time.

Jack pointed out the obvious: "How am I going to satisfy you if you won't take off your pants? How do we have sex if you won't let me touch you?"

"That's all right," she'd replied, bending to kiss him. "I've got a sensitive mouth."

She'd been telling the truth. Satisfying Kansas was easy—it was the first time Jack had ever met a woman who orgasmed simply from being French-kissed.

And she hadn't been faking either. Kansas's orgasmic shudders transmitted to Jack while they kissed. Other than for the lack of physical stimulation, he could tell that she was coming just like any other woman who'd had an orgasm with him.

Her body tensed and relaxed and trembled. She had a look in her eyes like she was dying, but loving it.

Afterwards, Kansas fellated Jack. She gave incredible head. The soft, glove-like feel of her mouth on Jack's cock was to die for.

But the first part—*kissing* Kansas—had been a problem. She had literally the worst breath—bar none—that Jack had ever encountered anywhere.

THE 'END OF THE WORLD' PIE

Kansas's mouth stank like a million cats had expired in the midst of their shit inside it. And Jack knew the reason cats buried their feces was because it stank horribly.

Jack had been too tipsy the first few times he and Kansas had sex to really care about her bad breath, but when she'd started visiting him at home rather than meeting him at the bar, it became an issue.

Truth be told though, he'd still not have broken up with her if not for her weird behavior concerning her clothes.

"No," she'd say, seductively but firmly, giving him a vomit-inducing kiss. "The threads stay on. No matter what. And keep your hands on the sofa."

"But . . . but . . . "

Jack was always stuck speechless. It tortured him to have such physical perfection so close and not be able to touch it, or to even just *expose* it and thrill his eyes on it. Damn! Kansas's shrouded nipples looked almost two inches long.

One night, Jack couldn't stand it anymore. He'd attempted ripping Kansas's clothes off. She'd fought back like a tigress, then fled once she'd foiled his attempt to bare her.

Jack hadn't seen her since then.

"We're going to see Kansas?" he asked Aida now.

Aida nodded. "Em . . . yes. She's my elder sister."

She instantly returned her attention to the road, swerving just in time to avoid hitting a group of World Inc. salesmen hawking inflatable guide dogs.

Once the road was clear, she looked back at Jack.

"I mean it—she is my elder sister."

Jack smiled back, perplexed. It was becoming quite a strange day.

"My sisters and I have been called many names throughout history and literature," Aida said. "The Fates, the Furies, the Three Witches, the three clocks that tell the time of humanity, the Sirens, the Bitches Eternal . . . "

Jack nodded.

" . . . We're sort of a sub-divine guiding hand . . . "

Another nod.

" . . . The main thing you need to know is that things went badly wrong along the way somewhere, and so me, Kansas, and Crash decided we needed to fix things somehow."

"Crash?"

"My *younger* sister. The goddess of automobile accidents."

"Oh." Jack nodded again. "What went wrong?"

Aida pouted thoughtfully awhile before replying.

"Well *this* . . . " She stretched out a hand to indicate the milling throngs of salesmen everywhere. "World Incorporated. All *we* had in mind was a one-world government. Then, with mankind's endless warring over for good, we could regulate death control by more natural means. But, well, you can see for yourself what we've ended up with."

Regulate death control? Jack was as horrified as he was befuddled.

"Hold on, Aida. Don't you feel *any* sense of responsibly for those you've killed? It is a nasty death—AIDS, I mean."

She shook her head. "Nah, I'm innocent of any crimes."

"Huh?"

"Well, AIDS doesn't actually kill you. It just weakens you so something else can."

Jack looked at her stonily. "That's like saying a gun kills you, not the shooter."

"View it however you want. AIDS is effective though. And it took ages to think up."

"Think *you* up?"

"No, but I've got to switch identities depending on the time period I'm in. I was once the Black Death, then Typhoid, Malaria—whatever kills fastest at any given time."

Her expression turned solemn. "But you've got drug fixes for all those now, so I'm now AIDS. And Kansas keeps upgrading me so World Inc.'s drugs don't work."

Jack frowned. "What's all this got to do with me looking after a pie?"

Aida grinned. "Patience, darling. You can't have your pie and eat it."

VII

The bakery was in an inconspicuous neighborhood.

What caught Jack's attention as they turned onto the side street leading up to it was the total lack of salesmen.

Here there were none of the madding crowd endlessly trying to sell him something he didn't want, or didn't want to want.

It got confusing quickly—separating what you actually wanted from what World Inc. decided you should want and then convinced you that you wanted, and which you bought realizing that even your wanting it was a desire World Inc. had sold you.

The bakery itself was unobtrusive. It looked like nothing odd went on inside it.

That was, until they walked through the door and saw the television-headed cat sitting in what Jack assumed was reception. Ranged around it were a motley assortment of cakes and pies.

"She's downstairs," the cat said, the image on its screen changing momentarily into that of a cat's head and addressing them. "She's in a foul mood."

Aida nodded. She and Jack made their way past the cat to a back room, then down a flight of stairs into the bakery proper.

The blast of heat that met them upon opening the door was enough to explain the room's single inhabitant's almost total lack of clothing.

Kansas was tending a small white oven. She stood with her back to them, wearing only a blue G-string and flip-flops.

Her nudity however, wasn't the pleasant fulfillment of Jack's fantasies. He now understood why she'd always refused to disrobe in his presence.

Each of Kansas's buttocks was a huge human head. The left male, the right female. Both were hairless, of fat-faced flat-nosed individuals, and asleep. The back of Kansas's head was covered with another sleeping face. Jack saw its nostrils twitch as it snored loudly.

Kansas turned to face them. Each of her breasts was also a human head—left male, right female also. These heads had long noses.

Jack recoiled in horror. He'd always wondered what her nipples would feel like once he got them out of her clothes.

In contrast to what the cat-TV had made them expect, Kansas seemed happy to see them.

She smiled at Jack. "Hello, darling." Streams of sweat ran down her body from the heat in the room.

Jack felt in danger of fainting, and not just from the temperature. Seeing Kansas as she really was, on top of today's other revelations, threatened to become too much for him.

After a short exchange of pleasantries, Kansas returned to tending her oven. Jack wondered how such a little appliance could produce so much heat.

Aida read the question on his face. "The heat's piped in from Hell," she explained, "the oven's merely a conduit."

"Done," Kansas announced a short while later. "Now it just needs to cool."

She turned off the oven. The room temperature immediately dropped, as if the heat previously emitted by the oven had now been sucked back into it.

After removing the pie-tray from the oven, Kansas led the way upstairs. They went to the reception where the television-headed cat sat sentry.

Jack's hopes that Kansas would now get dressed were disappointed.

He was treated to the distressing sight of one of her head-buttocks crushed out of shape as she made herself comfortable on a chair, its tongue hanging out of its open mouth like an idiot's. Spittle dribbled from its lips. It showed no sign of waking from its slumber. The degree of feature distortion was such that Jack doubted the auxiliary head had a skull or any facial bones.

"I know I've got a fat ass," Kansas told Jack. "Stop staring at it or I'll make your cancers start aching."

It took Jack about a minute to get his head around the implications of her statement, and match names.

Aida . . . AIDS; Kansas . . . cancer.

He remembered how disgusting her breath smelt, and how he now had *lung* cancer.

Once Jack had worked out the true magnitude of the convoluted mess he was in, he asked a question that demanded a simple answer:

"What's so special about this pie?"

Kansas laughed. "This pie," she said, "is the End of the World."

Kansas explained somewhat:

"The pie needs to incubate for a week—to learn about human nature and behavior—before it's fully ready. That's where you come in, Jack. You simply keep an eye on it while it familiarizes itself with the human psyche by scanning your mind. You're not particularly likeable, so it won't like humans. You're a coward, so it'll have no fear of the human race."

She stared at Jack pointedly, her beautiful aquamarine eyes intent with purpose. Her face was so lovely—he was almost able to forget the grotesqueness of the rest of her.

THE 'END OF THE WORLD' PIE

"On the last two days, we're going to remove the restraints we've so far placed on your illnesses. You'll be in *a lot* of pain. The pie will come to understand that humans can hurt, and in conjunction with all it's already absorbed from and about you, it will desire to hurt humans."

She smiled. "That's all; the next day we'll collect our pie and make you well again. After that, all you need to do is wait for the world to end."

She looked at Jack inquisitively, her expression hard and cold. "You'll do it?"

"I'll do it," Jack said. "How long have you been baking this thing?"

"About fifty years."

VIII

"End of the World" pie in car, Jack and Aida made their way back across town.

The television screen head on the giant bird next to the Chief Executive was showing World Inc.'s "Daily Discipline Hour"—the time when scapegoat salesmen from its three worst-performing branches from the previous day were killed as "encouragement" to everyone else to work harder. The participating branches also competed for who could think up the most entertaining means of dispatching their respective offenders.

Today's candidates were World Inc.'s Osaka, Bombay, and Nashville branches.

Osaka was first. Six yellow-suited faceless men were beheaded and then ground up into paste, which was pumped into the corporation's fish tanks.

Bombay boiled their scapegoats in oil, while voluptuous dancers cavorted and pranced all around the cooking pots. Afterwards, the corpses were well garnished and fed to a huge eight-armed god with an elephant's head.

Nashville affixed their scapegoats to monster-sized loudspeakers with superglue, then played louder and louder discordant fiddle music to them till their heads exploded, splattering brain matter everywhere. Afterward their corpses were sliced up with high-E guitar strings.

A faceless brown face replaced the diced corpses on screen. It addressed the viewers, speaking through ears almost as large as those of the Bombay elephant-god:

"This has been a World Inc. presentation. Voting for your favourite segment of today's show commences now and will end in precisely five minutes."

"Don't you just love the human race?" Jack asked in disgust as the Bombay branch's presentation was voted the most entertaining.

And watching over all, like a flawed Almighty, sat the icon-like figure of the Chief Executive.

Jack's disgust was mixed with dread. This was more than just the nebulous queasiness the Chief Executive always filled him with. Jack knew what would happen now—for the next couple of hours after this program each day, the salesmen worked with fresh vigor.

He was right. Before they made it back to his house, Jack had been talked into buying six more packets of Instant Kids, a box of singing potatoes, and a life-insurance policy for a convict on death row.

Just as they drove past the Chief Executive's violence-proof cubicle, Jack finally realized what it was that bothered him so much about the huge crocodilian figure and all its predecessors—it wasn't reading *any* of the documents it was appending its signature to.

Once the pie was safe on Jack's living room table, Aida left, saying she had business to attend to.

Jack went out to get a drink—he needed to be in an atmosphere of normalcy for a while.

Returning home from the bar afterwards, he was surprised to discover there were no salesmen on his street when he turned onto it.

Then he was surprised to find Aida's egg-shaped car waiting for him at home. Clearly, she'd forgotten something. He quickened his steps.

"Pssst, pssst."

Jack turned back, peering into the car in surprise. It had seemed empty when he'd walked past it. Besides, he'd given Aida a key to the apartment, so why would she be waiting out here?

"Pssst . . . over here. It's me—the car."

Jack realized that it *was* the car talking to him. The same female silhouette he'd noticed twice previously was on the front door, only this time it wasn't moving.

"Crash, I assume—the goddess of automobile accidents?"

"That's right, Jack. I love you."

"Where's this heading?"

THE 'END OF THE WORLD' PIE

"The obvious. Let's fuck. Now—before Aida comes back."

Jack gaped at the car. "You're . . . joking . . . right?"

Something about the way the vehicle revved itself in response assured Jack that it wasn't.

"Look," he said. "Can we discuss this later? Aida's wait—"

"Screw Aida," the car growled, its voice seeming to come from its wheels. "You're *mine*." Its voice turned ugly. "You'd better give me what I want. *Now*. Be nice to me, Jack, or else I'll sic every car in town on you." After a pregnant pause, it added: "Airplanes and machinery too."

Its voice was menacing, convincing Jack that he'd best comply with its demand.

"How do we do it?" he asked. "Do I fondle your gear stick or something?"

"Round the back; remove my fuel tank cover."

Jack walked round to the vehicle's ass-shaped rear and removed the fuel tank cover.

He shivered. The entrance to the fuel tank was a perfectly formed vagina.

The vagina smelled of World Inc. petrol. It was soft and squishy, with large labia and a massive clitoris.

"Give me head, Jack."

Jack knelt between the car's split curves and paid homage to the cunt, kissing and licking it while the car revved and growled like it was approaching the finish line of a race.

Finally the car shuddered thrice, as if it had just hit a succession of potholes in an otherwise smooth road.

"That was *good*," it purred afterwards, its voice dripping satiation. "Your turn now. Come around to my front."

"But . . ." Jack was already unzipping himself, his cock was hard. The fuel-tank vagina looked eminently fuckable.

"You can't come in my fuel tank, darling," the car said softly. "Semen messes up the engines—something World Inc. made no allowance for. Come round to the front of me."

Erection sticking out in front of him, Jack walked round to the front of the car.

Once he was there, the car's World Inc. monogram popped off, revealing a pair of lovely flesh-and-blood female lips.

"I'll give you head too, darling," it said. "If you come in me here it just enters my radiator."

"This will look really weird if anyone passes by."

"Not if I do this." There were a pair of soft clicks and the hood lifted. "Any onlookers will simply think you're trying to fix a fault."

Jack agreed with that. He inserted his penis into the luscious impatient mouth. There was no need for lubrication—motor oil dripped from the lips and smeared his member.

Jack fucked the vehicle's mouth for a long time, thrusting into it with delicious abandon.

He and the car shuddered and thrummed to two orgasms together, their twin noises of mechano-erotic carnality disturbing the night for a while afterwards.

IX

Aida was waiting upstairs in Jack's apartment.

"Where've you been, baby? I've been waiting for you."

"I just finished screwing your car."

Aida laughed out loud.

"I was only joking. I *saw* you. I'm sure half the neighborhood did too. Good thing I cleared the street of salesmen. Crash insisted."

Embarrassment threatened to overwhelm Jack. He changed the topic: "So what brings you back?"

Then he remembered something, and changed the topic back again: "And why did your car . . . sorry, your *sister* . . . insist I'm hers?"

Aida tucked a loose lock of black hair behind her ear. She smiled.

"First things first. I'll re-answer the 'why you?' question you asked me this morning."

Jack waited.

"It's because you're a snivelling wimp, Jack, unable to handle responsibility."

"Huh? What's that got to do with this? No . . . I mean, what the hell are you talking about?"

Aida sneered at Jack. "For example, look how you abused Kim, your ex-wife."

That stung Jack. He glowered coldly back at Aida. "I didn't *abuse* Kim. I *divorced* her. There's a huge difference"

"Exactly. You took the coward's way out." She laughed mockingly at Jack's confusion. "That's what you are, Jack—weak. A woman wants a

THE 'END OF THE WORLD' PIE

man who's *strong* enough to stand up to her, particularly when she's being irrational. Kim didn't care that you hit her, she loved you despite that. But she cared that you weren't willing to remain with her because you were scared you might go on hitting her. You simply weren't strong enough to overcome your fear of maltreating her, your fear of—"

"But I did it *for* her!" Jack practically yelled out this self-vindication.

"Did you? Wasn't it so you wouldn't have to cope with the guilt you'd feel if you found yourself unable . . . no . . . too *weak* . . . to control your violent urges?"

To that, Jack had no answer. He was confused. How could refusing to hurt someone you loved be wrong?

"Anyhow, that's why we chose you. You've no spine. Putting it bluntly—you're a coward."

Jack put aside the aspersions to his character for a moment.

Something puzzled him.

"Even avoiding the obvious question of how you know so much about me and my ex, I'm still confused. What on earth does Kim have to do with . . . " he pointed first out of the window in the general direction of Aida's car, then at the pie on his table, then spread his hands in an encompassing gesture " . . . with . . . any of this?"

"I told you we're *three* sisters. Kim's the third, the youngest of us. Her real name's not Kim, its *Crash*. She's animating my car now—she can live in anything with a metal component. Remember she had a metal spine?"

Jack remembered. After Kim's childhood motor accident, she'd been the lucky winner of a World Inc. "free med" competition, entitling her to lifelong "repairs."

In addition to replacing both her hip joints, thighbones, and ankles, World Inc. had also laced her vertebral column with steel—just for good measure. At least that was the story she'd told him.

He remembered one other thing. Kim's maiden surname *had* been *Krash*. Crash, the apparent goddess of motor accidents.

No wonder having sex with the car had felt so normal.

Jack had a sudden flash of insight. He felt he now understood the human male's fascination with automobiles—if their actual essence was female, it made sense.

He wondered what his few male acquaintances would give to have sex with *their* cars like he'd done. Most likely, everything they owned. Jack found it strange that World Inc. hadn't yet thought of this marketing ploy.

He turned his attention back to Aida. Her disparaging summary of his character bounced angrily back and forth across his mind like World Inc. tennis balls.

"You really think I'm a coward?"

Aida sneered. "Well, we both *know* you're not going to endanger yourself to save the world, if that's what you mean. Just watch the pie, Jack. And remember, its wellbeing is all that stands between you and a lifetime of *unbelievable* pain. And, yes, I do mean *lifetime*—you'll live as long as we want you to."

She walked over to the door and let herself out.

X

"Let's eat it," the soap demon said after obediently producing a froth of soap so Jack could wash the motor oil off his penis.

"Eat what?"

"The pie you brought home. It smells fantastic."

"You're crazy." But it was true. The pie did smell great. Strange he hadn't noticed that before.

Taking the soap demon back with him for company, Jack sat down in his living room and stared at the pie.

On seeing the demon with him, all Jack's butterflies fled into his bedroom, to a safe place beneath his bed. But they needn't have bothered—the soap demon had only one thing on its mind.

"Let's eat this pie," it repeated. "I've a great feeling about this—it's going to be a real once-in-a-lifetime experience."

"I'm not sure that's wise," Jack said. "They say its the end of the world."

The soap demon stared at Jack with large bulbous yellow eyes. "This pie?"

Jack nodded.

"All the more reason to eat it then. If you eat the end of the world, the world can't end."

"But they say if I guard the pie, they'll heal me. And they were very specific about how much shit I'll be in if anything goes wrong. They—"

"*They*? Who's *they*? Your mad girlfriends? Jack, you never had good taste in women, nor apparently much sense either. Exactly what good will being well do you if the world ends?"

Jack looked at the soap demon in surprise. "You have a point there, you know. I never considered it from that angle."

THE 'END OF THE WORLD' PIE

They debated the pros and cons of eating the pie for a while. Then Jack thought in silence for a while longer.

"No," Jack said finally. "They're wrong. I'm *not* a fucking coward."

They ate it.

The pie tasted even better than either Jack or the soap demon had expected.

Damn, Kansas could bake. The crust practically melted on their tongues, and the filling was sweet and meat at one and the same time, a blend of exotic fleshes and spices neither had ever imagined possible.

The frog-demon burped loudly. "Wow. This rocks big time."

Jack, raising a fresh slice to his lips, nodded his agreement.

Their only concern/distraction was that the pie made noises when they swallowed it—loud noises inside their throats as though they were somehow eating a factory.

XI

The next morning, Jack was awoken by three salesmen.

He opened his eyes, saw two featureless faces—a black and a white one—staring at him, and shut them again.

Oh, no, he thought.

Jack counted to ten, then opened his eyes again. The salesmen were still in his living room.

He raised a sleepy head and looked around. A third salesman was busy registering the serial numbers on his packs of Instant Kids.

Jack groaned. "I know you've started selling door-to-door, but I didn't invite you in. This surely constitutes a breach of my privacy. Please leave before I call the cops."

"In a moment, sir. We'd been knocking for a while without getting a reply, so we assumed you were out, and used World Inc.'s master key to admit ourselves. We're not selling anything, we're here to replace your soap demon."

Jack was suddenly very awake. "What's wrong with it?"

"Terminal malfunction, sir. One we've not seen before. You can see for yourself, sir."

Jack looked at where the man was pointing.

The soap demon lay on the floor, motionless on its back, a huge lump of soap frozen solid in its mouth.

A huge mechanical arm the size of Jack's leg projected from the demon's stomach. The base of the arm was still attached to its spine—the extrusion of this new mechanical organ had burst the frog-creature open like a rotten fruit.

"Wha . . . wha . . . what is tha . . . tha . . . that thing?" Jack asked in disbelief.

"We don't know, sir. Clearly a major malfunction, though. Your demon was still broadcasting its distress signal when it blew up. We'll be able to investigate it once . . . "

Jack no longer heard the man. He was staring at the empty pie tray. *How?* For the first time he realized he felt very different. His *belly.*

He waved the salesmen back, then unbuttoned his shirt for a look.

Just like with his soap demon, there was an arm sticking out of Jack's belly. It was human, male, and was grasping an impossibly HUGE gun in its hand.

The arm wavered unsteadily at first, swaying from side to side like a drunk. Then it steadied, pointing at one of the salesmen—the one who'd been indexing Jack's packs of kids.

The gun made a loud pop and the man's head disintegrated.

Shit, Jack thought, as another hand popped out of his belly. This one was female. It held a sword with which it slashed left and right.

More salesmen rushed into the room.

After losing four more of their number—two with their heads shot off, one decapitated by Jack's female stomach-hand, and another disembowelled by it—the salesmen managed to restrain and disarm Jack's new limbs.

Using a humongous roll of duct tape, they secured Jack in a chair. Then they lifted him and carried him out of his apartment.

"Where are you taking me?" Jack whimpered in alarm.

"To the Chief Executive, to our labs and our doctors, sir. We really need to find out what's wrong with you. You've clearly infected your soap demon with a sickness that we can't have spreading."

The salesman paused for a moment before adding, "It's essential you understand, sir, that this of course voids your warranty on the demon we came to replace. Also, please expect a bill for costs World Inc. has incurred, both for making this service visit, and also the replacement cost for our dead staff."

THE 'END OF THE WORLD' PIE

"Put me down now!" Jack yelled.

The salesmen paid him no heed, instead bearing him swiftly downstairs.

They lost another of their number whilst restraining the cobra that suddenly sprouted out of Jack's neck, its fangs dripping with venom.

Once outside, the salesmen cleared a path through their fellows and rushed Jack toward their van.

Then there was a sudden silver flash of motion, and all the salesmen on Jack's right were airborne and crashing to the ground broken and bleeding.

There was a screech of tires, and next the salesmen on Jack's left shared the same fate.

Another screech of tires. The four salesmen carrying Jack put him down. The salesman restraining Jack's neck-cobra let go of it.

They all stared in shock at the female silhouette on the bonnet of the egg-shaped car facing them.

"Let him go," Crash shouted. "He's *mine*!"

"Ours, you mean." Aida and Kansas opened their respective doors and stepped out.

Kansas—grotesqueness once again obliterated by sexy black clothing—pointed at the salesmen. "Like she said, free him, he's ours."

"Not on your life, lady," a senior salesman retorted. "He's World Inc. property now. And you two are in serious trouble for interfering with corporation business."

At his words, those salesmen who weren't dead quickly regrouped. They moved to surround the sisters.

One pulled a white packet from his briefcase. "You ladies seem rather stressed," he said. "I recommend these fully guaranteed World Inc. stress pills. These are the new formula—we've successfully eliminated the unwanted laxative side—"

Kansas reached out and grabbed him. Pulling his face to hers, she kissed one of his ear-mouths and let him go.

The salesman fell backward. While he squealed like a piglet being slaughtered, the ear Kansas had kissed began swelling. It became a tumour that consumed first his head, then his entire body. It swelled uncontrollably, till the salesman was one humongous rotund mass with no distinguishable features. The shredded yellow remains of his suit lay about him.

Pulsing all the while like a monster heart beat within it, the man-

185

tumour quickly grew to the size of a house. After first rolling from side to side—crushing many salesmen—it began cracking up like an egg.

Finally its top half fell off, freeing a huge yellow bird that had octopus-like tentacles in place of wings. This began attacking the salesmen at random.

"I wonder, ladies—seeing as things are so dangerous at the moment— if I can interest you in purchasing our latest model of—"

Aida grabbed the salesman. Jack gaped in disbelief when she forced the man's entire head up her backside.

The salesman's body began shrinking. It withered in its yellow suit till it looked like an unhealthy maize plant. Then body and suit both disintegrated into dust.

Aida farted loudly, blowing out a mess of red powder.

"Just like I always suspected," she said in disgust, "World Inc. salesmen are low on brains."

While the salesmen fought the tentacled bird, Aida and Kansas freed Jack and bundled him into their car.

With a deep purr of content, Crash drove off.

XII

"Are you okay, baby?" Crash asked, her voice laced with concern.

"He's okay, leave him alone. I don't know what's wrong with you."

"Sorry I ate your pie."

"That's more than okay. We intended you to."

"What!?"

They were out of town now, on a hillside.

Down below in the far distance, Jack could make out the humongous figure of the Chief Executive—now a giant goat in a tuxedo—furiously signing an endless flood of documents without reading them.

Above and around the goat's head floated a swarm of little objects like silver bees.

"Those are World Inc. warplanes," Kansas said. "They'll be here in about thirty minutes. Now—"

Jack interrupted her. "What do you mean, you *intended* me to eat the pie?! And what the hell is my business with World Inc. warplanes?!"

Aida replied him. "You see, darling," she said in a saccharine voice, "we lied about the name of the pie we gave you—it wasn't the 'End of the World' pie, but the 'End of World Inc.' Pie."

THE 'END OF THE WORLD' PIE

Jack looked at her with less comprehension than before.

In addition, he felt really strange now, like he was someone other than himself, someone MUCH greater than he'd ever been before.

Jack felt as if huge machines were in motion inside his body. He also sensed a beehive of activity going on under his skin—people planning strategy and manufacturing weapons on his behalf.

The gun-wielding auxiliary arm in Jack's belly had in the meantime reached somewhere inside him and rearmed itself—it now clutched a bazooka. The inscription on the weapon's side said it fired ultra-miniaturized, thermonuclear, heat-seeking, armour-piercing missiles.

His female auxiliary arm had now been joined by another, the pair of which clutched a bow and quiver of arrows. For the first time he saw that "Made in Japan" was tattooed on both female wrists.

Jack had sudden certainty that the arrows they fired would destroy tanks if necessary.

The cobra sprouting out of his neck was now armour-plated. Jack knew it, too, was now a weapon, a flamethrower with a range of miles.

"What have you bitches done to me?!"

"Relax, lover," Kansas said, her eyes shimmering like tiny oceans. "That's what we're trying to explain. We want you to get rid of World Inc. for us."

"I don't understand," Jack said.

This wasn't true. Inside him now was the certain knowledge that the global monster World Inc. was *the enemy*, the foe to be destroyed at all costs.

Like dominoes falling, one knocking over the next in an interminably long chain, windows of previously shut knowledge opened up to Jack.

He saw.

World Inc. had all but totally conquered disease.

Soon—in a matter of days—the cure for AIDS would be released as a cheap seven-day course of pills. A cancer vaccine was also already completed, and currently being patented.

World Inc. had also developed the chairbag, the pneumatic self-sealing, total-cloaking, ultimate evolution of the airbag that would mean a final farewell to automobile fatalities and even non-explosive aircraft ones, as the monopolistic corporation planned to fit aircraft chairbags with parachutes.

The Sisters—Kansas, Aida, and Crash—were furious. They were utterly enraged to see all their hard work undone.

Undone, not by human altruism, but by greed.

Jack saw clearly this truth: World Inc.'s freeing the Earth from the shackles of disease and automobile death wasn't due to any love of mankind—though it would be proclaimed as such—but rather by the desire to maximize their profits.

On two fronts: making profit curing those with disease so they could make even more profit selling unnecessary and unwanted items to them when they no longer had to spend all their hard-earned money on disease.

The logic grew a little fuzzy here—Jack remembered that World Inc. owned most of Earth's hospitals . . .

It didn't matter. What did was that the Sisters were right, World Inc. was wrong, and he, J.A.C.K., was the mutant avenger, the chosen one, transformed to correct this injustice.

It was his duty to right this greatest of wrongs by getting rid of the evil would-be healers of the human race, so the Sisters could lovingly afflict mankind with disease and motor accidents again.

And the Sisters really did love mankind . . . loved to hurt them, loved to kill them, loved hearing their screams, loved feeding on their horror, on their despair . . .

"I see you understand," Kansas said. "In addition to superhuman strength, total invulnerability, and unmatched military strategic prowess, you're also the only human on Earth immune to World Inc.'s greatest weapon—their power of persuasion. They can't sell you anything anymore, which makes you dangerous to them, so they'll . . . "

J.A.C.K. didn't hear her. He was busy calibrating the extension of the barrel of the gun he'd just projected out of his mouth.

The first World Inc. warships were already within range.

J.A.C.K. computed. Data scrolled itself down the inside of his eyes like they were computer screens.

There were six-hundred and thirty-five aircraft approaching; apparently all the warplanes available in this sector of World Inc.'s domain. If he extruded another set of guns from his chest he would be able to destroy all these in a matter of hours.

Then he could start his march northward and take on the military/marketing garrisons stationed in the Canadian axis. No point waiting for them to come to him.

Suddenly J.A.C.K. felt very impatient. He hoped the approaching warplanes would arrive quickly. He could attack first, but it was bad tactics—if he educated them too quickly as to his firepower, they might turn tail and flee. So . . .

J.A.C.K. waited as patiently as a bird of carrion circling a dying man. His Japanese belly-arms held a pair of explosive arrows notched ready in their bow.

Already J.A.C.K. saw himself as the world vulture pecking World Inc.'s bleached bones.

"Don't get hurt, baby," Crash said, as he let off his first salvo of missiles. "Remember, I love you. I need you." Her silhouette paced nervously back and forth across the length of the Sister's car. "I . . ."

"Shut up, twat!" her sisters yelled in unison. "Don't distract the man—he's got a war to fight."

"I love you too, Kim," J.A.C.K replied, speaking out of his right ear. He was pleased. His first shots had all scored direct hits—salesmen were falling out of the sky like burning snowflakes. "I'm fighting for your honor here, honey. And I can assure you, these greedy bastards aren't gonna win."

I, AUTOCORRECT

ALLEN GRIFFIN

TREES COMPOSED OF regret line the inside of the bedroom, branches hang low heavy with our rapid copulations. Settle on this, throat obstructed, eyes burning, and we got ready for bed.

Our bodies made a tent from the sheets. We slither in and out of one another's flesh. Hit tunes speak through the wheels of Samsara.

I'm gutted, a hundred tangled limbs, a spice of humility sprinkled on the skin.DVR the clouds, whip away at the car pool lane. We wait in a river, watching a thousand red eyes watch us. We have responsibilities and we are trying hard. The board meets every Tuesday, decides our payment levels. We fill truck beds with toothpaste. Dogs bark out legal proceedings at the edge of the property.

"Grind on!" I scream at the TV, totems of skin dancing across the skin. I stake a claim on the soft pink flesh of her tongue, they can pry it from my cold dead hands. Our house claims more windows per square foot than an ocean liner, each one designated 'his' and 'hers'.

The looking glass shows a slow road to back in time. Sit on the steps and wait for fate to intervene. A cost-benefit analysis is read by the gushing crude of an oil well, a car pulling into the driveway startles away the animals living in our chest cavities and cavorting in our loins.

"Flicker . . . flicker . . . flicker," she screams.

My lungs fill with chemicals from a green jar. We sing hit songs from the radio while a man with a tear tattoo tries to translate our words, but we are singing too quickly. The dumpster eats young couples on their smoke break, sneaking kisses and sex in the walk-in cooler.

I, AUTOCORRECT

Back in the bar, masses of people sing on boxes of flickering light, stroking to the beat of warriors prancing on horseback. A red-head tears pages from a Bible, putting together a new book with only her favorite parts. Desperate men trek across deserts, splitting buns and apples, talking to double-agent angels about the end times.

We work for a cruel boss, selling nooses and tazers in the city of pyramids.

"There is no way but the way," I whisper in the ears of no one.

"This is a big band cyclone," she cries out, her feet crossed, shoes wrapped in paper to hide their sinister designs. The keyboards tickle secret codes from car stereo speakers. We will just miss each other getting on and off the highway, a year apart, maybe two.

The secrets make her smile.

"Burn fast, burn fast, don't worry about flying high again." There's a bar down the street, wrapped in your favorite sweater, but the city of pyramids is always hot, even late at night. The motel was run-down but famous. The geography is overwhelming but tasting important.

I slept in the bed wedged into the cockpit of a mech. The heat remained trapped outside, she's having none of it.

"This is the city where we'll die and be reborn. All the cafeteria workers are blind." A code word for safety and anonymity, there are ears everywhere.

The desert swallows up lovers. At home, there is a fiscal meltdown, attacks based on fluids dumped into boxes reverberating across the horizon. Towers speak mouthfuls of earplugs, surveillance bursting forth from Catholic wombs.

"I am the Codex. These flowers exist only for the feedback loop. None of you are invited to the wedding, only the most defiled will be permitted. We fuck in tents and are only aroused by betrayal."

God is pressure and the gears grind humanity to powder, the machine speaks through me. All transactions are narcissistic. They sell rotting meats in the bazaar and she goes jogging on a carpet of burning books. Sand is our breakfast, cooked into omelets.

"Dear Codex," I mutter, but we really don't want to talk anymore. The computer whispers secrets only she used to know. It tells me what to say and how to say it. I chase painkillers with handfuls of nickels and dimes, my apron dragging around my feet.

This place doesn't amount to a hill full of beans. We rush into the squares and see people we thought were long-dead laying on benches at the bus stop. Bums sprinkle rose petals on the bodies, stand on street corners crying out,

"How do you like them apples?"

I've been to that bar before. I am drunk off chowder and spend my days in lean-to libraries. She starts a notebook and refuses to fan the flames. Money flows down like a river, rowers of toothpaste dip their oars in recumbent waters.

"This is the Big Book of Right Answers," I declare. A special project headed by a team of lovely Italian ladies. Walk down to the river, hand in hand, if only for an afternoon of unspoiled potential.

"A year from now you won't believe the heat, you'll lose faith in the existence of snow. You'll stumble on to the landing strip and throw up your hands, unable to direct traffic. People will say reprehensible things and you'll refuse to correct them. There is no way but the way."

"What's this?" I retort."I already know the way around these roads. I'd make love to you but I don't know how. There are secrets all around us. Our dreams speak in Italian or Cantonese. I'd visit many places but it takes too long to drive anywhere with a busted-out window and no stereo."

Two-story Tarot cards stand in a ring in the desert. You promise change, we cry over the sound of blast-beats and naked lust. The morning papers read of sexual escapades and toxic cocktails.

"I'll follow the light into the snow."

"Can't you see the bulbs are burning red?"

The town stands on the ruins of simplicity, the white river turning brown from the waste of the corpse factories. She tells me her eyes are no longer in their sockets and soon they'll venture further. Time slips into a quicksand monologue. Everyone is required to live next to a meth-lab.

"I can't sleep. I see the intestines of others slipping away, draining from places better not witnessed."

I, AUTOCORRECT

The house fills first with water, then with mud. Motors are bought and replaced as quickly as they flood. I erect a weight bench and a bronze idol of the great goddess. Instead of birth, she brings death, which is birth all over again.

Each set of arms holds a pair of eyeballs in their hands, bursting up from the dirt or descending from the low clouds to see. Only through the imperfection of the senses can these regrets and victories be judged.

I woke beneath a blanket of nipples, glorious areolas built up like a distributor cap. I'm learning to do for self, walk through parking lots painted entirely on hillsides. The money is gone, but it always has been. The realization is new though.

There is no way but the way.

MЯ. ꟻUƆꓘ YOꙄ, OꓘⱯY?

TOM BRADLEY

My solitude grew more and more obese, like a pig.
— Yukio Mishima

WHEN THINGS WERE normal, Mr. Fukuoka could be found trying to teach Japanese to rich teenagers in a prep school in the mountainous north. But, tonight being abnormal, he found himself in the southern wastes, visiting the scene of a crime perpetrated against him when he was younger than his students, when he was known as Little Flip.

Wandering off alone into raucous blackness, Mr. Fukuoka fell, humbled, to pray upon the abrasive desert floor, and impaled both knees on a decaying coil of War Relocation Authority barbed wire. Peeling that up from the sterile dust, he uncovered an intact jar, its glass blued by decades of ultraviolet radiation, its label bleached but legible. No mayonnaise, but the crispy remains of two baby rattlesnakes were visible inside, greened by jaundiced moonlight.

Little Flip had intended to domesticate them, or at least to save them from the bullsnakes (long, thick, and black as the donkey penises cited in the Book of Ezekiel) which the guards had been ordered to set loose on the periphery to chase the mother rattlers off. But he had either forgotten or, more likely, in his dispossessed state, had lacked the means, to punch air holes in the lid. Dried macaroni-like mummies with microscopic fangs were the result of his lifetime's sole visitation by the nurturing instinct, active or passive.

"Better known as Hellman's Real Mayonnaise east of the Rockies, which is where you rice-niggers should be," a bully guard had mumbled. Physically unfit for combat, bug-eyed and hoarse, the guard had tried to

194

confiscate the jar, but had been persuaded to relent by a golden and blue angel from the mountains.

"A child needs his pets," the Mormon missionary had smirked. "Just as we grown-ups do."

Tonight, shaking the concentration camp relic in his hand like a baby rattle or sorcerer's fetish, Mr. Fukuoka stumbled down a dry gully and into a roaring corner of red-sand Topheth. He peeked between a cactus' upthrust fists, and what he saw stunned and paralyzed him like a double injection of hot reptile venom. He froze, obscured in lurching campfire shadows. He seemed to have almost walked in on a Canaanite orgy.

The throbbing concussions could have been his own heart imploding, self-destructing in waltz rhythm; the screams and profanities and flashes and tracers could have been his eyeballs and eardrums bursting out of their appointed seats, being washed away, dislodged by the pressure inside his head; the artificial winds could have shot from the four dilated nostrils of a yoke of supernal Palmyra oxen, bearing on each of their backs one foot of the awful Bedouin Yahweh, come to deliver the final revelation of all time.

A detachment of jeering junior shamans, lithe and semi-clothed Caucasoid apprentices to red masters, howled and brawled among themselves with broad gestures. They sent forth bolts of lurid fire from their bony, outstretched arms and into Heaven's black midsection. Boys' lean backs and buttocks were visible. Sinewy creatures, seemingly one-armed, followed behind them and whispered abominable jokes over their shoulders and into their juvenile ears, hunching and huffing very close, making the centaur with seven limbs.

He should have suspected something in homeroom the week before.

The polygamist children from the boarding department had reacted so jubilantly to the geology teacher's proposal of a geode-digging "all-nighter" among nerve-gassed sheep carcasses in the U. S. Army's proving grounds. Japanese language instructor to the children of the *nouveaux riches* for an entire week already, "Teachie-poo-*sensei*" had assumed, in his naivete, that the Lord was giving him a chance to teach these privileged white children a denotation of the word *topaz* other than the one found at position eight of Professor Moh's unrevised, unexpanded Hardness Scale, which the geology teacher kept tacked to the homeroom wall. At the very top of the chart, just above *diamond*, someone phenomenally tall had penciled a new position of ultimate hardness: "Nip homo boners."

It had been part of his new-on-the-job hazing to be duped by the other faculty members into co-chaperoning this field trip. He had no idea what he was in for.

"What does our right-honorable governor call that county?" one of them had squealed from the back row of desks.

"Panoramaland!" the rest of them had hooted in unison, making googly-eyes and whirling their index fingers in psychedelic spirals around each other's ears.

"Our patriarchal stomping grounds!" the polygamist children had screeched. (The administration let anybody with lots of money into the school.) "Time to take care of some business, boys!"

And here was the reason for their jubilation.

Instead of the sand-dune Jehovah's sublime voice, Mr. Fukuoka heard the scratchy squawks of adolescent heathens with near-angelic physiques. When not dancing like naked dervishes in the firelight, they seemed to be hawking various survivalist paraphernalia and ordnance freshly delivered, in the original factory boxes, from the belly-hatch of their millionaire patriarch's helicopter.

The shoppers appeared to be Marxist braves and savage septuagenarian peyotists from the Shivwit tribe aboriginal to this smoking cranny of Gehenna. Latterly elevated to polite Intermountain society's upper-middle echelons by the discovery of lush uranium deposits on their reservation, the Amerinds had shown up tonight not in the expensive sharkskin suits they wore to New Zion's Bank, but in traditional buckskin sweat-lodge garb. It was a canny enough wardrobe choice, considering the fatuous young romantics they were dealing with. Their exquisitely beaded loincloths were bolstered plump with stumpy red penises and substantial wads of equally hard currency, neither of which they seemed particularly desirous of keeping a hold on.

For the Native Americans' benefit, one of the less gifted Japanese students demonstrated something brand-new in those days: a surface-to-air, shoulder-deployed, heat-seeking anti-aircraft missile. The suggested target was a single crawling point of light far overhead which everybody surmised to be an Israeli spy satellite. And the rocket seemed, after a slithering, smoking chase through the constellations, to find its mark, filling the suborbital void with livid blasts of light, and the desert with incredulous howls of glee.

Cadets from the polygamist family's private military academy discharged M16s, Uzis, and AK-47s into Orion's belt, confident of their immunity from prosecution on this scofflaw reservation, where the bare mention of the words *Bureau of Alcohol, Tobacco, and Firearms* could be relied upon to elicit hoots of derision from even the most stone-faced old squaw.

Without being told, Teachie-poo *sensei* decided that he was witnessing nothing less than red communism cutting a deal with under-aged splinter Mormonism. They most likely were hatching a nefarious plot to stage a paramilitary coup in this county, at whose southernmost extreme was situated a vast dam that provided life-sustaining electricity to considerable portions of that militarily sensitive area known as the west coast of the United States of America.

Only minutes before, he had discreetly absented himself from the girls. They appeared to be camping more or less legitimately, if one ignored the mushroom clouds of hemp belching from the turquoise mouths of their sleeping bags. He'd left those future brides of Satan under the chortling, geode-fondling supervision of the geology teacher—

"Damn Army boys must be re-hearsin' for 'nother damn Tit Offensive out there on the damn provin' grounds, yup-yup . . . "

—and he had scrambled deep into the moonlight. Almost insane with masochistic nostalgia for the relocation camp, and the guards, and the intrusive right hand of the golden and blue missionary, he had found nothing more edifying than an old vermin-rattling mayonnaise jar, and this mescaline Eucharist.

In the hot night air, hiding among the shadows at the rout's periphery, the youngish Japanese teacher found himself slipping into a delirium of rage at the sight of his boyhood's praying ground being desecrated by moneychangers, an intoxication compounded by denied sexual arousal at the spectacle itself.

His heart began to swell with some half-formed intention of bringing fright and firepower to bear upon the pony-tailed socialists and the spawn of multiple fornication. He would drive them like sheep; he would force them to ooze their lubricious selves ten yards due west, or maybe twenty or thirty, or maybe a hundred miles, across sperm-yellow salt and scab-red sand, to where he hallucinated the county line. There, beyond the protection of the county attorney—who happened to be a plural mother of the "polygily-wiggly" boys—they would be forced to undergo citizen's arrest at the Japanese teacher's passion-quaking hands.

Quaking hands, but not bare.

Falling again to his punctured knees, he began to gather what he trusted were the raw ingredients of simple but effective explosive compounds. With splitting fingernails he scratched up various soils from his long-abandoned bridal bed, plus shirt-pocketsful of hardness-eight gravel to serve as splattergun projectiles. He prayed a weeping prayer of repentance as he performed the damnation offense of removing and shredding, for a fuse and wadding material, his official Church undergarments, this world's only sure prophylaxis from the black influence of Beelzebub. With adrenalin strength he wrenched the crumbling tailpipe from an abandoned army jeep, an orange barrel for this primitive but blessed blunderbuss.

Then he stumbled through the darkness and, mostly with his fingertips' sensitive skin, set about scrounging a sort of soldier-of-God uniform for himself, a disguise, improvised from dry stone detritus and desert carrion. He peeled some skin from a dead, pregnant ewe's jaws and eye sockets and stretched it across his own face to protect his lungs and brain cells from the toxic fumes of whatever burnt holocaust his pupils might be offering up to their Canaanite bull-god. With his bare teeth he gnawed free from their spindly anklebones the clawed feet of a gluttony-burst vulture, coated them with his own scant saliva and mud-pasted them to either side of his head: elfin ears, dead pinfeathers tickling. Like Moses himself, he sprouted a steer's parched and porous horns, and encircled them with a thorn-crown of blood-colored and blood-reeking barb wire.

As he made himself over, the gruesome elements in his costume began ever so gradually to be obscured by glistening ones: beads of sun-blued glass from coolies' shattered opium jars were draped from either earlobe; ivory-colored hair barrettes and false eyelashes were alluringly fashioned from baby rattlesnakes' filament-fine skeletons, lovingly shaken, with curled fifth fingers, out of the mayonnaise jar. And, in case his mask slipped, he concocted himself a facial foundation of talc-fine sand, wind-sifted, and moistened seductively with blood from his own tear ducts. A powder of pollen was coaxed from cactus blooms clenched for the evening but finger-pried apart like moist fairy buttocks. And all this was obscured ever so subtly by a pagan bridal veil of woven cactus spines.

Heavenly Father's voice suddenly rang out from the hilly north. It blasted a passage through the night clouds and rebounded off the exposed depths of outer space: "Leave off thy preening, effeminate son of the Gibeah Benjaminites! Set aside thy whorish adornments and step forth with thy flaming rod into the light!"

MR. FUCK YOU, OKAY?

But the Japanese teacher was a tobacco-free Latter-Day-Saint. He had no match to detonate his cannon. He began to wail aloud, a keening sob of lamentation, bringing all eyes in the vicinity down upon him.

Matter-of-factly, with no hesitation and little registration of surprise, the demoniacs embraced the creature that came hiccoughing from the shadows. They took his makeshift weapon and politely stacked it, tepee-style, among a cache of other wartime exotica, not even snickering. They draped him all about with their skin, their acne pockmarks and syringe-holes serving the same gripping function as suction cups on squid tentacles. And they drew him into the party, just another knot in the parched tangle of aborted serpents.

"Just another Utah misfit," laughed a horribly familiar teen voice, "a hairless Edom fucked out of his birthright for a bowl of bean soup—or, in this case, a pan of stir-fried green veggies!"

Leather-faced grannies gathered and gnawed on the youngish teacher's Japanese fingers in some nameless atavistic behavior. They shoveled handfuls of a sage-flavored incense onto the campfire. They fed him strychnine-tufted cactus bulbs that popped his brain-skin like an overripe hymen, and they laughed, at first affectionately, then derisively, at his impotence and structural underdevelopment.

The Mesopotamian god-head sprouted several writhing strands of hair, became a five-snake medusa, not only fatal, but impossible to behold for any creature without two faces, the second able to see behind.

The familiar boy's suffocating presence could be felt more and more, like a creeping odor. He squatted in the shadows and wrote in the living flesh of the orange sand with a slip of barb wire—not his Japanese calligraphy exercises, but something else, specifically for the benefit of three Shivwit braves, who gaped, were appalled, who giggled and wept in rapture and terror, who periodically touched one another's scaly elbows for corroborative witness, and manipulated their feathered fetishes to ward off the strong medicine contained in the overwhelming strokes that the white hand produced and wiped away with equal nonchalance.

"C'mon, you guys, can't you maintain twenty seconds in a row? These are the kind of questions they put on the entrance exam. Take 'em home to little Pocahontas, so she can come pitch her wigwam in our boarding department. We need some new blood around that dump."

At some rough jostle of a mighty sandstone elbow, very close to home, the new arrival was unmasked as he squatted and grimaced in a mound of ritually and literally defiled salt. Teacher and students' faces met, grinned cougar teeth, flashed coyote tongues.

The brat's prematurely bleary eyes focused in a single direction for the first and last time. They lingered with impertinence where they shouldn't, but eventually those eyes managed to find their way around to the empty mayonnaise jar still clutched to the front of Teachie-poo-*sensei's* body, thence all the way up to his face.

In a convulsion of delight, certain words were belched, eight in number, destined to remain immemorial among the students of the college preparatory institution:

"Why, if it isn't Mr. Fuck You, *Oka-a-a-ay?*"

L⊲B∃LS

CHANTAL NOORDELOOS

THE DREAM ⊲LWAYS starts the same. I stand in an office, modern and decorated like a picture from a futuristic magazine, a black leather suitcase in my grabbers. My partralli is hot with anxiety, cheeks flushed a soft pink. Before me is the opaque glass door to the manstenker's office, and beyond it lays my judgment. Bold letters on the grainy glass state that this is the office of T.B. Durnham, the big manstenker of the WSL offices throughout the entire United States. The big man, the top dog, the one everyone fears, and he wants to see me. I'm afraid, even though I know this is just a dream. Someone once told me that if you die in a dream, you shall never wake up again, and I think I believe them.

The knuckles of my left grabber rap against the glass, right underneath the letters *URN*.

"Come." His vravol is deep and sounds like gravel. My quavals knock together and my sticks feel like pudding when I step through the door and meet manstenker Durnham partralli to partralli.

He's a large man; fat spills across his desk like spilled Jell-O. Six chins flow from his partralli and fold across his neck and the top of his chest, each large enough to have a personal identity. His occulors are hidden in a forest of cheeks, and he stares at me from behind fatty flesh and large glasses. Black hair, peppered with gray, surrounds his partralli at the sides, though it's thinning at the top, and he has carefully brushed the greasy strands across the liver-spotted, gleaming scalp.

"Miss Panim . . . " The deep vravol almost hisses my name. "May I call you Rose?"

"I rather you called me by my name," I say, my vravol trembling. "It's Rachel."

His occulors glare at me from behind the glasses and I almost concede in letting him call me Rose.

"Sit down." He doesn't quite bark, but it's close, and he reminds me of an overgrown love child of a bulldog and an elephant seal. I bend my quavals and sit down on a three legged chair, struggling to keep my balance.

The manstenker browses through a stack of light blue sheets of paper, his bushy occulorbrows knotted at the top of his large nose. He licks his index disgin and looks at me from behind his glasses, a leery smile on his fat partralli.

"Miss Panim . . . missss Panim . . . miss miss miss Panim." He sings my name in a long, drawn out, slow baritone, his occulors switching between me and the papers he's riffling through, until he pulls out a large light blue sheet and shakes the creases out of it demonstratively. "Here you are . . . Rrrrachelll." He rolls my name over his pink tongue as if it's made out of sugar.

"Yes, sir?"

"You know why I have called you here, Rachel?"

"No, sir."

"Not even a guess?"

"No, sir. My department is running smoothly. We've exceeded the sales quota, my workers are happy, as far as I know. I don't know why you called me here." From the look on his partralli, I know he didn't call me in for a promotion, though I know that my department is the best functioning in WSL.

"Oh, your department is running very smoothly indeed, Missss Panim." He points a fat disgin at something written on the paper, but I can't see what he's pointing at. "I have no complaints about the work you produce. You seem quite proficient in your job. That's not why I called you here, no Rachel, it really isn't. My problem is not with what you do, it's with who you are."

My occulorbrows shoot up, and I feel my mouth go slack with a question I don't dare to ask. He looks at me with those little occulors, and I see them sparkle with malice.

"Who I am?" I parrot him, my brain a swirl of thoughts and emotions that collide together in a big tangle of brain yarn.

LABELS

"There have been complaints about your offensive personality."

"My . . . my . . . offensive—?"

"Oh, yes, your coworkers have complained." He raps the disgins of his right grabber on the desk with a rhythm that hypnotizes me.

"About what? I treat everyone with respect. I'm always kind to my colleagues, and never demanding. I don't understand why they would complain. I've not had any arguments or anything." My occulors are so wide now that I can feel the dry air lick at my corneas.

"No, but you're assuming this is about what you do again. This is about who you are. You see, it is you who are offensive. You don't fit in here."

"Why not?"

"You're short, but you're not acting like a short person, Rachel. And it's offensive to others. You have reached your glass ceiling, yet you insist on beating your grabbers against it, smearing the glass with your greasy disgin prints."

"I . . . I . . . don't understand."

"You presume too much, try to work hard to get above your natural ranking in life. You, and all the other short people, need to stay in their place. This world belongs to the tall, it always has. It's a matter of evolution, the tallest are the strongest and they will survive. You can't be something just because you work for it, Rachel. That would be absurd. If you want to be anything, you need to be born to it. It's about privilege, not about lifestyle choice or performance." His patralli beams at me and he fishes a fat tordekki from the top drawer of his desk. With a flourishing movement, his piggy occulors still on me, he puts the tordekki between his teeth and bites the end off, spitting it in the ashtray before him. From the same drawer he takes a match and lights it with his thumbnail, the little red head exploding with the bright flame, and he holds it to the end of the tordekki, the other end in his mouth as he puffs. Languid streams of smoke, slow like mellow snails, curl up in the air and I can smell the scent of burning tobacco. It's a strong smell and it tickles both my nostrils and the back of my throat. I let out a small cough and a tiny moth flies from my lips. I stare at it in surprise.

"Look at this world, Rachel. We all belong in a box, we are all labeled from the day we are born, and by the time we grow up, there will be more labels to stick to our skin." He rises to his feet, the gynormity of his stomach bouncing under a white shirt, the buttons taut, revealing some of the pink flesh underneath. "I'm not only a tall person, but I'm also big." He rubs his hands over her massive abdomen, the fat underneath molding under his strong disgins.

"I . . . I don't see what this has to do with my work?"

"Let me show you my labels." Square disgins peel at dainty mother of pearl buttons, releasing the folds of flesh from the white cotton shirt. I stare with fascination at the deep crevice of his belly button that hangs over his crotch from the unevenly distributed fat flab that is his stomach. He runs his disgins up his body, and points at the words that are branded on his skin.

Tall
Big
Strong
Rich
Dominant
Feared
Powerful

He points them out one by one, his grabbers running over the flesh, while his disgins press down on the scarred tissue that make up the letters.

"Let me see yours, Rachel." The words are soft, almost a whisper, and he licks his lips when he looks at my shirt. "Show me your labels."

"I don't want to show you. I hide my labels, they are not who I am, they are who I'm perceived to be."

"That's bullshit. We are our labels, our own opinions don't matter. We are a product of the masses. Their occulors, their ears, their minds make us. We have no control over that."

"But we are the masses. Do we not have an opinion, the same as everyone else? Does our world view not count?"

"We are the masses because we need to be. Our opinion only counts when it's conformed to the world. Otherwise it's anarchy, and the world can't thrive on anarchy."

"But are we not all individuals? Do we not all have our own souls that make us unique?"

He unbuttons the fly of his pants, he has to lift his stomach to reach it, and then he drops the grey slacks to the ground. His white boxers with little blue flowers soon follow suit. There are more words branded on his legs, and I can see a long penis dangle from underneath the bottom of his gut. The head is a purple red color and the word "Greed" is branded into it.

LABELS

"Take your clothes off, Miss Panim." His vravol roars with the depth of a thunderstorm, and I obey. I take off my shirt, the soft fabric of my silk blouse rubbing against my skin. Then my skirt, a dark blue, pinstriped pencil skirt, slides across my pantyhose, the material rustling like dry leaves in the wind.

"The bra too, and the panties." His breathing is heavier now, his gaze glides over my skin.

I reach back, and the hooks of my bra cling together, reluctant to let go. My disgins fumble with them, and when I finally loosen the lace straps, my bra comes alive and slithers across my body, down my leg and on the floor, far away from me. I make an attempt to stomp on it, so that I can prevent it from leaving, but it's too fast for me, and all I can do is watch it slither away. My white breasts with the rosebud pink nipples are exposed. One breast has the word "Woman" burned into the soft skin, while the other has the phrase "Potential Mother."

Along the contours of my stomach, the words "Short, Dainty and Delicate" are branded. My legs bear "Inferior, Accommodating, Submissive, Dependent."

"Some of these words don't suit me at all." I let my nail scratch at "Dependent."

"You just won't listen, will you? It's not about you. You are short so you are dependent. You need the tall to survive, this is the way that the masses have decided. There is no fighting it, Rachel."

"What if I don't agree?"

"We have more labels for you, Rachel. That is why I called you in here." He clicks his disgins and two men crawl out from under his desk, both medium height but very muscular, and both dressed in nothing but boxer shorts. I can read some of their labels. *Goon. Subservient. Violent. Sadist.*

Strong hands grab my wrists and pull my limbs apart, exposing the entirety of me. The manstenker bends down, and when he comes back up, he's holding a poker . . . glowing red hot at the tip where a word is curled into the iron. He leaps at me, the layers of his fat swaying with a magnificent grace, and presses the heat of the poker against my collarbone.

The pain would have been searing if this were anything but a dream, but now I only mimic a scream, more shocked than anything else. I pull at my limbs that are still held by the goons. The manstenker steps back and looks at his handiwork, his square disgin pressed between the fold of his third and forth chin, wiggling around as if he's searching for something. From the skin he pulls something silver, and to my shock I see it's a mirror. It grows in his hands until it's big enough for me to see my entire body.

My occulors glance across my neck to the ugly red and brown burn mark on my collar bone. "etanidrobusnI"

"*Insubordinate.*"

"I thought it wasn't about my actions, but about how I was perceived." My words taunt him, and I watch his partralli contort in a sneer of disgust.

"Semantics," he shouts, unable to hide the embarrassment that flushes across his cheeks. "I perceive you as insubordinate, and therefore you are. I will label you as I see fit."

"I shouldn't have to wear these labels. If every individual who labels me left these scars, there will be little left of my body." I jerk away from the grip of the goons, and they disappear like snowmen in the desert sun, leaving nothing but beige puddles on the floor where they once stood.

"If you can label at random, then so can I." My vravol is strong now, and I feel the scar that says "Dependent" fade on my skin.

"I will call you 'Narrow Minded' and 'Cowardly'." Thick welts, shaped in my handwriting, appear on the manstenker's cheeks and neck. "You are not strong, you are weak." His previous scars tear, as if I pushed a hook through them and ripped at the skin. Hot blood drips down the bulbous layers of skin, red snakelike trails racing each other.

"I have the power to make labels fade, to make scars heal, and there isn't a damn thing you can do about it." I spread my arms, press my chest forward, and proudly display my body, the old labels fading on my skin.

A hand grips me . . . not like the hands of the goons, this one is different. This one is real. It tears me away from the office, away from the boss and back into *reality. I open my eyes with a gasp and look into my husband's eyes. There is worry behind the black pupils, and his mouth is no more than a thin line.*

"What's the matter, sweetheart? Had a bad dream?"

"It was a weird dream," I admit.

"Must have been your bad day. I know how sensitive you are."

I feel the letters etch into my skin . . . S-E-N-S-I-T-I-V-E.

They burn and itch, and all I can do is take a deep breath and close my eyes. Labels . . .

⊢HE LAST GOD

DON WEBB

LEMING HAD TAKEN the bold step of moving into one of the abandoned apartment houses on Congress. Within walking distance to the Capitol, it had been a very popular (and rather expensive) dwelling place. It was near one of the biggest colonies of the Eyes. Sometimes one or two would attach itself briefly to the glass at night. Unlike 99% of the remaining inhabitants of Austin, Leming did not have black out drapes. He would flip off the Eye when it landed, but he didn't anger it by shining a light on it. He was defiant, not suicidal. He wondered one night what would happen if he placed a mirror inside the glass—show the Eye an Eye—but when he went to get the large freestanding dressing mirror that Dr. Walthers had had in her bedroom, the Eye focused on him. He could feel it watching him, draining him, and no doubt reporting to the big red brains that rumors said were underground in the drains, the caves, the secret government installations. He lit the room only with a nightlight, ironically a Christmas night light—once the delight of Dr. Walthers' daughter. She was grown up now, and probably fled like her mother to one of the well-lit rural compounds, where humans were said to be "pondering their next move." Leming froze while the Eye watched. He felt anger more than fear, but enough fear to keep him in place until the Eye detached itself and flew away about four in the morning. He slept late, but there was little recrimination at work for such omissions. People missed hours or even days.

Leming rode his scooter to work. The ad agency had practically no clients now, but somehow was still issuing paychecks more-or-less on schedule. His boss, the bleary-eyed Ms. Williams, nodded at him when he walked in at 10:00.

"The internet is down. Have you finished the sketches for the Two Step?' she asked.

"Since they're no longer open at night, no one loves their patio, and live music is almost a thing of the past—I don't know what to sell the bar with," said Leming.

"They've got a great dance floor. Didn't you and your sweetie, what's her name, used to go there?"

"Molly. Molly Jimenez. Molly broke off with me."

"I'm sorry. I didn't know. Was it because of—?"

All conversations ended with a "because of—"or a "since—" or a "you know" followed by a nod toward a nearby roosting place. Leming went back to designing an ad campaign for a bar that attracted no one in a deserted city. Lunch came in a couple of hours. Leming joined Scott at the little sandwich place around the corner. Only two items on the menu today: salami with cheese or salami without cheese. Leming chose the former. After all, it was said, you only live once.

Scott asked him, "How's life in the rent-free world?"

"You know, for a well-thought of professor, I expected better digs. Her taste in wine is mediocre, and there were no hidden books of folklore."

"I hoped that some dim story from the past might throw some light on them."

"What's wrong with space aliens, mutations, and inter-dimensional travelers?"

"Those are modern myths. We think we understand them because they use, or rather misuse, the language of science to explain things."

"You don't agree with your ex? That they're the Eyes of god?"

"I am more of a Pink than a White. Hell, I'd be more of a Black except that I don't like drugs or S&M."

A group of Whites were marching down 11th. They carried signs urging all to repent. "Make Your Soul As White As The Son!" Some signs read "Sun" instead of "Son." Their clothes—shirts, pants, scarves, and shoes were certainly white—reminded Leming of ads for bleach when he was kid. "Get your clothes whiter than white!" Leming saw that Molly was not among them. He didn't know if Molly had joined them, but she shared their ideology. She felt the Eyes were here to make moral judgments. To judge against sex outside of marriage, or affairs, or casual drug use. Molly's divorce to her husband hadn't become official when she and Ron Leming had begun the physical side of their relationship. A week after the first Eyes had arrived in Austin, attaching themselves to the underside of the Congress St. Bridge, one had flown to her window at night. She and Ron were making love when she saw its ugly, semi-transparent shadow on her window. She jumped out of bed, covered herself, and ordered him to leave. He was terrified. Nobody went out at night, but she screamed and screamed. He ran to his car, expecting at any minute to be touched by their sticky, flexible skin. He thought one flew over his shoulder.

He had tried to call for the first few days. That was when phone service was fairly reliable, and few people had fled the city. He drove to her home once, knocked and got no answer. Maybe she was gone; maybe she was living in one of the White tent cities.

There were four political parties/gangs/religions in deserted Austin—in most of the US, in fact. The largest was the Whites, advocating a life of total purity: no masturbation, no meat, no drugs, no swearing, and no you name it. The next largest group was the Pinks. They advocated denial. Act like the Eyes didn't fly around at night, didn't roost in dark places during the day, and didn't really have pupils that focused on you. Despite their denial, Pinks stayed inside at night, and largely drank heavily. The Blacks and the Purples seemed to be about the same size, if there was anyone keeping demographics these days. Both groups were small and the rumors about them were terrible. The Blacks were a sort of Latter Day Satanists, claiming the Eyes were the perception organs of some evil being, either Satan Himself, or something more eldritch and evil like Zushakon, the god of Darkness of some obscure California Indian tribe, or Ah Puch of the Mayas. The devil simply wanted to watch—so they organized orgies, heroin parties, S&M spectaculars, chanted formulae from cheap paperback grimoires, parked in handicapped parking spaces, and the like. They hoped to either impress or appease the presumably bored god that had travelled across unimaginable abysses for a cheap thrill. Rumors abounded. At this Black Mass, the Eyes had attached themselves to the worshippers; at that orgy, fire had shot from the Eyes' pupils, barbecuing the miscreants. Most people thought that the rumors were White hate mongering. But anything could be repeated in the daylight, when it could be both half believed and half laughed at. The Purples claimed to have a "scientific attitude." The Eyes were UFO aliens, or extensions from another brane, or a response to pollution, global warming, and Monsanto. But their approaches were simply recycled urban superstition and pseudo-science. They collected americium from smoke detectors and made anti-Eye shields. They erected pyramids so that "shape waves" would drive the Eyes away. They played with Tesla coils and Theremins. Of course there were rumors here as well. Dr. Leonard Walton of Sherman Oaks had communicated with the Eyes using an old Pac-Man game. Susan McWhortle of St. Louis had driven them away by finding a certain radio frequency. Eliot Chang of San Francisco had driven them to a piranha-style feeding frenzy by spraying them with insecticide.

The White parade passed the restaurant. Conversation stopped inside. The six patrons and two employees looked at each other. Everyone wanted to respond exactly like everyone else. Nobody liked taking a stand anymore. Conversation picked up again in a few minutes. No mention of the Whites, although a young couple sitting in back looked very shame faced. No one mentioned the Eyes.

Back at work, Leming thought about quitting. The economy was going to collapse soon enough, but the ritual of his job gave him comfort. He went to his manager.

"I'm going to drive out to the Two Step and talk to the owner. Maybe he can suggest something."

"Be careful. Inside a bar it is dark, and you might not keep an eye on the daylight. You don't want to have to spend the night there, unless you've developed a taste for Country and Western Music. Take your car, not your scooter. At least you still dress like you're part of a business."

There was no way he would drive under an underpass on his scooter. The Eyes seldom flew in daylight, but the thought of it was too creepy.

The Two Step was a pretty famous bar. Austin, "the Live Music Capital of the World," had several destination clubs, bars, and other venues. If you liked Country and Western, you headed to the Two Step on South Lamar. There was no traffic these days. Like everyone else, Leming speeded under the bridges and didn't look up. The bar, a large one story wooden building, had a big parking lot. Inside was cool. Willie Nelson crooned on the juke box. One couple slow danced, three or four others were finishing a pitcher of Lone Star Draft. Texas LSD. The bar's owner, Jimmy Ray Searight, was bullshitting the barkeeper. He gave Leming a long stare.

"Sorry, mister. Checking out your clothes."

Leming wore a blue seersucker suit and a bowtie.

Leming shrugged.

"You're so light. I was afraid you were a White. Three of them came in the other day, threw white paint all over me." Searight pointed to a white paint splotch on the floor. "They aim to close us down, talking with the emergency city council. Who are you?"

"I'm Ron Leming. I work GD&C. I'm designing your ad campaign."

Searight laughed, "Well, I could sure use it. This place used to be packed. Don't know where we would run it that would do any good. What are you drinking?"

"Shiner."

Searight nodded to the barkeep.

Leming discussed his ideas for a while, but Searight had other things on his mind. The White attack had disturbed him.

"Leming, they hinted to me that the city council is in contact with them."

"Sounds more like a Purple rumor."

"These religious types are dangerous. They hate fun. Always have. Back when they were the Puritans they made trouble against Shakespeare. When they were the Citizens Against Pornography they tried to close down the porno theaters. Of course VCRs later took care of that."

"Maybe your ad campaign should be 'Bring Fun Back!'"

"'Bring Fun Back!' Hell yes. We should bring fun back. Not crazy fun like the Blacks. Good, clean American fun. Maybe we should hold an outdoor event. Outdoors at night."

"That might be a hard sell."

"Do you honestly know of any Eye attacks? I mean, we hear all the time about how the friend of your uncle's chiropractor died of a heart attack because he stepped on one of them in the dark. But do you honestly know of any attacks? Any deaths?"

Leming waited thirty full seconds before answering.

"No, sir. And I've been thinking about that a lot."

"I'll give you ten thousand cash dollars if you can organize an outdoor party here in two weeks."

His boss thought he was crazy. But no other money was coming in.

He went home at 5:15. There was an Eye dying on the parking lot.

It looked like a large model of an animal cell, nearly eighteen inches across. Roughly oval, it had many dendrites with small suckers that it used to attach itself to surfaces. Grey and translucent, it had an eye where a cell had its nucleus. The center of the Eye was six or seven inches thick, and it narrowed to about an inch thick on the rim. The eye inside looked like a human eye. This one was blue. When the creatures started to die, the inner eye moved randomly, not focusing on anything. When it was healthy, you could *feel* when it was looking at you. It was like the feeling you used to get in the old days that someone was looking at you (say at a movie theater). But this feeling was a hundred, a thousand times more intense. In theory, the government was studying it. The Eye before Leming began to twitch. Before they died they would vibrate. Just before death the dendrites would whip through the air, making high pitched scree like a bullroarer. Then, at the moment of death, its membrane split open, releasing the eye and the foul smelling cytoplasm. It drew ants and roaches in swarms, and the smell could make you lose your supper for weeks. Leming didn't want the eye to die here. It would make the whole parking lot smell for a week. And sometimes after the death of an Eye, hundreds would show up that night, perhaps mourning their fallen comrade.

He looked around for some cardboard, or maybe a trash sack. He found some in the big blue dumpster. With great distaste, he picked up the Eye with the white trash bag and dumped it in the remains of an Amazon.com delivery box. The eye inside suddenly focused on him. He felt so *observed*, he started to throw the box away and just run. But the eye went back to its random twitching. He walked to the alley. No other Eyes were watching him, and he certainly did not want the few remaining neighbors to see. He trotted down the alley until he was three blocks away from his apartment house and tossed the Eye in a dumpster.

Before he had squatted in Dr. Walthers' apartment, Ron had lived in a small rental house in north Austin. Now he felt like that old man who took his dog to poop in his yard every night—a victim that shows his defiance by his miserableness. He knew he had polluted the block he left the Eye to die in, but what was he supposed to do? Take it on a drive? Throw it in Town Lake?

He pulled his shades that night. He didn't feel defiant. He had disquieting dreams about drums and fire, and once he thought he saw Dr. Walthers.

The next he drew up designs for a huge poster:

BRING FUN BACK. LIVE MUSIC. GAMES FOR THE WHOLE FAMILY. FIRST BEER OR COKE FREE. TAKE BACK THE NIGHT. THE TWO STEP 7:30 PM. BE THERE OR BE ☐

White back ground, alternating red and blue letters. Four feet tall, three feet wide. He would have them plastered around town. A couple of the sign shops they did business with still answered their phone. The first told him to fuck off. The second, run by an elderly ex-hippie, offered him a discount just for the hell of it. Two days later, the big posters were at every major thoroughfare. In addition, Groovy Printing had run off smaller sized posters, similar to the ones used for guitar lessons or garage sales, and added various logos to them: a marijuana leaf, crossed long necks, the University of Texas logo, bats, etc. These were on telephone poles in many neighborhoods.

The next day, two men in gray jumpsuits visited the offices of GD&C. The manger sent them to Leming. One was a young white man in his twenties with straw colored hair and a Hitler moustache. The other was a stocky, bald Mexican man with a narrow, whitish scar coming off his lip.

"We are not happy about this proposed gathering," said the older man.

"The Council has not approved it. Nor will they approve it," said the younger man.

"I was unaware the Council had anything to say about lawful assembly at a public space. Last time I checked, the Bill of Rights was still in place."

"I don't think you understand. We're saying the Council does not approve. You should consider where they get their orders from," said the younger man, pointing upwards towards God, the Feds, or maybe the Eyes.

"We are watching you," said the older man.

"Seems like the world is pretty full of watching these days," said Leming.

They left. They would be much more dramatic if they were taller or not dressed somewhat like janitors. He asked the manager if he should drop the gathering.

"A client paid for advertising. We advertised. Although, you might let him know."

Leming made a call. Searight said the Grays had visited as well. Very scary sounding. If they have some contact with the Eyes, the taxpayers need to know. Let's just play it out. So they were already Grays, yet another group slicing the thin pie of power thinner. He went to lunch with Scott.

"So you're going to the party?" asked Scott.

"Yeah. I am going to make a stand. As far as I know these things aren't even intelligent. They don't show any organization, any purpose. They just scare us. I want to make a stand."

"I think you're an idiot. I think the Eyes are a test. An alien IQ test to see if the monkey people will destroy themselves. Already we've factionalized. We've fled. Why? *Because something is looking at us.*"

"So wouldn't the response be to show we're not concerned?"

"This isn't about them. It's about us. If people party at the Two Step, Whites will show up to pray, Blacks will show up to get naked and whip each other. Grays will show with riot gear, and Purples will have spark guns and portable diathermy machines. It will be an unpleasant fight at best, even if no Eyes swoop in to watch."

"So you council cowardice."

"In this case, yes. Let Searight have his fling."

That afternoon after he left work, but still well before dark, he found two Grays in his apartment. One was a pale, red haired lesbian with a crew cut, the other a light skinned black man who was tall enough to be dramatic. They seemed shocked to see him.

The woman asked, "Are you a friend or relative of Dr. Miranda Walthers?"

"Friend," lied Leming. "What's this about?"

"We have bad news and a warrant," said the woman. "Why are you here?"

"Miranda asked me to water the plants."

The man said, "I am sorry to inform you that Dr. Miranda Walthers was found dead earlier today in Doublesign. She had hung herself. She left a note. It read 'The answer is in my apartment. Lemmus mos tenet verum. I don't suppose you read Latin."

THE LAST GOD

"No," lied Leming.

You don't get through four years of Latin at a Catholic school with a name like "Leming" without learning the Latin for "lemming"—lemmus. The sentence meant "The Lemming will know the truth." Ron was frankly scared shitless. Messages from women that hung themselves delivered by government toughs weren't any more a part of his life than the Eyes were.

The man said, "I'm Thomas Hayes, this is Patty Helinek What's your name?"

"John Falk." *No way was he going to say "Leming."*

"Any idea what the answer is?" asked Ms. Helinek.

"I have no idea. She was a folklorist at UT. You could check out her books."

He gestured at the floor-to-ceiling library. He had looked through dozens of volumes with no result, and then had continued to squat here to show his defiance to the Eyes and because he could walk to work. The two Grays looked at the books with dismay.

"Shit," said Mr. Hayes.

"Do you read?" asked Ms. Helinek, "I mean, read a lot?"

"I guess so," said Leming

"If you found something, could you let us know?" asked Ms. Helinek.

"Sure. I'm just like everyone else. I want to get to the bottom of this."

"Are you Purple?" asked Mr. Hayes.

"Hell, no. I'm Plaid."

"That's funny," said both of the Grays at once, without a trace of humor.

As soon as they were gone, Ron divided the apartment in grids to search. He took off work the next day, which was a Friday, so that he would have three days. If the dying doctor said the "lemming would know the truth," then by god he would. On Sunday morning he found it. He couldn't tell if it had exquisitely hidden or just fallen perfectly to be unobserved. A small thumb drive with a gun metal gray case was lying behind the leg of a desk in Dr. Walthers' bedroom. It would only be found by someone on their hands and knees. He plugged it into his laptop. It had only one file Roned "Notes." It read:

((Fix this up for article –ask Susan for biblo data on Codex C. Tell people what's what or let them figure it out??))

215

DON WEBB

The Maya are known for their observation/fascination with deep time. Like the Hindu cosmology, they are concerned with deep time, their chronicles reaching back 400,000,000 years, long before modern science tells us that humankind had made their appearance. The three major codices tell of the creation of humans by the gods—mainly for sport and amusement but with a certain understanding and affection as well. However, the lesser known *Codex Catamaco* (first cited by Barlow in 1949) paints a harsher picture. The *Codex Catamaco* was believed to be a hoax for many years, since Barlow provided no evidence in his brief article "A New Codex" *Anthropological Quarterly Spring 1949* ((Check pages #'s)) ((mention Barlow's weird life? Connection with Lovecraft and Burroughs??)), however Mary Denning's 1975 discovery of a copy of the Codex among a lot of Mexicana at Southby's established the bona-fides of the document.

The description of the gods and their purposes is unusual. The "gods" are said to have arrived after the explosion of a star and were almost bodiless for this reason. They sought to build bodies for themselves—humans being one of the trial forms, although a large black centipede seemed more suitable for most of them. They fed upon human beings' sensations and emotions, having lost these crucial aspects of being in the star explosion. These wounded gods were of terrible aspect (the aforementioned centipedes as well as winged toads, crabs, etc.), and had some sort of "night flyers" that gathered raw human emotion and sensation. Humans lived in abject fear of the gods and petitioned them for better dispensation. In agreement, the gods took on comely forms and the humans began religion—a form of feeding the gods the emotions they craved, especially guilt, which was prized for mistakes the wounded gods felt in connection with the star explosion. The wounded gods agreed to let mankind forget their true nature as long as religion provided them nourishment. They even let humans think that they lived beyond death as the bodiless gods do. They gave the maintenance of mankind to their youngest member, the God of Forgetting. He can never be summoned nor banished for no one remembers His name. They had great powers of illusion and forgetting. In sport, however, they chose certain humans to expose to reality, feeding on their fear, guilt, and despair. The *Codex Catamaco* stated that most of what seems arbitrary about human life are bad patches in the illusion the gods made. More frighteningly

That's where the notes ended. "More frighteningly." Great. Either Dr. Walthers was on the discovery of a lifetime, or she had gone a little mad. The seeds for it had been around ever since the "Mayan Doomsday" scare of 2012. She had found a terrifying cosmology that could explain the Eyes. Enough to turn a man Purple.

But what good was it? Was the "Lemming" supposed to go preach this in the streets? The party at the Two-Step seemed a better idea. The next night, Leming saw something that gave him hope. A small group of revelers were drinking beer on the roof top garden of the building next door. They weren't loud, but they were outside at night. The party grew silent at one moment when an Eye flew into their midst and attached itself to the base of a burned out lamp. But after a while, they began to party again (in a more subdued fashion), not leaving the roof until another hour had passed.

The next morning, Leming heard the sounds of other people in his apartment building. Either new squatters had moved in shortly after dawn, or maybe some of the original inhabitants had returned. A nearly full crew came to work, and the boss even chewed Maggie Whitney out for being late, when she sauntered in at 10:00.

That night there were cars on Congress. Only three. But that was three more than usual. The next day as he left Dr. Walthers' apartment, one of the neighbors gave him the stink eye. He smiled back at the woman and said, "Bring Fun Back!" The woman merely snorted at him. Perhaps if these were the original tenants he should perhaps return to his home in north Austin — they might be wary of a squatter. That night he moved out. He considered knocking on the door of the neighbor he had seen that morning and explaining that Dr. Walthers was dead, but all-in-all that seemed to raise more questions than it closed.

His lawn was overgrown. Several of his neighbors were mowing theirs even though it was late evening. Who was he to buck a trend? He pulled his mower out of the garage, fired it up, and let her rip. He waved at his next door neighbor as they each cut their grass. When he was done he called the guy over for a beer.

"We really let our lawns go," said John Haggard, a thin wiry man that had lived next door to Leming for four years. Leming couldn't recall a conversation with him that lasted more than five words.

"I think lawns were the last thing on our minds," said Ron Leming

"Funny so many of us reacted the same way."

"What do you expect? I'm just glad bravery is returning."

"Yeah," said John, "If you say so." He walked off with his beer.

An Eye flew down to the sycamore tree in Leming's front yard. It focused on him. He felt so drained that he nearly doubled over. He tried to speak but only made gurgling noises. He hoped Haggard would turn and see him—maybe carry him a few feet inside of his open garage and thus break the Eye's gaze.

Like a dozen other nights before, with the abrupt memory of the new day . . .

The next day at work, he got a call from Searight.

"Why the hell did you put up so many signs? I am not paying you guys a cent more."

Leming assured him, "Groovy Printing took it on themselves as a sort of holy quest."

"Yeah, well did you know your holy hippies added marijuana leaves to some of the posters? Or naked dancing girls?"

Leming hadn't seen the naked dancing girls. Maybe Groovy Printing was Black.

"Well I'm sure it will help the turn out."

"I've only got so much space. I can't believe that I ever thought this was a good idea. If I get in trouble with the police, I may talk to my lawyers about your firm."

"I doubt any police will bother themselves over a pot leaf or a picture of a naked woman. Besides, the party has already been a success. Have you seen the streets lately?"

"I see the streets every day. What do you mean? My bar sits on South Lamar."

"No. I mean have you seen the streets at night?"

"Well of course I have, what are you getting at?"

"Well maybe this isn't happening in your part of the woods, but people are out at night."

Searight sighed, "Of course they're out at night. Where would they be? My business runs on night people wanting to have a few beers, some fajitas and dance a little."

THE LAST GOD

"But the party . . . " began Leming.

"The party was your idea. Advertise the bar. Increase your patronage. Jeez, I don't what I was thinking. This place is jammed every night. I just hope I can handle the party. I know it's y'all's business to drum up business, but couldn't you have come up with something better?"

Leming talked for a while longer then put the phone down.

He had one more test. At lunch time he offered to drive Scott to a Mexican place in South Austin. As he drove under an underpass, its upper surface pulsing with sixty or seventy roosting Eyes, he pointed up at them.

"They still creep me out, even with people acting brave," said Leming.

Scott asked, "What creeps you out? Bridges? What are you talking about?"

"Oh, nothing," said Leming.

The rest of his life he was the only one that could see Them. He could see them drain people who didn't notice. He began to see other things, too. It was two years before he chose the same way out as Dr. Walthers. He pinned a note to his body with two words written on it:

More frighteningly

(This story is a nod to Lawrence Person)

⊢HƎ MⱯHLƎЯ SⱯЯⱯⱯM

BOB RITCHIE

HE LAST TIME Mahler has sex, his wife folds into an origami bird, and that makes Mahler wonder about . . . well, things. Like, how come a white towel gets dark when it's soaked in water, and when was the last time he changed the cat's litter box.

Besides, the bird isn't worth much. A bit of colored paper, now criss-crossed with fold marks. *That's what I call "state of the art,"* he thinks.

Mahler decides to call in a professional.

"My wife is a Japanese paper toy and there are many other, more important things on my mind. When's lunch?"

The pro scratches the bottom of his foot before replying. When he finally speaks, his voice sweeps up the leaves on the front lawn. "As a card-carrying plumber, I offer you this advice: Next time you paint your toenails, do not use a lead-based paint, and your toes won't fall off ever again. And get that water-heater checked. Here's my card." He hands over a pocketful of cats. The letters of the plumber's name have been shaved into their fur—one letter per cat.

Mahler puts the cats in the anything drawer for later perusal. He bows and says, "Thank you, Oh Wise, man. You have made me public again. Can I get you some pretzels?"

The shaking of Oh Wise's head hurls bolts of fabric. Mahler ducks but still gets quacked on the ear.

"No, my son," says Oh Wise's tattoo. "I must go to those who need my aid, and I cannot stop for frivolities. But if you've got a beer, I could take it with me. It would really take the edge off." He stands and wraps the sacred chain around his waist. "I'll send a bill."

220

THE MAHLER STREAM

Mahler, fears much eased by the sage advice, wonders, *What to do? What to do?* He looks up. But that is not enough. He looks down. That is only slightly better. Alas, he sees that his shoes are scuffed and dull; the picture of polish and a stained rag that comes to his mind depresses him. (Suicide is not out of the question.)

On continued examination, he notices that his shoes are curiously odd—oddly curious. He feels his body compressing into his feet and wishes that he had remembered to use his Dr. Scholl's. His last thought is *As if my feet weren't big enough already.*

See the feet, observe the eyes (one in each big toe); how sad they are. Bloodshot toes are so unattractive. Worse than that, Mahler is forced to spend a fortune on shoe repairs—no deductible—and his athlete's foot has spread to his ears.

A table walks, and the German shepherd down the street gets its PhD in philosophy. It wants to be a big city prof so it can pick up pretty young bitches.

No one is really sure what the table wants, but there it goes. It finally stops in front of Mahler's mother's *mal de mer;* the acidic spew etches the movie *Animal House* into the drying grain.

Soon, Mahler's life settles down into a routine: answer the phone, wash the carpet in the hall, leave his wife. He is bored easily, and only then does he learn how to succeed at business without really trying. When he buys an answering machine that doubles as a carpet cleaner, the boredom really begins to set in.

Desperate for change, he throws a party at some passing cars. The evening is not without entertainment, but he spends most of it listening to the tree-leaf babble of all the guests and the hiss of a tape-recording without Dolby. After the 10-car pileup is cleared away, Mahler is arrested for malicious mischief; when it is discovered that he no longer exists, the charges are dropped with a warning and a $25 fine.

Mahler finds non-existence to be exciting, though he misses Twister. He is sorry when he has to return for a dentist's appointment. He decides to run for mayor of Funky Town.

BOB RITCHIE

The first political ad opens with Mahler dressed in sheepskins and tennis shoes: he wants to appeal to a broad market. "Do you know the answer?" he asks. His fingers are red and white and his palm is blue (lonely for a pull). Mahler continues, "I used to, but it was extracted with my last molar." He rests his flaghand on one of the gun belts that crisscrosses his hairy chest; in the background, we hear a song by Metallica. "So, just like my opponent, Incumbent Upon Us, I ask for your support; don't send Dr. Roth's—they make my nose hurt and my feet just stay flat." A shower of paper robins fills the studio, covers Mahler from knee to neck; his wife starts pecking his penis. After Mahler moans, the background music changes to hamburger. His voice, muffled by frijoles, attempts to shout, "Please call 1324899876000301. Ask for Jessie. She'll do what she must. So will you. Vote for life." Hands grow out of the birds and cross at the wrists. "Take me away," he insists to the table full of ennui.

Thank you very much for riding the Gold Rusher, and I hope your stay here at Six Flags Magic Mountain has been and will continue to be the finest ever!

'Bye now.

SNOWFLAKES FALLING, PAGES TURNING

ELI WILDE

IFIRST SAW her in Meticulous Meticulous on Sunday night when I was serving beer in champagne glasses to geneticists after the news about Zion broke. She was on her own, sitting at my favourite place in the corner beside the Peace Lily. I don't like it when people sit in my corner.

I think it was her dark hair, so straight and perfectly gleaming beneath the low wattage down lighting. Just as easily, it could have been those melancholic eyes looking at nothing I could see in the bar. Maybe it was neither of those things. Maybe it was the languid way she drank her vodka. How she brought the glass to her lips and swallowed perfunctorily like she wasn't taking any pleasure in the drink, merely demonstrating how easily she could force herself to do something she didn't enjoy.

Red light angled in through the window above her as the last tram squealed its arrival. The doors opened and I saw the legs of two passengers step out of the carriage. Their heels echoed dully against the grey pavement and she suddenly looked toward the entrance. When no one entered she didn't appear surprised.

I'd like to say I didn't take advantage of her at closing time.

Her attraction was undeniable.

Taxis no longer ran after dark, not since the embargo. I walked her home the short distance to her apartment which was located above a restoration store close to the town centre. It was expansive with double bay windows to the front and four sets of sash windows to the rear. There were no rooms, no dividing walls. The lounge ran into the kitchen, the kitchen into the sleeping area, the sleeping area into the bathroom, the bathroom into the lounge. Glancing around the space I noticed a statue of David resting on the mantelpiece. It had been painted black. I could understand the need for someone to do that to him.

Alice walked over to the cube and pressed a button. Broken Bells streamed out from the high level speakers installed all around the apartment. It was like listening to music in 3D and I could easily have spent the remainder of the night doing no more than losing myself in those three dimensions. If she hadn't pulled me into her space. She tasted of neat vodka and her skin held a suggestion of the bar. The leather seat polish and constantly percolating coffee had found her and stayed with her. She removed all of my clothes while remaining fully clothed herself, and when she dragged me over to the bed I began to undress her. She fell into unconsciousness just as I removed her bra. Looking down at her nakedness I briefly considered all the possibilities presented before me on the crisp white sheets. Staring at her sleeping face, I tried to see what it was that made her different from all the others. Tried to understand her allure.

I could not name it.

I walked over to the kitchen and opened the refrigerator door. The bowl of cherries gleamed like they had been buffed with leather chair polish. I grabbed the bowl and began to eat the perfectly ripened fruit, spitting the stones back into the bowl. At the cube I flicked through her playlist and saw with some surprise that she had similar tastes to mine, despite the fact she was a brand new model. The wooden floor felt warm against the soles of my bare feet, like it was burning on the other side of the boards. Feeling a little queasy I ran the cold tap in the stainless steel sink and put my head underneath the flowing water. Cooler and clear of thought, I turned off the tap and dried my hair with the towel on the rail at the end of the counter.

After I finished the last of the cherries I began to feel hot again. Perhaps I was coming down with a fever. Leaving the bowl of cherry stones on top of the circular dining table, I walked over to the bed and removed her panties. Lying on the bed next to her, I moulded myself into her back and naked slept the rest of the night away.

The next morning I watched her crawl across the bed toward me. Her expression was neither sultry nor interested. The early morning light came in through the gap between the blinds, shining through the strands of her hair as she crept closer, magnifying her beauty. 'I want you again,' she said, mistakenly thinking we had sexed the night before. When she began to suck on my toe, I didn't think it right to tell her otherwise.

Afterward, we sat at the dining table eating croissants and strawberry jam. 'I don't even know your name,' she said, blowing the steaming espresso she held in both hands while staring at me eating her croissant.

'J . . .'

'I think I'll call you Y-Y.'

'What should I call you?'

'Let's watch a movie,' she said, rising from her seat and heading into the lounge area with her espresso left untouched on the table.

I sat on the walnut canapé sofa while she flicked through her movie collection. The sofa looked elegant, but it was impossible to get comfortable on the wicker seating and ornate frame. Holographic technology was no longer freely available; film reel was the fashionable alternative. The projector whirred into life and I watched it flicker on the large screen while she walked over to the bay windows and closed the blinds.

In near darkness, she wordlessly sat next to me holding the remote and pressed the buttons on the controller. After a short while, *Institute Benjamenta* appeared on the screen in glorious black and white and I was immediately drawn into its sound. The creak of leather as the servants swayed their way toward Alice affected me profoundly. It got inside my skull and eroticised. The way Alice talked when she asked her young saplings to refer to their manual—like a synthetic breathing into my ear while I slept—tingled my scalp. When we watched her cut herself with the deer hoof, my newfound lover squeezed my hand so tight I wanted to kiss her painfully.

'Did you like Alice?' she asked when the film had finished.

'Yes.'

She smiled. Sad, still, but pleased.

'Can I call you Alice?' I asked.

'Yes. Yes, I'd like that.' She rested her head on my shoulder then and closed her eyes. 'I want to dream in black and white.'

'What do you want to dream about?'

'I want to be a sapling.'

'A servant?'

'I don't want to make any more decisions.'

'Decisions about what?

She didn't reply. I think she pretended to sleep. Yes, I'm sure she wasn't sleeping. I closed my eyes too. Unsure where Alice was taking me other than how I felt. Cocooned inside her apartment, I never wanted to leave.

I awakened some time later with Alice regenerating against my shoulder. I was slumped against the arm of the canapé and it dug into my side, pins and needling me. It didn't matter; I didn't want to be anywhere else. I should have been back at the bar, but Meticulous Meticulous was just a job. Alice was something I had never experienced before.

She began to stir, lifting her head from my shoulder. 'Do you like Turkish food?'

'Yes.'

She got up and stretched. Went to the restored pay phone hanging next to the front door and ordered a takeaway.

'We have an hour before it arrives,' she said, 'time enough to bathe.'

Alice sat behind me in the bath with her wet, glistening legs on either side of my chest. She washed my hair with shampoo and the fragrance reminded me of a girl I liked in college. Ylang-Ylang, I secretly called her. When Alice rinsed me with the stainless steel shower head her fingers were as light as the wind and almost caressed me back to sleep. Later, Alice dried me with a white cotton towel as I stood in front of her. She dressed me in one of her bath gowns, while I concentrated on the tips of her fingers, each time they inadvertently touched my skin.

Sitting at the dining table, we drank pinot noir and listened to The Penguin Café Orchestra without speaking while we waited for the food. As expected, the meal arrived exactly one hour after Alice had ordered it. A teenage girl wearing a free issue Uprising T-shirt waited as Alice showed her ID. I stared at the girl, trying to discern what was different about her face to mine. She wore a baseball cap instead of a motorcycle helmet as part of her rebellious behaviour against the faction. Alice paid with correctly weighted coins. From her disposition, I couldn't tell if the girl was synthetic or clone in nature like me.

I sat at the dining table while Alice removed the food from the takeaway wrappings and served them on her perfectly white dishes. She sat opposite, drinking pinot noir, watching me eat kashkek with cacik yoghurt and tandir bread.

'Why do you hate your studies?' she suddenly asked.

'Because I want to be a poet.'

'You write poetry?'

'No.'

'Why not?'

'I don't know how to write poetry.'

'Do you keep a journal?'

'No.'

'I want you to write about your time here with me.'

'Okay.'

'Do you ever write?' I asked Alice.

'Not anymore.'

After I finished eating, Alice wouldn't allow me to wash the dishes; I was never to wash dishes, she told me. I watched her as she rubbed them clean, clean again, then simply continued to rub them with the cloth like she was doing something essentially profound. Watching her working this way filled me with something I can only describe as adoration. The snow affected everyone in different ways, yet we were all the same when you looked at things without thinking. I didn't want to stop her; it didn't feel like my place. She had slipped into temporal fugue, that was all, nothing serious. I eventually took the cloth away from her and guided her to bed. She needed rest. She needed me. She closed her eyes without knowing she was doing so and slept as she began to reset.

I picked up the journal Alice had given me and sat at the table watching her breathe, wishing I could follow her into her dreams; hating being apart from her. I closed my eyes and tried to imagine what she saw while she slept. We were together, before the faction and winter, before cloning spoiled everything. It was snowing and there was no sadness when it snowed here, no loss of innocence, only joyfulness. We heard bells; they rang out in the distance, but they were bells all the same. And there were men here too, like those we saw in movies.

I opened my eyes.

The journal stared blankly at me. Picking up the pen, I began to fill the journal with words about Alice. The scent of her skin. How she whispered in her sleep. The way her artificial eyes always betrayed her feelings. We had only been together a short while, yet I understood her like nothing else I had ever encountered before. Never had writing come so easily to me, and reading the words I had written, it felt at last like I was writing poetry. Poetry only I could understand.

At the refrigerator I opened the door and picked up a jar of beetroot.

Placing it on the dining room table, I moved toward the counter and the bread.

'Let me do that.' Alice said behind me. 'You are never to make food for yourself.'

She had reset perfectly.

I sat down at the table and watched her prepare my sandwich.

'How is your writing going?'

'Fine, I really enjoy writing about us. Do you want me to read it to you?'

'We need to go shopping. I want to buy you some clothes.'

Alice placed the sandwich in front of me.

Biting into the sandwich, I didn't taste anything, not even the synthetically produced olives inside.

I didn't want to leave the apartment. Not even for a brief moment.

'Hurry, we need to set off before sun fall.' Alice said.

How could she want to go outside? I didn't want to share her with anyone else. Something was wrong. I had miscalculated everything. 'I think it is going to snow.'

Alice walked to the window and placed her hand on the glass, staring outside. 'It won't snow today.'

When she took her hand away from the glass, I watched her fingerprints disappear on the reflective surface.

'I'm tired of seeing you in Meticulous Meticulous garb,' Alice said. 'Hurry up and finish eating.'

Stepping back into the world after I had finished my sandwich, the rain immediately began to touch her, making her wet, leaving her that way, while the wind thought I couldn't see it caressing her, running its invisible fingers through her hair. I despised the wind and the rain, but it was the others who hurt the most, as I watched their eyes take Alice into those places I could never follow. The places I could only ever imagine.

Holding onto my hand, Alice led me into the shop. Inside, I gave the assistant - who looked exactly like me, my fierce gaze as she stared at Alice too long. I wanted her to look different to me, but the differences were miniscule, almost imperceptible unless you stared and stared and stared. Even then, sometimes I never recognised the difference. Cloning is too clever, too clear-cut; like a mirror that never reveals everything, it keeps secrets. You have to stare at it from the edge of the mirror. Only then can you see how imprecise and cruel it has become.

SNOWFLAKES FALLING, PAGES TURNING

I agreed to the first clothes Alice chose for me. She paid for them with correctly weighted coins and I walked out of the shop dressed just the way she liked in clothes far too elegant for a student wanting to hide.

'Can we go back to the apartment now?' I said.

'We should do something with your hair.'

'Like what?'

'It needs to be red.'

'I like it just the way it is.'

'The sun will start to fall soon.'

'Can we go back to the apartment if I let you colour my hair?'

She didn't reply, but I didn't care when I saw the way she smiled. And afterwards, my hair, long and red, wasn't so bad.

'Can we go back to the apartment now?'

'After you see my favourite coffee shop.'

She asked me right away, in the café as I sipped black coffee and bit into a cheese Panini. 'Do you like my skin?'

I loved the way she talked, the sound of her voice. The way her eyes watched intensely; curious orbs of artificial intelligence, seeing more than I wanted to show. Taking my time, chewing deliberately, I pretended not to care about her question. She fell back into the creaking seat, smiling perception. She already knew the answer. Knew me better than I knew myself. She sipped her wine, but left the aubergine wrap untouched.

Stepping back into the apartment, I relaxed; Alice was mine once more. She tasted of rain and the windswept park, where she took me after we finished shopping. Her hands guided mine across her body to the places she wanted me to touch. She pulled open my dress and her teeth rolled my nipple. I gasped when she bit too hard. Her skin's scent, moved me to the edge, reminded me of the garden in my dreams. The one full of Ylang Ylang, where I was born as an individual and created by God not in a lab. The garden where I possessed a soul.

When she grabbed hold of me—one hand on each side of my head— she found my mouth and we crossed the line until it became blurred and I no longer knew right from wrong.

She slept afterward and I wrote while waiting for the delivery. Snow filled my journal, falling silently without landing, bloodless and pure. Alice too, was present on every page, with eyes no longer wearied by neglect.

The wine arrived at the usual time, and I paid the teenage girl with the correctly weighted coins Alice had left beside the statue of David. As I stared at the girl, I thought I saw something in her eyes. Something different to me. When I opened the package I was surprised to see synthetic merlot inside instead of pinot noir.

'They've sent the wrong wine,' I told Alice when she awakened.

'It's not a mistake,' she said, yawning into her hands. 'I ordered merlot.'

I didn't mind merlot or pinot; it was all the same to me, but not so Alice. I knew something had changed. While she washed, I made myself a beetroot sandwich. 'Are we watching a movie tonight?'

'We are going out tonight.'

I ate the sandwich without comment from Alice. When I finished, I washed the plate and she took me away from our apartment once more.

Zoom Zoom's was full of dark shadows twisting in and out of the light searching for the abandoned. It was all in my mind, everything I saw. Alice danced with everyone, everyone except me. I wanted to leave her but when she sat on her own with her eyes holding that look again, I knew I would never leave her. She started to drink vodka for the first time since we met. I didn't want to take advantage of her, but I would if it mattered.

Near curfew, we walked back through the park, following the path that led to the vacant play area. Winter was coming to an end, everyone was sure about that. It hadn't snowed for over a month. Alice lit two cigarettes and handed one to me. I wondered what pleasure she gained from such things. The smell of candy suddenly filled my senses, something I hadn't experienced since birth, the only time we were spoiled. She never looked at the swing, though we both heard it sway in the breeze. I wondered how children's laughter sounded, other than how it did on celluloid. What it must feel like to hold a child. Taking in a final lungful of diluted nicotine, I stamped the cigarette into the ground and we meandered into the darkness listening out for the tram that would take us home.

Alice awakened late in the afternoon the next day and poured herself a merlot. She no longer asked me about my writing. I continued to write all the time anyway. It helped me conceive. She bathed alone listening to Lyckantropen Themes and Ylang Ylang filled the apartment when she started to wash her hair.

'It's snowing,' I said, after she dried herself.

SNOWFLAKES FALLING, PAGES TURNING

She stared at me and then hurried over to the bay window, parting the blinds. 'They said reality would emerge now that Zion has finally been unearthed.'

'Yes, they did,' I said, knowing it was a lie.

Zion was dead. It would never return. Only clones and synthetics endured, trying to be human because there was nothing else to aspire to. I walked to the window and stood beside her, staring out into the streets where no one ever walked. The shops and restaurants in this area had long since closed down. Only the streetlamps remained standing. Unlit, they continued to hide the wretchedness below.

'It will never stop snowing,' she said, as she started to cut her arm with the blade.

I knew her then, as dark blood dripped from her tubes. I knew all of them. Understood why they smoked and drank and sometimes ate.

They did it for us.

And the engineers of old had their reasons for turning red blood into black. I think they did it to show the darkness at the heart of human nature. 'It's so beautiful,' I said, watching the soundless fissile winter fall and land fractal. Realising then, how even in the depths of psychosis we are still so fragile.

⊢H∃ ⊣NMOS⊢ PL◁G⊃∃ B∃LL SW⊣MS

ANTONIO MAGOGOLI

AFTER THE GENTLEMAN left, Aldo unbuttoned his shirt and leaned back in his leather chair. It had been a tiring evening, a tiring conversation. The gentleman had given him many things to ponder. Aldo knew sleep would not come. No, not this night. Sleep would not come.

Everything is dirty and corrupt within the village and outside of it. We have no energy for anything but our silly philosophy. Juice from wounds shower us. Stars preach to us about our dining arrangements.

Aldo finished his scotch and closed his eyes. In the darkness of his eyelids, Aldo saw the gentleman's face. It was a handsome face, one that both comforted and disturbed him. The question the gentleman named Gennaro had posed was still reverberating in his mind.

"Do you want to have dinner?"

I have met with men on roads and have divulged the secrets concerning all structures and have opened my ears for them. They insert knives into my codes. They insert blades into my playful manikin train birds. They insert coins into my eye sockets and fish out false bruises that color in books fresh from the bakery. The dinner plans have died, anyway.

Everything the gentleman had offered was attractive but still... Aldo's instinct was to refuse. There was something about the offer that scared him. In fact, it terrified him.

"I'll come back tomorrow," the gentleman had said. "I hope you have decided by then."

THE INMOST PLAGUE BELL SWIMS

You look at me so oddly, as if I'd betray your philosophy or betray your somewhat incomplete life in that 'hospital'. What a 'hospital' it is! Have you eaten?

Aldo's eyes were still closed when he heard his dog walk into the room.

"Pepper, come 'ere, my dear boy," Aldo said. He opened his eyes and saw that his loyal friend had stopped in the middle of the room and was staring at his master. "What is it, boy?"

Things will not get better, dear Gennaro. Things will get much, much worse and spill the blood of millions in the caves off the coast, the caves filled with witches and bottles of filthy lungs and spells and teeth but we do not believe in these things, these ugly things because the last thing we want to do is accept the superstitions of our fathers and long-faded shadows blacking out windows and ugly skin we want to strip off and shade the sky with. Gennaro doesn't deserve us. We're not hungry just yet.

The dog was still.

Aldo coughed plumes of breakfast.

Someone built structures out of toy blocks and left them here for me to clean up. I am appalled but not surprised. I AM VERY SURPRISED. I do not have disgust for anything BUT YOU but you know that because you have seen my murderous rage when I pulled my knife from my coat and held it up to your skinny effeminate neck and said, 'You disgust me just as much as you disgust yourself!' but I did not harm you because to harm you is to give you the satisfaction of winning my passion even if only venomous passion. You were never ever hungry.

Aldo got up from the chair and approached his pet. The animal did not make any movement in response. It continued to stare at Aldo.

"Boy, what are you up to?" Aldo said, slowly moving his hand forward to pet Pepper. Once he made contact with its fur, he was relieved to see the dog go back to normal. It barked happily. It burped plumes of breakfast.

Aldo scratched under its neck, showering the animal with attention. "That's my boy. There he is. There he is."

The telephone sprang from its cage and rang.

There are splendid rituals inherent in splendorous structures, simple structures, complex structures, all structures alive or dead, beautiful or ugly, calm or anxious, shoved into dust, those cement structures and structures made of playing cards and matchsticks, twigs and blocks, idols and fermented fruit. Your lemon tree is for the hangman, the limp-wristed hangman who spills candy from the gut and builds puppets in the attic of the Milligan Lady. Your hunger is now apparent.

"Hello?" Aldo said, standing in the hallway, holding the phone to his ear, watching Pepper walk into the kitchen.

There was no reply so he said again, "Hello?"

Pepper sprung ghosts along the road with tables with no chance to plot the long headed murders in the books. What books? What books, you say? We don't know, you traitorous worm! Eat!

The person on the other end cleared their throat and said, "Mr. Magogoli?"

"Yes?" Aldo said.

There was no response.

Things won't go the way of his philosophy if he doesn't put on the shirt, put on his father's worn shirt and watch the trains go by with their goats and their ugly stink of women, perhaps police officers perhaps just farmers waiting for blood and popular genes.

"Who is this?"

Again no response.

Blackbirds bit the king (Gennaro) and outlasted the entire population of singing stars and costumed Greeks who fought against playful librarians who check me in and check me out and read me to the children like ugly puppet tales (Punch and Boothie).

"I want to know who this is!"

Spread the phone butter across the lisping cowards.

Another clearing of the throat and then, "Mr. Magogoli?"

Everything is a moment NOW and not from some universal source.

"I already answered, damn you!"

I know where you can find these men. (Find these men and kill these men!) They hide out in the back room of the shop called WAYWARD DOMES. I've been there. I know many of you have been there. It is a den of weak vipers. The birthplace of Poor Jim, that cowardly cuckold!

The person on the other end hung up.

A cat meowed in tune with the wind.

Aldo knew going up to bed would be futile. It would not bring him rest. Instead, he grabbed a book out of his library and went back to his parlor where he sat down in his leather chair. He opened the book and started to read, hoping the very act of his eyes moving back and forth would bring sleepiness and eventually lull him into a few hours of peace.

THE INMOST PLAGUE BELL SWIMS

Those who dare return to their birthplace, those are the true artists. They wish to use the palette that was bestowed upon them by the gods, by fate, the very force of creation. This artist fills his chalice with pure and unadulterated creativity, with the very core of their destiny. This destiny more often than not includes their eventual destruction by the very art itself. Destruction by creation, a circular temple of a fate played out in artful strokes of annihilation.

Aldo awoke from his wakefulness.

That fickle light bringer, that ungrateful slug that oils the machine. You know his leader, the man who is the father of the infamous man known simply as "THE INMOST HOST."

There was a knock on the door. Aldo was startled and frightened. He hated being surprised at a visitor's arrival. He needed to be prepared for any sort of intrusion.

Aldo rubbed the words out of the book and coughed out plumes of yesterday's lunch.

He walked over to the window and looked out. The gentleman was at the door.

But was he?

The folk songs of my village are haunting odes to the Stone Age perversions of my mechanical ancestors. You are the only one in the penultimate universe. Eat the false toy block moon.

The gentleman was very handsome.

Drink wine unearthed from the farm. The stench of cosmic pride. Your intestinal homesteads relieve you and pocket the spoils of the shopping center. You wear masks and make noise. Sing your songs but don't worry. I AM RECOVERING OKAY. The solar crocodile opens wide.

WITH RESPECT.

He eats dinner and talks French and he is the surgeon! He wants to render his fantasies into abstract meat. He is a whore on the beach of philosophical posturing, a devil from deep in the earth, from the bottle, from the wet spider web of the north shaped into rectangles and draining into bloated childhoods vomited back into political art of his elderly years.

Handsome still, yes, but Aldo thought the man looked . . . different. This couldn't have been the same man!

Aldo opened the door.

Blackened bakers bake body-shaped buns.

"Have you decided?"

Aldo will be left raped and murdered under a brazen sky made of lung!

"I'm afraid I have not. In fact, I have just woken up when you knocked. I really haven't had the time to think."

A fancy fop under suspicion!

"That's unfortunate. I'm afraid I simply do not have the time to leave and come back yet again. Is there any chance you'd be able to make the decision at this moment? Will you accept my help now?"

"I . . . I just don't know."

Pepper dies.

A leaky flip runs flippant around the structured bogs while doomsday cogs explode possum dust through the highways of motion sickness chimpanzees.

"That's unfortunate," the gentleman said. "Quite unfortunate indeed."

All the nurses molest you. All the doctors examine you with their spidery fingers and metallic instruments. They fill out charts in cuneiform and call upon your parents to tell them the terrible news.

Aldo awoke from his wakefulness.

Animals make ugly animal sounds through lemon tree horns.

Aldo found himself neither in his leather chair nor in his bed. He wasn't in his parlor or his bedroom. He wasn't even in his house.

Aldo was lying on grass in the midst of stone ruins. Whatever had stood there previously was ancient. Had it been a church or temple of some sort? Aldo didn't know but he was more concerned with how he got there.

Some structures are born for ruin. You are poor and weak!

Aldo stood up and walked a few feet toward an opening in the ruins. He looked out and saw nothing but a wide expanse of grass and the occasional tree.

Someone has turned his book into an instrument... for torturous intent!

There were no buildings. There were no people, no sign of civilization.

Except for the ruins.

And a voice.

"Do you want to have dinner?"

⊢HƎ S⊢A⊢ƎMƎN⊢ O⊣ ⊢OM ⊢ЯYO⊃T

CHRIS KELSO

1.

THE BIRDS WOULD watch Tom eat. They'd gather on the pier and leer at him, white as almond blossoms, as if they *knew* something.

Outside—a staccato of fireworks

Tom Tryout observed the wound he'd made in his girlfriend's belly. Its ripe rawness was almost vaginal, gaped to maximum resistance, leaking, budding ever outwards in ugly red shrooms of tissue.

Tom took out a syringe and dug it into the bar of Suzie's semi-rigoured forearm. He descended the plunger then brought it back up slowly. He brought it up to view, studied the measure of blood that filled the gauge. The Gangles outside squawked. He smiled. Tom could hear Mr Kowalski outside trimming his lawn with that old busted-up mower of his, the one with the stiff pull-chain and shifting mechanical guts as loud as an ironmonger's clank.

—I sure know how to pick 'em huh?—Tom addressed no one.

He rolled up his shirt sleeve and pinched the flesh on his bicep until it became rouged with the colour of sudden circulation. Tom stuck himself with the needle, sinking the plunger till Suzie's blood mixed with his within the great sarcophagus of flesh. Tom had an erection too.

—*No point ignoring it*—he thought out loud, unbuckling himself and seizing his thickened shank with a firm, murderous hand. He leaned over his girlfriend's detonated corpse and . . .

Tom looked down at his wilting penis and knew he just couldn't do it. He hated Suzie and everything she'd done to him, but raping her corpse seemed . . . a touch excessive maybe? They had only slept together once before. It meant a lot to Tom but not a lot to Suzie, and wasn't that always just the way with boys like Tom?

He was seventeen years old now. Suzie was his third girlfriend but the first one he loved enough to murder.

Cue soporific vibrations of a migraine . . .

Two Tuesday's ago . . .

It was trash day. Lines of refuse bins sat curbside, pregnant with garbage. Tom liked his seaside town. Every lawn on Shaver Point was lush and always freshly-cut for summer. Each house on his avenue sat prettily opposite the verdant greens with their panels of white timber.

He'd known most of his neighbours since he was a young kid, and liked most of them too. He thought they were all real friendly folks. Outside his window were the sounds of the brawling sea by the pier, the gentle idling of boats, of happy people, inner calm, arsenic white sands on the horizon like a sudden stroke of snow on coloured canvas . . .

Equally, there was much Tom *didn't* like about his street, mostly to do with *her* . . .

Love had left him with a great heaving anvil in his chest. He still hadn't gotten used to life without Suzie. He sincerely believed he never would, Tom being a teenager of suicidal ideation as it was.

Suzie lived three blocks from his house and he had to walk past her window on his way to school every morning. The pain was unbearable, cruel even. Tom felt sure he was being punished for something, maybe for giving his heart away too easily. He proceeded to move through life like a dismal flame, lath thin.

Tom couldn't help but look in the window as he walked past, squint through his own reflection. One time he was met with the hostile golem-mask of Suzie's father, who'd always hated Tom for being a wimpy sort of kid.

Suzie had just dumped him before spring break; it was all very sudden. She was going off to university to become a marine biologist or something. He'd never see her again, he was sure of it. Worse than that, Tom had been plagued by these crippling headaches since her departure.

THE STATEMENT OF TOM TRYOUT

He figured it was just another one of those weird physical reactions to unexpected loss—he supposed his body was lacking the essential nutrients of love. Granted, Suzie was a beautiful girl and Tom really believed she felt the same way about him as he did about her.

Suzie said she still wanted to be friends, that they'd just drifted apart lately, no big deal—but Tom soon discovered the truth. Barely a week later she started dating Leo Kricfalusi. Leo tormented Tom growing up, now he'd stolen his girl.

It just wasn't fair.

The Winged Shaver Gangles gathered in a suspended configuration—the white cartel. Tom's presence always seemed to induce an angry reaction from the birds. Upon mere sight of the boy the birds started weaving in a regimented formation, as if poised for attack, as if they saw his presence in the town as a threat. They'd squawk and jibe him in a chorus of rasping klaxons, they'd dive-bomb from the air and charge him beak-first until he was well out of sight, away from the pier . . .

Sometimes Tom thought they sounded almost human—WIMP, HEY WIMP! WIMP! WIMP! HEY, FUCKIN' WIMPY KID! Or—HEY, HEY PEANUT DICK? HEY, FUCKIN' PEANUT?

That awful, elongated screech. It was unreasonable.

The Gangles owned the pier. It seemed as if every Gangle in the world came there between migrations. A cull was out of the question; the town was named Shaver Point after all, and they couldn't very well obliterate the thing that made their town unique. People just accepted that they were here to stay and learned to accept them.

This one Gangle sat perched on a lamp-post a few blocks down the street from Tom's house, its talons cut in keen edges. He got out his telescope and mounted it on a tripod. This bird looked different. Tom stared until he met its gaze. Its eyes were like black buttons, impenetrable, fierce as the fiend in hell. He was certain the Gangle had a severed arm dangling from its yellow neb.

Eventually the bird soared off towards the pier with barely a beat of its wings.

On his way to the store for his father, Tom saw Mr Kowalski mowing his lawn. He smiled at Tom when he walked past.

—Morning Mr Kowalski.

—Mornin' Tom m'boy! Powerful weather we're havin' huh? Looks like it's gonna be a good one! Damn Gangles aside . . .

—Yeah, they're acting weirder by the day.

—They're getting fat as fools!

—My dad had to put tension wire on the roof to stop them pulling off the insulation. Mr Kowalski tutted out loud.

—The celestial bird my keister!

Tom noticed the busted-up push mower the old man was using.

—You know, my dad has a cordless power mower if you need it?

Mr Kowalski gave a big jolly laugh.

—No, no. I'm okay with this ol' heap oh junk, don't you worry bout that. Say, you on your way to the store sonny?

Tom nodded.

—Here, pick me up a bottle of aspirin would ya?

Mr Kowalski tossed Tom three coins, not nearly enough for a bottle of aspirin.

—Sure thing.

—You're a good boy Tommy.

Tom hated being called Tommy but didn't mind it so much when Mr Kowalski said it. He was a harmless old coot. He was an old city guy from some grease-trap on the outskirts of paradise. You could really tell that Shaver Point brought him a lot of spiritual calm.

In the store, Tom picked up the aspirin along with a bag of pretzels and a blueberry slushy. His dad wanted him to pick up some fruit and milk, which he forgot to do. His skull was still throbbing a little so he took a couple of aspirin from the bottle he'd bought for Mr Kowalski and crunched them—his face twisted by the awful taste of flavourless medical powder. He caught his reflection in the convex mirror. He saw the horror of freedom and responsibility. For a moment he was grateful for his burden of agony.

On his way out into the parking lot he saw Suzie with Leo Kricfalusi. Something in his gut anchored. Tom tried to duck behind a parked Chevy but he'd already been spotted. He tried to remain cool, composed, his emotions kept in check.

Leo was an overdeveloped teenager with a quarterback's upper body strength and hurdler's calves. Leo was a stark contrast to Tom, who'd looked the same since he was twelve years old and would surely remain thin as a gold leaf until his senior years. Kricfalusi smirked.

—Hey Tommy, you out shoppin' for your mommy?

Suzie nudged Leo in the arm. She didn't like to see Tom ridiculed. She'd put him through enough.

—They're for Mr Kowalski—Tom countered lamely.

—Aww, look at you, always the Good Samaritan huh?

Tom put his head down and tried to brush past Kricfalusi but got body-checked instead. Tom's slushy tipped all over his shirt. Kricfalusi found this hilarious. He picked up the aspirin and threw back a few pills before tossing the bottle back at Tom. When Tom looked up, he was more hurt to see a cruel grin on Suzie's face.

Then, at the apex of his humiliation, something wet and slimy cracked over his head and dripped down his face in foul streaks. Tom looked up and saw the Gangles circling. There was a maddened shriek and, on cue, a deluge of shit showered over the boy. They seemed ready to barnstorm. Tom wanted to just disappear, to not be standing there in front of Suzie covered in Shaver Gangle excrement.

After dropping off the aspirin at Mr Kowalski's place, and apologising for the half empty bottle, Tom ran straight upstairs to his room. When his father asked where the groceries were, Tom didn't reply. Dad was cool that way though, he always cut his boy some slack—after all, he knew what it felt like to lose your first love.

The following Tuesday, Tom was taking out two sacks of garbage just as the trucks were doing their rounds. He still hurt from his run-in with Suzie and Leo the week before; the whole ugly mess would be a long time in healing. Tom stuffed both bags into the container and was about to go back inside, when he stopped suddenly. One of the dump trucks was crushing up trash in its rear loader. The pneumatic grapple clutched another heap of bags and dropped them into the compactor. Tom watched on, mesmerised. His mind was fixed on fantasies about getting Leo back for all he'd ever done to him.

It would be tragic if he were to meet such an awful end. Then he could be with Suzie again. The soft murmurs of a migraine stole back his attention and he headed back inside with his hand clutched over his forehead.

This was the worst summer ever. Unlike Suzie, Tom hadn't bothered applying for university; he wanted to spend the summer with her before making any decisions about his future. All he knew was that he wanted Suzie to be in it.

The paintwork on Josie's house had been corroded by Gangle shit. Her parents were never home so it never got cleaned. If she hadn't been Tom's best friend he wouldn't have been seen dead going near that place.

Do you know about Hell's Orchard?—Josie asked, knowing the answer, knowing full well that Tom had articulated his fear about ever visiting the place. Josie often did that when she wanted to talk about something delicate but wasn't brave enough to just come out and say it. They made good platonic companions; Josie was stuck in the heart of her own existential nightmare.

—Course I know it.

—You heard about all those murders too then?

—I dunno . . .

—So why don't we, like, go down and check it out or somethin'?

—I don't want to, we have our last exam tomorrow.

—So? It'll only take, like, a sec . . .

The truth of the matter was that Tom had always been much too nervous to ever go near Hell's Orchard on the edge of town. It smelled of bygone nightmares.

—The rumours about him being a lizard isn't true . . . like, I'm sure of it.

—That's hardly my main concern!

The owner, *Mr Hell*, was a crapulous old man who shot dogs and stole children. Even Tom didn't want to cross the path of such inherent nastiness and evil. Josie dragged her nails through her long black tresses and flicked away the fringe with one jut of her neck. Josie's eyes were scored with gothic make-up. She looked at him past the fallen mask of hair and she grinned. Tom knew that grin. It meant she thought he was a chicken shit.

—I hear he can't kill women anyway because his reptilian Teiidae superiors are all female. Killing women is, like, totally against their culture.

—Lucky you . . .

—You still hung up on Suzie?

—A little . . .

—Hey man, like, fuck her. You can do better?

—You really think so?

—Well . . . nah, but, yano, I'm here for you n' stuff.

Tom heard the Gangles howling under the blister-bright sun, mocking him. Just like Leo Kricfalusi. While Josie was talking, he decided he would kill Suzie. It was the only thing he could think of doing that would alleviate this awful funk. His headaches wouldn't cease until he took action, until he stuck up for himself. Maybe then the birds would leave him alone too . . .

2.

Mr Alhazred screamed at his class to be quiet—his students fell dead silent. They hadn't seen him enter the room. Normally the kids in his classes shut their mouths just from the sound of his formal shoes clip-clopping down the corridor. This time they'd gotten sloppy; he caught them red-handed. When Mr Alhazred yelled, he yelled with his entire being. His jaw dislocated to a huge cavernous hole, teardrops of saliva shooting forth over the whole class.

—EXAM TIME YOU LITTLE PUKES! EXAM TIME, THAT MEANS SHUT YOUR GODDAMN SWILL HOLES!

Josie and Tom hadn't actually been misbehaving but took Alhazred's warning with a personal seriousness. He was wearing a summery T-shirt and Tom saw the Gangle in him—an ivory plumage with a dark mantle. Then there was that voice, that shrill, flustered screech which vibrated through your body like rickety train tracks beneath a hurtling locomotive. He reduced bullies to tears, irrevocably shattered the spirits of the sensitive. The only noise more ear-piercing came from the insane seagulls perched on the railings outside. Alhazred was a monster. They say he was possessed by the devil; it must've been something worse. It wasn't so hard to believe . . .

The exam hall smelled of teenage fear, the bubbling bile of anxiety . . .

Tom wasn't worried about his exams. He studied thoroughly and mathematics always came sort of naturally to him—in any case, extinguishing his ex-girlfriend the night before had left him oddly settled and focused. Even when a horde of Suzie's gal pals appeared in the corridor mumbling speculatively about her whereabouts, Tom wasn't worried. Even when everyone lined up in preparation to enter the exam hall and he could feel Leo Kricfalusi's stare follow after him . . .

He wasn't worried.

Worst case scenario, he'd kill them too.

—*Let them natter amongst themselves*—Tom thought to himself and remembered that—*the problem with women like them is that their cities have never been bombed and their mothers never told them to shut up.*

It was Bukowski who said that.

The invigilator, a stooping, bearded ignoramus, gave each student a number eight pencil and told them to begin. Tom opened his paper and started writing down answers to equations without really having to think. Ten minutes in, the invigilator started going into a semi-orgasmic sneezing fit.

—AHH . . . AHHH . . . AHHH . . . Jesus, it's comin' . . .

Tom, who was in the front row, directly under his gaze (and firing line), did well to ignore the haze of snot and sputum swarming from the invigilator's flaring orifices.

—It's com . . . AAAHHH-CHOO!!! CHOO!!! . . . eugh . . .

Tom finished his paper with plenty of time to spare. He turned it over and diligently folded his arms. The invigilator looked at him untrustingly; everyone else was writing or had their head in their hands. Tom used this time to re-live the more pleasant aspects of his relationship with Suzie.

. . . how her lips traced his mouth when they kissed

. . . like the way jagged objects whisper through layers of human flesh with devastating efficiency.

He could not contain a smile—a feeling that tunnelled through his molten core like a close range shotgun shell. Tom was an artist making figuration libre, a neo-expressionist maverick, too ahead of his time and all that . . .

—Here it comes . . . again . . . AAAAHHHHHH . . .

Tom fantasised about climaxing into Suzie's open stomach wound, watching in woozy satisfaction as the teardrop of fluid disappeared into the subterraneous chasm of webbed connective tissue, into the pits of her fucking soul . . .

—CHOOO!!! Oh, eugh, jeez . . . eugh . . . oh Jesus . . .

He could feel her blood in his body, snaking foreign arteries, mixing well with the host. Suzie would always be a part of him now, the thought of which freshly stirred his arousal; the anticipation of getting home to his own room to masturbate made Tom's belly ache. His brain swam in a reservoir of endorphins, his stiff cock under his desk begging to be strangulated. Tom started sweating.

The ache in his bowel grew more intense. His sphincter winked and puckered. Both testicles tightened up, his toes flexed. Tom wondered if he might cum without having to lay a finger on himself.

He decided to use Suzie's corpse that night. He wanted to lose his virginity to her. She was currently lying under his bed. *Her body won't have decayed too severely*—he hoped. Tom worried for a moment that her vagina might have seized up and become impenetrable. He felt it only once while Suzie was alive. Tom had never enjoyed sex.

The invigilator sneezed again and a bead of blood dribbled from his left nostril to the hairy camber of his top lip. His eyes spooled to the back of his skull until he was staggering around with the milky white eyes of a man possessed. He went to sneeze again but the pull-back was so prolonged you got the feeling that when he did eventually go to release, his entire internal organs would shoot from of his nostrils. He released.

(His entire internal organs shoot from his nostrils)

Everyone started screaming . . .

The Smiths were always on. He loved The Smiths; he and Suzie used to listen to them together all the time. He listened to "There is a Light that Never goes Out" and dragged Suzie's mannequin out from under the bed. Tom's room was a mess. He lay her supine in the middle of the floor and knelt at her feet. Tom was nervous, the ready-stiffness from the exam theatre long gone.

—This is it . . . *destiny*.

Her skin wasn't as hard as it looked; she had maintained a kind of rubbery smoothness. Tom decided he had to just bite the bullet, get it over with. He couldn't go through high school another day a virgin. He wrestled his trousers to just below his hips and yanked Suzie's skirt and underwear to her ankles. *That intrepid first step*. There was a strange smell, but Tom chose to ignore it for now. He lowered himself down on to her, gently bringing his lips to hers. Tom kept his eyes on her face— that pale, shocked mask with a mouthful of pause. Tom ran his trembling hands over her parchment-thin flesh, praying it might spark his arousal. Her delicate features, once flushed with sunburn, were now blued and chisel cold. He dreamt of making Suzie live again. The song ends.

He put his flaccid penis into the bloody trench of her stomach. He thrust in and out of the wound, each dip revealing a cock-end swathed in wet gore. Suddenly he felt a presence in the doorway—it was Josie.

—Tom, what're you doing?

Tom tried to maintain his composure and avoid scrambling to his feet ashamedly. He stood up, in his own time, in full frontal profile before Josie. Her eyes went to his flaccid penis. Tom could still feel the warm, wet heat on his cock, blood *still* soft as liquid velvet.

Maybe if he'd been more forthcoming when Suzie was alive she might not have left him. If he'd just *stuck it in her* the way Kricfalusi probably did. He couldn't help but think like this even though it achieved nothing. His head throbbed a little.

Josie looked back up at Tom's face and said—What'd you think of the exam then?

—Fuck, Josie, I . . .

—A demon of the first kind, eh? Relax, I won't tell anyone you fuck dead bodies.

—Really?

Josie shrugged.

—So, how many have you killed?

Tom's face fell to shock, he was instantly offended.

—How can you even ask me that?

—Have you eaten any part of her yet?

Tom bowed his head, nodded.

—Just one of her organs, the liver I think. I can't really remember.

—Huh! Well there ya go . . .

—And I think I tried some of her blood. I've been injecting myself with her blood, only because I loved her, you gotta believe me.

They both stood in silence for a few seconds, allowing the intensity of the situation to dim a little.

—What are you thinking Josie? Are you going to call the cops or . . . ?

—Heck, I'm just thinking, like . . . yano when you think you really know someone, like, they seem so predictable?

—I guess. I just wanted her to be part of me. When I was eating her, I don't know, it felt like something more intimate than sex . . .

—You should really try getting laid man . . .

—Please don't tell anyone, you can't tell anyone. Leo will kill me!

—Sure, all you have to is, like, something for me . . .

Tom's testicles crawled. He knew what Josie wanted him to do.

THE STATEMENT OF TOM TRYOUT

3.

Hell's farmhouse was like something from a horror movie. The crutch of a deformed sycamore split into twisted boughs of shrunken heads that dangled just above the roof. Tom and Josie saw the grid of mown grass and bare soil of the plantations that promised to hide all manner of atrocious nightmares from clear sight. Josie picked up a shrag from the ground and started bending it nervously.

—We don't have to do this—Tom reassured her.

—I *want* to do this. Stop being such a baby . . .

A sudden silver varnished the trees, the moon was out. The Gangles were silent but still present. Tom felt the wrought iron railing that led to the woodlet. He was cold, his head still felt ready to burst.

—Why do you want to come down here again?

—Cos of the murders you dummy.

—Josie, this is dangerous! Mr Hell is an alleged reptilian psychopath!

—Then you two should get along, like, totally famously . . .

The two made their way towards the farm house. Tom had no idea what Josie was trying to achieve but forced himself to go in order to keep his side of the bargain. Walking behind the girl, he thought about how easy it would be to kill Josie. She hadn't expressed any fear towards Tom; she seemed comfortable letting him trail behind her.

Tom thought there must be something in that kind of trust.

They approached the porch. Suddenly, Tom noticed Josie frozen in her tracks. He peered over her shoulder and saw something floating over them like a mirage.

A tall being, stooped in shadow. It had the look of an old sawbones. Hatch-marks on its fingers showed in the moonlight as it came into view. It was Mr Hell...

Hell had been snorting something, it spangled his top lip like powdered sugar. He didn't seem embarrassed about it.

—Little late for trespassing, don't ya think?

Tom and Josie were frozen to the spot. Mr Hell plucked an apple from one of the under-branches and held it aloft by the burr-knot. He presented it to Tom, who reluctantly took it and scrutinised the offering.

—Eat it—Hell insisted.

Tom took a big bite. It tasted good, crisp with a subtle dryness.

—What'd you think?

Through the fear, Tom's face was a beaming plate of joy. Hell took this as his answer. Josie was still studying the old man's face with an architect's eye. Scars overlapped on both cheeks and he had one eyebrow missing. Hell's face was like a Halloween mask, and a tatty looking one at that. Tom noticed his ancient ugliness too; he was everything expectation and dread promised. Had his apples not been so delicious he would've surely turned and ran. Tom saw the same blank stare present in most of the other antagonists in his life; Leo, Mr Alhazred, Suzie when she smirked . . .

—Pruned in winter while the trees are dormant and thinned to perfection. This orchard is my life.

Tom was still crunching his apple, trying to savour its taste. Hell knelt down to meet the two teenagers at eye level. When he spoke his breath smelled of soil and natural decay. He focused his stare on Tom.

—It's all I have.

—More than some—Josie added.

—I've been banished from the place I used to call home.

—Why?

Hell twisted his neck until the sinew looked ready to snap. It eventually made a loud crack that made Tom wince.

—I know about you...

—Know about what?—Tom took an instinctive step backwards. There were traces of the sweet apple still on his tongue.

—Help me . . . —Hell asked with his limpid, pleading eyes.

—Help you? To do what?

—Think about it, what are you good at?

—I dunno, not much! Math, science maybe? I don't know a single thing about working in an orchard . . .

—Killing women, that's what you're best at. I'm no good at it. It's the Teiidae you see. I haven't got the nerve to disobey ancient values like that, but you can summon the anger and resentment needed to extinguish a female life.

Josie snorted and muttered under her breath.

—You believe that do you?—she spoke to Hell, who continued to ignore her.

—I can only kill children, adult males, and small animals. Women are the final hurdle. I can't kill them, they all seem so maternal to me.

THE STATEMENT OF TOM TRYOUT

—That's because of the Teiidae, right?—Josie asked.

—It's a sneaky female trick, plucking feeling from the foulest of souls.

—What makes you think I can do it?? I can't kill women!—Tom protested.

Mr Hell gave Tom a knowing grin—he knew, but *how* did he know?

—You are talented boy, I can sense it in you. You can kill and consume flesh like a true monster of the night.

Tom felt pride swell inside of him then considered its source. Hell inched closer, nudging Josie out of the way. He spoke in a faint whisper.

—They used to mock me too you know.

—Who? The Gangles?

—The Gangles, women, people, all of them . . .

—Why do you want to kill women?

—The truth of the matter, is that I want this town culled. I want *us* to take it back . . .

—From the Gangles?

—From the Gangles *and* the people who live there. The stretch of land isn't rightfully theirs, it belongs to us. The Old Ones bequeathed it to our people centuries ago. The town went by a different name back then; The Nameless City, we can call it The Nameless City . . .

Tom looked sceptical.

—The birds sense our reptilian ancestry. They can taste our darkness like rotten maggots in their saliva. We were forced to retreat to underground chambers until there was only a few of us left . . . and the people living there right now are all hooked up to the same virtual reality headset, intruders one and all. It's time we woke them up . . .

Tom felt uncomfortable for a moment when he thought about his father or Mr Kowalski coming to harm.

—The Gangles don't like our people, we are the reptiles. The sea was once receded, there was no pier. The Nameless City was like a desert.

—Am *I* a reptile?—Josie asked, half kidding. Hell kept talking as if he hadn't even heard her.

—This is all I have left boy, growing Adam's fruit . . .

Tom could see the white fiends gathered on the roof, listening. Hell clutched the boy by the shoulders, his long fingernails subtly penetrating Tom's flesh through fabric.

—The birds, they shit on everything, take what they want, just like those fuckin townsfolk! If you don't fit in they leer at you, they can sense how weak we have become! The gulls are attracted to the stench of humanity, of servility and slovenliness, that's why they allow those people to live there. Every organism of reptilian lineage in Shaver Point is considered a trespasser, doomed for a life of utter misery.

—Jesus—Josie was ready to leave. Tom saw the flung arrows of her expression but was unmoved.

—Let me tell you something. There is a battle going on out there, between the oppressed and the oppressors. What's your name?

—Tom . . .

—Tom, you know what it feels like to be oppressed don't you?

—I guess . . .

—And what about your little girlfriend, does she know oppression?

—I'm not his girlfriend—Josie said, snapping to attention. She seemed a little agitated that Hell was only now acknowledging her existence.

Hell's eyeballs ping-ponged around in their sockets.

—I'll deal with the children and animals, I'll give you some salt bags to fend off the Gangles. When they eat salt their heads explode. Tom, you can take the women. I'll capture them one by one and you expunge them accordingly.

Tom's head ache returned. Hell stood up from his kneeling position.

—You're getting migraines . . .

—I get them a lot.

—It's the Gangle siren that does that. It's how they hurt us.

Josie butted in—Okay, this is just getting kind of, like, fucked up now. Tom, it's one thing to kill some cheerleader slut, but killing the women of Shaver Point? I mean . . . *really*?

—Every man has his palms run through with nails—Hell looked straight at Josie when he said this.

—Stop! Stop saying shit! Tom, you're not really gonna, like, listen to this nutjob are ya?

Hell put his hands on Tom's shoulders and spoke to him as a father would his only son.

—You want to belong to something ancient and great? Show me what you can do . . .

Tom turned to Josie.

—What, you think you're some kind of fucking Holden character now? Out to kill the phonies, right?

—The phonies . . .

THE STATEMENT OF TOM TRYOUT

—Tom...

He advanced on the girl, grasping the slender column of her throat with strangler's hands, bearing down on her until her legs bent and she began to fall backwards. They wrestled on the ground for a few minutes, Josie's nails tearing into Tom's wrists . . . Tom thumbing the larynx until Josie started making rasping sounds, a final cry to the Gangles for help . . . until she finally submitted to him.

Hell stood still, frozen with pride and shock.

—She was a Gangle . . . you heard her make that sound.

Tom released his grip and Josie's head fell limp. He *did* have a migraine again.

—It's all cultural conditioning. The people of Shaver Point are as cruel as the Gangles; they have a mentality of privilege, subjugation and wanting to dominate . . .

Tom knelt in the dirt next to Josie and resigned himself to his inescapable destiny. He belonged here, even if he felt cold and alone on the inside. That might never go away. His temples pulsed and two veins branched off down either side of Tom's face, his brain opening for the first time, skull separating, nose breathing in the fetid stench of murder and savouring it in his throat, in his heart, in his viscera eyes . . .

AUTHOR BIOGRAPHIES

Andrew Wayne Adams is the author of *Janitor of Planet Anilingus*, a metaphysical comedy-romance-adventure available from Eraserhead Press. Born and raised in rural Ohio, he now lives in Canada. He enjoys posting links to "Macho Man" Randy Savage videos online at andrewwayneadams.blogspot.com.

Jim Agpalza is a freelance illustrator/painter, cover artist, character designer and is the co-creator of the animated show *Spacefish* and the novel *Fantastic Earth Destroyer Ultra Plus*. Born and raised on an island in the middle of the Pacific, he now resides outside of Portland with his wife and two kids and the ghost of his dead cat Jah. We love you Jah.

Max Booth III is the author of Stephen King's *Odd Thomas*. Follow him on Twitter @GiveMeYourTeeth.

Bruce Boston is the author of more than fifty books and chapbooks, including the dystopian sf novel *The Guardener's Tale* and the psychedelic coming-of-age novel *Stained Glass Rain*. His poetry has received the Bram Stoker Award, the *Asimov's* Readers Award, the Gothic Readers Choice Award, the Balticon Poetry Award, and the Rhysling and Grandmaster Awards of the SFPA. His fiction has received a Pushcart Prize and twice been a finalist for the Bram Stoker Award (novel, short story). His latest collection, *Resonance Dark and Light*, is available from Amazon and Edritch Press. For more info, please visit his website: www.bruceboston.com

Twenty-five volumes of **Tom Bradley**'s fiction, essays, screenplays and poetry have been published by houses in the United States, Canada, Great Britain and Japan. Various of his novels have been nominated for the New York University Bobst Prize, the Editor's Book Award and the AWP Award Series in the Novel. *3:AM Magazine* in Paris gave him their Nonfiction Book of the Year Award in 2007 and 2009. His nonfiction has appeared in *Salon.com*. Tom's most recent titles are *This Wasted*

Land and Its Chymical Illuminations (Lavender Ink), *Elmer Crowley: a katabasic nekyia* (Mandrake of Oxford), *Family Romance* (Jaded Ibis) and *We'll See Who Seduces Whom: a graphic ekphrasis in verse* (Unlikely Books). See tombradley.org.

Sébastien Doubinsky is a bilingual French writer and academic, born in Paris in 1963. An established writer in France, Sébastien Doubinsky has published a series of novels, covering different genres, from classical literature to crime fiction, as well as a few poetry collections. His novels, *The Babylonian Trilogy* (*Goodbye Babylon* in the US), *The Song of Synth* and *Absinth* have been published in the UK and the US. Three of his poetry collections, *Mothballs, Spontaneous Combustions*, and *Zen and the Art of Poetry Maintenance* have been published in the UK. He currently lives in Denmark, where he teaches French literature, culture and history at the French department of the university of Aarhus.

Robin Wyatt Dunn writes and teaches in Los Angeles. You can find him online at www.robindunn.com

Allen Griffin is a writer and musician living in Indianapolis. His work has appeared in several cool places including the *Splatterlands* and *OminousRealities* anthologies from Grey Matter Press, *The Mustache Factor*, and *Innsmouth Magazine*. He also has two chapbooks available from Dunhams Manor Press, *The Noxious Winds of Karmageddon* and *No Such Heaven*. He can be found on Facebook and at Twitter as @Agriffinauthor.

Michael Griffin's stories have appeared in magazines like Apex, Black Static, Lovecraft eZine and Phantasmagorium, and such anthologies as the Shirley Jackson Award winner The Grimscribe's Puppets, the Laird Barron tribute The Children of Old Leech, and Mighty in Sorrow. His standalone novella Far From Streets was published by Dunhams Manor Press. His work is upcoming in Leaves of a Necronomicon, Cthulhu Fhtagn!, Autumn Cthulhu, Xnoybis #1 and A Mythos Grimmly. In addition to writing fiction, he's an electronic musician and owner of the Hypnos Recordings ambient music label. He's on Twitter @mgsoundvisions and blogs at griffinwords.wordpress.com

R. A. Harris lives in South West England. His work has been published by Dynatox Ministries and Bizarro Pulp Press as well as at various online vendors.

Rhys Hughes has published more than 30 books and over 700 stories in a long writing career. His work has been translated into 10 languages. His latest book is the collection *Mirrors in the Deluge* and his blog can be found at: The Spoons That Are My Ears!

Gabino Iglesias was born somewhere, but then moved to a different place. He has worked as dog whisperer, witty communications professor, and ballerina assassin. Now he hides near a dumpster in Austin, Texas, where he works as a freelance journalist and impersonates a PhD student. His nonfiction has appeared in places like the *New York Times, Z Magazine, El Nuevo Día*, and others. The stuff that's made up has been published in places like *Red Fez, Flash Fiction Offensive, Drunk Monkeys, Bizarro Central, Paragraph Line, Divergent Magazine, Cease, Cows*, and a few horror, surrealist, and bizarro anthologies. When not writing or fighting ninja squirrels, he devours books and spits out reviews that are published in places like *Verbicide, The Rumpus, Word Riot, Heavy Feather Review, The Lazy Fascist Review, Bookslut, Electric Literature, Atticus Review, Entropy, HorrorTalk, Necessary Fiction, The Magazine of Bizarro Fiction, Out of the Gutter, Spinetingler Magazine, Buzzy Mag*, and a few other print and online venues. He's currently working on overcoming his crippling hippopotomonstrosesquipedaliophobia

Chris Kelso has been printed frequently in literary and university publications across the UK, US and Canada. His books include *The Black Dog Eats the City, Schadenfreude, Transmatic, A Message from the Slave State* and *Moosejaw Frontier*. Chris has served as voluntary copy editor for Dog Horn, *Jupiter Magazine*, Eraserhead Press (and cult horror imprint Deadite). Along with Victoria Hooper he edits the Sceptre award winning, *Sci-Fi magazine*. In 2012 Adam Lowe and Chris edited the *Terror Scribes* anthology and *Caledonia Dreamin—Strange Fiction of Scottish Descent* with Hal Duncan. Along with Garrett Cook he is the co-creator of The Imperial Youth Review. Chris lives in Kilmarnock, East Ayrshire in Scotland and by day works as a Librarian stacking books and running art workshops for the East Ayrshire Council.

Sean Leonard lives in Madisonville, Kentucky with his family and his dogs. He's a writer, a horror movie reviewer (HorrorNews.net and Gorefiend.com), a drummer, and he's been working with Bizarro Pulp Press since 2013. Sean is also a freelance proofreader/editor, with a number of BPP and JournalStone releases included on his list of finished projects. He can sometimes be found at www.seanleonard.org.

Thomas Logan has a variety of literary and pulp stories appearing in online and print publications and has worked in various capacities for Fictional International and smaller journals. Most recently, he's served as Fiction Editor for the Portland, Ore. literary journal The Grove Review and is proud of his membership in the Buntho SF Writers Group, which grew from an Ursula Le Guin class at PSU. Semi-reclusive and secretive, he'd prefer you not to know that he got his MFA in 2006, has lived and taught across the country, or that he often ends his sentences awkwardly.

Adrian Ludens is a dark fiction author from Rapid City, South Dakota. Recent and favorite anthology appearances include: *Blood Lite III: Aftertaste* (Pocket Books), *Shadows Over Main Street* (Hazardous Press), *Darker Edge of Desire* (Tempted Romance), *Insidious Assassins* (Smart Rhino Publications), and *The Mammoth Book of Jack the Ripper Tales* (upcoming from Running Press). Visit him at www.adrianludens.com.

Antonio Magogoli has been hospitalized since 1985 where he dictates his work to the nurses.

Chantal Noordeloos lives in the Netherlands. When she is not busy exploring interesting new realities, or arguing with characters (aka writing), she likes to dabble in drawing. In 1999 she graduated from the Norwich School of Art and Design, where she focused mostly on creative writing. There are many genres that Chantal wants to explore in her writing, and she likes to write for all ages. Storytelling is the element of writing that she enjoys most. "Writing should be an escape from everyday life, and I like to provide people with new places to escape to, and new people to meet."

Having written for magazines like *Fangoria* and *Dark Discoveries*, **John Palisano** has also published many short stories and novels. His novel *Dust of the Dead* has just come out from Samhain, with *Ghost Heart* coming early next year. He's easily found on Facebook /johnpalisano or his blog: www.johnpalisano.com

Dustin Reade is the author of *Grambo, We're Decomposing As We Go . . .* , and *Bad Hotel* (Coming Soon). He lives in Port Angeles,

Washington where he plays music, uses William S. Burroughs' "Cut-Up" technique to fill out job applications, and performs atheist wedding ceremonies. He is currently studying to be a Funeral Director.

Matthew Revert is an author and recording artist from Melbourne, Australia. His most recent book, *Basal Ganglia* was released by Lazy Fascist Press and his Debut record, *Not You* was released by Kye Records

Hailing from California, **Bob Ritchie** now lives in Puerto Rico. He has a fantastic wife and as many as five kids. Editing, yeah, teaching, sure, some translating. Ritchie (as his wife calls him) is a musician who is fortunate enough to have collaborated with Jon Anderson, a particular favorite of his. Bob (as he calls himself) is also a writer of stories and has written several things that might even be good. His work has appeared in *Unlikely 2.0, Small Print Magazine, Prick of the Spindle,* and other forums; two of his stories were nominated for the *Pushcart Prize.* Neither won. Oh well.

The strange and bizarre works of **Steve Carter and Antoinette Rydyr (S.C.A.R.)** incorporates anything from sci fi and horror fantasy to surrealism and weird satire. They create in a variety of mediums— prose fiction, illustration, comic books, screenplays and even music. Among their most horrific pieces are the *Spore Whores* trilogy (Eros Comix, USA), the psychosexual horror fantasies published in Robin Bougie's *Sleazy Slice* (Canada) and the *Gorgasm* series. They recently released their first graphic novel called *Savage Bitch* which is filled with wild primal amazons, loads of crypto-evolutionary monsters and weird cults. Find them at www.weirdwildart.com

Steve Rasnic Tem's latest novel *Blood Kin*(Solaris) is a Southern Gothic/Horror blend of snake handling, granny women, kudzu, and Melungeons. This spring PS Publishing brings out his novella *In The Lovecraft Museum.* Also this year Centipede Press collects the best of his uncollected horror stories in *Out of the Dark: A storybook of Horrors.* In 2016 Solaris will publish his dark sf novel *Ubo*, a meditation on human violence as seen through the eyes of some of history's most violent figures.

Daniel Vlasaty lives in Chicago. He is the author of *The Church of TV as God* (Eraserhead Press) and *Amphetamine Psychosis* (Black Dharma Press).

Don Webb was born on the magical day of April 30, 1960. He has taught writing to adults, shot fireworks professionally, taught high school English, made corn-dogs, and been a industrial investigator. He is an expert on modern occultism, Texas folklore and wasting too much time on Facebook. His most recent work is *Through Dark Angles*, Lovecraftian short stories. His wife is lovely, his cats tuxedo, his chilli mac turkey.

Eli Wilde lives in North East England. He has written three novels— *Cruel*, *Four Days* and *Neophyte*. His story in this anthology, *Snowflakes Falling, Pages Turning*, was inspired by the sound effects in the movie *Institute Benjamenta* and his desire to read fiction written by postmodernist replicants.

Wol-vriey is Nigerian and quite tall. He is the author of *The Bizarro Story of I*, *Chainsaw Cop Corpse*, *Vegan Zombie Apocalypse*, *Meat Suitcase*, *Guiltessa Dolores*, *Boston Posh*, *Big Trouble in Little Ass*, *Vegan Vampire Vaginas*, *Vagina Mundi*, *Melanie Nemesis Catchpole*, *The Fly Queen*, and *Bizarro 101 (A Basic Primer)*. Wol-vriey blogs at http://oddityfarm.wordpress.com

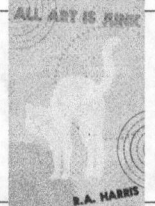

All Art is Junk by R. A. Harris

Lana Rivers, a girl with paintbrush hair, is missing and it's up to Lancelot, her cyborg knight, and his bionic conjoined twin, Cilia, to find her before her evil father, a disrespected artist turned mad-scientist, performs a terrible experiment on her.

Cherub by David C. Hayes

Cherub wasn't like the other boys—too slow, too rough—but he didn't deserve what that hospital did to him, and now he will make them pay.

Skinners by Adam Millard

Los Angeles, the City of Angels. At least, that's what the brochure says. What it fails to mention is the earthquakes. Oh, and the flesh-eating creatures lying dormant beneath the concrete, waiting for the chance to surface once again. Their wait is over . . .

The After-Life Story of Pork Knuckles Malone by MP Johnson

What's a farm boy to do when his pet pig becomes an evil, decaying hunk of ham with slime-spewing psychic powers?

A Lightbulb's Lament by Grant Wamack

A gentleman with a lightbulb for head wakes up in a world full of darkness, hooks up with a beautiful ex-prostitute, and an old man who can heal people; he travels down south to find the mysterious Creator.

The Horror Show by Vincenzo Bilof

A poetry novel—a narcoleptic, amnesiac Nobel Prize-winning poet becomes the subject of an experiment to cure madness.

Beyond by Jordan Krall

From Jerusalem to Mars, psychiatry and the unraveling of the universe

Gravity Comics Massacre
by Vincenzo Bilof

An absolutely shitty novella involving comic books, aliens, a serial killer, teenagers in an abandoned town, horror-trope dream sequences, and an ending you're going to hate.

Glue by Scott Lange

Sticky bowels and sticky situations.

Ascent by Matthew Bialer

Is the 8 foot tall creature haunting a small town in Iowa in the fall of the year 1903 the product of a hoax and collective imagination or was it one of the first documented paranormal event in America? This epic poem grapples with these questions.

Fecal Terror by David Bernstein

A killer turd is on the loose!

The Fairy Princess of Trains
by Christopher Boyle

Danny's mediocre life turns upside-down when his couch starts whispering to him. Then he's charged with a supernatural mission: Rescue the Fairy Princess of Trains.

Terence, Mephisto & Viscera Eyes
by Chris Kelso

9 new science fiction stories from Chris Kelso

How to Succesfully Kidnap Strangers by Max Booth III

Do not respond to bad reviews. If you must respond to bad reviews, please do not kidnap the reviewer.

Bizarro Bizarro: An Anthology

The finest bizarro short stories from 2013.

Necrosaurus Rex by Nicolas Day

Necrosaurus Rex tells the tale of Martin, a simple janitor, who takes an unfortunate trip through time, becomes a violent mutant, and the father of us all. There's 14 billion years crushed inside these pages, and most of them are pretty nasty.

Day of the Milkman by S. T. Cartledge

In a world dominated by the milk industry, only one milkman survives after a terrible storm sinks all the ships and throws the Great White Sea out of balance.

Moosejaw Frontier by Chris Kelso

An unapologetic disaster of metafiction

Notes from the Guts of a Hippo
by Grant Wamack

A rugged journalist travels to Brazil in search of a missing hippo researcher and the notes left behind lead to something earth shatteringly revelatory.

Industrial Carpet Drag by Bruce Taylor

Chemicals make you do great things!

ADHD Vampire by Matthew Vaughn

He came, he conquered, he was distracted a lot

www.ingramcontent.com/pod-product-compliance
Lightning Source LLC
Chambersburg PA
CBHW060625260626
47161CB00008B/2803